I0716753

Published by: GladEye Press
Interior Design: J.V. Bolkan
Cover Design: Sharleen Nelson
ISBN-13: 978-1-951289-19-5
Library of Congress Control Number: 2024949939

This is a work of fiction. All names, characters, places, and events are either a product of the author's imagination or are used fictitiously. Any resemblance to real persons, businesses, organizations, or events are totally unintentional and entirely coincidental.

10 9 8 7 6 5 4 3 2 1

The body text is presented in Garamond, 11 point for easy readability.

ASH VALLEY

THE PROMISE OF THE LAND

Book Three of the Risk of Being Ridiculous Trilogy

GUY MAYNARD

GladEye
Press

Springfield, OR

The Risk of Being Ridiculous

It's Boston 1969 and nineteen-year-old Ben Tucker and his tribe of long-haired freaks desperately seek lives that make sense in a world distorted by war, racism, and bankrupt values. Ridiculous takes you on a passionate, lyrical six-week ride through confrontations and concerts; courts and cops; parties and politics; school and the streets; Weathermen and women's liberation; acid and activism; revolution and reaction. And, of course, love—as Ben feverishly pursues the long shot desire of his life—Sarah Stein.

"Masterpiece . . . the book never hits a false note while charting some of the most turbulent times in American history . . . When my kids ask me what the '60s were really like, I'm going to hand them this book."
—Steven Hager, *High Times*

"Maynard captures both the essence of that one colorfully wild historical moment—the late 1960s—and the timeless yearning for meaning. In the end, [this] is a romance as tender as any you'll read."
—Ana Maria Spagna, author of *Test Ride on the Sunnyland Bus: A Daughter's Civil Rights Journey*, 2009 River Teeth Literary Nonfction Prize winner

Trial: A Long Year from Here to There
Where *The Risk of Being Ridiculous* ends, *Trial* picks up the story of a year of trials, culminating in a harrowing courtroom drama Ben Tucker faces in the aftermath of a violent protest.

Facing serious criminal charges resulting from a 1970 demonstration, Tucker navigates lawyers he doesn't trust, travels from the streets of Boston to the beaches of California through a country at war with itself, an improbable but passionate love affair and budding communal ties out west with a group of college dropout freaks—with a date with a judge and jury in a solemn Massachusetts courtroom always looming in front of him.

"A trip down memory lane for readers born around 1950, a peak into the storied land of sex, drugs, and rock & roll for those of later generations, a coming-of-age and achingly deep love story, Guy Maynard's *Trial* is perhaps most of all protagonist Ben Tucker's quest: his and his friends' examination of that maddening gap between what is and what should be—and therefore, how shall he—how shall they all— live? A reader feels that quest will stay with Ben throughout his life, as it may with the reader as well."
—Evelyn Searle Hess, author of *To the Woods*, winner of a WILLA Literary Award for Creative Nonfiction, *Building a Better Nest*, and *Shoulder to Shoulder*.

… Ben and Sarah's adventure continues in
Ash Valley: The Promise of the Land …

ASH VALLEY

THE PROMISE OF THE LAND

*Let me say at the risk of seeming ridiculous, that the
true revolutionary is guided by great feelings of love.*
—Ernesto "Che" Guevara

*Driving us was the absolute conviction that we were part of a global
uprising against war and greed and racism and the slavery of being
chained to a reality of pointless jobs and useless things. Along with that
came a mystical faith that if we leapt toward the lives we imagined, even
though no landing place was immediately apparent, we would get to where
we were supposed to be going.*

Spring

SPRING/1

State Highway 62 flows down, down, down through the wet green western slopes of the mighty Cascades. Just past dwarfing summit snowbanks not far from Crater Lake, we entered the thick towering forest of our long winter's dream. Down, down, down, riding the banks of the wild Rogue River, shrouded in a dense mysterious mist, something more solid than fog, less liquid than rain: a substantial translucence that felt like a passage from one state of being to another, from all that we had known to the possibility of all we had imagined, a daunting vaporous veil still reluctant to reveal whatever might be on the other side. Down, down, down to a junction town called Trail, where we took a right turn to head north at the first sign we'd seen pointing us toward Tiller.

I was driving the blue Ford van that we had bought for our passage to the West. Sarah was riding shotgun. Mike was behind me and Paulie next to him, with her dog Quinn Man curled nervously at her feet. We were quiet, almost numb from the 3,000 miles of road behind us, covered in four long days, mesmerized by this new world flowing by outside our windows, sort of stunned: months of adrenaline pushing us toward this place, now just thirty miles away, dissipating in the gray green watery light of late afternoon into a more solemn sense of anticipation.

We started climbing again toward the last summit we had to clear on Highway 227, a narrow curling mountain road lined with magnificent Douglas firs and steep sudden drop-offs that appeared around long, unsuspicious curves. As we began our final descent into the South Umpqua Valley, occasionally the wall of trees was interrupted by ugly patches of stark bald land, littered with remnants of dead trees and piled brush. Loaded log trucks buzzed by us heading south, hell-bent on dumping their last load of the day. It was all getting very real.

But we had made it, goddammit, to this wild place called Oregon that had come alive to tantalize and sustain us through our last struggles in the Old World. "Now," this dripping, fierce, proud landscape was asking us, "Now what?"

We began seeing signs of civilization as the downward slope began to ease and the road nestled next to a rippling creek. We saw a cluster of small, rough houses, exhaling floating clouds of wood smoke, and even a little store right after a small sign announcing a community called "Drew."

The creek twisted the road around, sometimes tight against sheer cliffs, which left little room for error on either side. I resisted the urge to get through these last few miles as quickly as possible and slowed way down. This was no time to miss a curve and fly down toward the water, now hidden by the slope covered in steeply slanted trees. So fucking close. A log truck steamed up behind, seemingly within inches of our rear bumper, the grind and grunt of its downshift piling on the anxiety pumping through me. The driver laid on his air horn.

The curves finally yielded to a soft sloping straightaway. Up ahead I saw a sign for a restaurant in front of a parking lot, the Tiller Tavern. I pulled in and let the log truck have the road. We got the finger as it roared past us.

We all looked at each other. Wide eyes slowly registering relief. Smiles. And then crazy laughter. We pulled back on the road and immediately crossed a bridge where the creek we'd been following emptied into the South Umpqua River. At the end of the bridge, a solid green sign with faded white lettering said: WELCOME TO TILLER.

SPRING/2

The TV didn't really even work. Maybe if the wind was blowing just right and the antenna happened to be pointing in the right direction, we might get a fuzzy picture that we could barely make out as channel 5, a CBS station out of Medford. But it was not watchable for any length of time. And besides, well, … fuck TV.

It was a spontaneous event. Mike woke up grumpy, saw the blank TV staring back at him as he scowled at the rest of us jammed into the White House "living room" with steaming cups of hobo coffee, "What the fuck is that doing here?" he asked. We all laughed.

"We should put it out of its misery," Dale said. "You know, if you shoot a TV, it implodes."

"What does that even mean?" I asked.

"It just kind of sucks in on itself. Whooooosh!" Dale said as he dramatically spread his hands wide and then drew them together.

"Cool. Do we have a gun?" I asked.

Turns out we did, an Enfield 303 that somebody had given Dale and Sydney. I'm not sure why. Maybe to shoot deer who wandered freely behind the house, in the small flat area—not even really a yard—that quickly gave way to a steep forested rise, which was characteristic of most of the fifty acres that went with the White House. I don't think they had ever actually shot at anything but we had a gun and some bullets and, now, a mission. Dale and I packed the heavy cabinet that contained the TV out over the front porch and loaded it into the back of Stu's white '52 Chevy pickup. And we all piled in.

A crowd had been waiting for us when Mike and Paulie and Sarah and I first arrived at the White House, jazzed and joyous at the end of our long trek. Jeffrey and Little Eddie and Walter had flown out right after our wedding and some Illinois folks—Huntsman and Swig and Rusty (who'd been with us on the California beaches the previous summer)—somehow beat us there. Tiller fucking Oregon, man, that's where it was happening. The house had five bedrooms but that wasn't even enough. In anticipation of all of us showing up, Dale and Sydney had moved to a cabin on a friend's property farther up into the mountains and Stu was staying at another friend's place just a bit upriver from Tiller. Sarah and I, and our new dog, Moonbeam—a sturdy mix of German Shepherd, husky, and, we were told, wolf, who Stu had given us as wedding gift—got a nice big bedroom, the only one on the first floor.

Mike and Paulie had the corner bedroom upstairs and Jeffrey had the nicest of the smaller bedrooms. Everybody else just kind of found a spot in the other rooms. It was apparent from the start that, as perfect as the White House sounded when there were just four or five people living there and the rest of us were dreaming of escapes from apartments in the city, it was not going to work as our long-term home, not enough living space, not enough farmable land. But it was a good landing spot, a base where we could orient ourselves and look for the right place.

Dale and Sydney had found the White House after our group of eight had split up north of Eureka, at the end of last August after spending a month and a half fruitlessly searching for a place for all of us along the California coast. Sarah and I had to go back to Boston for my trial. Mike and Stu decided to hang out with some folks they met along the Navarro River. Herschel stayed in Berkeley. Rusty got a drive-away car and invited Sarah and me to join him for the trip to Champaign-Urbana, which would get us two-thirds of the way to Boston. Dale and Sydney continued north into Oregon to see Crater Lake. On the way, they stopped at a little store, where they saw a crude note on the bulletin board: House for Rent 5 Bedrooms $50/Month.

We dove right into getting stuff done. We sold the van for $1,115 ($65 more than we paid for it—not counting the $175 we had to pay to fix it in Philly), planning to replace it with a pickup, hoping to buy one from the same guy who sold Stu his, an old man named Earl who lived a ways downriver and had taken a liking to our band of refugees from the East.

Paulie already had her eyes on a horse, her first Oregon dream, a ten-year-old gelding named Stormy. Sarah and I were going to chip in and the horse would belong to the group, but we all knew that it would mainly be Paulie's horse. Sometimes it seemed Paulie connected with animals better than she did with people. When we had to stay at Sarah's parent's house one more night after the van was fixed after the wedding, Quinn Man had to sleep in the van because the Stein's two dogs were not receptive to him hanging out in the house. Paulie opted to sleep in the van with him, rather than with Mike in the house. Soon, she would have a horse. At first, she would keep him at a stable on the place where Stu was staying with a guy named

Stephen, who was renting a cabin from a mother-and-daughter family on their place a few miles upriver.

Sarah and Jeffrey and I spent part of a day working in a small garden plot next to the driveway in front of the house. The dirt was still somewhat wet from all the spring rains, but we had a few sunny days when the temperature got up into the sixties and the soil dried just enough to be workable. We were anxious, too, to do anything that seemed to move us toward this new life we had imagined. Man, it felt good to get that good moist Oregon dirt between our fingers, to get dirty even if we didn't really know what we were doing. On Stu's direction, we covered the fresh-tilled ground with some hay, to keep it from turning to mud in the next rain and to, eventually, add some nutrients. Our next step was to plant some tomato starts in pots and get some posts for a fence to keep the ever-present deer out.

After working up a sweat in the garden, Sarah and I walked across the road to the river. The brush was thick on the short steep bank, but a narrow path, 12 or 15 feet long, led to a small natural gravel beach, where we could stretch out and soak in the powerful afternoon sun.

I had never really experienced the roar of a river up close. My childhood home of New Bedford, Massachusetts, was at the mouth of the Acushnet River. But I never knew it as a river. In my limited scope, that river was what went under the bridge to Fairhaven, just at the edge of the harbor, which opened on to Buzzards Bay, which was an extension of the Atlantic Ocean. The ocean, with its waves and tides and rhythmic rumble and vast horizons, was the water I knew, the water that mattered. In my Illinois teen years, the plodding brown rivers, which I took scant notice of, seemed no more than drainage ditches with names. One notable exception to my lack of awareness was a hot summer night when Scottie and I, after a band gig in Dubuque, Iowa, joined a party of strangers on the Mississippi River, floating easily in slow murky warm water with cold beers in our hand, a blissful sort of scene until we were attacked by a gang of unfriendly local greasers and had to escape through dense bank-side brush followed by a long slog along railroad tracks, stranded 250 miles from home. That river, it turned out, was no joyful glide but a lazy, dirty, dangerous trap.

When I went back to Massachusetts for college, I landed next to the Charles River. It, too, seemed slow, but much more civilized than the northern Mississippi, with sail boats and rowers in sleek sculls and carefully cultivated paths along its banks. In my early days there, lonely and lost in a new place with no friends, the easy flow of the river was soothing, a welcome contrast to the urban hubbub just steps away, and the constant clamor in my head. Walking the Charles had a certain philosophical weight, I thought, and in my first college days, I imagined I was destined to be a deep thinker. Walking beside the river with my hands studiously clasped behind my back seemed part of living that role.

Long after those fantasies of intellectual prowess had been exploded by pot and LSD and friends who humbled me, Sarah and I got to know each other walking along the Charles, about two-thirds of the way through our freshman year. I was deeply attracted to her, but she was just looking for a sympathetic somebody to talk to about troubles with her

Philadelphia boyfriend and how she fit into the tribe of freaks and radicals that our group of friends was becoming, the tribe that eventually would emigrate to Tiller, Oregon. We'd slip away from the near constant party in our dorms, navigate the grimy underside of the Mass Pike, dart daringly across Storrow Drive, and there we were on the tree-lined banks of the Charles. The more we talked, the more attracted I became to her, to her fundamental honesty, her natural empathy, her no-bullshit intellect—and the more I listened, the more I became the trusted friend, the safe *not*-boyfriend. It was an agonizing dilemma for me for quite a while. But it was, I believe, those thoughtful walks along that wide quiet river when I had little hope that showed her some part of me that eventually she thought she could love. There must have been some deep vibes beyond my understanding in the flow of that river.

But the Charles never roared. The South Umpqua, loaded from spring rains and snow melt, powered by its rapid descent from the Cascade peaks that rose to the east of us, positively roared—a roar that was a song, a soliloquy, and a symphony, a single powerful voice and glorious universal chorus. Hesse, I think, once wrote that all the sounds of the world could be heard in the river's music if only we learned to listen better.

I heard majesty and power as I lay in awe on the warm fine gravel next to Sarah, a welcome and a warning. This was the song of our new world, the mighty green trees a short stone's toss away on the other side, the deep blue sky emerging from fleeting gray clouds above us, the gray-blue mountain water rushing white over exposed boulders and scattered remnants of logs.

We shed our clothes and waded in gingerly through the shifty gravel and around sharp rocks. The water was fucking freezing. Sarah stopped when the water reached her thigh, balancing against the current, holding her arms across her pale white chest, laughing and grimacing at the same time. Sarah, naked in the South Umpqua River, sparkling with fresh wetness, framed by Oregon's raw splendor, beautiful in an entirely new way. I moved a little farther out until it was just deep enough for me to drop down and immerse my whole body in the river. A baptism. Shocked by cold, I jump to my feet as fast as I could in the slippery footing, and screamed as loud as I could:."Wooooooooh, ooooh, ooo." As thrilled as I was chilled to the bone.

I lunged toward Sarah still shivering in the shallows and before she could put up any defense, I had her in my arms, wetting her with the river water that dripped from me. We kissed deep and quick, completing the ceremony, then hurried to the warmth of the dry gravel. I was deliriously happy.

We presented quite a scene heading to the dump in Stu's pickup. We, of course, had gotten good and stoned before we left the White House. Most of us piled in the back around the condemned TV. Stu drove, with Paulie in the middle and Mike riding shotgun. Mike carried the rifle and occasionally would brandish it out the window to clenched-fist cheers and laughter from those of us in the back, and Dale and Sydney, following behind in their VW bus, would honk their horn. A merry band of revolutionaries we were.

We ceremoniously hauled the TV off the truck bed and placed it on the edge of the parking area, the lip overlooking the dump's pit. We had the dump to ourselves. Mike still had

the gun. It seemed only right that he would be the executioner.
We lined up loosely behind him as he knelt and brought the
rifle to his shoulder.

It was a goof, this ritualistic killing, just a fun way to get rid
of a broken-down old TV. But, man, what would be a better
way to declare our independence from all we had left behind,
consumerism and lowest common denominator entertainment,
false values and brain washing, a society so convinced that it
was the greatest fucking thing the world had ever seen that it
had lost the ability to think critically about itself. McLuhan had
told us that television had laid the groundwork for the cultural
revolution, that, as a "hot" medium, it taught us to expect
to have some control over our lives and our world. Maybe
there's some truth to that. There was no doubt that watching
the events around the Kennedy assassination and almost live
coverage of the war in Vietnam and the riots in the inner cities
and the Chicago cops gone berserk at the '68 Democratic
National Convention had made deep imprints on our
consciousness. But television was also the ultimate expression
of the vacuous materialism that we were trying to escape. We
had to kill it.

At the Tiller dump, nobody gave any speeches or deep
analysis. Mike made one shot to dead center, and then we all
heard the eerie "Whooooooosh" as the shattered screen sucked
in on itself. It was quiet for a few beats as we all looked around
wide eyed at each other and then somebody said, "Far fucking
out," and we rushed to kick the carcass down into the pit.

SPRING/3

Things had calmed down a bit. Huntsman, Swig, and Rusty had split. Tiller was not quite their scene. The Tiller Tavern, the only bar within twenty miles, was hostile territory. When they tried to hang out there one night, against Dale's advice, the dozen or so patrons stood at attention, some with pool cues raised like a flagstaffs, and sang "The Star Spangled Banner." They bought some beer to go and came back to the White House a little shaken and talking about moving on soon.

Their departure left only seven of us in the house: Mike and Paulie, Jeffrey, Walter, Little Eddie, and Sarah and me, all from the Boston tribe. To celebrate what felt like the beginning of some stability, the other Boston expatriates Dale and Sydney and Stu came for dinner. Stu brought along Stephen, who he was staying with to alleviate the crowding at the White House.

It was a feast. Mike, a big kid with big opinions, his cedar bark hair just starting to grow back after he'd cut it to testify at my trial, made bread. Sydney, thin with long straight dark hair and a face anyone would call pretty, reprised her role as den mother of our chaotic crew and led a bunch of us in chopping onions and garlic for a meat sauce to go on spaghetti and preparing lettuce, carrots, celery, and tomatoes for a big salad. Walter, short with hair all over the place, who'd lived with Sydney and Dale in Boston, was her chief assistant. Stu, roommate to Mike and me at our last Boston apartment, with a mound of curly hair and irrepressible East Coast wit, kept the woodstove cranking.

With the baking bread and gurgling sauce, the house was filled with an enchantingly domestic aromatic warmth. Eddie, the kid who'd escaped from a high-class mental institution to our apartment at Mountfort Street, kept the joints flowing, and Jeffrey, known for his fine taste in hashish and music, kept tunes blasting as we all kind of danced through our sundry tasks.

Stephen, the newcomer to this crowd, smiled quietly as he nursed an Olympia beer from the case he had brought as his contribution to the festivities and observed our loosely collaborative effort. I didn't know much about him. He seemed like a good guy. He looked strong, with a firm, angular jaw and straight brown hair reaching down almost to his shoulders. He spoke in measured sparse sentences that gave a hint that a lot of hard-won experience lurked somewhere behind them.

A few years older than us, he had spent some time in the army and seemed to know about mechanics and animals and working hard in ways the rest of us didn't. On the place where he lived, they had chickens and a milk cow and a few horses that he helped look after. That's where Paulie's horse was going to stay for now. I don't know how Stephen had ended up there or how long he had been there. He seemed a little ill at ease among us but was friendly, and it seemed like he had skills and knowledge that could be valuable to us as we tried to adapt to our new life in Oregon.

We put together two small tables to make one table big enough for the eleven of us. All manner of chairs from all over the house were collected and lined along the table. It was a scramble to pull together enough dishes and silverware but somehow we did and the table was set and loaded down with the platters and bowls of the food we had prepared. And we gathered around.

Dale, sturdy looking with thin blond hair that couldn't quite reach his shoulders, raised a can of beer and spoke as he scanned around the table. "Can you fucking believe it?" We all raised whatever beverage was in front of us to join the toast. "From West Campus and Comm Ave and Mountfort Street and wherever else in Boston and Cambridge we hung out. From our fruitless quest on the California beaches and serious trials and crazy weddings and old families and shit jobs and a thousand stoned-out sessions talking bullshit about moving to the country and growing gardens and creating communes and making a fucking revolution. Well, brothers and sisters, here we are."

"Right on!" I shouted with others and we tapped glasses and cans and shared hugs and clasped hands and victorious smiles. I caught a glimpse of Stephen, who now seemed even less certain of what to make of us. But he grinned too and shyly went along with whatever physical expressions of solidarity came his way.

Then we dove into the food, with a celebratory and dope-driven voraciousness. Everybody had just about filled their plates when we heard a knock on the door. It got quiet. Anybody we knew wouldn't bother knocking. Had we imagined it? Then a louder more insistent knock. I was closest to the door. I looked around the room. Expressions ranged from quizzical to paranoid. I looked to Dale and Sydney, the longest residents. Dale shrugged his shoulders, so I got up and went to the door.

A couple, maybe in their late thirties, looked at me nervously, a look that intensified when they saw the gathering behind me.

"Hello," the man said in a shaky voice. "We are the Zimmermans and we are supposed to move into this house tonight."

I heard the words he spoke but I couldn't really understand what he was saying, It didn't make any sense. This was our house.

"What?" was the only response I could muster, not challenging him, just seeking some clarification. I was thoroughly bewildered.

His voice was firmer. "We have rented this house as of today. Our kids are in the car. You were supposed to be gone by now."

"What?" I said again, but this time turning to look at my friends behind me, zeroing in on Dale and Sydney.

"All our stuff, our kids, our dog are in our truck," he repeated, trying to get through to me. "We've paid the rent three months in advance. The landlord, who is our cousin, said he sent you a letter weeks ago. The house was supposed to be vacant."

Dale was now beside me at the door. "Well, he told you wrong. We never got a letter like that. We've kept up with the rent. There must be some kind of mistake. You sure it's this house?"

"Yes. I'm sure it's this house," Zimmerman said. He seemed to be getting more confident and more frustrated that we couldn't accept what he was telling us. "Look, we can call my cousin if you want to get this straightened out."

"There's no phone here," Dale said. "We'll have to go to the phone booth at the gas station."

"OK, let's go," Zimmerman said.

Stu's truck was the last vehicle in the driveway besides the Zimmerman's, so he drove Dale to the gas station, following the fully loaded Zimmerman pickup.

We finished the meal in stunned near-silence. Sydney was certain she had never seen a letter from the landlord. The mail went to a P.O. box at the Tiller Post Office which was just a few hundred yards down the road. The postmasters, Mr. and Mrs. Potter, were particularly unwelcoming, we'd been told, and suspected of being overzealous in their inspection of mail addressed to any of us or the few other freaks living in the area. But, letter or no letter, the situation was still the same. A full-on family with all their earthly possessions was set to move into this house that we had been aiming toward for more than half a year, that was the base for our big plans for land where we could build houses and gardens and new ways to live, and that we had just moved into, just gotten settled in, had just got our hands dirty in its moist Oregon soil. Not much anybody could say. Just wait for Dale and Stu to come back.

We were all still sitting around the table when they came back, grim-faced. We had polished off the case of beer that Stephen had brought. We knew by the way they looked when they walked in the door that they didn't have good news.

Dale spoke. "Well, it's true," he said, matter of factly. "Old man Zimmerman rented the place out from under us. He claims to have mailed us a letter telling us to be out by today but I swear none of us ever saw it. That didn't mean shit to him. They're family and, he didn't say this, but I think the more he saw what was going on here, with more and more people and cars arriving, the more he just wanted to get us out. He wouldn't listen to anything I had to say. So, we have to clear out of here tonight."

Sarah looked at me, kind of panicked. I didn't have any answers. We'd lucked out finding this big house in tiny Tiller. How were we going to find another place with room for all of us? Shit, where would we sleep tonight?

"Fuck, man, we don't have to go," Mike said. "We're here. Let them find another place. Let them try to throw us out. Fuck 'em, man."

"Yeah, we could do that," Dale said. "I just don't think we're going to win this one, Mike. Did you see that family. Shit, they're just poor folks, too. They aren't trying to fuck with us. They're just looking for a place to live. They sold their house in California and want to try to make a go of things here. Nice folks. Shit. They feel bad for what's happening to us. But they've got no place to go."

"We do that, Mike, and that could end this whole thing before we hardly even get started," Stu said. "Is this the place we want to take our last stand for. I don't think so."

"Not good community relations," Walter added. "'Hippies battle homeless family,' doesn't sound good any way you look at it."

"Shit," Mike said, not yielding but sort of acknowledging that the consensus was forming against him.

"So what are we going to do if we leave? How are we going to find another place?" Sarah asked.

"Old man Zimmerman told me about a two-bedroom place downriver, near Russ and Sally, some freaks we know, good folks." Dale said. "I called the number he gave me. It's empty and some of you could move in there tonight. There are a few places around where people might be able to crash for a few nights at a time." Not exciting possibilities.

"Shit, we gotta start looking harder for our land," I said. "This sucks. Two bedrooms won't hold all of us."

"I was going to head back east soon anyway," Jeffrey said. "Tidy up stuff back there, convince Annie to come back with me. Maybe there'll be a place for all of us by the time we're ready to come back."

"Yeah, me, too." Eddie said. "And I'd like to find a woman to come back with me. Someone to keep me warm at night."

"Good luck with that," Stu said and some chuckles lightened the heavy mood a bit.

"Well, we ain't going back anywhere," I said. "So that leaves me and Sarah and Mike and Paulie and Walter without a place. That two bedroom could work, for awhile at least."

"And three dogs," Sarah added.

"Somebody could crash with Stu and me up at the Nielsen's place for a night or so," Stephen said. "There's not a lot of room, but ... "

The conversation subsided for a bit. A joint got passed. A nice buzz on, I looked around that funky old house that had meant so much from so far away and we had embraced so passionately in the two weeks we got to spend in it. Now, it was passing, disappearing from our lives. It had served its purpose: a West Coast foothold, that became, more importantly, we now realized, an Oregon foothold. We didn't even know, when we started looking for a house for all of us, that Oregon was where we were meant to be, and we never could have imagined that Tiller, Oregon, was our destiny. But now, there was no thought of going anywhere but somewhere in this South Umpqua Valley.

This was a setback, a stunning complication. Mike stayed pissed. Sarah fretted about the arrangements in a two-bedroom house. Paulie contemplated taking Stephen up on his offer so she could be closer to her horse. Dale and Sydney seemed a bit overwhelmed by the transformation from their quiet winter days in an underpopulated White House to feeling some almost parental responsibilities for the lot of us. Eddie and Jeffrey still had business back east but their hearts had been won by Tiller. Stephen must have been wondering just how he had landed in the midst of this mixed bag of freaks—but he didn't seemed turned off by us.

I was bummed for certain. But I knew we weren't going back. We were here and we would figure out how to stay here, without fighting it out with a hopeful family or some local eviction posse. This was just another little twist in the road from that dying *there* to this promising *here,* palpable now, but still just out of reach. This was nothing compared to the many more treacherous stretches we had already overcome.

We pulled ourselves away from that table and just started throwing shit into Stu's and Stephen's trucks and Dale and Sydney's VW bus. We were out of the White House in three hours and seven of us found places to sleep amidst all the stuff that just got tossed in the door of our new home, the Red House, the same song of the same river running through the rushing thoughts in our heads.

SPRING/4

The Red House was a tantalizing purgatory. We were still just across the road from the river but the bank was a sharp drop to the water and clogged with thick brush. No good beach spot. No garden spot. No land to speak of, really. Behind the house was steep forest probably owned by some logging company. We put in some time in a garden Stu was working on at the Nielsen's place, but that didn't feel like ours. The water in the Red House flowed thick and orange with sulfur so we couldn't drink it and bathing in it felt dirty—and, when the tub was full, it made the whole house stink like a fart factory. It was a small two bedroom and the five of us— Walter, Mike and Paulie, and Sarah and me—and our three dogs—Moonbeam, Abby, and Quinn Man—were on top of each other and living surrounded by unpacked boxes and scattered, miscellaneous stuff.

Russ and Linda, who lived in a very small house below us on the same driveway, were welcoming freaks who had lived a while in Champaign in the recent past. Getting to know them was cool. And at the bottom of the driveway, a family named Bolinborg—a mother and father, a grown daughter and her husband, and a son—lived in a little bit bigger house. They seemed like simple hard-working folks scraping by the way country folks do, seasonal jobs in town when they could find them, maybe some days on a logging site up in the woods, and getting what they could out of their surroundings: deer, firewood, fence poles, and the like. Most locals kept their distance, but like Earl, the Bolinborgs had been downright friendly to our friends who spent the winter in the White

House. Mrs. Bolinborg—her first name never did come up—brought them casseroles and pies and the son-in-law liked to come by and drink beer with Stu and Dale and Sydney. His name was D.K. Quarles but he was known as Squirrely. The story went that when he was in the army, he was told he had to have a nickname and he could choose Queerly or Squirrely, and it didn't take him long to make his choice.

With Russ and Linda and the Bolinborgs, our little neighborhood was cordial and welcoming enough. Nobody hassling us. We put up some block and board bookcases and tried to make the Red House feel something like a home, but we all knew this wasn't the kind of place we had dreamed about.

Oregon was still Oregon and we tried to get to know it. Sarah and I bought a red '52 Chevy pickup from Earl, who had sold Stu his white truck. We paid $200 each for the white and the red trucks, and they were good solid rigs, but they had both been worked hard over their nearly twenty years of existence. Their odometers were long past reflecting a true sense of the toll their mileage had taken on them. Keeping them running was an ongoing challenge. But the best part was that they came with a lifetime guarantee that if we could get them to Earl's packed-dirt driveway, he would figure out what was wrong and talk us through fixing it. And chances were pretty good that he would have just the part we needed at a much better price than any of those fancy auto part stores in town.

Earl was a classic. He was 73 years old and lived in a self-built compound of plank-sided sheds full of tools and parts and all manner of canned goods around a small house in Days Creek, a bend in the road sixteen miles downriver, between Tiller and Canyonville, the nearest town with anything more than a gas station-store and post office. Earl had built the Days Creek store back in the late forties and ran it for years. He'd been out of that for a while and his wife had died a short time before he dropped by the White House one day last winter to introduce himself to these strange young folks who had come from the East. I don't know if it was curiosity or old-fashioned good neighborliness or maybe loneliness that led Earl to knock on that door, but a remarkable friendship grew out of that meeting. Most locals were either openly hostile or avoided us all together. Earl didn't seem to give a shit what anybody else thought.

He had an almost rectangular granite face, plain brown-framed glasses, close-cropped gray hair—and the thickest fingers I ever saw, muscled and callused, worked to a machine hardness, worn to a leathery shine, fingers formed by a lifetime of hard work getting by in that lush and rugged country. Yet those blunt sausage fingers could nestle a quarter-inch nut and guide it around fans and manifolds and whathaveyou past the godawfulest crook of an engine and thread it on the barest tip of the bolt where it needed to be. And that, of course, after our young and nimble fingers had failed a dozen times. Earl, smiling, patient, encouraging, would wait as we tried and cursed and declared the impossibility of getting that particular nut on that stupid misplaced bolt—and then, matter-of-factly, do it. He was trained in the first class at the Ford auto repair school back east but Earl's automotive skills were wizard-like, magical, rather than strictly technical.

For years, I had disdained knowing anything more than I needed to about cars or anything mechanical. I loved to drive but didn't care how a car worked. But now, the owner of a '52 Chevy pickup, committed to some level of self-sufficiency and under Earl's spell, I was determined to rise above my absolute incompetence to learn how to deal with these vehicles.

His place, being right on our way to Canyonville, was also the perfect stopping place on our trips to town. Even when we had mechanical business to attend to, we'd always visit—his word—in the small living room of the house, kept hospitably hot by a corner woodstove. He served us instant coffee in hard plastic cups and told us stories of the days when salmon were "thick as cord wood" in the South Umpqua River behind his place, how any man could step outside his door and in no time get enough venison to can up to last the year, how he built his house out of lumber from a local mill in seven days, with a handsaw and a hammer and help from a few buddies. His little dog Queenie, with the thinning hair of old age showing patches of pink skin, always curled at his feet. Us city kids with our country dreams were mesmerized by his stories and his absolute acceptance and generosity. He got something from us, too, I guess, but that was harder for me to understand. Most of us Boston transplants had some level of mystical faith in our Oregon pilgrimage, and Earl seemed the personification of this particular piece of Oregon, its history and landscape, its culture of rugged self-sufficiency, its seasons and its creatures, a hard-handed, soft-hearted, plain-talking shaman of this valley that had drawn us from 3,000 miles away.

But from the beginning and for as long as we knew him, Earl never quite got Sarah's name right. Early on, he heard it as Sharon, and Sharon she always was to him.

Earl's friendship was a kind of orientation into the valley, and the trucks he sold us lent a hint of legitimacy to our quest to become Oregonians.

Behind the wheel of the red truck, shifting—smoothly, at last—through the on-the-floor, three-speed transmission around the sharp curves of the river road, I felt like less of a stranger, an intruder. When driving a pickup, I learned, someone driving a similar rig in the opposite direction, would give you a little nod and a quick flip salute to acknowledge you. I was thrilled the first time that gesture was directed at me and clumsily returned it. Even some of the locals who would shun us in any public setting would do it. In the blur of two pickups converging at fifty miles an hours, they couldn't focus fast enough to see I was one of those East Coast hippies. Speed and distance and the cover of an old pickup truck made room for just a taste of neighborliness.

Another step I envisioned toward becoming an Oregonian, I thought, was to learn to fish this river. As a boy, I had fished in Buzzards Bay, trolling for blue fish or striped bass. I loved those days, especially when we were on the water in the sun with a bracing sea breeze and felt the strike of one of those wild fish, see them rise above our wake, and wrestle them into the boat. No great techniques or skills were required, just the rudimentary reflex of reacting when you felt a strike. It was all natural and flowing. Now I was in Oregon, with its spectacular mountain rivers and its reputation for salmon and trout.

Stu could be the master gardener. Paulie was set on raising horses and spent more and more time hanging with Stormy up at the Nielsens, sometimes spending the nights there. Sarah was also into animals, learning about chickens and goats, and keen on developing her craft skills. Mike read Mao and baked bread. Walter was studying astrology, looking for lessons that could help us to live better together. I read a lot, too. Hesse's *Narcissus and Goldmund* struck home with its explorations of the dualities of mind and spirit, of body and soul, of freedom and stability, dualities that seemed to stare us in the face. "One had always to pay for the one with the loss of the other," Goldmund tells us. But why? Couldn't we have both? Couldn't we have it all? That's what we were trying to find out. I loved having the time and space to ponder such questions. But it was the unveiling of my first spring in Oregon, and I couldn't stay inside for too long without needing to get out into it.

So I would be a fisherman, learn these streams and the species who inhabited them.

I spent an hour one afternoon at the Canyonville Hardware Store, talking to the two guys working there, mid-forties and definitely straight but friendly enough, about how to get started fishing in the area. They sold me a mid-priced lightweight spinning rod and reel and a couple of lures, and they gave me a couple of small spools of line and some sinkers to practice casting. Rainbow trout were the only fish in the river at that time of year, they told me, and that season didn't open until May. There was a steelhead—another kind of trout—run in September and salmon also ran in the river, but it was illegal to catch any because they were getting so scarce. But, they told me, learning to cast in the river was the key skill, to get your lure or bait to the hole you were aiming at and then to work the current and get your rigging back in without getting tangled in all the debris and weeds. The finer points of knowing which holes to hit, how to set the hook just right, how to play them in and land them would only come with hours on the river, hours I was looking forward to.

The next morning before anybody else even got up, I gathered my gear and walked along the road upriver until I saw an opening in the brush along the bank with a flat rock shelf below it where I could stand right up next to the moving river. There was a slow drizzle falling but the sun hovered close behind the wispy silvery clouds, casting a soft diffuse light on the fast rippling water. I just stood there, absorbing it all for a while, tasting the wet fresh air, marveling at the magical beauty of so many shades of liquid gray, immersed in the intimate river song, the only sound I could hear until an early run log truck geared down to take the curve in the road above me. But that slowly faded, too, and it was just me and the river again and I knew that anything that brought me to this river was a blessing. Oregon. Oh, man, I loved it.

So eventually, high on this scene, I tried to focus and rig up my gear. I wasn't quite sure whether the reel and the eyelets on the rod should be on top or on the bottom. I know the guys at the hardware store had showed me but it seemed so simple when they demonstrated that I didn't really focus on the details. From my ocean fishing days, I remembered that the reel was on top, so I tried it that way. I tied the end of the line to the spool on the reel but when I tried to reel in more line, it seemed to be going the wrong way. Eventually I flipped the reel to the underside of the rod and got the line to come in. I attached some sinkers to the loose end of the line. I pivoted the rod over my head and whipped it toward the river. My "cast" was only the two or three feet I had pulled out to attach the sinkers, which went flying as the line came to a sharp stop. I could hear a faint "plink, plink" where they splashed into the river a few feet away. The line hung limp in front of me.

It didn't get much better. After a half hour or so of puzzlement and frustration, I figured out the reel should be below the rod and the eyelets of the rod should face down, that I had to flip the bail (the half-circle that sits above the line) open and hold the line with my finger when I drew the rod back. But even when I got those basics right, I struggled to coordinate the release of the line with my finger and the whipping action of the rod. Either I waited too long to lift my finger and the line would, again, stop abruptly short, sometimes sending more sinkers flailing into the river, or I would release it too soon and catch the brush behind me which involved extended untangling, or the line would release out of control and fall weakly just a few feet into the river. I kept trying while the morning slowly brightened and the droning log trucks got more frequent. I made two or three decent casts in all that time, but never got my line in clean, always finding a sunken log or a clump of water weeds to tangle in. I snapped my line off trying to get it free of the last of those. I thought about throwing the goddamn rod and the reel into the river, but I didn't. I just sat down on the cold flat rock and refocused on the river's song, the sweet light of the sun, floating in and out of the breaking clouds. Exhaled deeply. Man, I didn't want to fight this river, but it turns out it was a powerful, willful force, not some prop for my amusement or fantasy fulfillment. I'll be back, I told it, as I turned to climb up the bank and head back down the road to the Red House.

Just as I climbed the short driveway toward the house, Stephen's black Dodge one-ton truck pulled in. Stu sprung out of the cab, followed quickly by Paulie and Stephen. They all were beaming, radiant.

Stu caught my eye. "We found it, man. We fucking found it."

SPRING/5

"**I**t's perfect," Paulie almost sung.

"I've never seen a more beautiful place," even the usually stoic Stephen, who was becoming more and more a part of our trip, was grinning like a motherfucker.

Sarah, Walter, and I were firing questions at them but they were too busy gushing to get into any details. Mike hung back, reserved, barely cracking a smile.

Finally everyone took a breath and crammed into the living room. Stu took center stage.

"We went and looked at this place up Francis Creek, off the river road about ten miles up. It was OK. Forty acres mostly forest but with enough cleared land for a good garden and animals and stuff, a small funky house and a couple of outbuildings and the creek running along the edge. It was OK, a lot of potential.

"But then …"

He scanned the room, eyes big. Walter lit a joint and started passing it. "Somebody had told Stephen about a place farther upriver, almost to Umpqua Falls. I'm not even sure how we found it. It was on a Forest Service road. We went up a couple of wrong ones before we finally came to a locked gate and could see some cleared land beyond it."

The joint came around to Stu and he took a deep pull, milking the dramatic pause as he played us with his eyes. "Just wait," they said.

He exhaled and looked around the room again before he resumed his story. He even had Mike, loosened by the first couple of tokes, going now.

"So we're standing there, trying to see what we could see and wondering if we dared climb over the gate to check the place out, when a pretty clean pickup truck pulls up behind us and a short, stout weathered looking man wearing a Caterpillar hat, climbs out. 'What the hell's going on here?' he says, sort of gruff but not like really hostile or anything and he's looking us up and down. Stephen told him we had heard this place was for sale and we were looking for some land. He examined us again but with a different kind of expression."

The joint came back to Stu and he paused to take another toke. "You're driving me crazy, Stu," I said. "Come on."

He smiled big at me, now pretty stoned in addition to reveling in our rapt attention. "Don't worry," he said, "It's worth the wait."

"So this guy—his name is Willie Campbell—got friendly, 'OK let me show you around the place,' he said. And man …"

"You won't believe it," Paulie giggled.

"It blew my mind," Stephen added.

"One hundred and thirty-five acres of cleared land in a box canyon valley surrounded by virgin forest, all National Forest land. A pretty together house that Willie built for his family, another older funky house a little ways up the road, a couple of barns and a few other sheds and outbuildings, a year-round creek, three ponds. Willie's got cattle running on it now. He loved it up there but his wife's health has been declining so now they spend most of their time in Canyonville, where he runs the saw shop. You could just tell looking at his eyes how much he loved that place. But he's anxious to sell now. He wants 100 grand for the place but we could move on with a $5,000 deposit and a balloon payment of 20 grand in a year.

Regular payments after that. We could move on as soon as we do the paperwork and pull the deposit together."

Stu gave me a smug look. The joint was back to him but before he took a hit he said, "Did I tell you it'd be worth the wait?"

"Shit, we could do that," I said. No sweat. We had our wedding money. Stu had savings from the social security he got after his father died. Paulie and Mike had savings. We could put together five grand easy—and we had a year to get the $20,000 together. We really could do that.

"It's so beautiful," Paulie said and she walked across the room to give Mike a big hug.

I grabbed Sarah's hand and squeezed it. She pulled me toward her and we kissed, soft and sweet. Walter hugged Stu and then surprised Stephen by hugging him, too. Stephen was awkwardly cool with it. Our land, our land!, was in sight.

Walter threw the I Ching. "Is this place <u>the</u> place for us," he asked as he shook the three coins in his hands. He threw them to the floor: three heads, and he drew a solid line with a circle in the middle of it, the bottom line of the hexagram. Then he threw two heads, one tail, three times in a row, and after each one, he drew a broken line on top of the previous line. The fifth was like the first and another solid line with a circle was added. For the top line, he threw two heads and a tail which meant another broken line. The hexagram looked like this:

—— ——

———o———

—— ——

—— ——

———o———

Walter grabbed the I Ching book and found the hexagram. "OK. It's number three, Chun, 'Initial Difficulty.'"

"That's all right," Paulie said, "I mean what would you expect?"

"Maybe we've already had the initial difficulty," Sarah said. "Look at this place," she laughed as she looked around at the boxes piled all around us.

"Wait, wait, let me read it," Walter said, raising his hands. "That's just the title." He paused and looked around until he had our attention again. "OK, the Judgment says, 'Chun indicates there will be great progress and success, and the advantage will come from being correct and firm.'"

"All right," I said, smiling at Stu, "I think we're pretty fucking correct and firm."

"Come on," Walter said, "you've gotta listen to the whole thing. And the point is not to make it fit what you already think but to listen for advice about how to proceed."

We all tried to get serious, to pay attention, but we were all sort of giddy and stoned.

"OK, here's the Commentary," Walter continued. "'In Chun, we have the strong and the weak commencing their intercourse,'" he paused and looked around to see if anyone would make a wisecrack, but we were trying to be good, and he was sort of smirking anyway. He put on his serious face again. "'… and difficulties arising. Movement in the midst of peril gives rise to great progress and success through firm correctness.'"

"More firm correctness," Stu said. "How are we supposed to know what's correct?"

"Listen, maybe you'll hear something," Walter said and read on. "'By the action of thunder and rain, all between heaven and earth is filled up. But the condition of the time is full of irregularity and obscurity. Feudal princes should be established, but the feeling that rest and peace have been secured should not be indulged.'"

"Well, they got the rain right, but princes?" Stu asked "Who are going to be our princes?"

"You fucking guys," Mike said, frustrated with the banter. "You don't take it literally. This stuff was written in ancient China. You gotta interpret how the text applies to the question you asked. It seems to me it's saying the land is a good thing if we do it right, but that strange shit is going to happen and we will need leaders to get through it. Just getting the land is not going to bring peace and make everything easy." He scanned the room sort of smugly.

"That sounds about right on," Walter said.

"So how do we know what 'doing it right' is?" Sarah asked.

"Wait there's more," Walter said buoyed a bit by Mike taking the whole thing more seriously than the rest of us. He read some more which, he said, seemed summed up in the text about the changing line next to the top: "'The fifth line, undivided, shows the difficulties in the way of its subjects in dispensing the rich favors that might be expected. With firmness and correctness, there will be good fortune in small things. Even with them in great things there will be evil.'"

"What the fuck?" I said. "I don't like that."

"It's not a fortune teller," Walter said, a little exasperated with me. "It's an advisor. One more thing to read. The changing lines create a new hexagram, number two K'un, Receptive, "Resting in Firmness. 'K'un represents what is great and originating and having the firmness of a mare.'" Paulie smiled at Stephen with the horse reference. "'When the superior man'—that just means someone doing the right thing—'has to make any movement, if he takes the initiative he will go astray; if he follows, he will find his lord. The advantageousness will be seen in his getting friends in the south-west and losing friends in the north-east. If he rests in correctness and firmness, there will be good fortune.'"

"In other words, the princes are fucked," Stu said. "OK, Mike, you can be a prince."

Mike laughed. Walter tried to make sense of it all. "Man, I think it's just saying it's going to be hard at first, so we need to pay attention and try to stay righteous. We're going to need leaders but if they get too big for their britches they're going to have a fall. None of that seems surprising to me. Good advice and nothing that indicates that we shouldn't do this."

"That's all I wanted to hear," Stu said.

Walter lit another joint.

The next day, Stu took Sarah and me to the land. The Forest Service road that led to it was about eighteen miles upriver from Tiller, heading northeast up into the Cascade Mountains. It was a beautiful drive that we had taken before, exploring the river road up to Umpqua Falls, which was another couple miles beyond our turnoff. But it was all different now. Now that curling, majestic fir-lined road was the portal to our dreams. My adrenalin and spirit soared with the elevation as I tried to imagine that each turn, each rise, each magnificent river view could soon be the path to our new world. The gray, drizzly day, made the rich greens of the trees and the steel blue of the river all the more mysteriously stunning, like the cloud-shrouded passage that opened the door to other searching souls in *Brigadoon,* a childhood favorite of mine. Like those guys, I kept thinking this is too good to be true.

We drove a couple of miles up a steep bending gravel road before we came to the gate. It was locked, so we pulled over to the side of the road and proceeded on foot, glad to have been warned to wear rubber boots for this trek. We leaned against the gate in silence for a while, contemplating what lay on the other side. The rain had picked up, with hints of snow mixed in, and it enveloped the valley before us, with a level of wetness worthy of *Sometimes A Great Notion,* the book that had introduced me to Oregon during our last winter in Boston. Despite that, or maybe even because of it, the first view was breathtaking, a gray sodden aura rose from this sudden valley—an opening of rough muddy pasture 100-yards wide—that drifted into majestically forested slopes that seemed to climb forever into the clouds. A metal-roofed open barn sat humbly in the distance. And this panorama, it turned out, was only a hint of the full extent of the wide valley that waited around a bend just a healthy stone's throw up the road.

We hopped the gate, now with full permission from the owner, and walked along the rutted road that ran on a narrow shelf along the western edge of the valley. The cattle, who had had the place to themselves for a while, stared suspiciously. We slogged a mile and a half in the drenching rain through the sticky mud, trying to avoid the cow shit, all the while glowing with a growing awe as the valley broadened to 500 yards at its widest, near an almost middle-class looking house, with a fenced yard and a nearby chicken coop. The house seemed out of place in this gently wild setting. We peeked in the windows, could see the kitchen area with a propane stove and a sink, a simple table set under a stairway, and a paneled living room with a stone fireplace, so much nicer than the Red House or even the White House, so much nicer to our eager eyes than any place we had ever lived.

West of the road across from the house, was a cleared flat area with an odd collection of equipment from the life of the ranch: a Caterpillar, two old pickups, a beat-up army munitions carrier, box springs, stoves, toilets, and piles of scrap lumber. Two sturdy outbuildings stood at either end of the clearing. The one on the north end made of rugged logs was the first structure built by White men on this land, Willie Campbell had told Stu. At the far west end of the clearing, two man-made ponds—one for swimming, one for fishing—formed by circles of raised dirt mounds were set against the bordering forest.

And there was more. The valley slowly narrowed as the road rose higher above the valley floor and curved around a barn, whose substructure rose from the ground below with its main floor even with the road. A calving barn, Stu told us. Further on, we came to a second, more rustic, dwelling. There was no lock on the door, so we went in, welcoming a short break from the rain. The house—maybe it had been a place where ranch hands lived—was basic and musty from months? years? of sitting idly through the wet and cold and hot and dry seasons of the mountains, but the roof seemed to keep the rain out, and there were two bedrooms, a kitchen area with a place for a wood cookstove, and a central hearth for a heating stove. It was ready for us.

Across from the Second House was another man-made pond surrounded by brushy woods featuring, I came to learn from Stu, Oregon Ash trees. Willie Campbell had told him that, explaining that was why the creek running along the east edge of the property opposite the road was called Ash Creek and the land was known as Ash Valley—and this place called Ash Valley Ranch. After passing the pond and woods, we came to a small meadow, where scattered grasses led to a row of trees just beginning to leaf out. They marked the bank of Ash Creek. The property ended just beyond that meadow, where the road turned sharply uphill, heading north, and was intersected by another Forest Service road coming steeply out of the west.

We walked back slowly, not saying a whole lot. Stu pointed out a good potential garden spot. Sarah mentioned how cool it would be to have chickens right next to the big house, fresh eggs every day. I wondered if there were fish in the ponds— Stu said Willie had told him there were—or the creek. Mostly, though, we just absorbed the thick, mind-blowing vibes.

Every soggy step of the way, our certainty deepened that we had found *our* place.

How could we doubt that it was meant to be? That all that had gone on since our little tribe had met at a college in Boston—the parties and concerts and demonstrations and acid trips and love affairs and the confounding tribulations and gut-wrenching trials, the California beaches, and the discovery of Tiller—had led us to this magical valley. We had traveled 3,000 miles, left so much behind, in search of a promised land where "we might laugh again," where we could become the kind of people we hoped to be, the kind of people we never could be in the old country. Driving us was the absolute conviction that we were part of a global uprising against war and greed and racism and the slavery of being chained to a reality of pointless jobs and useless things. Along with that came a mystical faith that if we leapt toward the lives we imagined, even though no landing place was immediately apparent, we would get to where we were supposed to be going.

Here, all wet and wildly happy, we were.

SPRING/6

Word that we'd signed papers to buy Ash Valley Ranch spread quickly among the freaks in the Tiller area. Our Boston group plus Stephen, now firmly established as part of us, was nine people, and Eddie and Jeffrey were expected back sometime soon, getting us to eleven. We were sure that the land could handle a lot more than that and we could use more monetary contributions and more people to do the work of creating a sustainable community. And there was a sense that all of us had been drawn from distant places to Tiller for a purpose, and Ash Valley looked more and more like the center of that overarching purpose.

Russ and Linda, the ex-Champaign folks who lived down the driveway from the Red House, were intrigued but seemed hesitant. Tim and Nancy, who also had Illinois roots and had a small house just upriver, were more enthusiastic. Phillip and Jane, who had moved to the area from California about six months earlier and were renting a nice place with some land in a community called Drew about five miles south of Tiller, were way into it. They had three kids including an almost new baby so that would add a fascinating dimension to the trip. Phillip and Jane were a few years older than us and seemed very together. Good people. The other freaks—Todd and Karen, and Matthew and Missy—lived a few miles further south. They'd been around for a while and owned their land, so they weren't interested. Karen, Matthew, and Missy were friendly and helpful. Todd told somebody (Dale or Stu) that he was sure we wouldn't be around long enough so there was no point in making friends with us. We didn't see much of him.

Another guy from California, Jack O'Leary, who crashed around at different places, sometimes sleeping in an abandoned cabin down by the river was immediately gung-ho to move to the ranch. He was tall and lean, a little younger than us, with a hearty laugh and a bit of a biker vibe. He seemed strong and eager to work.

Shortly after we signed the papers, Phillip and Jane threw a party for all the valley freaks. We were excited when Phillip and Jane had so quickly decided to be part of the Ash Valley trip. They had chickens and were raising goats, giving us a great start on the animals we wanted up there. Phillip was markedly mellow and soft-spoken, seemed to have a spiritual wisdom about him. When we'd be discussing something, he would sort of hold back, slowly stroking his wispy, long beard and then make some deep-sounding assessment: "Well, you know, man, life has a way of sorting all this shit out." Not really offering answers but setting parameters for how to think about something. Jane was kind of the yang to his yin, outgoing, almost boisterous. She loved to party and was the animal tender. And she seemed like an attentive mother to her kids, nursing the baby, Rainbow, and always keeping half an eye on Kathy, 10, and Greg, 8, who seemed pretty grown up for their ages. Jane regaled us with stories about her past life, including her stint as a stripper in LA—how to maximize the dollar bill capacity of a g-string and stuff like that. Now, she seemed way into a hippified version of Christianity but didn't try to lay that trip on the rest of us.

The party was kind of a totally unstructured organizational meeting for the prospective commune that would soon move to Ash Valley, a free-flowing rap session that was as much—or more—fantasy as practical details. In fact, we didn't discuss many details beyond a target date to move in a couple of weeks and people rattling off some of the stuff they could bring, tools and equipment and animals and vehicles and such. Nobody took notes or anything. Any kind of hope we had about having a serious meeting went up in literal smoke as a friend of Phillip's from Southern California named Wayne was firing up joints laced, he told us, with a special THC oil. Man, we got blasted. The sensation was an odd mixture of soaring euphoria and a thick heaviness that seemed to dramatically multiply the force of gravity. So, I had brilliant thoughts but I could only slowly squeeze them out toward other people, a 78-rpm album playing at 33.

Wayne seemed to glow under the spell of whatever drug it was and somehow maintain his lucidity. He was tall and thin with straight brown hair and a thick beard—and one extraordinarily long fingernail that I couldn't help but stare at. Phillip, Dale, Stu, Jack O'Leary, Walter, and I surrounded him as he regaled us with a melodic monologue of all the skills and experience he could bring to Ash Valley.

"Man, I built palatial houses for rich folks down in Southern California, fucking movie stars and corporate executives," he told us. "Mansions by the sea or high in the mountains. I designed them and ran crews of the best carpenters I could find using only the most select grades of wood. Enormous rooms with cathedral ceilings and beautiful bay windows. You wouldn't fucking believe it. But, man, they were all rich pigs. Sure, they paid me well but, man, they were never happy, no matter how spectacular the house ended up.

"This, this ranch you cats are talking about. That's what I want to do, simple structures for the people, man, make a place that matters, where we can live free and support each other. Man, I would just love that and I know I could help you. You know man, I'm a fucking architect, and even though I was building those $100,000 mansions, I know how to build great stuff, cheap, using basic materials. And I've got some far-out tools, man, gas-powered tools. We don't need electricity. And man, this place, this Ash Valley you're talking about, just sounds absolutely outasight. Man, I would love it if my daughter and I could be part of that."

His daughter was Tammy, an incredibly cute two-year old who had light brown skin and straight, starless-night black hair. While Wayne held court with most of the menfolk, the women were equally transfixed by Tammy. How could we not invite these two to be part of a great communal adventure? Another one of those things that just seemed meant to be.

As much as Mike enjoyed the joints that Wayne spread around, he was not much impressed by his credentials. He and Stephen sat off in a corner, spacing out and chuckling every once in a while at how stoned and silly everybody was, except, it seemed, Wayne.

When Mike, Paulie, Walter, Sarah, and I staggered out of the party toward the red truck for the ride home, I was trying to say how impressed I was with Wayne and how great it would be to have him on the ranch, but complete, coherent sentences were a challenge for all of us. Mike managed to express some doubts. "Seems like a big-talk LA hippie," he said and grinned. "But what the fuck, lotsa room up there. Maybe he can help us. Got good drugs."

The ride home was sssssslllllllllooooooooowwwwww. The road followed Elk Creek which tumbled down out of the mountains to feed into the South Umpqua right at Tiller, lots of tight turns, wedged between steep banks on the uphill side, which was fortunately the right lane going home, and steep drop-offs on the creek side which still seemed perilously close. The truck felt like an unbroken stallion, wanting to gallop around those curves, and I had to concentrate as completely as I was capable to hold it back. Mostly I stayed in first gear on this 60-mph highway, though once in a while the road would head downhill enough to make the engine groan so badly, I had to go to second. Then I rode the brakes. If the speedometer worked, I'm sure it never would have gotten much past 10 mph. The three of us in the cab (Mike and Walter were in the other world of the back) were frozen in a stoned-out daze of fear. I clenched the steering wheel until my fingers ached and all of us stared fixedly into this impossible maze of a road, as though some magic power in our vision could hold us on the pavement, keep us from sliding out of a curve and down down down to the creek. I have no idea how we survived those five miles. But we did.

SPRING/7

As immersed as we were with preparations for the move to Ash Valley, we still kept informed about what was going on in the outside world, mostly from the day-old *Oregonian* newspapers from the Tiller Store. The war in Vietnam, for one thing, was still going on. American and South Vietnamese forces had attempted an invasion of Laos, which was a short-lived failure. Lt. William Calley was convicted of the premeditated murder of 22 Vietnamese civilians in the My Lai Massacre. As many as 500 unarmed people had been killed at My Lai that day in 1968 and Calley was the only person to suffer any consequences.

Certainly none of the higher-ups who got us in and kept us in that immoral, unwinnable war—the old men who put American boys into the mindfucking position of fighting against a people struggling for independence in their own land—paid any price for their many war crimes of which My Lai was only the most visible example. Nixon ordered Calley to be transferred from Leavenworth to house arrest. Was that some show of solidarity to the grunt for doing his dirty work?

A year after the Kent State killings had set off a national wave of protest, resistance to the war continued. In late April, a group of Vietnam veterans threw away their medals on the steps of the US Capitol, followed by a march of half a million people in DC, with other marches across the country. Those events were sponsored by a broad coalition, which specifically opposed any militant illegal action.

Another group made up largely of counterculture militants—descendants of the Yippies and Motherfuckers who mixed music, drugs, and radical lifestyles with their politics, our kind of people—were planning a different sort of action for the week following Mayday. "If the government doesn't stop the war, we will stop the government," was the slogan of the Mayday Tribe.

That was exciting for Mike and me, the most overtly political among our group, though everyone was revolutionary on some level or they wouldn't have been about to move on to a commune in the wild mountains of Oregon. Most of us had gone to the earlier mass marches in Washington and some of us had even met, during our early days at Boston University, at a sanctuary for a soldier who had deserted in protest of the war. But when protests shifted from peaceful rallies and marches to targeted militant actions, Mike and I were the only ones likely to be there.

The Mayday Tribe offered hope for the mostly nonviolent, truly countercultural elements of the Movement to set the tone for the Revolution among the young. The Weathermen had confused a lot of us for a while. They appropriated the counterculture into their doctrines, and their attempts to romanticize violence had challenged some of us: if we were really revolutionary why weren't we willing to stand and fight it out with cops and ideological opponents. But their attempts to connect to the music and drugs and partying of the counterculture always seemed phony and opportunistic, and their pointless violence—epitomized by the Days of Rage when they challenged Chicago cops to a street fight—which some of us kind of admired in a self-questioning way at first, turned out just to be stupid, burned them out, and drove them underground.

But the Mayday Tribe was proposing militant nonviolent civil disobedience against government targets organized by small groups of brothers and sisters who knew and trusted each other—called affinity groups. Friends of ours who were still back east were heading to Washington in such groups to join in the festivities. It was a model not just for an action, but for a revolution. And those of us about to move to Ash Valley certainly qualified as an affinity group and part of our challenge was to figure out how we fit into the Revolution.

Six of us—Sarah, Mike, Stu, Dale, Jack O, and I—loaded into the VW bus to go to Eugene, home of the state university about 120 miles north of Tiller, for a Mayday demonstration. From what we could gather, the disruptive activities against the IRS, military recruiting, and draft offices, like the disruptions in Washington, were scheduled for the following week. This Saturday march and rally were to be peaceful, which was just as well since I was still on probation for the Northeastern thing. But it was a great chance for a road trip to see more of our newly adopted state, to join in our first Oregon protest, and to get a feeling for how to connect with like-minded folks.

It was a beautiful spring day, a blue-and-white palette of sky and graceful drifting clouds, as we cruised through Canyonville and merged onto Interstate 5, which rolled over hills and valleys between the mighty Cascades to the east and the more modest Coast Range to the west, past cattle ranches and early hay fields, barns and fenced farm yards, cows and horses and sheep stretching their legs and nibbling the green shoots of replenished pastures. The West … it really felt like the mythological West, open spaces and hard-worked land, generations of farm equipment geared up for use or set aside to rust slowly away. Small towns off spread-out exits, Tri City, Myrtle Creek, then three exits worth of big city Roseburg, before Sutherlin, Oakland, Yoncalla, Drain, and Cottage Grove and the flat open farmland that marked the beginning of Oregon's dominant valley, the Willamette (Wil-a-MET? Wil-AM-et? Our stumbling attempts at pronunciation gave away our out-of-stateness).

Eugene is nestled on the Willamette (it is Wil-AM-it, dammit, locals eventually clued us in) River between two forested buttes. We came off the freeway over a big hill and down into a modest neighborhood on its southern edge, houses that could have been in Champaign-Urbana, single-story ranches and bungalows, on wide tree-lined streets. It felt friendly and welcoming, radiating that college town vibe. In fact, the street we found ourselves on as we looked for the county fairgrounds, where the march was to begin, was called Friendly Street. Seeing numbers of freaky type folks all moving in the same direction, we pulled over and found out we were just a couple blocks away. So we parked.

It was cool to be among a mass of our people—about 500 gathered at the fairgrounds—in fucking Oregon! The feeling among the crowd seemed somewhat mellower, less intently militant than more recent demonstrations on the East Coast— maybe a slightly older crowd. But, small differences aside, it felt a lot like gatherings we had been at in Boston and Philadelphia and DC and Champaign over the last three or four years. And all day, since we left Tiller, I was gripped by the sense that we were going to run into somebody we knew from somewhere from another time. I had told everyone in the bus that I was sure that was going to happen and we riffed for a while on who it might be.

Nobody guessed that it would by Dougy and Jill. Sarah saw them first, just as the march from the fairgrounds was reaching the downtown mall, where we were to meet up with a contingent coming from the university for the rally. Twenty or thirty feet in front of us, we saw a guy with a big thick Afro next to a women with straight honey brown hair. Eugene was a college town but still had a minuscule population of Black people, as did the whole state of Oregon. Sarah was the first to speculate that the couple we saw could be our old friends and never shy (like me) in situations like that, called out their names just to see if there would be a reaction. And when they turned and we all had that flash of different-time, different-place recognition, all of our minds were simultaneously blown. Dougy would later say that as soon as he turned he knew it was us because he never knew anyone with hair as blond as mine.

Dougy and Jill were good friends of ours during our freshman year at BU, when most of us lived in the West Campus dorms, including Dougy, who was not a student. Jill lived in the girls dorm, where Sarah also lived. Jill and Dougy had started hanging together at Greenwich (Connecticut) High School and when Jill came to BU, Dougy eventually followed her. He—and she most of the time—stayed with another buddy from Greenwich, Kit, who lived a floor below me at West Campus 1. Kit would give them his single bed and he slept on the floor. Dougy was as much a part of the scene as anybody. We snuck him into the cafeteria, or brought him food, so he could eat. He fucking lived there, man. We loved it.

Dougy and I hit it off right away, hanging out at demonstrations and getting into long stoned raps about poetry and politics. We even put together some homemade books of our poetry. I don't know whatever happened to those. He and Jill got their own apartment up Commonwealth Avenue in Allston after the first semester, the first among our friends. It was just a few blocks from West Campus, so I hung out there a lot, and Mike and Stu did, too. And when Sarah and I were going through the slow transition from friends to lovers, Dougy and Jill's place was a great escape from the scene at West Campus, where we could be together out of the crowd of our friends on campus, trying on being a couple. Dougy and Jill were almost like our guides.

Last time I had seen them was the summer after freshman year, almost two years before our reunion on the streets of Eugene, when they stopped at my parents' place and hung out with me in Urbana for a few days on their way west after they had left Boston behind. I think we exchanged a couple of letters after that but then we lost touch. Last I heard they were in Boulder, Colorado.

And, yet, here they were in Eugene, Oregon. Far fucking out. We hugged and just kinda stood in the midst of the crowd in the middle of the mall in our own little bubble, sharing our amazement. Finally we found a spot to sit all together and tried to pay attention to the rally, but we continued shooting the shit and wearing big grins. No matter what we accomplished on a political level that day, finding Dougy and Jill in Oregon made the trip more than worthwhile.

They'd been living in Eugene for almost a year. They'd originally come to Oregon to visit Dougy's brother Chuck in Corvallis and liked what they saw and hung there for a while. But a recruiter from Lane Community College in Eugene showed up one day, actively recruiting minority folks to come to the college and live in Eugene, trying to increase the tiny percentage of people who weren't White at the school and in the town. The deal was too good to pass up, so they moved the next day. Dougy was going to school and doing odd jobs and Jill was working at a place where they helped kids with mental and physical handicaps. They were real excited to hear about our land and the plans for our commune.

The rally downtown was cool. When the kids from the university showed up, we had around 2,000 people altogether, all peaceful and feeling good. The speakers included Eugene's mayor and a city councilor—that was pretty amazing—and a guy who described himself as "just a working guy," short-haired, older, who said he used to be afraid of hippies and radicals, but now believed that if we could learn to work together we could end the war and do a lot more than that. People dug that and gave him a lot of shouts and a big ovation.

After the rally, most folks went to a park along the Willamette River below the butte at the north end of the city for a huge picnic. Music and balloons and all kinds of great food. Joints and wine bottles passed around. It also turned out that it was Jill's twenty-first birthday and a whole bunch of people joined in when we sang "Happy Birthday" to her. She seemed a little embarrassed but she was beaming, too, with a radiant joy. Man, the vibes were just jubilant, all these freaks gathered by Oregon's signature river, under magnificent firs on such a sweet spring day. Oh, Oregon!

People gathered in small groups to discuss the upcoming actions and other ways to fight against the war and further the Revolution. When we told folks of our plans for Ash Valley and how we wanted to build alliances with people in the city, they got excited and we talked about inviting a bunch of them to come down to see us once we got settled in. We exchanged names and addresses.

Dougy and I had a moment to ourselves, sprawled on the lush green grass, a little stoned and pleasantly buzzed from the wine.

"Shit, Ben R., I can't believe I'm sitting here with you in Skinner Butte Park in fucking Eugene, Oregon. Shit, man, I thought I might never see your ass again …" his words dissolving in an incredulous smile.

"I know, man, I know. Pretty fucking incredible.," I said. "Man, I've been through some serious shit, but now, man, now … everything is coming together. Like we used to talk about in Boston, but more, man, more than we even dreamed about. Shit, we got land. Beautiful fucking land. And so many of us that you knew in Boston are here: Sarah and Mike and Stu and Dale and Sydney and Walter—and more on their way. And now … you and Jill! Shit, man!

"Something bigger than us is working here," he said. "I mean what are the odds of us finding you today … or ever. It's too fucking crazy to even get my head around yet, but I'm digging the shit out of it."

"Man, you've got to come to Tiller, to see the land. To be with us. I know you've got a good trip going here but … we've got a lot of room on the land and you guys have been part of this crazy ass tribe since the beginning. You gotta come. We're moving to the land in just a few days. You just gotta come."

"Count on it, brother" and he extended his hand to me and we clenched our fists together and drew in close and tight.

Fucking Dougy and Jill in Oregon.

SPRING/8

I drove slowly when I thought we were getting near the turnoff to Ash Valley. I'd only been there the one time to look at it and there were no signs marking the road. But after we followed the river around a long easy bend, there it was, easing off and up to the left, unmistakably—now the twisting, climbing entrance to our new home. We were dead quiet, as each curve and rise in the road heightened our already surging levels of anticipation.

Sarah and Jack were in the red truck with me, Moonbeam in the back with all our stuff and some tools and firewood we had picked up at the Nielsen's place, where Stu had been staying with Stephen. Stu's white truck with Walter and Mike—and dogs Winter and Abby—and Stephen's big black Dodge one-ton with Paulie and dogs Quinn Man and Sundance, both rigs also loaded with stuff, were not far behind us. Dale and Sydney and the Hammond family might already have been up there.

We were moving on to the land.

The gate was wide open. We didn't have to park and jump over it. Some mystical goodwill now seemed to pull us through, and, as we crossed into our promised land, I was overcome by a trembling sense of joy—and I joined the others in letting out a howl. This magnificent place was now ours.

The weather had eased up since our earlier visit, still shaded toward gray and a little chilly, but no rain in a week or so. The mud on the road had receded and the pastures were coming in a rich green. A little snow clung to the top of the surrounding hills. The cows, still as at home as ever, watched us pass with the same indifference they had shown on our last visit.

As we passed the first barn and the broader valley opened up to us, we all inhaled almost simultaneously. It was the vision of a western ranch, a wide open shelf of pasture set beneath heroic hillsides of the most spectacular forest of ancient majestic trees I had ever seen. So much more stunning than I could have absorbed on that muddy gray day when I first laid eyes on it. It was too much to take in on first sight. And it was so much more than we could have imagined in our stoned and desperate fantasies of last winter or even the summer before on the California beaches. We didn't know enough to imagine such a place. And even in our wildest dreams, we didn't believe enough to think we could find a place like this. Man, how far we had come from January's bleak fearful courtroom, just five months earlier.

As we exhaled with exuberant smiles, we could see Dale and Sydney's VW in front of the Main House, unloading. Fuck, yes! We pulled up behind them and let Moonbeam out. She seemed as excited as we were, running toward the house and then toward the empty chicken coop and the log outbuilding across the road, sniffing frantically, thrilled by the wild mountain smells. She was panting with joy as she ran back toward us. Dale and Sydney greeted us with hugs and crazy smiles. "Welcome home," Dale said.

We could hear the white and black trucks rumbling up the road and soon they were there, too, and their dogs were loose, joining Moonbeam in exploring this new place with their noses and checking each other out, running madly into the wide open space and then circling back, tongues hanging in joy, to the people lingering around the rigs. We breathed deep this new air, shooting the shit about what we had packed and what we still needed to get but also gazing off here and there, taking it all in, this ground we were standing on, the fence around the house, the fruit trees just starting to blossom, the ponds and structures behind us, the width of the valley, the bend in the road farther on and all we couldn't see beyond it. We had myriad practical things to consider, to get to work on, but no one could avoid the overarching awe of that moment when we arrived at Ash Valley.

"I bet you are wondering why I have called you here today," Stu said when the conversation subsided a bit. It was Stu who, when Boston started seeming like a dead end, first talked about a place in the country with a garden and animals. He was beaming, as his dog Winter panted by his side.

We laughed. Sydney pulled a box of pots and pans out of the VW bus, smiled sweetly at Stu, and said, "How about if we start unloading some of this shit and figure out where we are all going to sleep tonight?"

"Exactly what I was thinking," Stu said, smiling sweetly back.

And we joyfully went to work. The Hammonds had already arrived, dropping Wayne and Tammy's stuff off at the Main House and then heading up to the Second House to unload theirs. With the three kids, including the baby, it made sense for the Hammonds to set up in that place, at least for now. It was cruder but it gave them their own space to help the kids through the transition. Tim and Nancy were expected soon, which would give us nineteen altogether to get this thing started, with more on the way. That would mean fourteen people and five dogs in the Main House, which had five spaces which could be called bedrooms: two upstairs in the main portion of the house, a back pantry where a couple of people could sleep, and kind of an annex-like tower structure that had a bedroom on the ground floor and a loft above it.

So we packed in mattresses and suitcases and boxes of books and records (despite having no electricity) and dishes and other household odds and ends, and a few pieces of furniture. We knew it would be tight until we could put together some additional living spaces. We parceled out rooms through a kind of an intuitive consensus system.

Couples got first dibs on the regular bedrooms. Sarah and I (and Moonbeam) and Dale and Sydney got the two upstairs bedrooms, Mike and Paulie (and Quinn Man) were in the pantry. We gave Wayne a choice of whether he wanted the lower bedroom in the annex or the loft for Tammy and him. He picked the loft, and Stu (and Winter) and Stephen (and Sundance) decided to share the lower room. That left Jack and Walter (and Abby), who volunteered to crash with their sleeping bags in the living room. When Tim and Nancy arrived and got a sense of the Main House scene, they decided to find a spot to pitch a tent.

We were an amalgam of pilgrims settling into this place. A family of five, a single father and daughter. Five couples (three married, two not), five single men. Eight from our Boston tribe (with roots in Pennsylvania, Illinois, Virginia, Connecticut, New Jersey, and other parts of Massachusetts), eight most recently from Southern California, two from Illinois, one from Pennsylvania. An architect, an army veteran, a one-time porn star, a former stripper, and a bunch of college dropouts. Political revolutionaries, spiritual seekers, Jews, hedonists,

Christians, atheists. Everyone liked to smoke dope; most took psychedelics. We had people who could cook and bake, play guitar, write, and even a couple of people who knew how to build things and raise animals, but most of us had never lived on a farm or knew anything about mechanics or had ever worked with our hands.

Some of us had known each other for almost three years, others we had known less than two months, some as little as a couple of weeks.

We brought twenty-seven chickens, three horses (Stormy, Mona, and Morning Star), one goat, five dogs, and one cat. We had five vehicles: a one-ton 1949 black Dodge flatbed; two 1952 ½-ton Chevy pickups; an orange-striped 1964 VW bus; and a green 1963 Willys station wagon. And a tractor.

We all believed, I think, that we could build something extraordinary on this glorious land. If we could learn to combine the passionate energy within each one of us, freed from the pointless pursuits of material success and social status, we could fulfill our needs to express our deepest, truest selves and to serve humanity without martyrdom or self-imposed suffering. We could change ourselves and the world—and be joyful and free.

But the land was more than a receptacle for our fantasies. It was a 135-acre challenge. It had everything we could have wanted, far more in fact. What could we make of it? The land was perfect for us. Were we perfect for the land?

SPRING/9

We had only been on the land a couple of days when we found out that the Forest Service planned to seek bids from logging companies to clearcut a significant swath of the east hillside directly opposite the Main House. We freaked. Virgin forest completely surrounded Ash Valley, defined it, sanctified it. Human beings had never fucked with that forest. Never. Some of those trees were hundreds of years old. Indians, who had to have known and delighted in this sheltering valley, wandered among them, hunting and gathering and exulting in their magnificence. Those ancient trees were a vital part of the aura of natural holiness that we all felt when we first saw the land. A clear-cut would rip that aura to shreds, carving a deep dead scar where a fabulously complex ecosystem had been thriving. It would mean a road up that hillside and heavy equipment erected at its peak, snorting and grinding from sunup to sundown, crews of men running around, looming over us, chain saws whining toward the ominous crack, air-sucking fall, and the thunderous death thud of a giant destroyed.

"Fucking Campbell had to know about this when he took our check," Dale said. A group of us—everyone but the Hammonds—was gathered in the Main House. It was rainy and gray outside. We had a fire going and a pot of hobo coffee on the stove.

"We don't know that," Stephen said. He was rolling a cigarette from a can of Bugler. "Maybe he just found out, too."

"Come on," Sarah said. "You think it was just a coincidence he was so eager to make a deal with a bunch of hippies and then, suddenly, we find out they're planning to log?"

"We were eager to make the deal, too," Stu said.

"We didn't know they were planning on clear-cutting the hillside," I said and reached for the tobacco can from Stephen.

"Would we have not wanted this place if we knew that?" Stu asked.

"It would have made it completely different, maybe he would have negotiated the price more." Sydney said.

"And that would have made it all right for them to kill all those fucking trees?" Mike said

"Mike, you know I didn't say that," Sydney shot back.

We filled up the central section of the house, which included the kitchen, a table under the stairway that had benches that could hold about six people, a fireplace between the kitchen area and the living room, where we had an old wooden rocker and a couple of funky brownish upholstered chairs. People not at the table or in the chairs filled in the places on the floor between them.

"I don't think we want to give up this land," Wayne said. He was in the rocker in the corner furthest from the fireplace, his daughter Tammy playing with a quilted doll quietly at his feet. "And I don't think we can renegotiate the deal." Even though he was the newest person in our group he had been one of the people—along with Phillip and Sydney—who was working with lawyers to form a corporation that would be the official owner of the land. "Family Clan" is the name they came up with, sort of a stupid name, but it was just something to put on legal documents. I had no interest in dealing with any lawyers about anything so I stayed out of it.

"Remember," Wayne calmly continued, "right now, they're just getting ready to seek bids. We can fight it."

"Fucking right we can fight it." Mike said, leaning against the kitchen counter, "We gotta fight it."

"I think he's talking about courts and lawyers, Mike, not guns and violence," said Walter, standing next to Mike, smiling up at him.

"Whatever it fucking takes, man."

We did finally agree to send Dale, Philip, and Wayne to Eugene to find a lawyer to help us stop the logging.

We got a start on the garden. Stu had picked out a space just south of the Main House about 170 feet by 80, a little less than a third of an acre, much smaller than we planned for our long-term garden but still fairly ambitious for our first garden, especially with the late start we were getting with soil preparation and fence building. As soon as we knew we were moving onto this land, Stu had been deep into the Burpee catalog, ordering seeds for pole and bush beans, lettuce, radishes, onions, leeks, carrots, corn, cucumbers, tomatoes, and marigolds, which kept insects away. The garden was going to be completely organic, which meant no chemical pesticides or fertilizers.

It took a while to line out the garden area with stakes and strings, trying to make it reasonably parallel to the road and the sides even distances from each other. Stu and Wayne and Stephen directed Sarah, Dale, Phillip, and me. The four of us represented the corners and the three of them would view us from different perspectives and move us around and then we'd drive stakes and run strings between them. Wayne had a 100-foot tape measure to check distances and make finer adjustments. It was cool, even just being a human marker, delineating the space that would be such a focal point for us.

The soil, Stu had determined, had good potential for a garden. Willie Campbell had told him that Ash Creek used to run right down the center of the valley and another smaller creek still flowed in the rainy season from the west hills to just north of the garden spot—the same creek that fed the ponds in the field across from the Main House. Before Campbell built those ponds and diverted Ash Creek to the eastern edge of the property to gain more usable pasture land, the valley flooded every winter. Campbell's hydrological engineering had significantly reduced the flow of water into the valley floor—though it still got plenty wet in the depths of winter—but those years of floods had left behind rich river bottom sediment that was the main component of the topsoil in our plot. It had been pasture in the past but the cows had been fenced out more recently, so the cow shit that riddled it was old enough to be tilled directly in, adding more organic nutrients. The ground was still kind of wet as we mapped the garden, just barely tillable. But as we moved around on that cool gray day, shifting stakes and string until everyone was happy with the shape, I could visualize a flourishing garden of summer, feeding us in nutritious and delicious abundance—and the joy of that vision swelled in me, blotting out in that moment the surges of anxiety that had crept into my head around the prospective clear-cut and the general chaos of our crowded living conditions and figuring out how this mix of people was going to fit together.

And that joy was multiplied many times when Stu climbed up on the tractor, fired it up, eased over to the nearest corner of our newly defined garden, lowered the tilling tines and slowly started breaking up the soil. Man, I never saw him so happy. I flashed back to him coming back to our apartment at Mountfort Street in Boston, after he'd dropped out of school and was working at the animal labs at Beth Israel Hospital, bummed and grumpy. Or even on the beaches of California in our first failed search for land, when he got a little ground down by that futility of our search and the complications of group dynamics. The crazy-assed dream he kept talking about through the Boston winter and the California summer was to get his hands on some dirt he could turn over and nourish and stick some seeds in.

It wasn't really a smile on his face as he steered the tractor with his head facing back toward the tines, it was a radiant glow of beatific focus, the determined exhilaration of doing exactly the right work. In a way, I envied him the certainty he had about his place on that place and that he was deep into it already. It bode well for our enterprise, and the garden he was creating, gave us something foundational to build on. It did me—and all of us—a lot of good to see Stu so happy and to be a part of his happiness.

SPRING/10

We got one good day in on the garden before the rains came back. Some snow even fell on the top of the hills above the valley. Most of the garden was roughly tilled. The next step was to work a bunch more composted cow shit into it. We had found a seemingly unlimited supply under the second barn, which had been used for calving for years. The barn was at the level of the road about 20 feet above the valley floor, and all those years of mother-and-calf shit, mixed with the straw that had been used for their bedding had been raked and shoveled through the gaps in the rough-slatted wood floor to an open area below—to age and ripen for our use. Another gift of this valley to us. We would, when the weather broke, shovel the shit from under the barn into a trailer behind the tractor and haul it over to the garden spot and then shovel it out onto the soil. Dreams coming true, man. Shoveling shit.

That barn had been renamed the goat barn because our plan was to use it for our goat herd, as a place where the mothers could nurse their kids and have shelter through the worst parts of the winter. We were starting with one female goat named Sheika who the Hammonds had brought up and was now tethered near the Second House.

Tim and Nancy were working on cleaning out the goat barn, where they had stashed what stuff they had moved up. They still had their place in town near the Tiller Store and Nancy split her time between there and the ranch. Tim stayed on the ranch most of the time in a two-person camping tent in the woods just above the barn.

The rain aggravated the crowded living conditions for the rest of us. When the weather was good, we had 135 acres to spread out on. But the rain kept us mostly inside and mostly in the Main House. We kept the fire going. Mike made bread. His father was a baker and Mike had essentially apprenticed with him the whole time he was growing up. He made great bread and whoever was around would help by grinding, with a hand-cranked grinder, the whole wheat berries to the just-right degree of fineness for bread flour, according to Mike's demanding standards. Bread baking, the fire crackling, joints circulating, and five or seven or twelve or more of us created a hardy coziness. We had lots of plans to make: the garden fence, our houses, the animals, the people still coming, the Revolution.

Meal planning and preparation was a major activity with nineteen folks to feed. Walter had become sort of the de facto overseer of the kitchen since he slept about eight feet away. Sarah, Sydney, and Nancy also were active in getting meals together. The rest of us, to varying degrees, would help with cleanup or keeping the fire going. The Hammonds sometimes ate down at the Second House but usually showed up for dinner, Jane often bringing something she'd cooked at their place.

Our diet at first was sort of a continuation of the type of food we'd eaten on the beaches of California, the stuff Sydney made: noodles and sauce and ground beef, hot dogs and beans. And we immediately started getting a lot of eggs from our twenty-seven chickens. One of the cool things about being in the mass chaos of the Main House was that if you got up early—and I usually did—you could collect the eggs from the chicken coop, which was right next door. We'd get as many as twenty eggs a day, so eggs and potatoes became a staple. But even twenty eggs go fast when you are feeding nineteen people.

Walter and the California folks also introduced us to concepts of organic and macrobiotic diets, eating whole grains and legumes, brown rice and homegrown bean sprouts. Those types of food were supposed to be healthier and they fit with the whole natural organic way we were approaching the garden and our animals and the basic concepts of the commune. And, especially with the grains and rice and dried legumes like lentils, it was relatively easy and inexpensive to feed a lot of people. But some of that stuff took some getting used to. And Walter could get a little intense about food and eating, like telling us we should chew every bite fifty times. Man, I tried, but it was a hassle. Like so much of what we were doing in the first few weeks, figuring what, when, and how we were going to eat was kind of a new thing every day.

The crowding in the Main House was inspiring people to create alternatives. Jack sort of unilaterally claimed the outbuilding at the south end of the field across from the Main House. It was a hard-worn plank and tar paper shack, filled with the detritus of god-knows-how-many years of ranch life: scraps of mostly unusable materials, broken tools, discarded appliances, and piles of bags of household trash that never got hauled off to the dump. While others of us were working in the garden or cooking or tending to the animals, he just started pulling shit out of there, trying to turn it into some kind of livable space. When he announced his intentions one night to the group at dinner, there was kind of a nodding acceptance. He'd already established his claim through his work. Dale suggested it would be better for people to ask before making a claim like that and there was some grumblings about his doing that while most everyone else was working on more group-oriented projects. At Sarah's suggestion, we came to a quick consensus that the log outbuilding at the north end of the field, which had come to be called the root cellar, would remain a common building, not available for anyone to claim as a residence. The whole discussion got tense at times, but Stu broke the mood by telling Jack, "Hope you enjoy life in Shantytown," and that's how that building was known from that point forward.

We had heard that the Forest Service was selling three 8×16 cabins and a much bigger central building also made of logs from a fire camp near South Umpqua Falls. We put in bids of $50 a piece on them, and found out quickly that we were the only bidders. Then we had to figure out some way to get them to the ranch. It was only a couple of miles from that camp to the road up to Ash Valley but we'd want to keep them as together as possible so we could plop them down on some minimal foundation and move in with little additional work. Without much debate, we all agreed that those would be designated to Dale and Sydney, Mike and Paulie, and Stu. They each picked out nice spots along Ash Creek spread out in the central part of the valley.

Sarah and I picked a site also along the creek but at the far north end of the valley, beyond the Second House and the reservoir, as the large pond at that end was known. The spot was on the edge of a sweet small meadow, nestled in among ash trees along the creek. We planned to build a small house—with a lot of help from our friends—and had begun working on plans.

We had to start moving people out of the Main House because we were expecting new arrivals any day: Jeffrey and his girlfriend Annie—formerly Little Eddie's girlfriend—and Eddie himself. And we knew more would follow after that.

SPRING/11

Paulie spent most of her time with her horse, Stormy, the flesh and bones of her Oregon dream. That meant spending a lot of time with Stephen, who also had a horse, Morning Star, and not just tending to the animals on the ranch but also on runs to town and to Stephen's old place downriver for equipment and supplies. Mike wasn't much interested in the horses. He helped out some with the garden, but focused mainly on baking or hanging out in the Main House reading.

Paulie had blossomed ever since we arrived in Tiller but especially since we moved onto the ranch where she could focus nearly full time on Stormy (and her dog Quinn Man, of course). She emitted a growing radiance, a sprouting of an inner potential that hadn't been evident to me before. Her features, which had struck me in their plainness when I first met her, transfigured to shiny vibrance: an effervescence in her soft brown eyes, her chestnut hair (not long ago chopped maniacally by her mother on the day of her wedding to Mike) waving free and easy, a near swagger to her almost constant smile. She spoke up and took stands in group gatherings. I began to see the woman that Mike was attracted to, an attraction I didn't understand up to that point—just about the time murmurs started seeping around the ranch that she and Stephen were having something of a fling.

When those rumors got confirmed, things got heavy. We were living on top each other. Mike and Paulie were staying in the back room of the Main House and Stephen was in the annex-like tower 10 or 15 feet away. I don't think Paulie and Stephen were ever blatant enough to sleep together in the

Main House. There was almost no privacy. Especially on rainy days, there was no avoiding each other—unless you went on a town trip, which all three of them seemed to do frequently, in varying combinations. It never got to the point where Paulie switched bedrooms or anything like that. It never was exactly clear to most of us how it all went down but there was no avoiding the fact that something was happening with the three of them.

Mike was stoic about the whole thing, isolating himself as much as he could, even more than he had been, not talking about it.

Of the first nineteen people on the ranch, there were five couples and five single men (as well as the four kids). Three of the couples were married, but even the two who weren't seemed to be in committed monogamous relationships. But, when we crossed that gate into Ash Valley, we accepted that we were embarking on an entirely new sort of social arrangement. We never had explicitly talked about what that meant, except in fairly broad terms of sharing work and resources. In the broader fledgling counterculture, monogamy was being challenged both culturally, in the guise of the so-called sexual revolution, and politically as the increasingly radical critique of the women's liberation movement raised fundamental questions about the oppressive nature of traditional familial and sexual relations.

It just kind of blew my mind. Paulie? And Stephen? And Mike the "victim" from my perspective? I understood on an intellectual level that we needed to redefine what a family was and the way relationships between men and women worked. But in the flesh and blood world, I wanted a monogamous relationship with Sarah and I think she felt the same. The idea of open, free flowing sexual relations among all of us scared the shit out of me. But the Mike-Paulie-Stephen triangle made me aware of the reality for the single men among us—no single, "available" women on the ranch, eighteen miles from the nearest (tiny) town, prospects of meeting an unattached female near zero.

Mike and Stephen finally got into it during a "family" meeting about the way work was going in the garden and for meals and other common responsibility. Mike verbally attacked Stephen, saying he was so involved with the horses and other animals and running back and forth to town that he wasn't contributing his share of work for the good of all. And, Mike said, Stephen was hurting the group by not letting other people use his truck which happened to be the only vehicle running reliably at that point (except for Tim's truck, which he made clear was not a communal vehicle). There was some truth to that, but we all knew the vehemence in Mike's attack—and he could be verbally brutal—was about a lot more than work and vehicles. Stephen knew it, too, and was kind of conciliatory and low-key in his response. Eventually, with some other folks joining in to defend Stephen, Mike backed off a bit and there seemed to be some sort of reconciliation. Paulie did not join in that discussion, keeping her eyes down and maintaining a neutral smile as it went on around her.

SPRING/12

The vehicle situation continued to plague us. The red truck was the first to stop working. It just wouldn't start. Philip and a visitor named Larry helped me work on it. Well, they did most of the work or, at least, the thinking. I let them direct me. They were convinced the generator was the problem, so we took that off and cleaned it up. We jumped-started the truck and let it run for a while, hoping that would charge up the battery. That didn't work. Jane came by with a joint, so we smoked it and then gave up for the day. Similar seemingly minor problems plagued the white truck, the VW bus, and Phillip and Jane's Jeep. Even the tractor only ran sporadically, meaning at least some part of most garden working days were spent tinkering with it. Walter told us that Mercury was in retrograde, which meant trouble with mechanical things. As good an explanation as any, I guess.

After we gave up fixing the red truck and got stoned from Jane's joint, I felt like avoiding the crowd in the Main House for a while on that drizzly day. I wandered toward the end of the property where our house site was. Just past the goat barn, I met Dale and Mike who had dropped acid a couple hours earlier. Dale was beaming and grinning, but Mike looked morose.

"You OK?" I asked. He looked into my eyes for a second without changing his expression then looked away.

"He's freaked about his woman, man." Dale said, still grinning. "What would you expect?"

"Man, it just doesn't make any sense," Mike said, staring away from Dale and me, out across the valley. "No sense.

That's what freaks me out. I'm not hung up about the sexual shit or anything. Fuck that. I ain't a saint. But shit man, who *is* Stephen? What is Stephen? Where the fuck did he come from? You know, man, maybe it makes too much sense. You know?" he said, finally looking back at me, then Dale.

I, stoned but not tripping, wanted to laugh, but held it back. I could see how freaked out Mike was. I didn't want to push him over the line. I looked to Dale, who also seemed on the verge of laughing, but just raised his thick eyebrows toward me.

"Hey, man, you're fucking tripping, no time to be figuring out what makes sense," I told Mike and he managed a half-hearted smile. "Let's walk," I said.

We walked in the direction I had been going, toward the north end of the ranch, but headed up into the woods and followed a deer path that meandered amidst imposing firs, so towering we couldn't see the tops. We were insignificant, tiny, crawling bugs buzzing through the very bottoms of their brawny trunks. The wind above was a distant flowing swoosh, like the firm easy breath of a watchful god. We came to a clearing on a short flat ridge, with a panoramic view back up the valley. "This is where I'm going to build a house for Sydney," said Dale, shining and proud. "I haven't shown her yet but I know it's going to blow her away."

We followed another deer path back down toward the road. We passed the Second House, where we could hear the Hammond family going about their day inside, and then followed the road past the reservoir and the scrub ash woods that surrounded it. We crossed the open meadow at the end of our property to sit under trees next to the creek, near where Sara and my imagined house would sit someday. All the rain we'd been having made the creek—only about four feet wide behind our site—roar. It was a different, higher pitch than the South Umpqua down by Tiller, sweeter, more intense. I shut my eyes and got lost in it, imagining Sarah lying next to me, a transparent roof above us, rain tap dancing through treetops moving to the rhythm of the rushing water, me diving into her watery eyes, deep and daring. This *was* a good spot. I could only imagine what my tripping friends were experiencing.

I opened my eyes and saw Mike staring across the meadow to the slowly rising hill across the road, but his look seemed to go way beyond that.

"Hey, man, things will change when we get out of the Main House, into our own places," I said, sounding loud as I broke the silence we'd all been drifting in. "Dale and Sydney up on that the hill, you and Paulie by the creek, me and Sarah here. This is too insane, now. But it's gonna change. It's gonna change soon."

Mike looked hesitantly at me. A soft smile. Acid humbled him, like it does to most of us, I think. With that and the sort of tender vibe enfolding the three of us, good friends taking deep stock of this new reality we had raced into with such fervor. "I don't know, man," Mike said, shaking his head slowly. "I don't know." It got quiet again.

After a time, the rain picked up and the trees could no longer shield us from it, so we stirred ourselves, exchanging warm and knowing looks—as though we had discovered something together—and decided to head back to the Main House.

Just as the Main House came into view, we saw an unfamiliar beat-up old pickup pull up and a scraggly looking guy with a six-gun strapped around his waist got out. Mike and Dale freaked out and waited by the root cellar while I joined a few folks coming out of the house to see what this guy wanted. He said that Stephen had been arrested in Canyonville. Some woman named Ruth had charged him with assault. This guy—who introduced himself to us as Bart—told us he had hung out with Stephen some at a bar in Canyonville, mostly before all us freaks showed up. That's where Stephen met Ruth and they did have a bit of a thing, Bart told us. But Stephen wasn't really that interested in her since he took up with us. So when she saw him in town, she got pissed and went to the cops with this story. "It's a bunch of bullshit," Bart told us. But the Canyonville cops jumped at the chance to arrest him, now that he'd let his hair grow and clearly become one of us.

Tim and Nancy volunteered to go bail him out, since they had the only functioning vehicle, beside Stephen's, which he had driven to town. Shit, man, Stephen was wreaking havoc with women all over the county. What was that about? We really didn't know that much about Stephen, except that he seemed like a nice guy and knew a lot more than us about the kind of work we'd have to do on the ranch.

When the commotion had settled down, I saw Mike and Paulie head off up toward the ponds, just the two of them. When they came back a while later, they were holding hands and laughing.

I came across a recipe for dandelion wine in *Mother Earth News*. The valley had a bumper crop of dandelions and any alcohol that made it up to the ranch got consumed in a hurry, so I thought this wine could be a good renewable source of a boozy buzz. Early one gray morning, I picked three gallons worth of open dandelion blossoms—with the dew still on them—put them in a pot, poured boiling water over them and covered it with cheese cloth. Let that sit for three days, then squeezed all the juice out of the flowers and threw the remains in the compost. I put the liquid in a big pot and added three pounds of brown sugar. You were supposed to add some oranges and lemons, too. We didn't have any of either, but I think that was just for flavor, nothing to do with the fermentation process, which was the important thing. I boiled that for 30 minutes, added 2 packages of yeast, covered it again. Then I had to wait two to three weeks before I could drink it. Bummer. But the recipe promised it would be worth it, describing its kick with a simple exclamation: "Whammy!"

SPRING/13

The rain kept up—more snow on the hills above us—which prevented us from working in the garden.

When the sun finally came out for a couple of days, we hustled into the garden, finishing up spreading the manure and working it into the soil. The tractor didn't work about half the time, so we had to do a lot of it by hand, using a wheelbarrow and shovels. But that was cool, too. It was good hard work with almost everybody putting in some time. With temperatures getting up into the seventies, people were shedding clothes, working close to naked—and getting completely naked when we'd go jump in the swimming pond just across the road in the warmest part of the day. Those were the best times. We'd smoke a joint or two and the chilled water was thrilling as it washed away the sweat and muscle aches of manual labor.

Sarah was a bit more shy than the other women about nudity outside of the swimming hole. I guess I was a little reluctant, too. But especially when it was just the people who lived at Ash Valley—no visitors, which was not that common in the early days—it became sort of natural and unremarkable. Sometimes when straight visitors came, we would forget that a topless woman or a bottomless man might disturb some people.

On warm working days, Sarah's standard look was worn blue overalls with nothing under them. She looked great. Being on the land had intensified her sensuousness. Maybe that was true for all of us. There was a physical rawness, a moral wildness, a spiritual openness, a social nihilism about being in the mountains, ten rugged miles from our nearest neighbors, no rules, no masters, nobody who could tell us "no" except we ourselves, to each other. The land itself was sensuous, the open vestal valley beneath the fierce verdant virgin peaks. You couldn't deny the physically sensuous tension sparking among all of us, especially after it flamed up in the Stephen-Paulie-Mike triangle. The casual nudity was just more kindling under that seething fire.

I was terrified of losing Sarah to a communal orgy—or worse, I think, to one of the single men—but I loved the stoked passion I saw in her, seeing her naked in the warm Oregon sunshine, or even just catching a glimpse of a breast peeking out from her overalls. And even though privacy was hard to come by, when we did have the space to make love, it was fervid, almost desperate, something a little scary about it—though undeniably wonderful. We both had minor freak-outs where insecurities about our relationship came up—how could they not in that environment?—but long walks and talks away from the Main House, down to our site in the little meadow by the creek reinforced our commitment.

On the day we were set to plant the garden, Stu was up early studying a thick bank of clouds that had rolled in overnight. He called off the planting, and within an hour, snow was falling on the valley floor: snow on May 20. We had much to learn about the seasons and rhythms of this place.

Most of us were just hanging out in the Main House, drinking coffee with the homey aromas of Mike's bread wafting around us, watching the snow dust our garden plot, when our Days Creek automotive guru Earl pulled up in his old beige Nash Rambler station wagon with his buddy Ernie. He had a big smile when he got out of the car and did a 360-degree scan of the place.

"Why, I think you kids did all right for yourselves," he said to Stu and Sarah and me, who had come out to greet him. "I do believe this is the finest spot of land I have ever seen in this country. By gosh, it's a pretty place. Don't you think so, Ernie?" he said, looking to his friend, who was short and tubby compared to Earl who was a tad over average height and stout as a tree trunk.

"Oh yes, Earl," Ernie said, following Earl's sweeping scan of the ranch. "It's a mighty pretty place. Finest spot I've ever seen. By gosh, I think you're right about that." Ernie had been Earl's friend, sidekick really, forever, back to the days when the two of them had built the Days Creek store with fresh milled lumber and a hammer and a handsaw. I'm not sure Ernie felt as warmly toward us as Earl did, but if Earl thought we were OK, then Ernie would go along with that.

Earl's stamp of approval meant a lot to us. He'd been in the South Umpqua Valley longer than any of us had been alive, which made it all the more amazing that he had never seen Ash Valley before. But it was way off in the literal middle of nowhere—only hunters and loggers were likely to just stumble upon it.

Earl and Ernie came in and we made them some hobo coffee and gave them some of Mike's fresh-out-of-the-oven bread, which they complimented heartily. We cleared spots for them to sit at the table, but it was apparent that the ambient chaos of so many of us crammed into the house on a bad weather day made them uncomfortable. After we introduced them to the few people who didn't know them and shared some awkward small talk about our garden and our plans for more housing, Earl asked about the red truck. I told him we'd spent some time working on the generator but that hadn't solved the apparent electrical problem. Earl took a gander outside, saw that the drizzly rain that had followed the snow had let up, and suggested we go out and take a look at it. Earl was much more comfortable standing around the open hood of a motor vehicle than sitting in a house—other than his own—with a bunch of people.

Earl gently supervised me removing the generator from the truck and then the armature from the generator. He pulled a small silver pocket knife out of his stiff jeans, held up by suspenders. The blade was worn down but keenly sharp. He scraped the grooves where the armature ran across the brushes. "I think this is your problem right here," he said smiling calmly as he worked the knife back and forth in the narrow grooves, making sure to remove the built-up gunk without damaging the copper beneath, essential for the flow of electrical juice in the generator. I thought we had cleaned those very grooves when Phillip and I had worked on it a few days before. But we didn't have Earl's knife or his deft touch. He handed the armature back to me to put back in the generator. "Let's give 'er a try now," he said. "That just might do it."

Of course it did. But somehow, I don't understand how, after we jump-started the rig, Earl was able to tell that the generator was generating plenty of juice but the voltage regulator and the starter were shot. "If you kids can come on down to my place tomorrow, I think I've got just the parts you need in one of my sheds. We'll get 'er running like a top in no time."

We all loved being on the ranch, but people were way into town trips, too. Nearly every day somebody needed something and other folk were only too anxious to fill whatever other seats were available heading downriver. The day after Earl had visited, we needed to take the red truck to his place. Stu, his garden work stymied by morning rain and who loved hanging out with Earl any chance he got, went along with Sarah and me. We had to push-start the truck and couldn't turn it off when we made the ritualistic stop at the Tiller Store. Most of us had specific treats—nonmacrobiotic, nonorganic, semisecret treats—we'd buy at the store, a little splurge and escape from the limited diet at the ranch. I always got one of those fat red spicy sausages floating in the gallon jar by the checkout stand. Sarah got a "mini-pie," artificial tasting chocolate filling inside a rectangular sugar-coasted crust, and Stu got a Fudgesicle. There was a disproportionate amount of enjoyment in these cheap treats because they were just a little bit illicit.

Earl was glad to see us, had his woodstove in the living room cranking and hot water ready for cups of Nescafe. He went on and on about how great he thought Ash Valley was and how lucky we were—how he wished he'd found a place like that when he was a young man. After we visited a bit, he dug around in his shed for about ten minutes and found a voltage regulator and a starter for the red truck. He kept an eye on me, offering a few gentle tips, while I tried to put them in with a little help from Stu. When I had finally passed his inspection, we jump-started the truck and let it run for a while to see if the battery would charge up, and shot the shit in the drippy drizzle. That seemed like a quintessentially Oregon moment: rain and grease on my hands and the sharp scent of burning wood and Earl telling stories, laughing, and treating us like we somehow belonged.

At a pause in the conversation, Earl decided the truck had been running long enough. I climbed in the cab, turned it off, waited a couple of beats and tried starting it. It fired right up and everything seemed to be in working order. He charged 25 bucks for the parts but the consultation and the company were free. And he gave us a bunch of miscellaneous stuff out of his sheds: canned salmon and venison in quart-sized Mason jars, a couple of cartons of empty jars, pots and pans, odds and ends of silverware, plastic cups and glasses, some colorful fabric that Sarah thought we could use for curtains, a box of sundry sewing supplies. He just kind of started pulling stuff out and loading us up. "Hell, I just don't think I'm going to be needing this stuff anymore. It's just cluttering things up, and I reckon you kids can probably put it to good use up on your ranch." What a guy. We could sense that Earl's world was turned upside down in ways he could never verbalize when his wife Lorna died not long before the first of us arrived in Tiller. The remnants of her feminine presence in Earl's thick-fingered, black-and-white masculine world seemed sadly dissonant and likely a source of some pain for him.

By the time we got back to Ash Valley—the truck running smoothly all the way—in the early afternoon, a rich blue sky and some sunshine had started to break up the clouds and Stu and I spent a couple of hours spreading shit on the garden. It was a fine productive day. Walter and Sydney made a good meal of lentil burgers and fried potatoes. The clearing skies seemed to lighten everyone's mood and the spirit in the Main House was more harmonious than it had been in quite a while. After supper, Dale offered up some LSD jujubes someone had given him and Mike, Walter, Stu, Wayne, and I took a couple each.

As the acid rush separated us from the rest of the folks hanging out in the Main House, we all wandered outside to the front "yard"—an area of low scrubby grass with a couple of small fruit trees, fenced to keep the cows out. We had a picnic table and a couple of wooden chairs that we pulled out from under an awning that hung over a flat concrete porch area in front of the house. The clouds were gone and we watched in silent awe as the stars emerged, faintly at first, but brighter and brighter as near absolute darkness crawled over the valley. The moon was the slightest silver crescent sliver, rising over the hill across the valley. I moved further from the house and its insistent hum of voices blended in conversation and lay flat on my back on the cool moist ground.

The stellar light show surrounded me. I was a star among the multitude of stars moving quietly through the glittering sky. Free but connected to everything else. Radiant. The light emanating from me was a deep warm vibration, lifting me above the valley floor, radiating out in all directions, touching every blade of grass, all the trees, the cows, and the chickens, and the goat and the horses, the dogs sleeping on the porch, the silent deer in the hills, the rushing waters in the creek. It surrounded the Main House and bathed it in a white-hot glow, filling everyone inside with the same warm vibration. The now serenely distant voices sounded like an angel choir. Everyone was smiling and laughing. I loved them all. We were made to be in this place. I was made to be in this place.

"Hey, Tucker, you OK?" It was Mike. I opened my eyes. He smiled softly. He looked unimaginably tired. "We're all going inside. It's getting cold out here."

"Yeah, OK," I said, realizing suddenly that I was cold, still laying on the ground, feeling dampness permeating every part of me. I sat up and shook myself. "Hey, man, that was good acid, huh?"

"Yeah, man," he said. "Let's go inside."

The living room was empty. Everybody else was already asleep. When I crawled next to Sarah, she was in deep sleep, a gentle snore escaping her slightly parted lips. I relished her warmth and the comfort of the covers. I was crashing, but still not ready to sleep. Man, I thought, that love I felt when I was lost in the cosmos was real, as real as anything I felt when I was stone-cold straight. But what do I do with it? We were in the right place at the right time. I was sure of that. But what am I supposed to do? What was my spot in this thing? I still didn't know the answer to that.

SPRING/14

We could finally start planting the garden. It was hard work. We laid out the rows for the various crops with stakes and string, following Stu's plans and direction. Using the strings as a guide, Stu and I made planting trenches with a hoe, with seed planters following a ways behind us. The soil was pretty well broken up and the manure mixed in, but we had to chop at it with the hoe to loosen it up more to receive the seeds. Each row was 80 feet long and we were going to end up with something like 100 rows.

It took us most of two days to plant half of it. Stu, Sarah, Nancy, Paulie, Dale and I focused on planting, and Wayne, Phillip, Stephen, and Jack worked on the fence. Mike, Sydney, and Walter would work in the garden in short spurts but then go in the house to get food together. The kids, Greg and Kathy, tried to help as much as they could. Jane was looking after the baby and Wayne's daughter Tammy, and she would bring us joints and treats for breaks. Tim was somewhere doing his own thing. We worked five or six hours a day, until it started getting hot, then did our ritual swim and cleaned our weary bodies with Dr. Bronner's Peppermint Soap, which was biodegradable so it didn't screw up the water. We'd get high and wait for the kitchen crew to clang the dinner triangle—we really had one hanging on the front porch—to tell us food was ready.

Those were fine days in many ways, but hassles continued. Dale, Walter, and Wayne got sick, Dale sick enough to go to Canyonville to see a doctor, who told him he had an ear infection. We had a bunch of visitors, too. We'd only been on the land three weeks, but word had spread on the hippie grapevine and a steady stream of guests showed up, somehow finding their way to our place two miles up an unmarked logging road. It was cool in some ways. It was great to see unexpected old friends and to meet new freaks, to show off our beautiful valley. Some brought dope or food. Some helped out in the garden. But all these extra people—hard to even keep track of how many, with people coming and going all the time, friends and friends of friends and friends of friends of friends and so on—made our crowded living conditions worse, made meals more complicated, and distracted us from dealing with simmering interpersonal conflicts among the people living there.

One night after a long day in the garden—and the swimming and the getting high—I was really tired and hungry and, by the time Sarah and I made it to the Main House (we'd lingered to mess around by the pond after everyone else had left), the line for supper was insanely long—like being back in a college dorm. Who were all these people? I thought. When I finally got to the food, I loaded as much of the spaghetti and sauce and salad and bread as I could fit on my plate. I turned sharply to find a place to sit and bumped into one of the visiting women and spilled my entire plate on the floor. People started laughing but I looked up and scanned the room, pissed, with my grumpiest glower and everybody got real quiet. Then I looked at all my food spread out at my feet and let out a furious, "Fuckkkkkk!" Everyone was staring at me, with looks that wavered between concern and an urge to break out laughing again, and finally, I couldn't help it—I had to laugh, too. And they all joined me. Sarah came over to help me clean it up and everyone else was supportive, patting me on the back, helping me get a new plate. When I finally sat down with my food, I had mellowed out, marveling and dismayed at how quickly I could become an asshole. The food was really good.

Sarah and I took a day off from the garden to go to Medford to take the rest of our wedding money, $1,750, out of the bank, to put into the communal funds. The red truck barely made it over the pass on the Tiller-Trail Highway. The engine overheated and when I pulled over to add water to the radiator, I saw that it was also leaking oil like a motherfucker. I added oil and more water in Medford and we limped back home, but I knew the truck needed serious work before it left the property again.

The drizzly weather returned, slowing down progress in the garden, and I got sick and spent most of two days in bed in our room, upstairs in the Main House. What a drag. I could hear the life of the ranch going on downstairs but I couldn't be part of it.

On the second day, Sarah came up after lunch and brought me some bread with peanut butter on it. We had just gotten a new baby goat who was immediately christened "Billy" and she had been down at the Second House playing with it with Jane and Paulie.

"He's so cute, Ben," Sarah said, giggly. "He's like a puppy or like a tiny pony but he bucks like a ram." Her good mood hit me wrong.

"That's what you did all morning?" I asked.

She could hear my annoyance in my tone. "Yes," she said sharply, "and it was fun. It was nice to get away from all the bummed out sick people here. What's wrong with you?"

"I don't know. Seems like there's more important stuff to be done."

"Sorry you don't approve." She got up to leave. "Sometimes you're a real bummer, Ben."

"I just wish I could be out there doing something." She stopped in the doorway and looked back. "This is such an important time for us and it just feels like every time we start moving in the right direction, we slip back into chaos. I feel so shitty I don't feel like I can do anything about it, just be a useless spectator."

"Relax, Ben. You're sick and we need you to get well. And, surprise, surprise, we're somehow managing without you. I had a lot of fun this morning, and the goats could be an important part of our trip, so I'm glad I got to hang out with them. Things will come together if we relax and let it happen. But I don't appreciate you telling me what to do." She smiled curtly and left.

We were out of dope, scraping resin out of pipes. After dinner one night, we had a spontaneous family meeting about whether we should try to buy a couple ounces of pot to tide us over until Little Eddie and Jeffrey showed up with what promised to be a bigger stash. We had about $5,000 in our communal fund, which came from Sarah and my money, what was left of Mike and Paulie's wedding money, money Stu had pulled from his savings account, as well as smaller amounts, a couple

hundred bucks here and there, that other folks had chipped in.
I was fine with our money being absorbed by the group. Some
people didn't have anything to put in, and that was cool, too.
We were betting our lives on this thing working. Money seemed
sort of trivial in comparison. Sarah and Sydney had been
selected to keep track of the money.

The meeting went all over the place, as all kinds of shit
came out about people feeling inequities about living spaces
or the amount of work different people were doing, the
management of and access to our vehicles, how we were
dealing with visitors, the kind of food we were eating and how
prep and cleanup were being done, the ways the kids among
us were being treated. Nothing really got resolved—except we
decided that we weren't going to buy pot, that we could wait—
but it was a healthy release of pent-up tension and everyone
seemed to feel better. The discussion seemed about over when
the Volkswagen bus, which was overdue from a trip to Eugene,
pulled up with Dale, Sydney, and Jack—and Little Eddie
with his wiseass smile and three ounces of fine Colombian
marijuana. We partied long into the night.

SPRING/15

Everybody turned up to merrily finish the garden. At first, it was everybody but Tim. Dale had asked him to join us when we first started in the morning and he had said he didn't want to and headed back toward the goat barn.

But after we got going with everybody else—even Little Eddie, though he mostly just kept us entertained with his acerbic commentary—and it became apparent to us that this was a breakthrough moment for the commune, Dale stormed up to Tim's tent in the woods to get him (Nancy had been staying in town most of the time lately). When they came back, we all gathered in the corner of the garden and tried to communicate to Tim. Dale did most of the talking, saying that we wanted a community that was more than a loose collection of individuals living on the land. We wanted to learn how to share our lives toward a common purpose for us all.

Working together on communal priorities like the garden was vital to learning how to share, how we fit together, as well as actually accomplishing goals we defined together. What could be more important than the garden, growing our own food, a first step toward self-sufficiency and freedom from the capitalist economy? That common purpose, we told him, allowed space for individuals to pursue their particular interests, but not to operate totally independent of the communal will. It was a good rap, maybe the clearest expression of our commitment to each other we had yet had. Tim seemed to sort of get it, and, still a little reluctantly, joined us for the final push.

It was a deep blue sparkling sunshiny day and our spirits soared. In less than a month, we had moved on this extraordinary piece of land, laid some rudimentary foundation for a communal living arrangement, and—despite rain and snow, failing vehicles and equipment, and, among us all, almost zero experience ever doing anything remotely like this—had turned one-third of an acre of rough pasture into 100 well-defined, mounded rows of dreams. Dreams of corn and tomatoes and lettuce and radishes and broccoli and so on and on and on. Our sustenance. We were cultivating life from the land with our soft city hands, and the loving camaraderie we shared as the last seeds were planted and final furrows filled was fucking mind-blowing. The power of the people, our power as a people committed to each other and this land, was no longer an abstraction or a dream, it was even now germinating in the soil we had broken and fed and worked and fondled between our fingers. It was alive. We had birthed it with good honest shared work. When all was done, we passed joints and jugs of cheap wine, the laughter and hoots of our euphoric celebration filling the valley with tribal joy.

SPRING/16

The day after we finished the garden, the Main House came slowly and groggily to life. We had earned a day of rest. I nursed a cup of hobo coffee with powdered milk and a big spoon of sugar, sitting at the kitchen table with Mike and Walter. We talked about some of the great concerts we had seen in our Boston days. That conversation always started with the first Led Zeppelin show we'd seen at the old Tea Party in January 1969, one of their first shows ever in the US. The place only held about 400 people and the only seats were two rows of old movie theater seats right in front of the stage—the suicide seats, we came to call them after that night when Led Zeppelin blew our minds with crazy loud, hard rocking blues like we'd never heard before. Most of the Boston folks who ended up at Ash Valley had been there that night and in those seats. It was a major event in forging the identity of our tribe.

Then Stu walked in and jumped into the conversation, talking about seeing the Allman Brothers at the new Tea Party—when they opened for the Nice and blew them away. Walter chimed in about when he saw them at the Cambridge Common—even before the Tea Party. Mike had been at both and joined in the superlatives about just how fucking great they were. The sad truth was I had never seen the Allman Brothers, a major hole in my musical experience. I'd been in Philadelphia with Sarah both times. I didn't regret doing that but I sure wished I'd seen the Allman Brothers. I could only hope I'd get another chance. Just as Stu was really getting into rubbing in just what a major mistake I had made, we heard vehicles—our road was a Forest Service road and technically public—and then saw two pale green pickups coming toward us.

The pickups stopped in front of the house and four men climbed out, three of them from the Umpqua National Forest headquarters in Roseburg and the other was head ranger of the Tiller district. The five of us who had been talking greeted them and slowly other folks—Sarah, Dale, Wayne, Jack— wandered out of the house and joined us.

After stiffly cordial greetings, the Tiller district ranger spoke. "We've just spent some time inspecting the proposed timber sale on that hillside bordering your property," he said, gesturing toward the east. "We understand you are concerned. …"

A cackle of response rose from our group, Dale's "Hell yes, we're concerned" rising above the rest of us. We had found a lawyer to represent us, a former congressman who was known as a liberal firebrand. He said he'd do it for a reasonable fee because he was sympathetic to our cause. He had already begun the process of trying to get a temporary injunction to stop the sale. That might be why these gentlemen were paying us a call.

The ranger, in his early forties with a buzz cut and a rounded belly pushing tight against the buttons of his Forest Service green shirt, paused and surveyed the group surrounding him, showing some concern himself. "We understand that and we want to keep you as informed as we can." He looked to his colleagues and then back to us. "We've concluded that the units meet all our criteria to be successful and safe clear-cuts." Again all our voices rose at once—angrier, more strident this time.

He held up his hand to try to quiet us and spoke, louder now. "Now I know it may seem strange to you but we are professionals"—snide chuckles greeted that, as Little Eddie, Stephen, and Paulie joined us. You could see his eyes counting us up, calculating the relative strength of the opposing forces here, the odds of them extricating themselves and escaping in their pickups. He raised his voice even louder. "We are professionals and we understand the science of forests. We have a lot of years of experience among us. And our experience and our science tells us that clear-cutting that hillside is the most ecologically sound method of managing it."

"That's just crazy," I said, trying to make a rational argument. "That's the same kind of logic that drops bombs on Vietnamese villages to save them. Insanity."

"What if we bought the rights to the trees?" Wayne asked.

"Well, you'd have to bid on them," the district ranger said. "To do that, you would have to show you were a qualified bidder, that you are capable of doing a responsible job of harvesting the timber."

"But we don't want to 'harvest the timber,'" Sarah said. "We'd just want the rights so nobody would cut the trees."

"Well, you can't do that," the ranger said, trying to show a patient smile. "If you qualified and won the bid, you'd have to harvest the trees."

A collective angry roar went up.

"Bullshit!" Mike shouted. "I ain't listening to this pig anymore." He looked straight into the ranger's eyes. "Just try and cut those motherfucking trees." He turned to go back into the house.

"It's going to totally fuck up our land," Paulie said. "Don't you care about that?"

"We understand why it might seem that way to you," one of the guys from Roseburg spoke. All four of them were almost imperceptibly backing toward their trucks. "But that is National Forest land and it is our jobs to manage that forest, both to keep the forest healthy and to make the natural resources in the forest available for industry and society. The wood from those trees will provide good jobs and lumber for houses. And we'll do everything we can to minimize the impact on your land."

"Bullshit," Dale said. "All you care about is making money for the logging companies and mill owners." He shook his head and offered them a challenging smile. "I guess we'll see what happens in court."

"We sure wish we could avoid that," the Tiller ranger said.

"Then don't sell the trees," Sarah said.

"Our plans now are to proceed with the bidding process. We'll try to keep you informed as best we can as things go forward. Thanks for your time."

They made a quick exit.

SPRING/17

More rain. A brother and sister from LA named Ray and Caroline—friends of Wayne and Phillip, I guess—showed up with a trailer full of stuff. After a short discussion among the folks who happened to be hanging out in the Main House, we told them they could store their stuff in the goat barn temporarily but we'd hold off any discussion of them moving on until more people were around. I helped him unload. He seemed like a nice guy, but kind of intense. He talked a lot about how crazy the city was becoming, lots of racial tension, cops hassling freaks, everything getting expensive and crowded. He was desperate to get out. I understood that. We all had been pretty desperate to get out of the various places we had come from. But it was slowly sinking in for us that—even with 135 acres, ten miles from the closest neighbor—we could not invite every desperate friend of each of us to move on the land. But we hadn't quite figured out yet how to make those kind of decisions and how to say no.

During a break in the rain Stu and I planted the last few cabbage plants, which we had started in small pots, while Wayne, Stephen, Dale, Sarah, and Jack finished the garden fence. Little Eddie rolled joints and walked around giving everybody hits. Radishes were already poking their sweet green shoots out of the ground. Far out. Phillip and Jane returned from a town trip with the mail. I got a pissed-off letter from my father about my student loan. I had borrowed $2,500 to go to BU and since I had been out of school more than a year, I was supposed to start making payments on it. My parents had been forwarding me the letters the bank sent but I figured

that, in the mountains of Oregon, I was out of reach. When
we had first heard that Fletcher Riley, one of the cops that I
had been convicted of hitting with a brick (the charge I was
completely innocent of), was suing me, my uncle, the big-time
Boston lawyer, told me: "They can't get blood from a stone.
Go to Oregon. Enjoy your life. Forget Fletcher Riley." Just
what I wanted to hear. I figured the same logic applied to the
student loan. But this was a little different in that my father was
involved. I immediately went into the Main House and wrote a
letter to the loan officer at the bank.

> *Dear Mr. Ford,*
>
> *At the outset, I apologize for not having contacted you sooner. The
> past year has been very hectic and full of crisis situations which have made
> it difficult to keep everything in order. I don't know if you are aware
> but on January 29, 1970, I was arrested in the midst of a police riot.
> In May of that year, I left college and still have no plans of returning.
> Through the fall, I stayed in Boston working and waiting for my trial.
> On January 5, 1971, I was convicted of two charges of assaulting a
> police officer. I will not belabor you with what that experience taught me
> of American justice, let it suffice to say that there was little or no justice
> involved. I was given an eighteen-month suspended sentence and placed on
> probation for three years.*
>
> *Following this, after obtaining the court's permission, I was married
> on March 13 in Philadelphia and immediately came to Oregon to try
> to put the pieces back together. Since that time, a group of families most
> of whom I met in Boston have gone together and purchased some land
> on which we are farming, raising animals, and learning many skills and
> crafts.*
>
> *I have virtually no money. What little my wife and I did have was
> spent on moving out here and the initial expenses of moving on the land. I*

am being sued at the present time by Mr. Fletcher Riley, one of the police officers I was convicted of assaulting, for $25,000 and my lawyer expects the other officer will soon also file suit. The land is owned by a corporation whose tentative name is Family Clan, Inc. The incorporation procedures are still pending. I own no shares in the corporation. I am an employee of it. I receive room and board and normal expenses, but, as yet, no salary. It may be several years before we are able to get any profit since it will take us a while to get the operation underway. The point of all this is that at this time, I am in no position to pay off this loan. I regret this. There are many things I didn't foresee happening but which nonetheless have happened and have changed my situation dramatically. I would also like to say that my father is in no position to aid me in this and that, although I'm not sure of the regulations, I don't want him to be responsible for anything save that which he agreed to, paying the interest. If there are to be legal repercussions, which I hope we can avoid, I would ask that they all be directed at me and not him as I am responsible for the developments which make it impossible for me to pay you at this time.

In closing, I'd like to thank you for your patience and to express the hope that I may be granted an extension or that together we can work something out.

Sincerely,

It was funny putting my life and the ranch into terms that might make sense to a banker. It was all essentially true. And I didn't, as I did in the letter I wrote to my parents to accompany the copy of the letter to Ford, write, "You said it, pop, 'banks are banks and pigs are pigs' and they're not worth hassling with when there is so much we have to do. Money is a myth! It's a symbol of wealth. The wealth is all around us and the pigs hoard it. That's why everybody isn't materially satisfied. The answer is to concentrate on liberating the wealth, creating ways of living that don't spawn greed, not putting a lot of energy and hassle into a negative, constrictive myth. Myths are only as strong as the energy that is put into them. That's why I refuse to take money seriously and why I will put only the slightest bit of energy into money necessary to function, as much as I have to, in this society. When I reach the point of putting no energy into it at all, I will feel a lot freer."

After I finished those two letters and stuck them in envelopes, I headed outside. The rain had subsided, and an unexpected late afternoon warmth softened the flat grayness of the day. People were hanging out by the ponds. I could see Sarah, Stephen, and Little Eddie, and the kids, Greg and Kathy. As I got closer, I saw that Stephen was fishing the upper pond with Greg sitting on the bank next to him, and the others were chatting and watching from the dock by the swimming pond.

"Cool, man!" Greg shouted as he jumped up to watch Stephen reel in a fine looking rainbow trout. We tried to treat the kids like equals as much as we could, but there was no mistaking the eight-year old boy in Greg's eyes as he hovered close to Stephen, reaching out his arms toward the flailing fish, trying to help bring it in.

"Relax, you'll frighten him back into the water," Stephen laughed as he calmly unhooked the fish and tossed it into a bucket. He had a big smile as he watched Greg hesitantly poke his finger into the bucket, just to touch the fish.

"Wow!" I shouted. I was feeling some of that eight-year old boy excitement myself. "Looks like they're biting today," I said to Stephen.

"Well that one was," Stephen said, with a soft smile, as he cooly threaded another worm onto his hook.

"Cool," I said. "I'm going to grab my stuff." I kind of waved and nodded to Sarah and the others on the dock and took off in a dead sprint to the Main House to get my rod and reel. I tried to walk slowly on the way back, get calm, but I couldn't help myself. Man, I'd been waiting for a chance like this.

Stephen had plenty of worms to share with me and I took up a spot on the bank opposite him across the 25-foot wide pond. Greg came over to offer encouragement as I struggled to get the worm securely on the hook. The rig, set up as Stephen had guided me, was just a small hook below a few split shot sinkers with a bobber about 18 inches above them. While I was trying to get it all set up, Stephen hauled in another fish. Sarah, Kathy, and Little Eddie on the water bed (which Wayne had contributed to the ranch) cheered and Greg looked longingly across the pond, wanting to be where the action was but being a good brother by offering me his help.

When I finally got my rig set up right, I drew my rod back with a few feet of line let out. I swung the rod over my head and released my line, but my timing was off and the bobber landed just a few feet in front of me, splashing in shallow and muddy water. Shit. I looked around. Stephen was focused on his line. The water bed folks tried to restrain their laughter, but I could see it in their eyes.

"It's OK. Don't worry about it," Greg was reassuring. "You just need a little practice."

Well, my casts slowly got better. And I got a few nibbles but nothing that felt like a real strike. Meanwhile, Stephen was hauling in trout almost as fast as he could get his line in the water. Greg slowly worked his way back to Stephen's side.

"Maybe, I've just got the good spot," Stephen offered when he had six fish in his bucket. "Why don't you come over here and give it a try?"

Sure, that must be it. I moved to where he had been and he moved 10 or 15 feet away. He got a strike on his third cast and landed a beauty. And I still got nothing. How do the fucking fish know who's throwing the damn line in the water?

Dinner activity was starting to happen in the Main House. Sarah, Little Eddie, Greg and Kathy, bored now with Stephen hauling in fish after fish and me not, started moving in that direction. Just as they left, I saw my bobber take a sudden dive and felt an unmistakable tug on my line. I pulled my rod up sharply and could feel the certainty of the hook setting and started reeling in.

"All right," Stephen cheered. He'd been rooting for me. I could tell he felt bad that his success had served to accent my failure. The fish broke the surface a couple of times as I brought him in. He was a good-looking one. I got him to the base of the three-foot bank where I stood and took the line in my hands to pull him up. And there he was, pretty as can be, dangling in front of me. I could see Stephen's broad smile in the background just beyond him.

And I turned around and saw Sarah and the others about halfway to the Main House.

"Look," I shouted, and lifted my catch high so they could see. Before they could respond, the fish slithered off the hook and plopped with a splash back into the pond.

The reaction went swiftly from near joy to sympathetic anguish—YAYyayyaaaahhhhhhhhhhhh—to unavoidable laughter. Stephen shrugged with an amused but supportive smile.

But I wouldn't give up. With the audience gone and my ego completely popped, I just kept casting. Stephen and I didn't say much as the day started to darken, focused on the quiet hum of our lines going out and the gentle splash of our bobbers. I did finally land one. And carefully pulled it up on the bank, safe from the water's edge. Stephen pulled in his line and gave me a gentle pat on the back. I added my one to his eight and we headed to the house for dinner.

The next night, after Stu and I had spent most of a town-trip day dealing with the white truck breaking down (again!), Matthew, a friend from Drew, showed up with some powdered mescaline, which a few of us snorted to top off an evening of joints and cheap wine. The pot and booze made us spacey but the mescaline made us wise. We got way down deep. Six of us, all flying on the mescaline, gathered around the kitchen table and passed around a copy of *The Realist's Last Supplement to the Whole Earth Catalog* with Kesey's article about the Bible, where he talks about the Revolution needing all sorts of tools and that the Bible was one of those tools. I actually read the whole thing. Others took in varying portions of it. Man, I just couldn't grasp what Kesey was getting at, but Dale picked his concept up and ran with it. "Jesus and all of them were hippies. The Bible is this freak manifesto that the Catholic Church and the straight-ass Baptists have distorted and manipulated to serve the capitalist Satan. The Bible is more revolutionary than the *Communist Manifesto*. You just gotta know how to read it. Kesey gets it."

"That's complete bullshit," Mike, every bit as high, retorted. "I think Kesey just had a bad trip and Krassner was high enough to think it sounded smart or something. All religion is bullshit—you know, opiate of the masses—and you're just shooting that shit up. That ain't revolutionary, man."

"But maybe," I said, digging the energy, "Both things are sort of true. Jesus was cool, a freak, a revolutionary, but the Bible was all these later people trying to capitalize on his trip, spinning him in ways that gave them power. So maybe there is some truth to what Dale says—if you can cut through all the religious bullshit, and whittle it down to the things that Jesus actually said and did, then maybe that is a tool for the Revolution. But, man, I think it means ignoring about 95 percent of the Bible, which is different from what Kesey is saying."

"It's all true," Walter said, scanning around the room, deadpan expression staring at each of us in turn. "But we can't understand it, so that's why people who claim to understand it, from the Pope to Kesey to Dale, keep fucking everything up. All imperfect messengers. It's beyond intellect. No use trying, man."

"I can go for that," Stu, eyes blazing, said, "so you guys should all shut the fuck up about this stuff. I mean who gives a shit. Fuck Kesey. Fuck the Bible. Fuck whatever book you think has all the answers." Everyone got quiet for a second and Stu's look softened, "Unless you're talking about Rodale's *Guide to Organic Gardening.*"

"Now that's some heavy shit, there, Stu," Little Eddie chimed in. "Heavy, heavy shit if you do it right. Right?"

Slowly, almost like a sequential reaction, the clever absurdity—and truth—of Eddie's comment hit each of us, and a wave of uncontrollable laughter roared around the table and filled the room. The few others who were awake and engaged in quiet conversations in the corners of the room, couldn't help but join in. It was delightfully infectious. Around that table, spastic with laughter, we fell into each other, some falling off the benches onto the floor.

What the fuck had we been talking about anyway?

SPRING/18

Jeffrey and Annie showed up in a rental car in the middle of the morning. Naturally, Jeffrey had some great pot, so everything stopped for an instant welcoming party. Jeffrey went way back to our days at West Campus at BU, and Sarah and I hung out with him a lot last winter when we were waiting for the trial. An interesting blend of intensity (seeking order) and mellowness (accepting and soft-spoken), he'd always been solid and a lot of fun. Annie was a few years younger, eighteen or nineteen, and quiet. She'd been a schoolmate and girlfriend of Eddie's in Boston, but she showed up with Jeffrey. Eddie and Jeffrey had an interesting relationship.

Stu and I got it together in midafternoon to catch a ride with Matthew to go to Earl's to get the white truck, which we'd had to tow there the day before. Earl had it ready to go, after replacing the fuel pump that he had determined was the problem. We hung out long enough to drink a cup of coffee with him and fill him in on the latest developments on the ranch, the garden and house plans and such. We got back in the late afternoon. Sarah met me as I was headed into the Main House and suggested we take a walk.

We headed out toward the pasture that ran down the middle of the valley as the chilly grayness was just beginning to darken. Walking on the road, you were more than likely to run into other people and that could always lead into an entirely different trip. Sarah seemed anxious for us to have some time alone, which was hard to find in the Main House. Sometimes on the rainiest of days when all of us were clustered inside together, Ash Valley felt so small and confining. But in the pasture, at the broadest part of the valley, feeling small between the defining peaks to the east and west, you could feel a sense of space and distance from the seemingly all-engulfing intensity emanating from the Main House.

We ambled north, toward the reservoir and the meadow where we hoped to start building our house in the next few days. I told her that Stu and I had run into Tim at Days Creek and that he basically told us he was leaving the ranch. Nancy had already essentially moved back to town. We both agreed that it was probably for the best that they leave. Nancy was righteous, a great worker and sister—she would be a big loss, but she had sensed early on that it wasn't going to work for Tim so she eased herself out.

Tim wasn't into sharing work, money, vision, anything. He was just looking for a place where people would leave him alone—and that wasn't going to happen at Ash Valley. That's not why we came here. Sarah and I agreed that the number of people living on the ranch was getting out of control, adding stress to all our other challenges. We didn't know where Jeffrey and Annie were going to sleep and one possibility was for them to share our room. We kind of said we would be open to that, but alone out here in the middle of the pasture, we could say to each other that we were bummed about that and resolved between us to focus our energy on getting our house built as soon as possible to get the hell out of that house.

We moved up to the road by the Second House to walk around the reservoir. We stopped talking for a little bit to try to get by without anybody noticing us. Safely past the house, Sarah brought up what had obviously been on her mind from the start.

"Looks like we have a new triangle," she said, with a look between a wary smile and troubled disbelief.

"What? No. Who?" I said. "This shit is killing us."

"Dale and Sydney—and Jack."

"What . . . . the fuck? Really? Are you sure?"

"Yup. Sydney basically told me and Paulie today that she is into Jack. She didn't get into any details about what that means, but it seems like trouble to me."

"No shit. Does Dale know?"

"I don't know."

There was something about Dale and Sydney that made this feel heavier than our earlier triangle. They had always been kind of the grown-ups in the tribe. Their apartment in Boston at 1387 Commonwealth was the main off-campus place where we gathered. Mike, Walter, Jeffrey, and Stu had all lived there. I crashed there and met up with Sarah there the summer after freshman year. Mountfort Street, our apartment sophomore year, was the party house and the permanent crash pad (folks at 1387 would send wandering freaks to us), but 1387 was sort of neat and had regular meals and an air of stability and homeyness that Mountfort Street never had. Dale and Sydney had the VW bus that led the way on our summer quest for a West Coast house the year before. They were the ones who found Tiller and the White House and kept it together through a winter until the rest of us could get out here. At least us Boston folks still looked at them as the central rocks that we built around. Now this.

We had come to the meadow of our house site. We sat under the trees near the creek bank. Close and quiet for a while.

"Are we OK, Sarah?" I finally asked.

"Yes." Her looked flipped from certainty to just a shimmer of doubt. "Right?"

"Yes. Such crazy shit all around us. I really think things will mellow a bit when we all get out of the Main House and the weather turns."

"It better. We can't keep going like this."

We sat on the moist, ragged grass where our house would sit soon and kissed a long slow kiss, a kiss less of passion than of reassurance and faith. Then we moved around the space and imagined what it might be for us to live there.

The next day, we followed Jeffrey to Medford in the red truck, so he could return the rental car. It was rainy when we got back to a gloomy mood that permeated the Main House where most everyone was hanging out. Sarah and I, determined to avoid the gloom, found Wayne and huddled with him in a corner to talk about our house plan. We quickly decided we didn't want anything rectangular. We played with a circular shape and then a hexagon but finally decided on an octagon. Wayne took the crude drawing that Sarah and I had been passing back and forth and made it look architectural. Wow. That was a big step. It was still raining, but Wayne and I decided to go to the site with a tape measure and some stakes and begin to figure out how that paper plan would look on the ground.

The small grove of ash trees along the creek provided a perfect framing for the house site. The ground was fairly level and high enough to be safe from flooding. The creek ran strong and loud stoked by all the rain and snow melt from the hills above us, probably close to its maximum level. The house would sit about 10 feet away from the near bank with the front facing out toward the open meadow and the road. It was far out going through the process with Wayne. He calculated that making each of the eight sides six feet long would fit the site well and give us the room we wanted. We did a crude layout of how the house would sit on the site with the stakes—and I could stand inside and begin to imagine living there. I got chills, man. It sorta seemed like Wayne had superpowers to look at space and conceptualize how to put a structure on it. We had a fucking plan!

I was soaking wet but soaring when we got back to the Main House—and I hadn't smoked any dope all day. I found Sarah, who was chopping stuff for dinner, and pulled her to me and gave her a big hug: "Man, it's so fucking cool," I told her.

"What the fuck are you so happy about," said Mike, who was also working on dinner a few feet away. "Got your palace all planned out?"

"Fuck you, Mike. It's fucking cool. And it's good for all of us, too, to start clearing out this house so we have some breathing room." The words came out more intense than I meant them, but, shit, couldn't he let me feel good just for a little while?

"But it's especially good for you. Remind me why we are building your house first?"

"Because we're ready. Because Wayne thinks we can do it pretty quick. Because we are driving each other fucking crazy cooped up in this house. Shit, man, why do you always have to be such a bummer."

Walter, also working on dinner, intervened, "Why does something good happening for Ben and Sarah mean something bad for you, Mike? Lighten up and get your bread in the oven."

Mike grumbled but carefully put his two nicely risen loaves into the oven of the woodstove. We had replaced the propane stove because we didn't want to keep filling the propane tank. I went upstairs to get out of my wet clothes before he could say anything more. Fucking Mike, man, such a solid brother in so many ways, but he could be such an asshole.

The tension only seemed to intensify during dinner. I couldn't take it, so after washing my plate, I went outside and sat in the front yard. The rain had stopped and the evening temperature was surprisingly warm. Stu joined me and then gradually Sarah, Mike, Paulie, and Jeffrey came out, too. Everyone kind of exhaled and shook their head as they took their places in a ragged circle we were forming.

I apologized to Mike for the intensity of my response to him. He smiled. "Hey man, you know I was just fucking with you. Don't take shit so seriously."

"It all seems so serious here—and pretty damn glum," said Jeffrey, wide-eyed and not even through his second day on the ranch. "What the fuck's going on?"

"Welcome to utopia," Stu said. "Guess the rain and living on top of each other is making people crazy."

"Like Sydney? And Dale? And Jack?," Sarah said. "Where did that come from?"

"Well …," Paulie started, looking self-consciously at Mike and then around to all of us. "It is kind of like going crazy. I don't know. Something comes into your head that you hadn't thought of before and it seems like it's a good thing and it makes sense and then … for me, at least, it took a while to snap out of it and see what I was doing and know that it was the wrong thing to do. Maybe that'll happen with Sydney, too."

"Fucking Stephen," Mike said, just loud enough for all of us to hear.

"No matter what causes it or whose fault it is," I said, "when this shit goes down, we end up with people sneaking around and others pissed off and nobody trusting nobody. Hard way to build a commune."

"But you all are in couples. At least for the moment," Stu said with his wiseass smile. "Things are different for us single guys. Not saying what's right or what's wrong—just the way it is and you've got to understand it."

"Paulie, I really appreciate what you said," Jeffrey said. "I don't know you that well and I can't quite imagine how someone who seems as sweet as you would end up with Mike," now Jeffrey had that wiseass smile. "But that sounded real honest and healing in a way, I guess. But … Dale and Sydney? … I know them real well and I just can't imagine how this happened and what's going to happen now."

"It just seems," Sarah said, "we all need to do a better job of talking about this stuff. Things simmer and then blow up and people jump all over each other and, like Jeffrey said, it's just no fun. I didn't come here to be bummed all the time."

The conversation felt genuine and such a welcome break from the whispering and gossiping that had fed the uneasiness that was hovering over everything, so we decided we should include everybody in the discussion. Jack and Sydney were in Shantytown and Sarah yelled over there to tell them to come to the Main House. Dale volunteered to go to the Second House to get Phillip and Jane. Everybody else was already in the house, where we spread out in the living room.

Mike launched right into a rap aimed at Stephen. "I just got to say, man, I felt betrayed by you … and Paulie. Paulie is a big girl and knows what she's doing, but I felt like you kind of took advantage of her. The whole horse thing was such a fundamental dream for her. We all saw that glow, that magical happiness when she got her horse, the kind of happiness that I think all of us are looking for here … and you kind of wrapped yourself into that and became an intrinsic part of that dream for her. I mean I was stupid not to see that and I was into my own stuff so wasn't paying as much attention as I should have but I don't know what I could have done."

Stephen listened, staring down mostly, but occasionally looking up into Mike's eyes, respectful and focused. Paulie watched Mike and looked around the room, watching each of us react.

"Listen, man," Mike said directly at Stephen, "Paulie and I are OK. I think we learned a lot about each other through all this. And I know you are an important part of this trip, that you've got skills we need and people that I like and trust like and trust you. I want to be your friend, your brother, but it's something we've both got to work on. I'll try if you'll try."

The room was really quiet for a few long seconds. "Thanks, man." Stephen finally said with his quiet gravelly voice. "I'm sorry. I think we got swept up in this whole new thing together and didn't think … didn't think about a lot of stuff. I guess. I want to be here. I want to be your friend. I'll try, too."

Mike and Stephen exchanged straightforward nods as we got quiet again. I couldn't help noticing Dale glowering at Sydney and then Jack, who had diplomatically positioned themselves in different corners of the room. One seeming, welcome resolution. One deepening dilemma.

Phillip and Jane entered into the silence, their hustling energy quickly subdued as they observed the somber looks in the room.

"Sorry to be late. We had to deal with the kids," Phillip said. "But, hmmm, looks like the party hasn't quite started yet." He half-laughed with his eyes darting around the room.

"We're just trying to talk some stuff out," Dale said. "Grab a seat."

"Which brings up something for me," Little Eddie said. "I haven't been here that long, but I'm just wondering why Phillip and Jane have the Second House all to themselves, while we're all fucking sardines in here? How many are we in this house? Thirteen? Fourteen? Me and Walter are sleeping on this very floor which is groovy, I guess, but we have to wait for everybody to leave at night and get woken up when people start showing up in the morning. I know you have the kids but it seems like you could take another person or two until we get other houses to get some people out of here."

"Hey, man, I can dig where your coming from," Phillip said. "The thing is, man, that house is really not that big. Really, it's tight with just us."

Jane lit a joint and started passing it around. "I feel for you, Eddie, for all of you. This is crazy," she said. "Greg and Kathy are cool. They could pretty much sleep anywhere and put up with anything. It's the baby, Rainbow, I worry about. She needs a stable scene. Routine. Quiet times. It's a huge deal taking care of a baby with no running water or electricity—and the two older kids running around being kids. I just don't think adding people, spreading the chaos of this house to our house would be good for her. I really couldn't do it. Sorry." The joint had come back to her. She smiled and took a deep hit.

"That makes sense," Sarah said and everybody, even Eddie, nodded their agreement. "We just gotta get more places for people to live. Soon. While we're talking, though, I gotta say to Phillip that sometimes I feel like you talk down to me and other women, like there are things you don't think we should know or do, that men should do the serious thinking and hard work and the women should cook and clean and take care of the kids. Traditional bullshit. I'm not into that."

Phillip reacted with a disbelieving smile. "No, no, hey, man, that's not where I'm coming from at all. Don't know where you get that idea."

"I sense that too," Sydney said. "Sometimes it's just the way you talk to us or who you talk to when you're thinking something is important. Not me. Not Sarah. Maybe Dale or Mike or Ben or Stu. I don't know about Jane. Maybe you don't do it consciously. Maybe you don't even realize you do it. But you do and it's uncomfortable for me and I suspect most of the other women, too."

Phillip now looked flustered. "You're right if I act like that … I don't know it and I sure don't mean to do it." He looked around at Sydney and Sarah and Paulie and Annie, the newcomer. "Hey, man, I'm sorry if I've made any of you uncomfortable. I'm just getting to know you as sisters and you are all righteous chicks"—groans from Sarah and Sydney—"righteous women, whatever. I'll try to do better and expect you all will help me with that."

Progress? Maybe. Another pause. Wayne calmly stroked his long beard and spoke in a gentle soothing voice.

"It seems like all these issues one way or another relate to having compassion for one another. This a wild social experiment. A lot of us hardly knew each other a couple of months ago and now we are trying to build something really complicated together. A working ranch. Communal relations. An example for others still stuck in the straight world to follow. And right now we are trying to do that with the handicaps of shitty weather and difficult living conditions. We've got to lighten up on each other. Keep working. Keep growing. But believe in your brothers and sisters and let's cut each other a fair amount of slack."

"We're all bozos on this bus," Walter added. "But man it's a fucking groovy bus and there's no bunch of bozos I'd rather be with. We just gotta keep trucking, man."

That sort of summed up the lesson of the evening. Things were said that had been festering among us and everyone seemed willing to try harder to communicate and be more understanding of each other. But the whole Sydney-Jack-Dale thing never came up, so it's not like we solved everything.

Later, I was writing a letter to my parents and Sarah was sleeping when Dale came in with a seeming sense of urgency and asked me to wake Sarah and come into his and Sydney's room, which was just across the small landing at the top of the stairs from ours. Sarah was confused when I woke her but I told her it seemed real important. When we went in, Sydney looked upset and Dale had a scary intensity about him.

"So it was cool that tonight we all talked about how we all need to help out our brothers and sisters more," Dale said. "Well, here's a chance for you." He was staring at Sarah.

The room was small. Sydney was curled in a far corner of the mattress on the floor. Dale was on the edge closest to Sarah and me. We sat on the floor leaning against a wall, just a few feet away from him.

"Sydney and I have been together for a while. We met early at West Campus and got into each other, had a cool romance and eventually had sex, which got a lot easier when we moved out of the dorms to 1387." Sarah subtly caught my eye with a mildly panicked look. She'd been woken up and pulled into this. "We were in love," Dale went on with an exaggerated smile. "You guys know all about that, right? The sex was cool and all that and frequent enough to keep me happy. But ..." Sydney was staring down, wouldn't look at Dale, wouldn't look at us.

"The sex was always about love and tenderness and that stuff in pop songs and fairy tales. Sydney was the first girl I ever really made love to. I never just had sex for the sake of having sex. You know this free love stuff that our generation is supposed to be all about. I never had just raw and physical sex. Sex for sex's sakes. And, well, it seems that Sydney has now experienced that. I'm feeling cheated and pissed about that."

He looked back and forth between Sarah and me. His eyes were huge and maniacal. Sarah stared down into the floor. I looked from her to Dale to Sydney. There was no air in the room, no space to back away. I couldn't think of anything to say to change the direction he was going. I wanted to grab Sarah and get out of there but there was no escape.

"Ben," Dale went on, "You've been open about the fact that Sarah is the only woman you've been with sexually. Maybe you feel the same way. A lack in your experience. So … sister and brother," he said with extra emphasis. Sarah looked up at him, having been directly addressed. "I propose a swap. I sleep with Sarah. Ben sleeps with Sydney. One time. Purely sexual." He stopped talking and leaned against a sidewall, with a crazy satisfied expression, confident he'd made a compelling case.

Sarah looked at me, with a horrified, pleading look. Did compassion for our brothers and sisters go this far?

"I don't feel that way," I said, trying to look and sound sympathetic. "Cheated. I'm sorry for whatever you're going through. I want to be a good brother and help but I'm not into this. Sorry, man."

Dale sat up, gave me an incredulous look, "Thanks, *brother*. I don't think you quite get how important this is to me. How important it is for *us*. What does *sister* Sarah have to say?"

She looked at me, at Sydney, still curled up and quiet in the corner of the bed, finally at Dale, staring intently, demandingly at her.

"Whatever is going on with you, Dale, I'm sorry," Sarah said. "But I don't think this is the answer. I mean how would it help?"

"We'd be even," Dale said looking at Sydney. Nobody had said anything about Jack and Sydney, but that reality was thick in the room. "Then I would *know* better what's going on. Maybe it would just take the power out of sex for me. What would it hurt? Aren't you willing to try, *sister*?"

"I just don't think it would help anything," Sarah said. "And I'm just not into it. It looks like, three of the four people you want to do this aren't into it."

"Three people who claim to care about me won't do this for me. You all talk about being liberated and compassionate. Well it's clear that's just a bunch of bullshit."

"Caring about somebody doesn't mean doing anything they ask you to do," I said. "It means trying to doing something to really help. And I think we all would like to find a way to really help you. But not this. Sorry."

"Well, if this isn't happening then I'm going to town tomorrow to find me a whore or somebody to pick up in the bar." Nobody said anything for a while. "Can I at least get a chance to talk to Sarah alone for few minutes."

Sarah nodded her OK to me and Sydney pulled herself up out of the bed and we went across the hall.

"I'm sorry," Sydney said when we settled into our room. "He's crazy. This whole Jack thing has got him crazy and, understandably, he's not listening to me anymore. He doesn't realize he's just making everything worse between us."

We were both blown away and exhausted, so we didn't say much else. Sydney was indisputably attractive but I did think of her as more of a sister and having sex with her would just seem weird—not raw or fun or liberating in any way—especially under these circumstances. I really was kind of conservative about sex, I guess.

It seemed like a long time but it was probably only ten minutes before Sarah came in, visibly shaking.

"He's so desperate and obviously hurting," she said. "I don't know what to do. I really want to help him, but I just can't get into it. It would be terrible, but he's convinced himself that him fucking me is the only thing that can help. He told me," she said, looking at Sydney, "that Jack told him that you two had slept together." Sydney grimly nodded. "I just can't do it, Ben."

"I know," I said, relieved, and I reached out to rub her shoulder.

I went across the hall and told Dale that this swap was not the answer, that I understood his hurt and his anger, his need to do something, but neither Sarah or I were into it. He talked more about Jack and his confusion about Sydney. Jeffrey, who had ended up sleeping downstairs until one of the bedrooms opened up and was one of Dale's best friends, joined us to help try to talk him down. Eventually, Dale ran out of rage and told us all to go to bed. Sarah and I cuddled close and soon I could hear her soft snoring.

Dale went to Eugene the next day.

SPRING/19

As we scouted the forest north of our property, crunching in the soft sweet-smelling duff on a crisp blue early June morning, I was overwhelmed by the marvel of my being there, doing this, a crazy dream come true. Stephen and I were searching for the first pieces of our house, a house we would build with our hands and the help of our brothers and sisters.

We needed poles for the framing: eight for the perimeter uprights, 6 inches in diameter and straight for 8 to 10 feet; one twice as thick and about 16 feet long for the center post; and 16 smaller ones 6–10 feet long for the tops of the walls and the roof rafters. After an hour or so, we found a few young firs about the right size.

Watching Stephen cut the first tree down, I was awed and a little scared by the power of the roaring chain saw—the chain whizzing around its huge 36-inch bar, a whining blur slicing easily through the bottom of the tree—and the smooth sure way Steven cut a notch on one side and then a straight cut on the opposite side to send it crashing down in a narrow clear spot in the midst of the thick cluster of trees and brush that surrounded us. He held out the still rumbling saw to me, pointed to another pole-size tree a few feet away and said, "OK?" with a smile that had a little reassurance in it.

I had never used a chain saw before or any kind of power saw, for that matter. Truth is I could barely use a hammer. And yet, just over two months on Oregon soil and we were getting ready to build our own house. Anybody who had known me for the first twenty-one years of my life would have laughed at the thought of it. But I couldn't continue to be mechanically inept and incompetent and do what I wanted to do on this land and with this commune. I had sorta hoped I could be the grunt of this work outing, carrying the gas can and ax and humping the poles out of the woods, while Stephen did the saw work. But with firm kindness and patience, Stephen insisted I take the saw. We both knew I had to learn.

Well, it wasn't OK at first. I got the saw bound up cutting the top part of the front notch too deep. I killed it. Doing the back cut, I over-revved the saw and it kicked back at me. Stephen just smiled when I looked at him, thinking he might want to take over. When I finally managed to get all the way through, the cut pole pivoted on its trunk and fell about 90 degrees off from where I was aiming and hung up in a nearby monster tree. Stephen was still smiling, amused but encouraging, as we worked the pole out of its entrapment and got it to the ground. "You did all right," he said. "You're just pushing it too hard. Relax, let the saw do the work."

I tried to believe that and did better on two others I cut down, though never getting close to Stephen's smoothness. We got six good poles that morning and dragged them down to the road, where we chained them together for me to pull to our house site with our tractor—another exotically powerful and utilitarian tool for me. It wasn't that long ago that I'd finally learned to use a stick shift. Man, did I feel on top of the world sitting on the tractor seat, sweaty and sore in ways I'd never been before, looking back at my load—the real stuff of our house. Stephen followed on foot, directing me and carrying the chain saw with the blade resting on his shoulder, thoroughly digging me digging the sense of power that comes from making something happen through hard physical work. Sarah was waiting at the house site as I drove the poles across the meadow toward her. I don't remember ever being prouder of anything I had ever done in my life.

Stephen taught Sarah and me how to skin the bark off the poles with a draw knife, a tool with a sharp beveled blade about eight inches long between two handles. Neither Sarah or I knew that such a tool existed or could have imagined the use of it if we did. It was hard work. You had to get the blade just under the skin of the bark and pull it steadily toward you, ideally without digging into the meat of the wood, which would slow and eventually stop the momentum of the pull, or jerking it up and through the bark layer and out. That was frustrating because you just got little chunks off and had to get a new bite under the bark—and also kind of dangerous because you were pulling this sharp blade with some force directly at yourself. It was sweet if you got a nice steady peel of a foot or two, the bark sort of curling away from the pole like a well-peeled apple skin. But that didn't happen often, especially at first, for Sarah who straddled the first pole and began pulling determinedly as Stephen and I went back to the woods to find more.

Over the next four days, we leveled the site and laid out the frame of the structure more precisely with stakes and string, finished gathering the poles and cut the ones for the perimeter to rough length (still learning the lesson of letting the saw do the work, I broke a Skil saw blade—not easy to do—on the second one, so we had to cut the rest with a chain saw), dug the holes for the uprights in the thick clay soil with a post-hole digger, raised the poles and cut them off at the finished height (we didn't have a ladder, so one guy sat on another guy's shoulders), put up the horizontal cross pieces between them, set the center pole, and placed the roof members, with a notch to sit flat on the outside pole and an angle on the other end to hit the center pole just right. Our vision had a shape in the real world.

We had lots of help. Stephen and Wayne were the structural brains, providers of tools, and the patient teachers of skills. Stu provided his strong back and kept us laughing. Dale, Jeffrey, Mike, and Jack all put in time, especially when we needed extra hands. Jane, Little Eddie, and Sydney would appear with joints or wine and to cheer us on. Walter could be counted on to bring us snacks and share some wisdom. It was going to be Sarah and my house, but the love that was building it was communal, shared—powerful, proof in the tangible transformation of dirt and wood and space that Ash Valley could work. *We* could work.

In addition to sort of learning how to use a chain saw, a tractor, a Skil saw, a draw knife, and a post-hole digger, I learned about chalk lines and plumb bobs and squares and levels and string lines and how to swing a damn hammer with some degree of efficiency. Sarah became highly proficient at skinning logs and showed a natural talent for understanding spatial relations as we, encountering the realities revealed by actually putting the pieces together, continually adapted our plans for the house to make it just how we wanted.

When we finished placing the last roof pole, righteously tired after five days of steady hard work, we let out a collective whoop and I hugged Sarah tight, both of us with traces of tears in our eyes. Then we hugged Stephen, Wayne, Stu, the core crew. And we were quiet for a minute or two and the creek's steady song became an anthem of triumph for us. Unthinkable, this eight-sided skeleton of a structure in front of us, such a short time ago when we were all so far away from this magic little meadow.

While we were so focused on getting our house built, we got good news on the legal front. Dale, Phillip, and Paulie came back from Eugene with news that we had set legal history by getting an injunction to stop the National Forest Service from selling logging rights to the land bordering our property. Douglas County sheriff's deputies halted the in-progress timber sale, flashing the injunction from federal court. The Forest Service was in the middle of opening the eight submitted bids when it got shut down. Cool! Our lawyers had heard from a couple of liberal ecology groups who had taken notice of our suit and expressed interest in helping somehow.

The injunction was only temporary, in effect until there was a hearing in which we could argue for a permanent injunction (a legal procedure that had been aimed at me in Boston not long ago). And our potential allies hadn't yet committed to anything beyond sympathetic interest. But still these were big steps: both the courts and activists were taking us seriously. That night we partied with some wine they brought back from Eugene and I decided my dandelion wine had been aging long enough and broke it out. It was potent but had a bitter taste (that's what I got from skimping on the sugar and fruit). After initial sips, nobody wanted to drink it but me. I was fine with that. Whammy!

We got word that the assault charge against Stephen had been dropped, but Mike and Stephen got into it again about some things Stephen said that upset Paulie, something about how she handled the horses. Shit, man, never ending. Mike blows up and even when he might have a valid argument, he ends up acting like an asshole, so Stephen looks like the wronged party. Stu and I tried to explain that to him, and he kind of got it. He and Stephen rapped it out and there seemed to be at least a show of peace again.

We also got into a discussion among everyone who was in the Main House about how to deal with new people, especially Ray and Caroline, who had decided they wanted to stay on without consulting the family as a whole. We decide to tell them not to build any permanent structures and to stay only until they could find somewhere else to live. We set a policy that anybody else who comes—besides those who we already expected—will be considered visitors and only become permanent residents if it happens organically, it's obvious to all of us, and we welcome them unanimously.

SPRING/20

After we finished the frame of our house, we took a day to haul the three 8 × 16 Forest Service cabins we had bought from the South Umpqua Falls fire camp up to the land. Willie Campbell, who we were buying the place from, provided the equipment and the expertise, and about ten of us provided the grunt labor. We had to put cross braces along the inside walls to try to keep the structures together through the rough four-mile trip up to Ash Valley, jack each of them up off the pier pads that served as their foundation and high enough for Willie to get the bucket of his front-end loader under them. We put blocks of scrap wood under the corners to hold them stable.

Then Willie expertly maneuvered the leveled bucket under the middle of the closer 16-foot wall, tipped the bucket back toward him, nestling the near side of the cabin against the back of the bucket and raising the opposite wall, which hung out in space. He then slowly raised the bucket, picking up the whole structure, which sat seemingly stable at a low angle with about five-and-a-half feet extending beyond the bucket on either side. We divided into two groups, five of us on each side, serving as spotters to keep the house from shifting as Willie very slowly steered the machine with its awkward load the 20 feet or so over relatively flat ground toward the trailer behind his truck. He pulled up along the side of the trailer and extended the bucket as far as he could over the bed, centering it between two 6 × 6 beams we had positioned about eight feet apart. We all jumped to take our positions around the cabin on the trailer. Willie then reversed the loading process, lowering the bucket as far he could, leaving room to pull it out, then inch by scary inch lowering the front end down, first toward a level position and then gradually creating a downhill angle. We all now positioned ourselves against the farther 16-foot wall that would, when the bucket reached the critical angle and gravity went to work, begin to slide out and off the bucket. Our job was to keep that slide steady and controlled as Willie continued to increase that angle as he backed the bucket off the trailer, leaving the cabin resting securely, we hoped, on the 6 × 6s.

It worked! We Ash Valley folks were just the reach of our twenty arms and the force of our combined weight, like an accessory tool to Willie's front-end loader, following his clear and direct commands, though our responses were not nearly as quick and precise as his machine's. Mostly, we watched with awe his organic connection to that machine and his hard-earned instincts for managing this situation, which we might not have been able to solve with all the right equipment and months to think about it. He pulled the levers and controlled the steering and the movement of the machine with a steely hint of a smile, a humble pleasure in the masterly skill that made that rugged piece of equipment do exactly what he wanted it to do, and a kindly patience with us less well-tuned instruments.

Willie's years of logging and transforming Ash Valley— creating ponds, moving creeks, building structures—had given him, like Earl, a power over the challenges of this daunting spectacular hard-ass country that still seemed, to me, a far reach for us. Willie and Earl were Oregonians who had known and thrived in an Oregon that seemed to be slowly slipping away—salmon thick as cordwood in the creeks, infinite trees in the forest, wildly clean and raw rivers, free space enough to engender a dogged independence. Ash Valley in its isolation from neighbors and communities, its lack of modern conveniences like electricity and phone lines and plumbing, its surrounding untouched ancient forests, was one of the few surviving vestiges of that Oregon. Could we handle it? Could we ever become Oregonians like Willie and Earl, people of this land? Both Willie and Earl were latter-day settlers of the Umpqua Valley, men who loved the vast and beautiful resources that they killed and harvested and tamed to make a life here. What were we—who had the audacity to both aspire to and question that way of life? Had we just stumbled on this land through a crazily random continuum of circumstances, bringing half-baked city ideas about "living in the country," destined to flail until we failed? Or had we been destined to come to Ash Valley, as it sometimes seemed, to save it from the ravages of clear-cuts and development, city kids saving Oregon from Oregonians?

On that day, Willie was our hero and, it was apparent as he led us that he dug the effort and heart and humor we brought to the work. I don't think he really understood what we were about and why we were there but—with another trait displayed by what seemed to us like the best Oregonians, like Earl—he didn't need to. He liked us and he liked working with us and that was all that mattered.

It was a slow ride to the ranch with the loaded trailer, but once we were there, the valley floor was dry enough for Willie to drive across the flat pasture, starting just before the garden and heading northeast toward Mike and Paulie's site, across from the goat barn in a crook of land following a bend in Ash Creek. Willie backed the truck up close to the site, so the trailer was roughly parallel to the creek. We placed a series of poles of about 4-inch diameter under the structure as we eased it off the 6 × 6 beams to roll it to the back of the trailer. Now, Stephen and Wayne stayed on the trailer to push while the rest of us—the original crew now joined by Jeffrey and Sydney and Walter and even Little Eddie—gathered on the ground, half on each side of the cabin as it came off the trailer and then easing it down to the ground when its balance shifted. We let it rest there while Mike and Stephen shoved two pier blocks under the downhill corners. Willie crept the trailer forward and the cabin slowly slid off until we all screamed together for him to stop, with just about a foot of cabin resting on the very back edge of the trailer. Mike and Stephen kicked two more pier pads under where we expected the back corners to land. We all, now seven on either side, at Stephen's count, "1-2-3 lift," raised the back end of the cabin off the trailer as Willie pulled the trailer out from under. "And now down—slowly," Stephen said, more calmly but still firmly. And we eased it down onto the pier blocks, reasonably smoothly. And there it sat—on the ground. A new home.

We whooped it up good after that. It took almost everyone on the ranch along with Willie's equipment and skills to get it done—and we did it. The power of the people! But it was getting to be late morning and we had two more to do, so the celebration was short as we all loaded up to go back for the next one. But we were now fueled with a profound sense of accomplishment and a new confidence.

It was getting dark by the time we dropped the last cabin on the southern end of the property near the creek across the pasture from the hay barn. This one was supposed to be for Dale and Sydney (until they built their house in the woods), but who knew what was happening with them? The middle one, across from the Main House, and on the other side of the creek, which was only a couple of feet wide at that point, was Stu's. We'd go another day for the much larger central log building, which we would have to almost completely disassemble to move.

Walter and Jane and Sydney had cooked us up a great meal of spaghetti and salad and biscuits. Willie joined us, as delighted as we were, I think, in being part of this deeply communal effort and impressed that we so eagerly did the work as he laid it out for us. Some wine appeared from somewhere and he drank his share. He even dared, despite everyone else's warning, to take a pull on my dandelion wine. Afterwards, he made a sour face, "That's some foul-tasting hooch," he said to me, with a quiet laugh. In many ways, Willie was worlds apart from us, but we'd found a connection getting those three cabins onto the land.

We couldn't talk him into spending the night—that would have crossed a line he wasn't ready for—but he decided to leave the trailer and the front-end loader and come back and get it another day.

SPRING/21

Most of us divided up to work on the different houses. All the cabins needed some work, fine-tuning their leveling, shoring up framing that had been jarred in the moving, repairing roofs and windows, and things like that. On our house, we had started putting planking on the roof, 1-inch lumber between the roof poles. Sarah and I planned to move down there as soon as the roof had tar paper on it, basically protecting us from any rain. Sydney, Jack, and Little Eddie headed off to LA to sell the old VW bus and score some pot from a friend of Eddie's. Dale was not too happy about that, but Sydney needed to be there to sign over the title and Jack had family to visit and places for them to stay, so there was some logic to the makeup of the traveling party.

After we had put up almost five sections of planks for our roof, the Skil saw blade was so dull it wouldn't cut anymore. I had hit a few nails cutting through the salvaged boards we were using. And every board we put up had to be cut on an angle at both ends—hard to do accurately with a hand saw—so we packed it in. The next day, while we waited for Stephen to go to town to get the blade sharpened, Sarah and I gathered shakes, which would be the final layer of the roof. How cool was it that almost all the materials we needed to build our house, we could get out of the woods or salvage from the ranch? When Stephen finally made it back, he had some dope, so we decided to smoke a joint before getting back to work on our house. About the time we finished that, Jon and Sheila, who had been expected for a while, arrived. With beer.

They were part of the Boston tribe but I didn't know them all that well. Jon was good friends with Walter, Jeffrey, and, I guess, Dale and Sydney. He lived next to Jeffrey in Cambridge but we never saw him much in the time leading up to my trial. And, in another one of those small world flukes, Sheila and Paulie had hung out together in high school in Springfield, Mass. Jon and Sheila had just gotten married and arrived in their clean-looking VW bus and announced they had a moving van full of stuff on its way. I'm not sure how well prepared they were for the realities of Ash Valley. I knew somehow that Jon, who was tall and thin with neat long hair and a well-groomed mustache and long beard, came from a family with money and that he had been more on the cultural (sex, drugs, and rock and roll) side of things, rather than the political, in Boston. I knew nothing beyond the Springfield connection about Sheila, who had long black hair that she wore in pigtails and a sort of delicate prettiness. Through their ties to others in the tribe, they were on the "expected" list, so they were in on arrival. And they did have a van full of stuff coming. Good thing people were starting to move out of the Main House to make room for them.

The party was in full swing by the middle of the afternoon when another car pulled up in front of the Main House and everything got suddenly quiet as Mike and I went out to see who it was. Fucking Rabinowitz, one of the original boys from New York. Wow. We had no idea he was coming, or how he possibly found us, but he had that killer loony smile as we hugged and the rest of the folks streamed out to greet him. Last time any of us had seen him was at our wedding when he showed up in a straight gray suit beneath his wild electric hair and gave us a $25 dollar US savings bond. Crazy fucker. The party soared to another level.

We did not put any more planks on the roof that day. But that night, we turned over our room in the Main House to Jon and Sheila (Jeffrey and Annie had already taken over Dale and Sydney's room) and gathered sleeping bags and blankets and pillows to make a bed inside the frame of our new house.

I was pretty high from the long afternoon and evening of partying when Sarah and I, with Moonbeam trailing just behind us, started the mile-long walk to our home meadow. But as we left the light and the noise of the Main House behind us, we were engulfed in a spectral luminosity that reached out over the valley. Sarah, not nearly as high as me, almost glowed under the load of bedding she carried, her face lit by the near full moon just rising into the clear deep sky above us. Something about her shine and that light eased me into a mellow lucidity, gradually grounding me into the momentousness of this moment.

"Wow. Can you believe this night?" I asked, looking into her. I was also carrying an awkward pile of blankets and pillows, the two of us sort of stumbling along. "It's like a guiding light taking us home."

"It's perfect," she said, her eyes sparkling through me. She giggled sweetly at our mutual clumsiness. "Everything feels different already."

We stopped to adjust our loads at the goat barn, while Moonbeam eagerly checked out the latest smells. We could have driven the tractor to our house or the red truck, which

was running well enough to make it that far. It would have
been a lot easier with all that stuff, which ended up being more
than we expected. But without even talking about it, we both
knew we needed to make this first walk home.

I stretched around her rebalanced load and gave her a
quick kiss Her lips were cold but soft and giving. There was
a hint of innocence in her smile that followed. We were so
exposed out in the uncanny brightness of this night, just the
two of us, away from the coverings of the collective: two
young lovers, free in an unfamiliar way. We ambled now. The
loads seemed lighter. We had, in some ways, already gotten
what had driven us so determinedly out of the Main House
and into this night. Not another night there, we had promised
each other, even with our roof not done. Aside from the
occasional rustling of the loose gravel under our feet we were
as silent as the valley as we came upon the Second House, quiet
too with just the light of a single kerosene lamp jarring the
natural radiance that was brightening as the moonlight crept
all across the valley. From there, it was an easy stroll past the
reservoir and into our meadow, where the half-finished roof
of our house-in-progress seemed almost to be grinning in
welcome.

The moon gave us enough light to arrange our bed:
sleeping bag on the ground under the portion of roof that
had planks on it, then sheets—how civilized—then another
sleeping bag on top, then two blankets. Then we stacked three
pillows (two for me, one for her) at the end by the center
pole, so we faced out toward the meadow. We moved without
speaking, the creek serenading us, not hurried, but with certain
purpose. It was a cold night. We crawled, each from our own
side, into the covers, and just beheld each other for a few

minutes in the dark shade our unfinished roof provided, lovers' smiles meeting one another. And kissed. Long, deep, solemn.

"Man, am I happy to be here," she said, the smile, now bigger, celebratory.

"I know. Me, too," I said. And we wriggled out of the layers of our clothes, staying under the covers, until we were both fully naked, and drew together in luscious warmth, and made sweet, sweet love in the bare bones of our cabin by the singing creek.

SPRING/22

After waking up for the first time to the beautiful tunes of Ash Creek and a quick cup of coffee at the Main House, we got right to work. In an on-off drizzle, we finished up the planks, got all the tar paper and one section of shakes on the roof. It was real fine listening to the rain pitter-patter above us as we slept dry in the open air that night.

The next day, Sarah and Phillip and Annie went to Roseburg to do some shopping and take Sheika the goat to the vet because her milk had dried up. We got a late start working on the house. We couldn't get the tractor—our means for hauling tools and materials to the site—to start. I tried to get the red truck going but before I made any progress, some bigwigs from the Forest Service showed up. I'm not sure what their purpose was beyond spreading more bullshit about the ecology of clear-cuts and what a tidy job they do when they rip all the trees off a hillside, maybe trying to talk us out of pursuing the court case. Dale and Wayne were going back and forth with them, and I just kind of hung on the periphery, frustrated by all the silly obstacles keeping us from getting to work. I was hoping to have the shakes all done before Sarah got back from Roseburg.

By the time the Forest Service dudes left, Stephen had the tractor going, so we headed down to our house with a solid crew: Wayne and Jon as well as Stephen and me. We were cruising, working on two sections at a time, Stephen and I on the roof and Wayne and Jon, tall guys, passing shakes up to us and cutting them to the angle we needed when we got to the end of a row. We were almost ready to start on the last section when Jane showed up with five joints she had gotten together from sifting seeds. After all we had done, we were ready for a break and it was cool hanging out, leaning against the perimeter poles, passing the joints around, shooting the shit. We got so into it, we were all surprised when we realized we had smoked all five. Nobody wanted to climb back up on that roof. The others split on the tractor but I stayed to clean up or try to do something else productive. I was really stoned, too, but the last section still black with tar paper between the finished sections of the silvery brown shakes just kept staring at me. Shit, I had to at least give it a shot. Moving slowly, with a bit of fumbling and breaking a couple of shakes in the process, I got the bottom row done. That left ten rows to go, each one with a couple fewer shakes as the piece of the roof pie narrowed as it climbed toward the peak. I stacked as many shingles as I could on the adjoining sections and saved my cuts to do several at once, so I didn't have to climb up and down so much. And, like the vanishing joints, the rows just followed one after the other, until I found myself fitting the very last shake against the center pole, which I then straddled and slowly spun around on, taking in all the angles of our finished roof and the creek side trees it now stood proudly among and the gentle meadow that it rose splendidly above. I just sat there awhile, my butt on the top of the center pole, just digging the shit out of my perch. Really, really high, man.

I realized how hungry I was and headed to the Main House, which was a different scene these days. Sarah and I didn't live there anymore. Mike and Paulie and Stu had moved into their cabins. Sydney was off to LA and Dale was just kind of crashing in the third cabin, but hadn't really moved in. So, relative newcomers Jeffrey and Annie and Jon and

Sheila now lived there along with Wayne and Tammy, Stephen, Walter, and Little Eddie (who was also in LA). It felt less like a crash pad, and the vibe, especially from the newest people, wasn't as loose—maybe those people felt more like it was *their* house, while we never really thought of it that way. We always thought that we had a temporary room there but the house was everybody's. Even in just the few days we had been sleeping at our house, it felt different walking in that front door, sorta like we were visitors. It was cool, though. With the new houses, the whole living dynamic had changed. We *had* a place that was just ours, so how could I begrudge the new folks for feeling more possessive of the Main House.

Sarah and the others who had gone to Roseburg had arrived just a little while before I got there. They had a good trip, though the vet didn't have any good answers about Sheika. Sarah picked up a few knick-knacks for our house, a vase and a painted metal box to keep matches in. Silly, little things, maybe, but it warmed my heart that she was so focused on making our house feel like a real home. I told her we had a good day, working on the house but didn't say we had finished the roof. I wanted that to be surprise. She was real happy when she saw it when we finally made it home that night.

The next day, the sun came out along with a spectacularly blue sky. I spent most of the morning with Stu trying to fix the brakes on the red truck, but it turned out we needed some kind of special tool—that we didn't have—to reattach the spring to the shoes. The next step on the house was the floor and Stephen and Wayne decided it made sense to use 2×4s for the boards supporting the floor planks—*joist* they called them— rather than poles, to give us a more uniform surface. So, Sarah and I started scavenging through a pile of scrap wood near

Shantytown, looking for eight decent 2×4s that were long enough. Soon after we started, a car came creeping up the road and stopped when they saw us. Two young men with sideburns and safely long hair (the back just touching their collars), one with a camera around his neck, got out and introduced themselves as being from the Roseburg *News-Review*, said they heard about us from the lawsuit we had filed against the Forest Service and wanted to talk to us for a story.

Sarah and I looked at each other, not exactly sure how to respond. Finally, I said I thought that would probably be all right and that most people were in the Main House just up the road and asked the reporters to give me a little time to check with them.

People were eating lunch or just hanging out. When I told them about the reporters, Mike freaked.

"No way we should talk to them or let them take pictures. We should tell them to get the fuck off our property right now. Shit, Tucker, you should know that. You want them taking pictures of you?"

"Wait a minute," Wayne said before I had a chance to respond. "I think it would be good. They're here because of the lawsuit. Good publicity could help us, get us more supporters, make us look like legitimate concerned citizens."

"Sure, man," Mike laughed. "You think they're going to check out this place, talk to us, and then write a story about what good fucking citizens we are? Keep dreaming. You can't trust these guys to tell the truth and, besides, we're *not* really very good citizens in their terms. "

"Well, we don't have to talk about the Revolution and killing pigs, Mike," Walter said with a half-smile. "We can be smart, talk about living in the country, growing our own food, loving the land. All that stuff is true, too, and it helps explain why we don't want them to clear-cut the forest. We are going to need more support to fight the Forest Service."

Most people seemed to agree with Wayne and Walter. I did. These guys seemed sincere, respectful, kind of digging what we were doing. We had to be careful about trusting straight people but we definitely needed allies, not just in the logging fight, but for the longer term struggles that were coming. We had to cultivate people who were open to what we were trying to do, not push them away.

"You fuckers can talk to them," Mike said as he and Paulie headed for the door. "I ain't. You're fools if you trust them."

I went out and told the reporters they could come in and talk to us. They sat in chairs on the far side of the living room. One guy asked questions while the other guy took pictures. I was half behind the staircase, which I hid behind every time I saw the camera pointed at me.

How many of us were there? Where had we come from? Why had we come to this part of Oregon? How did we end up here? What were we doing? What about the kids and school? What was our long-term plan? Why were we suing the Forest Service?

They were good questions and almost everybody chimed in with answers, good answers about the cities we'd left behind, the beauty we had found and come to love in Oregon and especially Ash Valley. We wanted to work hard and become self-sufficient. We'd send the kids to school in Tiller as long as we needed to but our long-term goal was to have a school on the land. We were trying to stop the clear-cut not only because it would destroy the pristine beauty of the place but because it would dramatically alter the ecological nature of the valley, with runoff from the bald slope mucking up our creek and flooding our flat land. We even steered them away from describing us as a "commune"—a word that carried some clichéd baggage—and told them we preferred to think of Ash Valley as a "community."

We sounded like good, reasonable people with a sensible plan. And the newspaper guys seemed to be eating it up.

It was a little strange that Wayne, Jon, and Stephen were centered among us, sitting on the table bench directly opposite the reporters and, thus, sorta like our central spokespeople. Wayne and Stephen had certainly been key to our efforts since we got on the land. But they were both relative newcomers to the long strange trip that had brought the Boston tribe, still the core group of this endeavor, to Oregon. Jon had been part of the scene in Boston, but, from my view, on the periphery. And he'd been in Oregon and on this land a total of three days. And yet, there he was in the middle of it, speaking, sometimes eloquently, about what we were doing there.

After an hour or so of talking in the Main House, our visitors asked if we could go back to doing whatever we do on a normal day and allow them to roam around the land and take pictures and ask more questions. After a brief discussion, I spoke for the group and told them it was OK but that they needed to respect people who didn't want to talk to them or get their pictures taken.

Sarah and I finished gathering the 2×4s and some planks for the floor and I chained them up to drag them to our site. She and Stephen walked behind me. When we got to our meadow, the reporters were there taking pictures. The photographer snapped a couple of shots of me driving the tractor across the meadow. I loved that image of myself, but

I sort of reluctantly asked them not to print any pictures of me. They agreed not to without me getting into the details of my probation and not really wanting to be a public face of the ranch.

I couldn't help but flash back to Sarah and I posing in the dean's office at BU for a photographer we thought was a freak and a friend. We had taken over the office as part of the anti-military campaign during the spring of our freshman year when our friendship was starting to bloom into some kind of romance. Most everyone else had gone to a big meeting to try to get more support. We volunteered with a few others to stay to "hold" the office, but mostly we thought it would be more fun hanging there than going to the meeting. So we posed, laying on the dean's desk and all kinds of stuff like that. We thought of it as a goof. But it turned out, those photos were key evidence when the administration decided to file disciplinary charges against me and twenty or so other kids. And that probably had something to do with me later being named in an injunction during protests supporting GE strikers, which I was barely involved in, and coming to the attention of the Boston cops, which might have had something to do with the Red Squad cop coming after me that night at Northeastern. On the other side of that chain of circumstances was the reality that Sarah and I got much closer during the anti-military campaign. The first night we ever slept next to each other was in the dean's office. And getting named in the disciplinary charges and being told to come to Boston (I was home in Illinois when I got the letter) early that following summer gave me an excuse to reconnect with and visit Sarah, which helped boost our relationship to another, better level. So was it ultimately a bad thing?

They did take some photos of Stephen pretending to put shakes on the roof, which was cool. After they left, we unloaded the 2×4s and planks. It had gotten hot, so we decided to wait to start building the floor and we jumped in the creek behind our house, a little pool about five feet in diameter and three or four feet deep. It was really cold but refreshing, down to our bones.

SPRING/23

Sarah and I barely made it to the Main House in time to catch the bus—Jon and Sheila's VW—heading to Eugene for the Renaissance Faire, a countercultural gathering that we'd heard about through the hippie grapevine. We didn't have much money to buy stuff, so I copied some of my poems on nice paper, Sarah made three colorful macrame wall hangings, and other folks made candles to trade.

The fair site was about ten miles west of Eugene near a small town called Elmira. When we got close, traffic was backed up, so Jon found a place to pull over and park on the side of the two-lane highway that led to the entrance, though we didn't really know how far we were from the fair—couldn't help but have some bummer flashbacks to Woodstock, where Sarah and I couldn't connect and missed all the music.

But it wasn't that far to the fair site and it was another beautiful sunny day and the other folks streaming along the road in all kinds of flashy freaky clothes exuded such good vibes that we got swept up in the exuberant energy. We were surprised they were charging an admission fee but it was only fifty cents. The whole scene was pretty chaotic, a powerful invigorating chaos, but definitely chaos: crowds of people wandering dusty paths through woods that ran along a meandering shallow river. I drifted in a daze at first, overwhelmed by the sheer number of freaks, lots of folks from Eugene and the surrounding area, for sure, but also people coming out of the rural valleys and mountains all over Oregon and Washington and even Idaho. It all felt very tribal. Sometimes the isolation of Ash Valley, which I relished in many ways, made me feel like we were fighting a lonely battle. But, man, it was mind-blowing and heartening to see how many of us there were. Everybody was smiling; everyone seemed happy. The air was full of pot smoke and exotic food smells and incense, all simmering sweetly in the warm sunshine. The craft and food booths varied from blankets laid on the ground or small carts to elaborate crafty booths made of tree branches and salvaged wood.

This was the fourth Renaissance Faire we later found out, the first taking place at a small farm in Eugene in November 1969. There had been two in 1970, the one held in October was the first on the current site along the Long Tom River.

Paulie got into the spirit right away, checking stuff out and bartering. She traded three of my poems for a really fine candle, a piece of art compared to the basic candles we had brought. I smoked a joint with the candlemaker, who was from a small commune up in the Coast Range west of Portland. He really dug my poetry. We exchanged addresses and promised to visit each other's places. I gave my last poem away to somebody who overheard our conversation. That was cool, too.

Sarah traded one of her wall hangings for a cool purple pitcher made by a young woman who lived near a town called Cave Junction in southwestern Oregon, where, she said, there was a happening freak scene. Stephen and Jeffrey got new knives with carved wooden handles. Paulie scored a big pottery bowl for three candles and got into a long rap with the potter about horses. Transactions and conversations like that were happening all over the place. The intimate one-on-one interchange of artists and the people appreciating their work was inspiring, a model for a decommercialized art scene, a vision for how things could work after the Revolution.

The information booth had a place for people from communes to share information about what they were into, if they were open to visitors, and how to contact us. We signed up and jotted down information from some other communes not far from us in southern Oregon. I'm sure we were all going through similar struggles. Just getting together to talk could be enormously useful and maybe we could find ways to work together, exchange goods, combine forces for big projects— great possibilities in connecting. And in the big picture, we knew that there were limits to what Ash Valley could become as a lone island in the conservative sea of rural Oregon, but if we could build a network of communes, we could multiply our effectiveness and our influence.

But beyond the bartering and information exchange, a capitalist overtone still permeated the fair, which was a drag. Some of the crafts and food seemed incredibly expensive. The beer garden—which I gravitated toward though I couldn't afford more than one beer—was run by a nearby commune and things got intense there. First the commune folks started arguing with each other—too much sampling of their product maybe—and then a bunch of bikers tried to "liberate" it and started a silly brawl that was quickly quashed. I appreciated their sentiment but they were all acting like jerks.

Of course, we ran into Dougy and Jill, our old Boston friends who lived in Eugene and who we had totally unexpectedly bumped into at the May Day protest. There was no real way for us to plan a meeting in advance but we knew some way or other we'd find them. Sarah and I hung with them, and when the rest of the Ash Valley folks were ready to leave, Dougy and Jill said we could crash with them and they would drive us back home the next day. So we stayed. We copped beer and Camels—store-bought cigarettes a real treat for us—on the way to Eugene. Jill made us a great meatloaf dinner. It was a fun night with them, and a bit of a treat to sleep in a house with walls and heat on a cool night. But I realized how acclimated I'd become to the quiet and seclusion of Ash Valley because even a fairly mellow city like Eugene felt crowded and frantic.

We went back to the fair the next day, a Saturday and just about when we arrived, it started raining hard. The dusty paths got muddy and slippery quickly. People started slipping and sliding all over the place, sometimes falling on top of each other in zany chain reactions as people tried to help others as they slid. Most people were laughing about it. We hung around long enough to score more cool stuff, trading Sarah's other wall hangings. She got a small ceramic vase, and at another booth with a tarp overhead to keep us dry, we got a stash box and a hash pipe carved from a deer antler with dental tools by this guy from somewhere in the mountains of Washington. We hung with him for a while. He was soft-spoken and modest about his wares, which we thought were amazing. He was intrigued by what we were doing at Ash Valley, especially that we were hoping to get into producing arts and crafts items both as creative outlets and to exchange for other goods. He promised to come visit us. After that, the whole scene kind of disintegrated, so people starting splitting, including a bunch of the vendors—and us.

We had a great time at the fair and hanging out with Dougy and Jill, but I was ready to get back to the ranch. We left Eugene in late afternoon.

All the way up the river road, I felt a surging sense of pride as Dougy and Jill were noticeably astonished by the beauty of the South Umpqua and the forests that rose on either side of it. This is only the prelude, I thought, just wait.

As we cruised through the ranch's front gate, the sun was just beginning to set behind the western hills above the valley, casting a low diffuse bronzy light that gave the fields in front of us an enchanting patina.

"Here we are," I said, pulling myself up to stick my head between Dougy and Jill in the front seat.

"Holy shit, Ben R," Dougy said. "This is it?!"

"This is only the beginning," Sarah said, nestling her head next to mine.

"Oh, my God," Jill said, real awe in her voice, as we rounded the first curve near the hay barn and the whole wide valley opened up in front of us. "This is unbelievably fantastic."

All of us were beaming almost as one when we pulled up at the Main House. Dougy got out and caught my eye as I did, too—and shook his head in emphatic approval.

Before any more could be said, people started pouring out of the house to greet Dougy and Jill and welcome us home.

"Hey, youse guys are just in time for supper," said Walter with a big stoned grin.

Home!

SPRING/24

There was a letter from Luke Vaughn waiting for me. He was about to get out of prison. Luke had been the leader of SDS at BU during the anti-military campaign in spring 1969. Sarah and I were with him when we went to Boston English High School to hand out leaflets and the kids attacked us. Sarah and I got away from them pretty quickly but Luke got caught in the middle of the mob and tried fighting back. He was eventually rescued by Black students who formed a circle around him and escorted him to safety. That was a big turning point for him that eventually led him to become a leader of the Weatherman faction of SDS.

That group believed that we needed to start fighting back against whoever was attacking us and that the role of White radicals in the revolution was to support Black militants (and other people fighting for liberation like the Vietnamese). Luke's Weatherman group went back to Boston English and basically challenged the White students to a fight. Later, they attacked the offices of the Center for International Affairs at Harvard that had developed some of the theories and strategies behind the Vietnam War. Unfortunately, McGeorge Bundy and Henry Kissinger, two of the center's more notorious members, weren't available that day, so, reports said, they attacked secretaries and other lower echelon office workers. Luke went underground to avoid the charges that resulted, but he got caught shoplifting long underwear in New Hampshire and ended up serving almost two years in prison. We had corresponded off-and-on for a while. He even confessed that, when he heard about the charges against me, he almost hoped that I would get jail time so we could hang out together in prison. This letter, written in clear but frantic black ink, was in response to a letter in which I told him about our move to the ranch and some of our hopes for it.

Tues. June 15

dear brother ben,

the revolution must be <u>mainly</u> fought in the cities - that is where the misery, the people, the explosive combination of Blacks, Chicanos, Puerto Ricans, universities, high schools, near chaotic social "services," corporate business offices are, and where we must be.

after the revolution we must destroy the cities as they're presently constituted. in fact, the revolution will do that primarily as a military-pol. necessity, but also as a service to humanity - cities were originally built for commercial-capitalist reasons centering around the need for a common trading market, but soon expanding to meet the capitalists' needs for concentrated, convenient, close-by banks, theaters, stores, raw materials, labor supply (PEOPLE!) - after the revolution we must construct new small village cities, spread thruout the country fairly evenly to allow OPENNESS, relative smallness. there will also be a need for even greater non-cityness + somehow that must be shared because both lives could be beautiful - communal, dynamic, intense village life, less intense country life - but the distinctions will not be nearly as great - in Amerika now the country people are mainly tight assed, narrow, individualist, racist, uncultured + the city people are mainly tight-assed, narrow, individualist, racist, "cultured" - the distinction is hard to see at times once u strip the superficial "culture" most of us have been brought up to believe is desirable, but the country folks shouldn't be glorified.

but <u>now</u> we must find a way to integrate the country into our lives 1) because it <u>is</u> incredible + a real joy + and that is not contrary to the rev. per se 2) because a rev. that is all no no is a loser, it is <u>mainly</u>

*- not completely - the pigs role to close off our options not ours 3) bec.
many of the rural skills - in terms of breaking out of our middle class
helplessness, technology paralysis - are vital - as u describe.*

*but there is the opposite, the limits of the country - a long discussion
i want badly to have w/you - all of you - not as a stern father but as
a comrade. it mainly revolves around your apt - and not fully conscious
- description of the "magic" of how the money appeared + how that
alienation from the urgent, non-magic <u>very clear</u> relationship most people
in this country see between money and unhappiness - e. g. my choices are
1) slave labor to the man (either boss or husband) 2) crime - high % of
detection, <u>jail</u> 3) prostitution 4) welfare - is ultimately the source of <u>non-
freedom</u> for you.*

*i think the solution lies in some form of revolving door country
institutions where people are able to experience the country but not
permanently root there, where many people are given the opportunity to
experience the wonders of anti-city living but also see their main task
as working in the cities. obviously this presents problems - e.g. tourism,
exploiting the full-time country people, senses of superiority/inferiority/
ego/guilt, technical problems of how we can make a farm a viable
economic and social unit w/openness to many city people, many others we
<u>must</u> resolve, a lot thru experiment + practice. i could go on, but tonight is
my next to last night here - hopefully - and i don't want to write even this
much but your letter was wonderful + turned me on a lot - I love you, ben,
feel very good vibes about you and very much hope we can become really
close friends.*

let me close w. 2 impt things:

*1) i respect you, your letter showed a real desire/ability to cope w/
a lot of complex realities and wasn't at all - nor did I expect it to be - a
defensive, cop-out. I feel our struggle will really <u>help</u> all of us - Mike,
Sarah, others - and is essential. Tiller, Weatherman, Bread + Roses -*

all are not the answer, but all - unlike many other experiments which contributed nothing or set us back - are good, have taught us a lot, are part of the answer. we are <u>losing</u>, the man is winning, we must do much better, immediately, and i think i have some ideas about how last year was a horrible year, a year of a movement falling in on itself because of its own errors - during that year a few of us grew, found experiences that were building - mine was one, yours was another, but we must figure out + change the <u>collective</u> experience of our generation which is badly dead-ended now.

2) I am extremely anxious to come <u>live</u> with you all perhaps for a month - August - it is a dream now. i am still writing this from prison, a totally <u>situationally</u> powerless human being locked in a hot bathroom as I write this, if I am released, as i expect, I still face a 3-yr probation, the reality of which i don't fully understand yet, in fact don't understand at all.

when i am out so many things may happen i am unable to plan w/ any sense of seriousness - BUT - i want to come to Tiller so bad it hurts. i was there with you today but had to come back to preserve my own sanity.

BUT - i will try <u>very</u> hard to come out - as of now that will include - in terms of <u>my</u> needs - 1) coming w/ my daughter Rita, an incredible person, if my ex-wife allows me 2) i will be working on my book a lot, typing, will need some quiet 3) i want very much to share in tasks - probably not full time because of my need for some lack of resp. after here + Rita + my need to do the book - but i also have a deep need to <u>work</u>, to share, and in no way want to be a guest - i don't want to do token work either. i love heavy physical work, i am 6' 2", <u>170 lbs</u> now, down from 200 when i came to jail, 196 9 mos ago when I was transferred here, i am in very good shape, want to work/ love w/ the kids, do dishes, do what must be done, there are many hours in the day and i hope i can make work an up. 4)i will either teach you to do with you or learn from you yoga - or all 3 - which i am into seriously but not as seriously as i would like

*to be 5) i want so badly to sun bathe w/ no clothes on - to tan my ass - i
can't believe it.*

*i don't yet drive a car - if Rita and I flew from San Francisco where is
the nearest Oregon airport - could you meet us there?*

love,

luke

Wow. I read the letter sitting at the table at the Main House,
conversation and joints swirling around as everybody
welcomed Dougy and Jill. Luke at Ash Valley? What a
trip. I liked Luke. I admired him, a brilliant man and,
clearly, dedicated to the revolution. His thoughts about the
relationship between what some of us were doing in the
country and the struggles going on in the cities were right on,
something Mike and I and sometimes others talked about a
lot. They complemented some of the discussions we'd had
at the fair in Eugene, though the Weathermen and that scene
were opposite ends of the counterculture. Luke would bring an
intense energy to the ranch, would challenge us in ways I think
we needed to be challenged. I was so happy he was getting out
of prison and glad we had established something at Ash Valley
where he could come to help transition back to the outside
world, where he could come to tan his ass.

But, still, it jarred my senses a bit to wade through his
detailed analysis and careful consideration of his plans in the
midst of a stoned-out Main House party. We were, I think,
what I had tried to describe to him in my letter—freaks trying
to build a working community to serve, in some way or other,
the Revolution—that had turned him on so much, but we were
also this fun-loving, odd mixture of kids with 130-acres to
play on, who were rarely as sure about the point of our being

there as Luke was about the five conditions of his potential one-month stay. And we all, in our way, did believe that magic lurked along the paths that had brought us here and floated mysteriously among us still in this beguiling valley we were trying to make our home.

Dougy and Jill made the chilly stoned-out walk to our house with us and Moonbeam in the soft half-moon light filtered through a thin layer of wispy night clouds. Sarah and I had come to relish the transitory passage of that walk and, like so much of Ash Valley, sharing that with D & J reinforced just how fucking special it was. They rolled out their sleeping bags on the dirt under our roof on the opposite side of the center pole from us, facing the ash trees bordering the creek. Our very first guests. We all slept well that night.

After a quick trip to the Main House for coffee in the morning, Dougy helped me get started on the floor, laying the 2×4s on end between the center pole and the eight outer poles, so the frame looked like a pre-cut pie. Phillip, Walter, Stu, and Stephen showed up just as we were ready to start laying the planks, which ran across the top of the 2×4s. Each board had to be cut on an angle at both ends, like the roof planks, the boards getting shorter as we got closer to the center. So it worked out great with the six of us, Dougy and I would mark the boards where they needed to be cut and nail them down when they came back. Stephen and Phillip would make the cuts. Walter and Stu passed the marked boards to the cutters and the cut boards back to the nailers and tried to keep us entertained.

"The nail, Tucker, you're supposed to hit the nail," Stu helpfully reminded me after I'd creamed my thumb with the hammer and shouted curses toward the cloudy skies.

"Easy for you to say," Walter chimed in. "The only thing you've been hitting lately have been joints and I have seen you miss a few of them."

"Not nearly as painful," Stu smiled. "Speaking of which …" He looked around expectantly.

"I got a couple," Phillip said, "you ready for them? Or … ?"

"Let's finish these two sections," Dougy said. "You guys get me so stoned I can't do shit. I want to sleep on a floor tonight. How about you, Ben?"

"That sounds good," I said. "And probably safer for my hands."

We kept going, getting in such a good rhythm that we pushed on to do a third section before we each found a spot on the brand-new (salvaged-wood) floor to rest our butts and smoke Phillip's joints. We talked about the Renaissance Faire—Phillip, Walter, and Stu hadn't gone—and the connections we'd made there; Dougy's scene in Eugene, the hassles of being a young Black man in a very White town, especially a young Black man living with a White woman; and Luke's letter. Nobody else sitting on our floor knew him, though Stu and Walter definitely knew who he was from our Boston days.

How do we connect to our brothers and sisters outside our valley and whatever it was The Movement was becoming? That seemed to be the question that had forced itself in front of us.

The personal connection with Dougy and Jane was already defined. A base for us in Eugene would be really useful. That's where the legal stuff was happening, in federal court. It was a city bigger—and friendlier—than Roseburg or Medford, with an airport. And we could offer them a safe refuge in the country where they could recharge from life in the city, exactly the kind of thing Luke talked about.

We were all into connecting with other communes. We could learn from each other and share resources. There were, it seemed, lots of communes in southwestern Oregon, hidden among the conservative small towns and wide-open rural spaces. If we figured out ways to work together, we could make a deep impact in these sparsely populated areas. We just had to make the effort to make it happen. As we were getting close to summer, everybody was busy and it wasn't easy communicating. Nobody had phones. I volunteered to write a letter to folks I'd met at the fair from a commune called Cedar Flats near Sunny Valley, less than two hours away, where there were a bunch of other communes. That could be a good first step.

But Luke and his potential visit freaked people out. Walter and Stu knew his reputation from Boston and were leery. Phillip heard the word *Weathermen* and talk of a revolution destroying the cities and didn't want any part of it.

"Man, I am not into violence at all," he said. "I don't like the shit the Weathermen have done. I'm not sure I want this dude coming to the land and being around my kids."

"He's my friend," I said. "If he comes, which is still pretty doubtful, he's just looking for a place to get his head together, with *his* daughter, just a little younger than Greg, I think. He's not coming to fight. Maybe he'll make us think about how we fit into the Revolution, which some of us think is important. I don't think you should be scared of that."

"Sure, sure, man. I'm into the Revolution, man, " Phillip said. "But it's got to be peaceful, you know, a head thing not a fighting thing."

"It's got to be more than a head thing," Dougy said, looking straight on at Phillip. "Shit man, look what's going on with Huey Newton and the Panthers. It ain't no head thing, man. I don't know exactly what this guy Luke is into, but if he's Ben's friend then I'd listen to what he had to say."

"Maybe we could mellow him out some," I said. "He's a really smart guy.

SPRING/25

It took us just two more days to finish the floor and the sleeping loft—and get all our stuff down there and really move into our house. Having Dougy there to help kept me focused and others picked up on that energy and joined in. It was fun and tremendously fulfilling—especially when we hoisted our double mattress up on the loft. A real bed in our summer palace. No walls, but a rain-shedding roof, our wood cook/heating stove on the northwest slice of the pie, a table in the southwest, a dresser under the loft, and a couple of old wooden straight-back chairs. Home. Home sweet fucking Home. We'd even dug a healthy-sized hole for an outhouse about 20 feet away and built a crude seat out of some of the wood scraps.

Most everybody who was on the ranch that day showed up as Sarah fine-tuned the arrangement of things. As many as we could fit—six or seven—climbed onto the loft and sprawled out on the mattress. I was happy and a little relieved that the loft held that load without a hint of strain. Walter claimed a central spot and rolled joint after joint to finish off an ounce of some fine Colombian we'd been smoking on for the past week or so. Could be our last—didn't really know or care at that moment. Those who hadn't made it up on the loft lingered nearby, joint-passing close. Our first party in our house. Almost everyone had contributed in some way to making this basic octagon shelter come to life where a little meadow met our spunky creek, and all seemed to share in the joy that enveloped Sarah and me. Communal action, communal reward. It was tangible in our poles and planks and bruised thumbs and laughter and soul-penetrating satisfaction.

When all the joints had been smoked, everybody slowly wandered off, leaving Sarah and me to marvel at our new place. We hadn't ever really had our own place before. Every place we had slept before had been a room in somebody else's place: Mitch's in San Francisco, Jeffrey's and Justine's in Cambridge, Leslie's in Boston, the White and Red houses in Tiller, the Main House. Always temporary. The longest stay was at the Western Ave place in Cambridge, three months. But this was ours for … for as long as we could imagine into the future. Nothing was hanging over us that was going to dictate what was going to happen next. Our place, our time. Freedom like we had never known.

After everyone left, we were both pretty stoned as we lolled on our bed, Moonbeam curled up at our feet. Stoned and stunned by our good fortune, we kissed soft and sweet. Sarah pulled away, and started running through the list in her mind of what still needed to be put away and talking out loud about where things might go. I couldn't really focus on the details of her plans. I didn't really care. I could only laugh and take pleasure in how into it she was. I flashed back to the stoned stroll we had taken in Allston when she had come up to Mountfort Street during Christmas vacation, on the day of the night we would make love for the first time, the New Year's Eve that took us from 1969 to 1970. We ambled down Harvard Ave, digging just being together out in the world, and she would linger long in front of antique store windows, carefully sizing things up and selecting furniture and accessories that would fill our imaginary apartment someday. I had no opinions to offer but I loved her thinking of a life, a real life, with me.

She could pick all the fixings. That was such an outlandish fantasy in the chilled dusk that winter evening.

In the real word of our real house, I listened and nodded and offered an occasional word of encouragement. At some point, she realized that she was almost speed rapping and I couldn't really keep up with her. She stopped, took a deep breath, and snuggled in close to me. We kissed again and had a moment of smiling into each other's eyes, and held each other tight. Things felt easy in a way they hadn't been in a long time. Everything seemed a little less urgent, a little more relaxed. After a bit, I heard the rumble of her sleep breathing— the woman was a world-class sleeper—slowly rising in an enchanted syncopation with the rhythm of the creek. I didn't sleep but I was serenaded away into a dreamlike bliss.

We had just begun to stir when Dougy and Jill returned after hanging out in the Main House to give us a little time alone. They both looked bummed, a sharp contrast to our buoyant mood.

"What's the matter?" Sarah asked.

"You two are so lucky to be down here," Jill said, shaking her head. "That place is just a downer."

"Really?" I said, "Everybody seemed so happy and together when they left here."

"Well, things changed fast," Jill said, looking to Dougy.

"First of all," he said. "Paulie and Annie were talking shit about Sarah, saying she took some stuff to bring here that wasn't yours?"

"What?" Sarah said

"I don't know exactly, something about there were a bunch of boxes together and you took all of them when only one was yours," Dougy said.

"That's bullshit," Sarah said. "I only took one box—that was ours. I know for sure. What bullshit. Why didn't they say something when they were down here, acting all happy for us."

"I don't know but they were acting kinda self-righteous about it and talking to other people about it. 'We gotta confront her' kind of shit." Dougy said.

"I couldn't believe it," Jill said.

"Fuck," I said.

"Fine, let them confront me," Sarah said. "I didn't do anything wrong. Somebody must have moved the other boxes someplace. That's just what we need around here, made-up problems."

"And that's not even all of it," Dougy said. "We moved outside to get away from that shit and Dale sorta corners us and starts laying this crazy rap on us. Telling us that the Revolution is happening here and it's all about 'country consciousness' and people in the cities just didn't get it and unless we got tuned into that we couldn't be part of the Revolution. Fuck, man, he had kind of a maniacal look in his eyes and this shit just flowed out of him like he was preaching. We split as soon as we could get away from him. What's going on with him, man? He used to seem so together."

I looked back and forth between Dougy and Jill. "Man, I'm sorry. Dale is in a strange place. His political or spiritual or cosmic view or whatever you want to call it has always been sort of out there—definitely acid tinged. But now with all the shit going on with Sydney and Jack and just the general insanity of this place … He's seems like another level of out there. But

I hope you know that's his trip not my trip or anything that represents this place."

"Yeah, man, I know … but shit, you guys got a lot to work out," Dougy said.

We hung out at our place that night, didn't even go to the Main House. A nice mellow evening for a change.

I couldn't go to sleep for a long time. Our first night in our loft, I lay in bed, listening to the creek and the human sleep sounds around me and the occasionally whispering of the breeze in the trees looming over us. I thought about Luke's letter and Dale's rap and the petty bullshit that keeps getting in our way. Is this just an escapist trip or the beginning of a revolutionary way of life that could work for us and will teach us how to tear down the empire? In some ways, Ash Valley *was* kind of a bourgeois escapist dream, living in a lush valley with all your friends with enough resources, for now at least, to get by without working for the man. It would be easy to let our possession of this land imprison our consciousness. Good people have been imprisoned by—sold out for—far less attractive situations. I had to believe that we would never allow that imprisonment to set in, that we could struggle through the bullshit and work our way to some common and clear understandings of how we connected to the world beyond our gate. We had to because I also believed that as soon as we forget or deny that we're part of a worldwide revolutionary movement we're going to lose this land, our mellow heads, and our souls. But no matter what, Dougy's right, there is so much still to be done.

SPRING/26

We woke up to Jill singing reveille, which was cool. When we arrived at the Main House, Paulie and Annie greeted Sarah like nothing had happened. She called them on it.

"I heard you two were accusing me of taking things that weren't mine," she said directly. "That's bullshit and it's even worse to be saying stuff like that behind my back."

Paulie and Annie looked at each other and then passed us to Dougy and Jill, who they knew had to be the sources of our information.

"Oh, that was no big deal," Paulie said. "We just didn't know where the other boxes had gone. They turned up later, so it's all cool now." She smiled. Annie smiled, too, but with less confidence than Paulie, a guilty kind of smile.

"Well, it's not really cool for you to assume that I tried to steal somebody else's stuff."

Now Paulie looked more harshly at Dougy and Jill. "Nobody ever said anything about you stealing anything. We thought you maybe took them by mistake."

"Well maybe talk to me before jumping to any conclusions. OK?"

Paulie and Annie kind of nodded. It didn't exactly feel like anything was resolved but just then a little, bright, deep maroon sporty car pulled up in front of the Main House, a type of car we hadn't seen on the ranch before, so that got everyone's attention … and then Little Eddie emerged. We all got excited and rushed out to meet him because we'd been expecting him back for a few days—and because we knew he'd have dope. What wasn't coming out of that car was Sydney and Jack—who had gone to LA with Little Eddie.

Eddie saw the burning question in Dale's eyes and said, "They decided to hang out in San Francisco for a while," which caused Dale to freak out. He let out a beast-like scream and stormed off toward the cabin where he'd been crashing. Jeffrey tried to go after him, but Dale, seeing him coming up behind, turned around sharply and said, "Leave me the FUCK alone." The rest of us recoiled from that burst and Sarah voiced the other question we all were thinking. "Where did this car come from?" It was a fairly late model Karmann Ghia.

Eddie smiled as he looked toward the car. "Got a good deal on it in LA. We needed something to get back here after we sold the bus. Cool, huh?"

We headed into the house and Eddie passed out mail he had picked up from our post office box before he started rolling joints. There was a letter from my mother, which was great. We had a good correspondence going. My father, too. My letters tended to be to the family as a whole but I got individual responses from each of my parents and sometimes my sisters, too. They were genuinely supportive and curious about what we were trying to do. Sarah tended to communicate with her folks by phone calls from the booth next to the Tiller Store. She'd call them—collect—every two or three weeks. I hardly ever called home. Letters worked better for me.

As I was reading my mother's letter—she was curious about our plans for school for the children among us—a big groan came up from Stu. He'd gotten his draft notice. The fucking "Greetings" letter telling him to report for induction in Portland on July 17. Shit. As far as I knew, he was the only one of the men on the ranch in jeopardy of being drafted.

He had somehow passed his physical while high on LSD, shortly before we arrived in Tiller. My two felony convictions had disqualified me. Stephen had already been in the army. Everybody else either had high numbers or some scam already in place. Dougy told Stu about a shrink in Eugene who had got him out of the draft and could help Stu, too. But what a fucking hassle.

Little Eddie looked kind of shell-shocked. He'd been off the ranch almost two weeks, been on the road for the last few days with only a brief stop in San Francisco and had already encountered two significant freak-outs in his first ten minutes back on the ranch. He lit one of the joints. He passed that one and lit another. Before long, so many joints were in circulation that two or even three would collide at one person, who would somehow try to smoke and hold and pass all at the same time. Finally, somebody laughed and then everybody WAS laughing uncontrollably. Little Eddie beamed: "Mission accomplished."

The pace slackened and a dull hush settled into the room, when Mike yelled, "What the fuck?" as he looked out toward the road from the kitchen window. We all scurried to get a view of what had alarmed him and saw the lights of a cop car flashing, leading another dark sedan down our road. After a stunned second or two of disbelief, there was a mad scramble to stash the dope and try to clear the cloud of smoke from the house. I was immobilized at first, wondering how I could get away from there without the cops seeing me. I was on probation, a bust now would likely send me back to Massachusetts to serve out that three-year sentence pronounced in that bleak courtroom last winter. Mike shouted at me, "Get the fuck out of here," his eyes steering me toward the back of the house, where Sarah and I could slip out the door and try to find some place to hide.

When we opened the door and peeked out to see the best route to take, we saw the two cars, still on the road, one still flashing its hostile fucking lights, moving quickly toward the Second House. We exhaled, took deep breaths together and decided to head quickly and directly across the valley toward Ash Creek and follow that to our house.

We made it without incident. We had crossed to the far side of the creek when we got close to the Second House, the brush shielding us from direct view. The two invading cars were still at that house when we passed it. I felt almost teary when we finally made it to our open-air home. We quickly climbed into the loft and huddled under the covers to make us near invisible to the road … and waited.

Finally, it was Stu and Mike and Dougy and Jill who showed up to convey the "all-clear" to us. The cop car was escorting Jane's probation officer, who had come to give her shit about not reporting fully about her new living situation. I guess the cops had heard something about a bunch of hippie radicals living on this commune and wanted to make sure the probation officer would be safe here. Jane, whose conviction was for some kind of welfare fraud, had handled it well apparently, convincing her probation office that although the group owned the land together, her family was doing their own distinct trip, which was actually true in some ways, more ways than she and Phillip would probably acknowledge.

That was good for me, too. My probation had been transferred to Oregon and I had met with my probation officer once in Roseburg, where the offices were. That meeting went fine and he said he would come see me sometime, but it hadn't happened yet. Technically, it was against the rules for two nonrelated people on probation to live together, but so far, our respective probation officers had not put that together and apparently nothing that happened that day had clued them in.

That night we decided we had to start locking the front gate. The Forest Service had keys to it since it was their road and cops could probably get in anytime they wanted but it might slow others down. It would be a hassle trying to keep track of a key but we had to at least try to slow down uninvited guests.

SPRING/27

Dougy, Jill, Sarah, and I spent the first part of the day finishing up a few details at our house, building a ladder up to the loft and a bookcase that fit neatly underneath it, all out of salvaged planks, like we used on the roof and the floor. I also fit some tar paper into the gaps where the roof met the center pole, which jutted up above it, to try to eliminate the last few drippy leaks that snuck through in heavy rain.

We still made it to the Main House by midmorning. Stu, Jeffrey, and Mike were already out in the garden, so we went out there to help them dig ditches for flood irrigation. A few hot days in a row had helped the garden to flourish. Leafy green plants lined up neatly in row after row, adding a third dimension to the dark mounded dirt. Lettuce and radishes were almost ready to eat. Stu took special pleasure in the potato plants that filled two rows proudly with thick clusters of varyingly shaped and sized rich green leaves. Potatoes were a key element of our diet.

While we took turns digging, we got caught up on the latest ranch gossip. Dale had split first thing in the morning, catching a ride with a town trip to Canyonville, and then planning to hitchhike to San Francisco to try to find Sydney and Jack. What good could come of that? Jeffrey, who'd been tight with Dale since the dorm days at BU, was really concerned about him. We all were, but it was hitting Jeffrey especially hard.

"It freaks me out," he said. "I've never seen him like this," Jeffrey said. "Never." Of course, as long as most of us could remember, Dale and Sydney were a pair, a team. I'd never really known Dale without Sydney. "I don't know how to help him," Jeffrey said. "It sucks." We all shook our heads in agreement.

And while that movie had moved off the ranch for a while, a new one with a similar theme was just premiering, Jeffrey reported. Sheila was apparently hanging out with Stephen, leaving Jon to play the role of Dale in this new drama.

"Fuck," I said, "How long have they been here? Two weeks?" Time passes slowly in the mountains.

"Fucking Stephen," Mike said. "What's with that dude?"

That hung in the air for a while. Dougy and Jill told everyone they were heading back to Eugene the next morning. Stu asked if he could cop a ride to try to see the shrink who might be able to help him with the draft.

"And I think Wayne might want to go along, too," Stu said. "He's got some business stuff to deal with."

Wayne and Phillip had just returned the day before after attending a court hearing about our lawsuit to stop the logging, which turned out to be just both sides filing motions. Our temporary injunction was still in effect but no decision was made concerning our request for a permanent injunction. Wayne had also started looking into his "business stuff."

During the past couple of weeks, we had started talking about how we could come up with the $20,000 for our balloon payment for the land due next May. Thanks to Willie Campbell we had a good hay crop growing in the field closest to the front gate. We could harvest that in about a month and sell most of it. That would bring in some money. Willie also told us he could help us get a start on raising pigs, another potential moneymaker. But $20,000 is a lot of bales of hay and pigs. Wayne had started talking about some connections he had in the marijuana trade. He was confident he could raise the twenty grand quickly selling pot, but he needed some money to get started. We still had a little over $4,000 in our communal fund, mostly from money Stu had saved from social security payments he starting getting when he was very young after his father died, but also money from Mike and Paulie's and Sarah and my weddings. Wayne had proposed taking some of that—$2,500 was the number he finally decided on—to buy pot to launch this "business."

I mostly stayed away from those discussions. Like with the legal stuff, I just as soon leave that to other folks. I wasn't against it in principle, but I felt like I was holding up my communal responsibilities in other ways, and dealing was just never my thing. Stu and I had somehow managed to lose money on some shitty wild Illinois pot we had brought to Boston from Urbana after a Christmas vacation, pot we had gotten for free. Hard to lose money when you start off with a free product. But we did.

And I was on probation. We were breaking laws with regularity on the ranch but something about making pot sales our major source of income took things to another level. Wayne and Phillip were the main advocates and Stu was into it. Jeffrey, who'd been successful dealing in Boston, gave some advice but wasn't into playing an active role. That was part of what he'd been glad to leave behind on the East Coast.

Wayne swore that none of this activity would happen anywhere near the ranch. He was convinced that he could get the money to secure the ranch and even get us a surplus to invest in our future. I liked the sound of that. And he had been righteous in helping us build our house. Even though we'd only known him a couple of months, he felt like a brother. Mike always had some reservations about Wayne, something about his hyper-mellow LA attitude and big talk that came off as bragging a lot of the time. But they had seemed to get along since we'd been on the ranch. Mike had the same attitude as Sarah and me and others. It was not his thing, but he didn't oppose it. And, shit if we could get the money that way, that would ease a lot of pressures.

We finished up in the garden and, during a lunch of peanut butter sandwiches on some bread Mike had baked, Dougy and Jill asked Sarah and me if we'd like to drop some mescaline they'd been saving for the right time. I said a quick "yes," and Sarah said an equally quick "no." Sarah had never taken any psychedelics. Nothing about it appealed to her—loss of control, new perspective, hallucinations. All the things that I dug. I'd tripped plenty of times when I was with her and she was almost always a good sport. Sometimes, when we were in a crowded scene, like a concert, she would be my guide, leading me to the front of the crowd and just kinda looking out for me. But she never was tempted to join me on the other side.

After the three of us dropped, we decided to take a hike up the east hillside behind Stu's cabin. I'd never been in the forest on that side. It took us a while to find any break through the creek-side brush, and what we finally found was a narrow and steep deer path. We headed up, Dougy in the lead, and then Jill, then me, as the surging energy engulfing us drove us with a silent and sharp focus. The skinny path we tried to follow was barely visible, as clusters of lush green ferns arched over it and smoothly yielded to our strides, with a whispering whhooooooooshhhhh that sounded loud in the dominant hush that surrounded us.

I didn't see a tree root that straddled the path, and I stumbled, almost crashing into Jill in front of me and then I was lying on the ground nearly swallowed up by the ferns. Dougy and Jill turned back to look, startled and questioning, and I answered, laughing—silly, relieved laughter. Once they realized I was OK, they joined in and we made a racket of laughter that seemed to ricochet around us. Taking a breath, I looked up and, ohmygod, the trees, they went forever. Too many to count, too high to comprehend. Walking upright, beside them, viewing from a horizontal perspective, I was astonished. But sprawled on my ass, with a chipmunk's perspective, strictly vertical, they were inscrutable gods, too awesome to do anything less than worship. They rolled to a steady rhythmic breeze, shifting from dense green to ocean blue to day-glo purple and became one solid mass of movement, a gentle sea flowing over me.

Hallelujah and Amen. I looked to Dougy and Jill who had followed my gaze upward and were as transfixed as I had been. Slowly, all our eyes met again and the hysterics and the veneration had given way to easy fulfilled smiles.

"You ready to push on?" Doug asked me.

"Yeah," I said. "Wow!"

"Wow, yes!" said Jill as she straightened up and extended her hand to help me to my feet again.

The trail continued its steep climb. The ferns became less dense and the path more defined as slightly compressed red-brown duff worn into greenish ground cover, weaving through the giants. The thick millennia-old culture that surrounded me transformed from scenes of exaggerated clarity—bold bright colors, each and every diverse element in exactly the right place—to darkened chaos, chilling with a visceral sense of danger. But we kept walking up.

We didn't talk, the crunch of our footfall our only conversation. I felt my eyes swiveling to take in as much as I could in front, around, above—and down, to try to avoid another pratfall. Occasionally, I'd stop and look back to where we had come from, an entirely different perspective, the rise growing behind us. Every once in a while, through the density of the forest, I caught just a glimpse of our open valley below, smaller and smaller as we climbed.

We saw sunlight shining up ahead and came upon a clearing below a rock face jutting proudly out of the mountainside. Dougy led us around it and up one side until, near the top, we saw a flat shelf that we could get to with just a short scramble over some craggy boulders. He looked back and Jill and I nodded, and we all climbed up and found spots to sit and exhale.

I don't know how high we were above the valley floor. 500 feet? 700 feet? 1,000 feet? My legs were tingly warm and ached a bit as I stretched them out. Deer apparently don't need switchbacks. We were high enough to see above the trees to view much of Ash Valley, the west side from the front gate to the reservoir, a light green, long, narrow squiggle on the huge dark green palette of the encompassing forests. I could make out the buildings and the ponds, see the vague movement of a vehicle—the tractor, I think—moving down the road and hear the distant, delayed straining of its engine. The humans—or what I thought were people—were insignificant specks. When the vehicle got to the goat barn and turned its engine off, the valley was silent, perfectly peaceful. The warm wind of this blue sky day at the end of spring swept across our faces with a soothing swish.

Jill spoke first. "My God, this is so beautiful." She looked at me, beaming. "You live here, Ben. Can you believe that?"

"No," I said. Staring down at the valley, I couldn't believe I lived there—and didn't even know how small I was, how small we all were, from here. Looking up from the valley, I sometimes mistook this hill, this miraculous mountainside, for a flat movie background to our silly dramas and schemes. Some days I hardly even looked up.

"You know," I said, as a cold chill shook through me. "This is what they want to cut." I did a slow 180 degree scan of the centuries of life that thrived between Ash Creek and where we sat. "These trees."

"Fuck no, they can't do that," Dougy said, his sudden anger a sharp jolt to my dreamy sadness.

"Well, that's what they want to do," I said. "We're trying to stop them, but …"

"But nothing, man, you gotta stop them. By any means necessary. Right?"

"Sure. Right," I said. But I was still more sad than angry. How could they even want to rip this all apart? For money?

"I'm sure they'll do everything they can," Jill said to Dougy.

"Yeah, yeah, I know," Dougy said. "But, man …"

We got quiet again for a long time, listening to the wind and an occasional groan from the treetops, a high-pitched bird call, the crackle of snapping twigs as some local inhabitant went about its day with no regard for us.

"Shit, Ben," Dougy finally said. "This is so good. I mean this whole place. The ranch. And yet … there is so much fucked-up shit going on. I don't know how this all is going to work." He looked at me with soft eyes, his anger all gone now, too.

It was true, what he said. I didn't have an answer. "I know," I said. I was, in that moment, so humbled by all that I saw: the broad panorama of hills rolling like waves all around me as far as I could see in every direction, the mighty firs that surrounded where we sat like spires of the holiest church in the universe, the secrets and powers of this mountainside, and the patch of flat green so far below us that I dared to hold some claim to. How could I know how to become worthy of this place?

The sun had moved all the way across the valley and was sneaking below the hills opposite us. We all knew that it was time to head back down the same path we came up. The mescaline was wearing off and tiredness creeped over us. My legs really burned going down. But somehow as we were tromping beneath the giant firs, my sadness slowly lifted, giving way to an overpowering openness. I was in the midst of indescribably powerful beauty, here, free from so much that I had long been trying to escape. Let it come as it will. Let me live in it. So many things were possible that could never be possible in another time or place. Let's see what happens.

We came to Stu's cabin and peeked in but he wasn't around, so we decided to go to our house to mellow out before encountering the Main House.

As we approached across our meadow, we heard laughter and saw Moonbeam and Sundance sprawled out in front of our house and Stephen and Sarah hanging out "inside," sitting on our two straight-backed chairs. They were passing a joint. Dougy shot me a funny look. They greeted us with stoned spacey smiles. Jill, leading us now, took the joint from Sarah and took a deep toke and passed it to Dougy. I came up last and took the joint after Dougy had taken a hit. It was a little awkward.

Jill, exhaling, said, "You guys wouldn't believe how beautiful it was where we went today up in the hills above Stu's."

"Cool," Sarah said. Stephen smiled and sort of brightened his eyes toward Jill.

Sarah looked at me. "Jane decided she doesn't have enough energy to ride Mona as often as she should, so she asked me if I wanted to help take care of her and ride her sometimes," she said, with an excited smile. "Stephen's going to help me learn the things I need to do," she looked at him, still excited. "We took a ride this afternoon. I loved it." Mona was a sweet eight-year-old pinto mare, one of the three horses on the ranch.

Feeling a slight buzz from the joint on top of the emptiness of coming down from the mescaline, I wasn't quite sure how to formulate a response. I looked back at stoned happy Sarah and then at Stephen, whose smile had been toned down a bit.

"Cool," I said.

SPRING/28

Dougy and Jill split right after a quick breakfast, taking Stu and Wayne with them. Stu left me a long list of stuff to do in the garden while he was gone—a watering schedule, crops that needed to be thinned or cultivated, where weeding most needed to be done. That was cool. Gave me near-official status as his top assistant in the garden, a clear role—and that made me feel good. Sarah and I went to work on it right away, thinning carrots. It was a beautiful morning, cool, blue skies. Jeffrey and Eddie joined us, Jeffrey to help with the work, Eddie to chat and pass a joint. Jon also pitched in. Annie came out for a while but the strange vibes between her and Sarah seemed to be lingering, so she split pretty quickly. But we got a lot done as the day drifted to warm and then hot, which was our cue to break for lunch.

After a productive morning and lunch, we decided to move the water bed, which needed refilling anyway, from the grass near the swimming pond to the dock next to the pond, which seemed like a better place for it. You could just roll off the bed into the pond.

Eight of us were hanging out at the ponds as we stretched the hose we used to water the garden to the dock to fill the bed up. It was a slow flow, so we took turns monitoring it, while we jumped in the water and smoked the joints that Eddie kept producing. It was getting nearly full when we heard the first groan from the dock. Everybody, standing on the bank or swimming, froze in place and turned to stare at the bed and the dock. The groan shifted keys and became a series of crackling snaps of wood breaking. Nobody had moved.

"Turn off the fucking hose," Stephen yelled, and I ran toward the spigot back by the road near Shantytown. Others, now in fast motion, tried to pull the hose from the fill valve on the bed—but the whole thing was slipping away. Then—a decisive "Pop"! and the dock broke free from its posts on the bank and collapsed into the water, the bed plopping awkwardly on top of it, half submerged.

We all froze again, watching the bed settle in the pond like a leaky water balloon into a bucket—then Eddie started laughing maniacally and everybody joined him, Walter and Jeffrey falling down on the bank and rolling into the water. I was walking slowly back toward the ponds laughing along with everybody when I heard a rig coming up the road. It was the red truck, which had been running pretty well for a few days, with Mike and Paulie back from their town trip. I stopped to greet them.

After they got out and saw the commotion by the ponds, Mike asked, "What the fuck's going on over there?"

I was still half laughing. "We tried to set up the water bed on the dock and it seems like it couldn't quite handle the weight. It kinda all crashed into the pond."

"The water bed on the dock? Whose brilliant idea was that?" Mike asked, with an exasperated smile.

"I don't remember. It seemed like a good idea."

"Fucking idiots," he said, laughing and shaking his head. Looking to Paulie, he said, "Can you believe these fools." Paulie laughed.

The three of us walked up to the ponds. Some people were forcing water out of the bed to get it light enough to pull out. The rest hung around the edges, offering sometimes helpful suggestions and also providing a running commentary—and lots of giggling. It was a challenging operation since the bed was mostly below the surface, some of it tangled with the broken pieces of the dock, though it still seemed to be in one piece.

"Can't leave you people alone for any time at all," Mike said, chuckling as he surveyed the scene. "Hey"—he remembered something—"we got the newspaper with the stories about us—two stories. Too bad they weren't here to take a picture of this. The real story."

SPRING/29

We were the featured attraction in the *Roseburg News-Review* on June 19, 1971: Page 1: "Family Clan Seeking to Halt Timber Sales;" Page 24: "Family Clan Creates Rural Area Community." (I still hated that name).

The first story reported on the hearing in Eugene, where not much happened beyond both sides submitting motions for the judge to end the case in their favor—and the judge putting off the ruling on either one. An old story. But the story also told the details and background of the case, describing the arguments we were making and how we got the temporary injunction. Our primary lawyer was a former congressman from the Eugene area and known to take on controversial cases, and we also had a younger lawyer who had worked with the Sierra Club.

Willie Campbell was a co-plaintive with us and having that in the newspaper was sure to get him a lot of shit down at his saw shop in Canyonville. I admired him associating his name with such a controversial action by a bunch of hippies. But he loved Ash Valley (the article mentioned that the place had long been known as the Erlebach Ranch) maybe even more than we did and he knew that clear cuts on that east ridge would be deeply disfiguring scars that would forever change the essence of the place. Our primary contention, as the newspaper reported, was that "strip clear-cutting would lower the property value of the 135-acre valley." And that was true, but the "value" we were trying to defend had almost nothing to do with money, though that would be the measure we'd have to present in court—sorta like my criminal case, where truth was not as much of a factor. The value we'd lose with the loss of our ancient and wise neighbors was an irreplaceable connection to a human humbleness that moves people to try to fit in the world rather than to dominate it, to a way of thinking and being where value and money were not synonymous. That point of view had no standing in a court of law.

The newspaper story reported our other contentions, which were that the logging would damage the valley drainage, including Ash Creek; that the logging in itself could do damage to the valley through mudslides and other natural consequences; and that it would mean loss of privacy and scenic value. All true. Two forestry experts—one from South Umpqua Community College and one from Oregon State University—had submitted statements that reforestation (growing new trees) would be difficult because of the steepness of the slope (as my legs testified on the hike with Dougy and Jill) and because it was facing west.

The story reported some facts I didn't know: the 54 acres (in five parcels) they wanted to clear-cut on the hill above the ranch were only part of the sale, which totaled 786 acres, most of which would not be clear-cut. The total "harvest" was to be 7.2 million board feet of Douglas fir, 750,000 board feet of sugar pine and similar species, and 950,000 board feet of incense cedar and related species. It was a fucking machine we were fighting. But this story made us sound like legitimate adversaries.

> 'Tis the gift to be simple, 'tis the gift to be free,
> 'Tis the gift to come down where we ought to be,
> And when we find ourselves in the place just right,
> 'Twill be in the valley of love and delight.

The feature story about us started off with the Shaker hymn and lyrics from Dylan's "Time Passes Slowly." The writer cast our aspirations in a good light. "A slow-paced realized dream, freedom, and simplicity," he wrote. "Three difficult things to find. But all three are real possibilities if you have a $30,000 down payment, can wander in a 135-acre valley, and live without conventional conveniences. 'When I was living in Boston, I had almost forgotten there were stars in the sky,' says a long-haired young man from Boston in his middle 20s." That could have been several of us who were from Boston with long hair, though none of us were yet in our mid-20s. Any of us might have said that. And our initial payment had been $5,000 toward a $25,000 total down payment. The story overstated the number of people living on the ranch, but that was often hard for us to keep track of. Reality could be an elusive thing inside the gates of Ash Valley, and the writer did make us sound as nonthreatening as he could (except for that lawsuit threatening local livelihoods).

He didn't name any of us. But we could identify some people by his descriptions. Stephen was "a younger man wearing wire rim glasses": "We're basically people who want to live in the country," he said. Wayne was "formerly an electrical contractor in Los Angeles" who said he'd been working on this dream for six years (when most of us were still in high school) and said of his "2-year-old suntanned daughter"(Tammy): "She's free." Sarah was a "dark-haired girl" who said, "Our greatest shock was to purchase this valley and then discover they were going to cut off 50 percent of the trees." Jon was "an intense-eyed man wearing the bib overalls favored by farmers," who said, "In terms of ecology, taking down the trees will mess up the whole thing."

The writer filled in more history about the ranch. The Erlebach Ranch had been homesteaded in 1916. Willie Campbell had bought it from that family in 1956 and cleared the brush and restored some of the early log buildings, including what we called the Main House. "Paneled with old boards, the six-bedroom house appears to be new, but it is actually a log cabin with 18-inch walls."

He tells the world, as we had hoped, that we prefer to call ourselves a *community* and not a *commune* and are not "stereotype 'hippies'" but more like early San Francisco cultural dropouts: "They want to be self-sufficient, away from the crowds, free of mainstream culture." True.

The photos with the story are of Stu alone on the tractor in the garden with the lower parts of the clear-cut-designated eastern hillside in the background; little Tammy walking alone down the road; and Wayne (with his long-nailed pinky extended for some reason), Jon in his farmer overalls, and Stephen smoking a cigarette, all on the bench by the dining room table in the Main House.

All in all, it was as sympathetic a story as we could expect from a Roseburg newspaper. I sort of knew the writer dug us when he came down to our house and hung out for a while. He closed the story with more from Dylan and the Shaker hymn. The last quote from us was from "the Boston boy:" "We're waiting for it to mellow out." And that was the absolute truth. "'Twill be in the valley of love and delight."

GUY MAYNARD

Summer

SUMMER/1

Walter had scored some peyote buttons for a summer solstice celebration. Most of us had read Carlos Castaneda and admired the sort of deep meaning he found on his peyote adventures. I really dug the whole concept he laid out about finding your *spot*—the one place where we could be our true, very best selves. All of us were looking for that, I think. I hoped we'd found at least the broad parameters of our spot in Ash Valley. But Castaneda meant something more individually specific than that and I knew I still hadn't found mine.

Walter was as close as we got to a spiritual guide, throwing the Ching when we faced challenges and doing everybody's astrology charts. His was definitely a freaky spirituality, wisdom coming from the Grateful Dead and the Beatles as well as more traditional teachers. Summer solstice had a long tradition as a day of celebrating the transition from spring to summer, the day with the greatest amount of light. And we all felt in our bones that we were on the edge of a fundamental transition as a community. The garden was all in and producing. We'd begun to work our way out of the housing crunch. We'd started thinking about raising our balloon payment. We'd drawn the lines in the battle for the trees. And, though interpersonal conflicts still plagued us, at least we'd begun to understand the issues and the need to resolve them. We were past the rush and chaos and the excuses of being at the beginning.

So it was perfect to take a psychedelic step back with Walter as our gentle guide, to absolve and cleanse, to prepare for the real work that lay ahead.

When we got to the Main House that morning, a big pot was boiling over a fire in the pit in the front yard. Walter had dumped in a bag full of dried peyote buttons that were now riding the bubbling surface like floats in a turbulent sea.

"How many doses is that?" I asked.

"I dunno. Enough," Walter said, focused and grinning. Most of the men gathering around the pot planned to drink the tea. Most of the women did not. Paulie was considering it. Most of us had taken synthetic mescaline, which is the psychoactive part of peyote, but no one had tried the natural version. But it seemed more organic, more tied to the Native Americans who must have spent time in our valley, whose connection to the earth and natural systems inspired us and we hoped to emulate. It also can make you sick.

"I'm warning you, this might make us puke," Walter reminded us as he started ladling the hot steeped liquid into mugs. Little Eddie backed away. "I'll see what happens to you guys before I take any," he said, laughing.

Mike stepped up and took a cup, then Phillip, Jon, Stephen, and me. Everyone else hung back so Walter took a cup for himself and started sipping. There was still more than a few cups worth left in the pot.

The taste was bitter but not as intense as I expected. The five of us found comfortable places to sit and wait, while the others scrutinized us curiously. Sarah, Annie, and Sheila lost interest in that pretty quickly and went into the house to make some breakfast. Paulie left soon after. Eddie and Jeffrey hung out, giggly at our awkward anticipation.

After about fifteen minutes, Walter asked if anybody felt anything.

"My stomach's a little weird," Jon said, "but I don't feel sick … or any high."

"Want me to roll a joint to get you started?" Eddie asked.

"No, I don't think that would be a good idea," Walter said dismissively. "It would fuck up the peyote high."

After half an hour, as the sun came over the ridge and we started feeling the heat, Mike said, "Hey man, maybe we just didn't take enough. Let's split the rest of it."

"Sure," Walter said, and he ladled out almost another whole cup to each of us.

By this point, everybody else had finished breakfast and started going about their days, laughing as they passed us sort of patiently trying to will ourselves into a psychedelic space.

Eventually, we heard the rumble and saw the dust of Willie Campbell's pickup coming up the road. He got out of his truck and beheld us all sitting there, decidedly not high. He chuckled, "I'm not even going to ask," he said, surveying us, all no doubt showing our awkward frustrated anticipation. "But, I could use some help moving some of my cattle from one pasture to the next. Any of you got some time?" He chuckled again.

Stephen looked at me and then Mike, and said, "Sure, what the hell." I nodded. Mike nodded. Jon nodded. Turns out, we found out later, that you need to eat about a dozen peyote buttons for a good high—and that's what makes you sick.

Helping Willie with his cattle was a lot of fun. Ten of us joined in. That was everybody who was on the ranch at the moment except Annie and the Hammonds and the four kids; Annie and Jane were taking turns looking after Tammy while Wayne was away. The hayfield closest to the front gate was almost ready to harvest. The grass in the field north of that, where the cattle had been since we moved on, was coming on strong. To allow that hay to mature, Willie wanted to move the cattle to the next pasture, closer to the Main House, just on the other side of our garden.

We spread out all around the perimeter, circling the cattle, while Willie opened the loose barbwire gate between the two fields. On his signal, we started closing the circle. As we approached them, the cattle lazily looked up from the chunks of grass they were chewing on and stared dumbly at us. Willie let out a high-pitched "WHOOP!" which sounded funny coming from him, and started a loud clapping of his hand. We all joined in. "WHOOP! WHOOP! WHOOP! WHOOP! WHOOP!"—A cacophonous chorus filling the valley accompanied by an almost rhythmic clapping and a lot of laughing. The cattle looked perturbed now. We were closing in on them but none had budged. Willie started waving his hands and shouting "Shooo, shoo, shoo." And we all did the same. Laughing more. The cattle started slowly moving away from us toward the open gate. "Shoo, shoo, shoo …" Eleven voices, high, low, shrill, melodic, "Shoo, shoo, shoo." And more laughter.

"Ataway," Willie yelled as the fifty or so head of cattle clustered toward the middle of us, ambling in the general direction we wanted them to go, as our circle tightened further. "Not too close," Willie yelled, "Keep 'em in front of you." Just then a calf bolted from the crowd and, suddenly moving quickly, breached our perimeter, running through the gap between Sarah and me. Mama cow, we have to assume, stopped ambling and stared at her fleeing offspring and, almost resignedly, started trotting after him. Almost by instinct, Sarah and I closed the space between us, to block her. "'S'alright," Willie yelled, "Let her go. We'll deal with the stragglers later."

It took us what seemed like an hour to get most of the herd into the other field, with seven stragglers (four cows, three calves) in the old field behind us. Then the fun really began. We had to zero in on specific cows—or a pair when a calf and a mom stuck together. So we had to cover a whole lot more ground. I took on the role of a runner—running with the animal to get it turned so it was between me and the gate, then others would join me to surround it and keep it moving the right way. I was running near full speed. The calves especially could move surprisingly fast.

In the broad open field beneath the thick blue sky, I felt like a kid playing capture the flag at Camp Nonquitt when I was ten or eleven, free and breezy, heart pumping with pure unfiltered life. Of course, now between my runs, I'd cough and my chest would ache a bit, reminding me that I'd put a lot of shit in my lungs since I was that little kid in South Dartmouth.

It seemed like another hour getting the last seven through the gate. Willie was tickled as he hooked the gate closed. "Well, that's a little different from the way we usually do it, but goldang, it was kind of fun, too."

We hung out a while in the newly cleared field, Willie leaning against a fence post with a long piece of straw dangling from his mouth, the rest of sprawled on the ground around him. Maybe this was the perfect way to spend our first solstice in Oregon. We'd been horseless cowboys, doing real ranch work. It sure felt good. We hadn't been sitting there very long before Jack came strutting up the road.

"Looks like I timed this well," he said with a chuckle. "Whatever you were doing, it looks like the works all done." We all laughed. Jack had hitchhiked back from San Francisco and been dropped off at the bottom of the road. He said he didn't know when Dale and Sydney would be back, but things had been relatively mellow between them all—so much so that they were considering trying a triad, the three of them living together. "Whatever," Jack said, laughing and throwing his arms up in jovial ambivalence.

There were lots of subtly expressive looks shared among us, but nobody said anything. Willie played with the straw in his mouth and we could see just a hint of raised eyebrows when he must have caught the drift of what Jack was talking about. The quiet hung for a while.

"Well, good day's work, boys … oh, and you girls, too," Willie finally said, smiling at Sarah, Paulie, and Sheila. "Better be getting back down to town and see what mama's got planned for me." He eased away from the fence, heading toward his truck. "Be seeing you all soon, I guess."

Because everybody had been out in the fields with the cows, lunch was pretty much bread and peanut butter and jelly or whatever else was easy to grab and eat. With the fun and fulfilling collective effort helping Willie shifting our mood, Walter was able to laugh about the peyote fiasco. "It could have been fun doing that tripping our brains out," he said. "Though it might have been hard to keep track of whether we were the herders or the herded. Come to think of it, Willie and the cows had the easiest jobs. Willie just stood by the gate directing us and the cows got to watch us making fools of ourselves, with our whooping and hollering and running around. They just kind of eased into a field with some fresh grass. Not a bad deal for them."

The afternoon started drifting by and most of us headed toward the swimming pond. We'd managed to salvage the water bed and had it set up on firm, almost flat ground just below the bank of the swimming pond. We all tended to crowd on it when we weren't swimming. Most comfortable spot for sure. As the sun was starting to angle down toward the western slopes, Stu showed up, dropped off by a semi-friendly local, who took a few minutes to shoot the shit with Stu and not so subtly check out the mostly naked folks hanging out by the ponds across the field.

Stu had his letter. The shrink had diagnosed him with something called "group delinquent disorder." We all laughed when he read that.

"What the fuck is that?" Mike asked.

"How the fuck should I know?" Stu answered. "She tried to explain it, but I didn't pay much attention after she told me it would get me out of the army—something about an 'oppositional disorder' and being part of a delinquent peer group." He stopped and slowly scanned all of us, barely any clothes among us, in varying degrees of stonedness. "Oh, I get it now."

"Think she hit the old rusty nail on the head," Walter said, as we all laughed.

Stu told us he had talked to Wayne over the phone before he left Dougy and Jill's, and Wayne said things were going well in San Francisco.

SUMMER/2

When Sarah and I arrived at the Main House, Walter, Mike, Stu, and Paulie were the only other people around. Walter told us that Dale and Sydney had come back the night before after we'd left. Sydney had decided to move into Shantytown with Jack. Walter said Dale was, as we'd all expect, blown away, and he took off immediately for his cabin. Nobody had seen him since.

"Man, what's going on here? What are we doing?" I said. I had fixed my coffee with powdered milk and lots of sugar and sat at the far end of the table under the stairs. "We just seem to be totally mired in bullshit. I feel pretty good when Sarah and I are hanging out at our house or when we all get into work like the garden or helping Willie with his cows. Sometimes it seems like it all makes sense, there is a reason for all of us being here. But it's so strange other times … I mean, who are all these people? What do they want out of this place? Sometimes I'm not sure how to talk to some of them."

"I know exactly where you are coming from," Stu said, as he sat at the opposite end of the table on the same side as me, to accommodate his left-handed drinking. "Being away a few days, I really started missing this place. But I come back, and … all these strange vibes. When we work, especially for me in the garden, and when we party, which is a lot," he stopped to grin at all of us, "everything seems fine but just living together feels so fucking complicated."

"I have to say," Sarah said, as she squeezed in between Stu and me "there are people here I trust completely—all of you," she looked around, slowing a second at Paulie, who sat opposite me and smiled gratefully, their spat apparently behind them—"Eddie, Jeffrey, Stephen, but there are others, I just don't have that feeling for. Annie? I have no idea what's going on with her. She's got some weird thing with me."

"I'm with you guys completely," Mike said as he took his place opposite Stu with a fistful of bread in his hand. "There are people I definitely don't trust. Fucking Wayne?" he looked to Stu, who shrugged. "Phillip? And Jon?—what's up with him and his fucking moving van full of shit. We gotta be careful with these people, man."

"Jon's OK," said Walter, standing between Paulie and Mike. He, who along with Dale and Jeffrey, knew Jon best in Boston. "He comes from a lot of money, which has fucked him up some. But he knows it. He's got a good heart. We were pretty close in Boston last year while you guys were gallivanting all over the country. I think he really wants to try to be a good part of this scene. Not sure how well it fits Sheila. I don't know her very well. Give Jon a chance. I think you'll get to like him if you do.

"Wayne?," Walter continued, "I dunno. He sure knows a lotta shit. Sometimes some of his rap sounds like bullshit." He raised his eyes and shrugged. He was withholding judgment. "Phillip and Jane? I like Jane, though she's kind of a head case. Phillip? I often wonder where Phillip's coming from. He's like a straight hippie or somethin'. I dunno."

This was the first time in a long time that a group from the Boston core had a chance to talk like this among ourselves. "I'm telling you, man, we've got to watch them," Mike said, "especially fucking Wayne with our fucking money."

"And we have to look out for each other," I said. "Us here with Eddie, Jeffrey … and Stephen, I guess. Dale and Sydney were kind of like the most together of us, back to the 1387 days … the ones to find Tiller and get things going here … but now … Dale is sort of out of his mind and who knows what's going on in Sydney's head right now. Jack's another one. He's a fun guy and a hard worker when he wants to be, but …"

Just then, Jack and Sydney came through the front door.

"Morning, y'all," Jack said with a hearty grin. Sydney followed with a slightly sheepish smile. "You all look so serious," Jack said, loud and energetic. "It's a beautiful day out there. Get out and enjoy it. We're just moving some of Sydney's stuff into Shantytown. Never imagined it would be a cottage for two, but looks like we can make it work." He looked to Sydney, who broadened her smile for him, but avoided eye contact with the rest of us.

Sarah, Stephen, and Sheila went to Medford in Stephen's truck to do some shopping. Bill Williams, our lawyer for the tree thing arrived for a visit. Willams, fiftyish, was tall and lean, almost bald with heavy black-framed glasses. His mellow demeanor made it hard to believe he had a reputation as a hell-raiser during his two terms in Congress in the late fifties. Phillip, Jon, Stu, and I took a walk with him along the creek on the east edge of the property, below the hillside that was part of the proposed timber sale. Williams was duly impressed with the beauty of the ranch and the forested hills rising above it. His bad news, which he tried to explain as we walked, was that we had lost a critical motion. The court had ruled that as private landowners we had no standing to sue the Forest Service, which voided the temporary injunction.

"We'll appeal, of course, if you want us to move forward," he explained. "The appeal process can take a long time, which effectively serves the same purpose as the injunction. The

Forest Service won't proceed as long as there is an active dispute. The last thing they want would be to go through the whole process of the sale and then have it nullified. So, this is only a temporary and procedural set back. There is still no ruling on the merits of our case, which I still believe are very strong."

"So … what's involved with the appeal," Jon asked, as we passed Stu's cabin. Williams looked closely at the cabin and smiled before responding.

"Well, it involves research," Williams said as he looked back to the four of us. "As far as we know, we are the first landowners to sue the Forest Service to stop a timber sale, so we have to see if we can find precedents in other areas that we can apply. My assistant can help with that." His expression got a little more serious. "We will need some more money, though."

It got quiet for a while. We stopped to look straight up the hillside. "So this it?" Williams asked. "Steep ground?"

"Yeah," Phillip said. "They'll build a road around the back side to the top and then work down the hill, cutting the trees and then pulling the logs up to load on the trucks."

"They really are right on top of you," Williams grimaced. "Unfortunately, the aesthetics of it all—the ugliness that you would have to stare at every day, the noise you'd have to listen to—is probably our weakest legal argument. But I can certainly see why it's so important to you."

We all stood there, quiet, staring up, as a little gust of wind made the treetops swirl in a smooth flowing dance.

"How much more money?" Jon finally asked.

"I can't say for sure," Williams replied. "But I think maybe $500 could get us a long way down the road."

Jon looked to the other three of us and then back at Williams. "Sure," he said. "We'll do it." Back to us: "We have to do it, don't we?"

We all nodded, understanding that Jon was offering up the money to do it. His and Sheila's money was not part of our communal fund—yet. None of us knew just how much money they had, but we all assumed it was a lot.

Maybe Walter was right. Maybe Jon was OK. Part of the reason I had tagged along on the walk with Williams was I hoped to discuss my probation situation with him, especially about how to deal with the fact that Jane was on probation, too, theoretically putting both of us in violation of the rules about two felons living together.

I didn't get a chance to bring that up to him until after we got back to the Main House and had filled everybody in on what we had discussed about the trees. By then, it was late afternoon and he was ready to head back to Eugene.

His quick answer—I was kinda getting a freebie because we weren't paying him to counsel me—was that he doubted the authorities would hassle me unless I did something more serious. To charge me with violating my probation, they would have to fly me back to Massachusetts, a lot of trouble and expense. Cursory advice but it eased my mind.

Sarah, Stephen, and Sheila got back from Medford right before supper. It looked like they'd had a good time. Sarah bought a funky old rocking chair from a second-hand store for 35 cents and some other cool stuff for our house—and a .22 rifle, something we'd been talking about for a while. We collectively had one rifle—the 30.06 we'd shot the TV with—and Stephen had a shotgun, but we wanted something lighter for target practice so all of us could get comfortable shooting.

They also got another rocking chair for Annie for her birthday, maybe something of a peace offering from Sarah, though it was presented as coming from all of us.

Everybody who was on the land, which was everybody but Wayne—twenty of us, including the four kids—was at the Main House for dinner, which became a birthday party. It was Kathy's birthday, too. She was turning eleven; Annie, we found out, was turning nineteen.

Even Dale showed up, clearly brooding and keeping as much distance as he could from Jack and Sydney, but he was there and even loosened up a bit after a couple of joints went around. Walter made lentil burgers. Mike had baked some rolls. And Paulie and Sheila had managed to put a salad together with lettuce thinnings and radishes from our garden, a monumental first for us. Then Jane surprised us all—and especially Annie—with four cakes, two carob honey and two ginger spice. We all sang "Happy Birthday" and it was a joyous solidarity riding on that old familiar melody. I think I even saw Dale crack a smile. As Annie and Kathy together blew out an odd assortment of candles, I thought back to the doubt-filled conversation of the morning. Maybe there was still a way for all of us to work together. The cakes were great. The ginger spice was a little dry and carob ain't chocolate but it was a real treat to share them, all of us together.

Soon, after the cakes had been ravenously consumed, Jack and Sydney started easing toward the door. The Hammonds, too, started gathering their stuff to head out.

Walter raised his voice, "Hey, wait a second," he almost shouted. When Jack and Sydney froze and everybody else got quiet, he lowered his voice. "Man, this has been a lot of fun, right?" The response was a lot of head nods and murmured agreement. "So … as I see people start shuffling toward the door, I can't help but thinking," he paused and looked around the room slowly, then spoke sternly: "Who the fuck is going to clean all this up?" Silence.

"Well, I tell you who usually cleans up." He stopped again, staring now at each of us in turn: "Me." He said that quietly. "You all wander off to your sweet little cabins and houses, stoned and stuffed, until suddenly it's just me and Eddie and a big fucking mess. Sometimes, Sheila or Jon might help a little or Annie or Jeffrey, but most nights, it's me and Eddie at the end. And, well, you know Eddie …" A little laughter at that. "This is our fucking bedroom, man. We can't split and imagine that some mystical spirit comes out and cleans up before you people start showing up in the morning to start messing it up again."

"Wow, man," Dale was the first to speak up. "Sorry. That sucks."

Then Eddie, "I know I'm not that much of a help, but sometimes I try a little, right?" He smiled questioningly toward Walter, who gave a half-hearted grin in response, "But it does suck man, how people just leave a mess. And it's especially bad when people just hang out so we can't go to sleep and then split without cleaning up after themselves."

"I try to help, too." Sheila said. "But it's like Eddie says, people just hang out without thinking about the people who live here, who sleep here. We're upstairs so it's not as bad for us, but some people stay late, other people come early, so it affects us, too." Jeffrey and Annie, who also lived upstairs (in Sarah and my old room) chimed in their agreement.

"Hey, man, I totally dig where you're coming from Walter— and all of you," Philip said. "We don't hang out here nearly as much as everybody else. And we've got the kids so we always split pretty early. But, man, yeah, you shouldn't be stuck with the mess like that."

"You could wash a fucking dish before you split," Walter said matter-of-factly staring stone-faced at Phillip and, in case anybody was thinking they were exempt from Walter's wrath, he swept the room with the same look. "All of you. Please wash your fucking dishes!" He eased back from that expression, rolling into an almost merry smile. "OK, I'm done."

Jack and Sydney came back into the kitchen area and grabbed some dishes off the table. Jane gathered plates from the people sitting around the edges of the room. Dale put some water on the stove to heat up, Sarah and I started scraping food remains off the plates into the compost. All of us were almost tripping over each other trying to do something to help clean up. Nobody said anything, Walter had taken a spot in the upholstered chair in the corner and was lighting a joint Eddie had rolled for him. As he exhaled, he grinned contentedly.

It was amazing how fast the cleanup went when almost everybody pitched in. Jack and Sydney left as soon as they could gracefully exit, followed shortly by the Hammonds. The clean house, the shared effort, the reduction of the crowd from twenty to twelve—a number that could almost comfortably fit in the dining/living area of the Main House— had left us in a mellow mood. Like so many days at Ash Valley, this day had been so full, so variable, so much a mix of the best and the worst of us, distrust, defeat, looming uncertainty, hope, profound pettiness, celebration, ongoing questions, and ephemeral answers. Walter, still flush with his seeming triumph, decided it would be a good night to throw the I Ching.

He tossed the coins and then thumbed through the book until he found the right hexagram.

"Number 58," he said. "This looks promising. The two trigrams represent lakes on top of each other, like our ponds, and it's called 'Joy, Pleasure.'"

"Cool, that's all I need to hear," Stu said. "I fully back more joy and pleasure."

Walter assumed a vexed expression. "Listen," he said.

"The judgment says, 'Tui'—that's the name of the hexagram—'intimates that there will be progress and attainment. It will be advantageous to be firm and correct.'"

"Wait," It was Eddie now. "How do you get joy and pleasure from being firm and correct." Walter ignored him.

"The commentary says, 'Tui has the meaning of pleased satisfaction' and indicates 'that what is most advantageous is the maintenance of firm correctness. Through this there will be found an accordance with the will of heaven, and a correspondence with the feelings of men. When such pleasure leads the people on, they forget their toils; when it animates them in encountering difficulties, they forget the risk of death. How great is the power of this pleased satisfaction, stimulating in such a way the people!'"

"Power to the people!" I said.

"Well, that's sorta what it's saying," Walter said, taking me more seriously than I deserved. "If we pursue pleasure and joy the right way, we will be stimulated to do the work we need to do and overcome difficulties. That sounds like power to the people to me."

"What's the right way?" Jon asked. He was serious.

"Well, there's more," Walter said. "The great symbolism says 'The superior man'—the good guys—'encourages the conversation of friends …'" He paused for a second … "to figure out their 'common practice.' That's basically what it says."

"So we've got to keep talking until we figure out our 'common practice,' Right on, I guess," Dale said.

"That's not exactly a major breakthrough," Sarah said. "We pretty much knew that already."

Walter sighed. "I'm not done yet. The changing lines are really important. They kinda fill out the meaning of the main hexagram." He looked around and everyone was still paying attention. That in itself was a victory for him. "The first changing line 'shows the pleasure of inward harmony. There will be good fortune attached to the pleasure of inward harmony that arises from there being nothing to awaken doubt.'"

"So," Mike said, seriously thinking about it, "if we have no doubt then we have inward harmony, but …" He looked around the room, eyes scrunched in doubt.

"Still not done," Walter said. "The second changing line talks about 'trusting in one who would injure him, making the situation perilous.'"

"So that fucks up the whole inward harmony thing," Mike said. Great—so, the Ching is telling us we have someone we can't trust. I remembered all the candidates that came up for that role in our conversation that started the day.

"You gotta take it all together," Walter said. "One more thing to read. The changing lines create a new hexagram, which adds further meaning. In this case, it's Chieh—or Removing Obstacles. The judgment says, 'advantage will be found in the southwest.'"

"The hayfield?" Stu asked.

"Or maybe LA," Jon suggested, thinking about Wayne's pursuit.

Walter continued. "'If no further operations be called for, there will be good fortune in coming back to the old conditions. If some operations be called for, there will be good fortune in the early conducting of them.'" No comments from the peanut gallery.

"And the commentary says, 'By movement there is an escape from the peril. Advantage will be found in the southwest. The movement will win all.'" Realizing people were starting to lose interest, Walter read the rest to himself and offered up this summary: "Some of the movement should be about getting back to doing things in old ways but when it's necessary to change, that should be done quickly. And the last line says: 'Great indeed are the phenomena in the time intimated by Chieh.'"

Walter shut the book. We all were waiting for him to say something, to tell us what it really meant. But he didn't. He just sat in the corner, calmly.

Pleasure. Joy. Progress. Attainment. Correctness. Satisfaction. Friends. Conversation. Common Practice. Harmony. Doubt. Peril. Misplaced Trust. Deliverance. Movement. Return. Quick change.

Yes. Of course, it all made sense. Like this day. Like the weeks since we'd move on this spectacular land. Like the stream-of-conscious circus parade in my head, smiling beauties atop prancing horses, sad clowns, plodding elephants, and graceful acrobats, sometimes flowing so smooth and jubilant and sometimes a jumble of chaos and confusion, all collapsing into each other as they run into an invisible impenetrable wall.

"Great indeed are the phenomena."

SUMMER/3

Mike and I went to Canyonville in the red truck, which had been running fine for a couple of days. He needed to see a doctor because he'd stepped on a big old rusty nail while we he was working with scrap wood to fill in some holes in the siding of his cabin.

It'd been a while since Mike and I had hung out, just the two of us. Outside of Sarah, he and Stu were the people I felt closest to on the ranch. In day-to-day work, Stu and I spent more time together in the garden, and Stu was more likely to wander up to our place to shoot the shit. Mike and I were allies in trying to make sure that revolutionary political consciousness was a fundamental part of our common principles. But beyond that we were really good friends who had been through a lot together. In a group, especially in a group that extended beyond the core of us who'd come from Boston, Mike often assumed a hard-ass blustery persona. But the smaller the group, and the closer he felt to the people in the group, the more likely we were to see the whole Mike, which could be sensitive and open.

We talked about the contradictions that seemed increasingly apparent on the ranch. Mao taught that it was only by identifying and analyzing the contradictions that exist in all situations that we could figure out how to deal with them. The I Ching—sort of the spiritual complement to Mao's political analysis—Walter had thrown a few nights before had told us that joy and pleasure awaited us as long as we were "firm and correct." I think the same phrase—"firm and correct"—had come up when Walter threw the Ching when we first heard about Ash Valley. "Firm and correct" was also the sort of phrase that Mao would use.

"So, I see that as the principal contradiction," Mike said as morning clouds yielded to a determined blue as we navigated the twists of the South Umpqua road. "Can this group figure out what is 'firm and correct' for us as a whole or can we survive with fifteen different versions of that?" Mike talked a lot with his hands, which made me glad I was driving—besides the fact that his vision was weak and he was a shitty driver. "Politically, of course, I support some sort of democratic centralism. Talk the shit out of this stuff but once we make a decision, we all live by it. But …" He paused and looked at me with a pleading kind of smile. "Do I want fucking Wayne telling me what is correct? He's got some people fooled. Not me. But I even wonder if I trust this group as a whole to define what is correct?

"So the secondary contradiction within the larger contradiction is the other thing the Ching brought up, peril caused by someone we trusted. Man, like we were talking the other day … what is this group? How do we identify who we trust, who the fucking betrayer is? I mean even fucking Stephen. I think he's a good guy. I don't know how we'd have gotten a lot of stuff done without him. But the shit he pulled with Paulie and now Sheila. He's like some fucking quiet phantom lurking in the background and then, boom, rumors and sneaking and … shit, and the whole Sydney-Dale-Jack thing—I love Sydney, she's my sister, but man that Jack is another one. All this sexual bullshit just scrambles everything up, especially when we *really* don't know where some of these people are coming from to begin with."

He was wound up as we cruised through Tiller. He kind of paused to catch his breath.

"Yeah," I said. "All that shit kind of eats away at us. Sexual freedom makes sense in the abstract. But gossip, distrust, hurt feelings makes any kind of solidarity hard. Shit, man, that's another big contradiction. And that gets beyond principles and beliefs and stuff, into biological urges and emotional attachments. Sometimes I even worry about Sarah and …" I stopped. I hadn't said this out loud to anyone before. "… Stephen." Mike looked at me, astonished. "I mean I don't really have any reason to … but did you have a reason to think something was happening with Paulie? Sometimes she just looks at him in ways that worry me. And now the horses thing—that's how it started with Paulie, right?" He nodded. I didn't often find ways to shut Mike up, but this seems to have had that effect.

"He's such a man's man kind of guy, so different from me. I can see why she would be attracted to him. Is he the trusted one who will cause peril for me—personally? Sarah and I are one of the few couples that hasn't had something like this happen to us. Are we immune? I would have thought Dale and Sydney were immune. Shit, I hate even thinking like this, but that's what I'm saying—all this shit going around feeds on itself, makes us paranoid or whatever."

I stopped. Sorry I had started, but that stuff had been rattling around in my head for days and, feeling safe alone with Mike, I just spewed.

Mike laughed. "Man, you are fucked up. I know you're not expecting *me* to give you marital advice, but I think you probably are just being paranoid."

We were quiet as we crossed the river in Days Creek. Things lightened up for the rest of the trip, and, after Mike got his tetanus shot, we laughed as we told stories over burgers and fries at the Airport Cafe, a very rare and not really sanctioned activity. On the way home, we stopped at the post office where there were letters from Barry and Luke waiting for me. Luke is out of prison! Both of them said they were coming to the ranch in August. That'd be a trip to have them here at the same time, two outlaws from different realms, the revolutionary and the pot dealer, but both important friends, though my ties to Barry went much deeper.

Given some distance from the commune, Mike and I had a chance to remember the depths of our one-on-one friendship and that gave me a boost as we returned to the ranch to dance some more with all the confounding contradictions.

A big old Cadillac was parked in front of the Main House. "What the fuck?" we both said at the same time. Then we could see Sarah next to the car with a couple of extremely straight looking people. They all smiled at me.

"Ben," Sarah said, "Do you remember my Aunt Bertha and Leonard." I didn't really but I remembered that Sarah had told me that a couple of her relatives were doing a West Coast road trip and were planning to stop by and see us. We never expected they would actually find us.

"Sure, sure I do," I said as warmly as I could muster. They were dressed up, like they were going out to eat at some place fancy. "I can't believe you made it here." I gave Bertha a hug and shook Leonard's hand. "This is our friend, Mike," I said. "He was at our wedding, too." I remembered that Bertha was Sarah's father's sister and the mother of her cousin Albert, the rabbi who had married us, along with my Uncle Nathan, an Episcopalian minister. She and Leonard had just gotten married and were on their honeymoon.

"Hey, man, what's happening," Mike said and shook their hands. They smiled politely.

"They were just getting ready to leave," Sarah said. "I'm glad you got back in time to see them."

"Me, too," I said.

"I gave them a little bit of a tour," Sarah said. "We drove down and looked at our house and took some pictures."

"This is such a beautiful place and your house is just so darling," Bertha said with a genuine smile. "I'm so glad we stopped and I'm sorry we have to run off so quickly. But this was a little farther than we expected and we've got quite a drive to our next stop."

"Well, we're so happy you took the time to come see us," Sarah said. "It's really very special."

"OK," Bertha said, looking to Leonard, "One more picture and then we really have to go."

"Let me take it," Mike said and Leonard passed him the camera. The four of us gathered against the Cadillac, Bertha and Sarah with their arms around each other, flanked by Leonard and me.

"OK, everybody smile," Mike said. We were all being such good sports. Then we all hugged and they climbed into their car and drove off down the road.

"I can't believe they really came," Sarah said. "… and left so quickly. To think, I was worried they might want to stay here."

"Yeah," I said. "Wow. I wonder what they were expecting. I wonder what they are saying now."

"Can't wait to hear the stories that get back to Philadelphia."

What a trip, a reminder that we were not in Shangri-La or Brigadoon. Anybody with the tenacity to find Tiller, navigate the river road, and turn left on the right gravel road could drop in any time. The world was just beyond our gate.

SUMMER/4

The hay in the field near the front gate was ready to harvest. It was a big field, 10 or 12 acres, according to Willie. Dale and I helped Stu with the mowing early one morning. Willie had left his tractor attachments and gave us a few tips on how to use them and on the whole process of haying.

Stu did most of the driving, while we walked alongside or in front looking for obstacles or big holes hidden in the waist-high grass, and then helping Stu avoid them. Once in a while we took turns up on the tractor, giving him a break, which was cool, but we knew Stu was our number one tractor man.

It was another beautiful blue sky sunny day. A gentle breeze rippled the grass, which was just starting to show seed heads, an "America the Beautiful" kind of scene. We finished the mowing near lunchtime, and after taking stock of how we had transformed a piece of our land in a morning of steady work, eased down the road toward the Main House, Dale and I following the slow moving tractor, all of us wearing satisfied smiles.

As Willie had advised us, we gave the mown grass now transforming to hay most of four hot, sunny days to dry before putting the raking attachment on the tractor and getting back in the field. We were now joined by Sarah, Paulie, Mike, and Jeffrey and shared two pitchforks and a couple of rakes among us. Stu was fully in command of the tractor now, while the rest of us swept hay that had been missed by the mechanical rake into the neat rows that formed in the tractor's wake. We probably didn't need that many people out there but it was fairly easy work made fun by the camaraderie we shared.

The next day, we waited until the sun was high overhead to start the baling. Everybody came out, even Jane, who set up a kind of picnic and break area in the shade of the hay barn, an open-sided structure with a tin roof, about 20 feet wide by 40 feet long. That's where we'd be unloading and stacking the bales. Jane could hang out with Rainbow there, and she had brought jugs of water and biscuits and cookies she had baked.

The baling went amazingly smooth. Stu, of course, drove the tractor. The rest of us were divided in three basic groups. The largest group followed close behind the tractor, and as the bales were formed they would, in groups of three or four, drag them to a central spot until there were eight or ten, and then start a new pile farther ahead. Behind all that, Stephen drove his flatbed, to which we had added side panels, to the piles. He would then join Mike and Jack in the truck bed. Philip, Dale, Jon and I, working in twos, would heft the bales, which someone said weighed close to 100 pounds each, up to the bed and the guys up there would stack them. When we thought we had enough, usually three piles worth, with the bed not quite full and room for us to climb up to sit on the tail end, Stephen drove to the barn, where we would unload, reversing the process, and stack the bales in orderly rows.

We grabbed drinks between loads, and folks from the pile crew would take a break now and then. Annie and Sheila took turns helping Jane with the little kids. Stu took quick breaks when his back-and-forth trajectory brought him close to the barn.

But we kept going through the hottest part of the day, the momentum of the communal purpose a powerful stimulant.

Those first bales I lifted with Dale to the truck felt so heavy. I wondered if I was strong enough for that crew. I couldn't imagine doing that for more than an hour or so. After we finished stacking the first load in the barn, I was sweating like crazy and questioning how long I could hold up. But the second load seemed a little easier and by the time we'd finished the fourth load—close to 100 bales worth—I was hustling to climb back on the truck to get back out to the field, where the piling crew was laughing, giving us shit about falling behind them. And then it didn't seem long before I looked around and realized more than half of the field was baled and stacked in the barn. The spirit, the energy, was contagious and we reveled in our defiance of the heat and the lurking aches of our bodies.

Then the tractor started sputtering. We had just finished stacking a load in the barn and were heading back out when it died. There were still six piles of baled hay that needed to be loaded—and about a quarter of the field still had loose raked rows. Phillip went to help Stu try to figure out what was wrong and during the delay everybody else came to help us load and unload those last piles.

When we finished with that, Stephen and I went out to the tractor to see what was going on. Everybody else stayed in the shade of the barn, snacking and stretched out in various positions of repose. Only when we stopped did we feel in our bodies just how hard we'd been working.

"Fuck, I don't know what's wrong," Stu said as Stephen and I approached. "It was running so good." He looked around the field. "Man, we were getting so close." We had more than 200 bales in the barn.

"Hey, man, we've done great," Stephen said. "Come and sit in the barn for awhile."

As we approached the barn, everybody started cheering for Stu, and he broke into a smile for the first time since the tractor broke down.

"You guys are too easy," he said. "Imagine what I'm going to expect when I actually finish a job."

We all laughed, except Paulie.

"Why can't we finish it?" she asked.

Stu looked at her like she was not quite grokking what was happening around her, which was not unusual for Paulie. "Umm . . . because the fucking tractor is dead."

"So why don't we just load up what's left loose? There's still plenty of room in the barn and, at least, it will be protected from rain?"

There were a few dismissive chortles from the men, but Sarah said, "Why not? It would be great to get this done while we're all out here."

"You know that might not be a bad idea," said Stephen, one of the few of us who had any experience with hay. "We'll never fill this place up with bales, so it wouldn't hurt to have a pile of loose hay.".

"Fuck yes, let's do it," said Dale. "Divide in two: half in the truck, half on the ground."

And suddenly, despite the fact that we were at the peak heat of the day and we were all tired, we were all jumping up to get out there and finish the job.

And, man, we did it! It was a hay party. Those on the ground, used pitchforks or just their wide open arms to gather the hay from the windrows and tossed them up to the truck bed where we used rakes or pushed or kicked the hay up toward the cab until the bed was so full there was barely room for us and then we would leap on top of the pile to ride back to the barn where we were met again by the ground crew to unload and try to create a reasonably compact pile. It was a fucking blast for all of us. And when, after another couple of hours, we had scooped the last of the hay from the field and deposited it in the barn, we all, covered now in strands of straws and thick coatings of hay dust, collapsed where we stood and laughed and laughed.

We all piled into the back of the truck to ride back to the Main House, no one, it seems, with the strength left to make that less-than-a-mile walk. We were a pile of worn bodies, quiet and content and glowing with a sense of collective physical accomplishment that few of us had ever known before.

SUMMER/5

Phillip and Jane and their kids had spent the night off the ranch. They went to a party in Drew that nobody else was invited to and had not returned. Walter sometimes hung out at the Second House just to get a break from the Main House, usually when the Hammonds were there. But today they weren't and he had, somewhat accidentally, "discovered" Jane's stash. The rest of us were out of dope, so he rolled a few joints from it and brought them back to the ponds where most of us were hanging out. He was a people's hero.

The Hammonds came back as we were cleaning up after dinner. They stopped by the Main House and brought some carob brownies that were left over from the party. They were in good spirits until Walter told them that while he was looking for some herb tea, he had found Jane's pot.

"Um, and maybe it seemed kind of bogus to me that when we're all out of dope, you're sitting on a healthy stash," Walter said. "Especially when you're off getting high at some party. So I took it upon myself to roll a couple for the rest of us. Just thought you would like to know. I didn't take it all."

Jane and Phillip looked stunned. "Man, what are you doing going through our stuff?" Phillip said. "That's fucked up."

"What's fucked up is that you are holding out on us," Mike said, grabbing one of the brownies. "You've got no problem coming down here and smoking dope that Eddie or someone else brings but then you got your own private stash, too. That's bullshit, man."

"I keep a little pot down there because I can't get up here all the time, with the kids and all, you know," Jane said, still standing just inside the door. "I share when I can, but you know anything I bring here just disappears, so I keep some. I'm sure you all were happy about that when Walter brought you some today." She smiled, pleased with her response. "'Judge not lest ye be judged.'"

"So some of us share everything," Dale said, sitting at the table, looking over his shoulder at them, "our money, our rigs, our dope …"—he shot a quick look at Sydney—"everything. But you folks in your own house with your own food and the rig that you don't let anybody else drive, only share when you feel like it."

"Things are different for us, man," Phillip said. He took a couple of steps toward the center of the room so he was addressing everybody. "You really don't get what it means to have kids. I know everybody loves to hang out with Greg and Kathy, but we're still the ones responsible for them."

"I see that," Sarah said, glancing at Phillip but focusing on Jane. "It must be hard with the craziness that sometimes happens here. But if we are in this together, which I hope we are, we can't have two completely different set of rules, or whatever you want to call it, for you guys and the rest of us. Like Dale said, some of us have put everything into the commune—and I don't care that much about the dope—but you two seem to hold back a lot."

Phillip shook his head and forced a smile. "Man, I don't know what you all expect from us."

A bunch of us tried to answer at the same time, finally yielding to Stu, who raised his hands toward Phillip. "Just to be more a part of it all. That's why we're here, right?" Phillip sort of nodded. "I see it in the work, too," Stu said. "I know Jane has got a lot on her hands with Rainbow and that's cool. And

Phillip sometimes you contribute a lot, but it's like you're not quite all the way into it, more like it's always on your time and your terms and not about what needs to get done."

Paulie had moved from the far corner of the room to stand at the end of the table. "I think just not hanging out with you so much makes it hard," she said. "I know it's easy for you to hang out at the Second House and not come up here so much. I know it gets crazy here sometimes, but if you were just here more, you'd know better what's going on and it wouldn't have to be such a big deal."

Phillip looked to Jane, who had sort of a blank expression. "Hey, man, we brought you brownies, right?" Phillip said, kind of laughing. "But I get a lot of what you are saying." He looked around to all of us, and then to Jane. "But there's not a lot of order about how things happen around here, so it seems like we sometimes do better just doing our own thing. Maybe if we had a little more structure about how we do things as a ranch, it'd be easier for us to fit into it all, with the kids. We could try if everyone else is willing to."

"It'd be far-out if we could make this place a little more kid friendly," Jane said, "I could sure use some help and I'd love to be more a part of what everybody else is doing."

Jane, with Rainbow on her lap, and Phillip sat down, as Eddie and Stephen made room for them around the kitchen table. Kathy and Greg found places on the floor, Greg leaning against the wall next to me. They had all been standing, their backs to the door, since they had come in. A vibrational shift had swept the room. I stood up and grabbed a brownie, and most everybody else did the same. The pan got empty fast.

"I love this," I said. "Confrontation transformed to communication. We need this. We need to just keep talking until …"

"Until we get to some place of fundamental trust," Jon said. "I love this place, I love you all but in my few weeks here I've seen a lot of mistrust. That makes it all pretty uncomfortable."

"Why are you here, Jon?" I asked. I'm not sure why. It seemed like a good place to start. He recoiled. "That's not meant to be a threatening question. Sarah, Mike, Stu, Dale and Sydney and me have talked about that a lot—since we first looked for land last summer. Paulie, Jeffrey, Eddie, Walter, too, as we were planning to come to Tiller. Less but some with Stephen, Phillip, Jane, and Wayne since we've been here, but with you hardly any at all."

"Why are you here, Ben?" Jon turned the question around. "Since you've thought about it so much, maybe that would help me." That was fair.

"I needed to get far away from Boston," I said. Jon nodded "I want to be with the friends, the brothers and sisters, I'd gone through so much with there, but far away in a totally different environment, to develop ways we could all live together and support each other without stupid jobs and playing all the capitalist games, not only for us but to be a model for other people. I want to work hard with my body, learn how to build things and grow things and develop my mind free of the cog-producing bullshit of the educational system. I want to nurture my relationship with Sarah in a non-chauvinistic way and free from the pressures and expectations of our families. I want to figure out what the next steps are for the revolution and what our part is in that. And, shit, yeah I want to have fun, smoke pot, drop acid, swim, and laugh."

"Does anybody here disagree with any of that?" Jon asked. Nobody did. "Essentially, that's why I'm here, too, Ben. We might—and I think we do—disagree about what the revolution is about and about how we go about living together but the broad outlines I think we all pretty much agree on, it's the details that are the challenge."

"So let's talk some details," I said. "About the revolution. I think that it's really important that we don't isolate ourselves from the Movement out in the big world. Trying to stop the logging here is really important—maybe part of the cosmic reason we ended up here, to save those trees—and it's great that we are united about that. But did everyone know that a bunch of Black kids rioted in Tennessee last month when a rock concert got called off. They fought for several nights, facing snipers and the racist pigs. And just last week, more Black kids, led by political militants, rioted in Jacksonville, Florida. Man, we gotta know about that shit and figure out how what we're doing relates to that, how we support it. And there's stuff coming out, defense department documents that somebody is handing over to the *New York Times,* that proves we were right all along about the war."

"Big surprise there." Stu said. That was about as political as Stu got, pointing out the stupidity of the other side.

"Yeah, I know, but it proves it for anybody with half an open mind. In our little world of the ranch, especially on these beautiful summer days, it's easy to forget there is serious shit going on out there, so we have to consciously try to stay connected to it and work at being part of it."

"Right on," Mike said. "Part of that is education. We throw the I Ching and do horoscopes, we should also be studying Mao and Huey P. Newton."

"'If you go carrying pictures of Chairman Mao, you ain't gonna make it with anyone anyhow.'" Walter said, grinning at Mike.

"Great song," Mike said, "but that's also kind of bullshit. Mao is a wise man and a brilliant revolutionary, but we could also study the revolutionary aspects of the Beatles and the Airplane and John Sinclair and the White Panthers in Michigan and the Motherfuckers in New York. It's the whole fucking thing, man, and if we don't understand it then how can we ever be part of it."

"My friend—our friend—Luke is coming here later this summer," I said, "just out of prison for shit he did as a Weatherman. I think that will be healthy for us to rap about how this place connects to what his vision of the Revolution is. He has some criticism, thoughts about how this could be an escapist trip."

"Man, I'm just not into any kind of violence," Jon said, most of the room nodding and murmuring in agreement. "And that seems more and more what freaks who talk about revolution are talking about. I'm totally into saving the trees."

"Well, there is violence—against the Panthers and the White groups who support them most strongly," Mike said. "Shit, man, I'm all for love and good times, but how do we get to love when the pigs are killing Panthers? What if we can't stop them in court from cutting the trees?"

"Maybe we build our love here in this place so strong that it just radiates out from here," Phillip said. "I mean that's where it's got to start, right? Maybe we become a place where Black brothers and sisters and other folks can come to get away from the violence."

"Nobody wants violence," Paulie said. "But we can't just pretend it's not happening."

"It's not like we're talking about forming a guerrilla army here or anything," Mike said. "We just gotta be real about what's going on and figuring out how we fit into it."

At that, Walter walked across the room and theatrically kissed Mike's forehead. "There's your Revolution, brother."

Everybody laughed, even Mike once he got past the initial astonishment that had overtaken him.

"So . . . how about a little love *and* a little revolution right here where we live," Sarah said.

"Right on to that," Stu said.

"Can we talk about some basic organizational stuff," Sarah said, "so people have a better idea of what needs to be done and how we should be doing it."

With the switch from the big R Revolution to the little r variety, almost everybody joined in the conversation enthusiastically. In a fairly short amount to time, we decided to divide into work crews:

Building: Stephen, Phillip, Jack

Garden: Stu, Ben, Jeffrey, Jon

Clean-up: Annie, Dale, Sheila

Kitchen: Walter, Sarah, Mike, Sydney

Miscellaneous: Eddie, Jane, Paulie

People could shift around based on the nature of the work, but this gave everyone a sense of where their main responsibilities were. And it kind of reflected the reality of where we had all gravitated to. The miscellaneous crew recognized Jane's maternal responsibilities, Eddie's almost constitutional aversion to work (we could have listed him as a one-man entertainment crew), and Paulie's devotion to the animals. We didn't think we needed a whole crew for the animals.

We figured Wayne would be part of the building crew, but he could decide when he got back. We also decided to get an early start as the temperatures were heating up and afternoons were best spent around the ponds. So, we'd have a light breakfast at dawn and then a big lunch late morning, try to put in an hour or two after lunch, then mellow out until a light supper in the early evening and go to bed when the sun goes down.

We had just started talking about weekly education sessions where people could share their expertise in certain areas like Stu about the garden or Jane about raising goats or Mike and me about politics when Charles Vernon, a good friend from Boston who'd been a dealing partner of Jeffrey's, showed up. We stopped the meeting for a bit to greet him and introduce him to the people who didn't know him. But when he started breaking out some pot—some fine Colombian, he told us—we asked him to wait until we were finished. That's how serious we were.

Of course, when we were done, we smoked a bunch. As Sarah and I and Moonbeam staggered our way home beneath the brilliant stars and a bright quarter moon, we marveled at the progress we seemed to have made and looked forward to an early morning.

SUMMER/6

We really did get up at dawn. We had a windup alarm clock that Sarah had gotten as a bat mitzvah present that startled us awake at 5:00 a.m. Coffee and rolls were ready at the Main House. Stu, Jeffrey, Jon, and I—joined by our visitor Charles—went out to the garden, which was like a fresh-faced friend in the gray dewy morning. Working in the first light of day felt so organic, rooted in the deep soil of human activity before we knew how to manipulate the illumination of our lives. I had a quick flashback to the days of detasseling corn in my early Illinois teen years, when heading to the fields at the crack of dawn was entering foreign territory. This morning, it felt like a lost home rediscovered.

We spent most of the morning weeding. There were lots of weeds. All the water we put on the garden and all the sun that shined down on it were just as nourishing for the weeds as for our vegetables. But the soil was loose and the conversation was absorbing. We were spread out around the garden but the quiet of the valley made it easy to hear each other. And the work was not so demanding that we couldn't stop for a minute or two and stand up and share a monologue, which Stu, our leader, was the most likely to do.

Stu and I had been riffing off and on about getting together a rock and roll band. I did have some experience, singing lead and playing harmonica and tambourine in a band through high school, but hadn't done anything like that for almost three years. Stu didn't know how to play a musical instrument and I'd never heard him sing. Same with Jeffrey, Jon, and Charles. But he was, like Jeffrey, like Jon, like Charles, like me, a fanatical music fan. We'd all been to many of the same shows in Boston—Led Zeppelin, Neil Young, Jefferson Airplane, Traffic, Grateful Dead, the Rolling Stones, The Who, The Band, the Kinks, and on and on—and we knew it would be cool to have a band. Stu, we decided, was a classic bass player type, in the mold of Jack Cassidy and John Paul Jones. Jeffrey had a striking resemblance to Eric Clapton, so he was destined to be our lead guitar player, with Jon on rhythm guitar. Charles, though he was only going to be with us a week or so, volunteered to be our drummer. We hadn't yet approached the three people on the ranch—Walter, Dale, and Eddie—who could actually play.

We'd made good progress on the weeding and put together a kick-ass set list for our band when the dinner bell rang. Sarah had volunteered to be in charge of the meal and it was great. She made chicken soup with mandlen (sort of Jewish oyster crackers; her mother had sent us a box), potato pancakes, and two challahs with sesame seeds. We were all in good spirits. Our work system had gone well. We'd gotten a lot done. We ate good food. We were all settling in to have a siesta, hanging out in the front yard of the Main House or up by the ponds. Phillip and Jane were heading off the property for a quick town trip when, just beyond the gate, they were met by four squad cars of state police.

They arrested Jane. One of the cop cars with Jane in the back followed Phillip back up our road to the Second House. Phillip stopped to tell people hanging out by the road what was happening. She'd been arrested for misuse of welfare funds, a felony. Phillip was going to take Rainbow to town to stay with some friends and get some stuff for Jane. Man, it was hard to look at Jane in the back seat of the cop car, even though she was smiling at us, looking somewhat oblivious. The cops in the front didn't budge, but kept a close eye on all of us surrounding them. People were yelling and freaking out, but we couldn't do a fucking thing to help her. That old sense of helplessness in the face of abusive authority overcame me and I started quietly weeping. Even here, even now. They could swoop in and rip us off. How could we defend ourselves? How could we ever build anything revolutionary in any sense when we were so vulnerable? It was a somber, quiet afternoon.

Jane was out on bail and back on the ranch the next day, cheerful and seemingly undaunted. She had an incredible ability to shine on whatever difficulties got in her way, a remarkable skill but a little scary, too. Made me question her grip on reality—a question that a lot of people would ask of all of us. But we were all relieved to see her out of jail.

We stuck with our work and meal schedule, making real progress in the garden and fixing up the root cellar in preparation for harvests to come. The kitchen crew kept producing great meals. Eddie even came out to the garden, helping as he could but mostly just joining in the conversation. He reminded us he was a drummer, so he claimed that spot in the band. Charles moved to being our keyboard player. He had as much skill on keyboards as he had on drums—that is, none.

Everybody seemed really focused on working together. Stunned and motivated by Jane's arrest, I guess, we hoped that if we could strengthen our internal harmony we could build stronger defenses against external attacks.

Over the next several days, we had an influx of people returning or coming to visit and, some, wanting to stay.

Patrick was first. One early afternoon, he just appeared, walking up the road. We sorta knew he was coming but had no idea when. He had been one of us since the West Campus days, had lived down the hall from us at Mountfort Street, been beside me at Northeastern, and made occasional appearances last winter in Boston, including at my trial and our wedding. He'd made a meandering trip west. His last stop before us was Mount Rainier in Washington State, which he climbed with a couple of buddies. They wanted to do more stuff up north, so Patrick hitchhiked down to Oregon. He'd slept in a cemetery in Canyonville the night before his arrival and then got a ride all the way to the Ash Valley gate from some local kid, who'd heard about those hippies up in the hills.

Next came Roger and Liz, friends of Mike and Paulie from Amherst. They pulled up in a big old box of a motorhome that was kind of startling to see sitting in front of the Main House. We weren't really expecting them. Maybe Mike knew, but he hadn't said anything. I'd met Liz briefly at a party in Amherst. I didn't know Roger at all. Paulie was happy to see Liz, who also had been friends with Sheila during high school. Mike never seemed excited to see them, but Roger pitched in with the crew working on the root cellar.

Herschel, an early Tiller pioneer who'd been with us at Mountfort Street and on the California beaches, dropped in as part of a West Coast tour, stunned at how the scene had evolved from the early quiet days at the White House.

Wayne came back, getting a ride from Eugene with Dougy and Jill and Dougy's sister Mabel. He told us the money was still working for us out there, and that things were going well—and he brought back plentiful samples of his products.

Two of Patrick's roommates from #8 Mountfort, the guys he had been traveling with until they split up after Mount Rainier, also showed up.

So, as we planned for a day off and a full day of partying on July 4, we had the most people we'd ever had staying on the ranch—somewhere around thirty.

SUMMER/7

I took a lot of LSD. Wayne had brought back a plentiful supply of what he said was pure acid. I took a double dose. Most of the Ash Valley men dropped, many taking a similar amount. I don't think any of the women did. Guests—mostly other South Umpqua-area freaks—had already started to arrive for our party. We had even filled our generator with gas, for only the second time since we'd been on the land, so we could have tunes. Music, so long a vital part of what connected us, was a rare treat at Ash Valley. But it was blasting Grateful Dead songs as I got off quickly and utterly. My first instinct was to get away from the Main House and the crowd as quickly as I could.

I wove my way into the house and found Sarah who was organizing the food that most of us had helped prepare the night before, and let her know I was going to disappear for a while. She smiled kindly, laughing at my urgency and however high I must have looked to her. She gave me a quick kiss and said, "Have fun."

As I left the house I saw Stu, Patrick, and Dale heading out of the yard toward the open valley. I rushed to catch up. They all laughed when they saw me coming, welcoming me, knowing exactly where I was on my ascension. The valley was shining as we glided into its gaping width. The cacophony building from the Main House sounded like it was coming through a tunnel, boring right into my ears. No one was leading or even thinking about where we were going. We were instinctively taking the most direct route away from what was behind us.

We came upon the creek about halfway between Stu's cabin and the reservoir. We stopped to listen. Our little creek, its flow starting to slow with the siphoning toll of consistently dry days, still sang a powerful song. Dale kneeled down and dipped his cupped hand into the brazen blue water and splashed his face. Eyes shut, smile radiating, he turned to us. "Sweet Jesus," he said. And we all splashed the chilled glistening water in our faces. The jolt was thrilling, sweet, awakening. The party noise sounded miles, days away, a distant memory.

We decided to cross the creek at a narrow spot not far away. It was an easy jump, three feet or so. Patrick went first, then Stu and Dale. But when I approached, it suddenly seemed like an uncrossable chasm. I stopped and saw the others waiting, curious looks on their faces, questioning.

"Come on, Ben," Stu said, his eyes piercing into me. "It's easy. Don't think about it, just jump." I laughed. I looked up and down the creek bank, thinking there might be an easier spot nearby. But there wasn't.

The others seemed to be patiently waiting, gazing up and down the valley and turning to look into the rising forest that loomed above us. I walked to the edge of the bank and assessed the jump one more time, turned and walked three of four yards away from it. Crouched a bit like at the start of the 880s I ran in ninth grade and then took off, getting as much speed as I could. When I hit the bank, I shut my eyes and leaped, a running broad jump that felt momentous. I tumbled into a landing a few feet on the other side, rolling into Stu, almost knocking him over. He regained his balance and smiled at me.

"You made it," he half laughed, "Wanna do it again?"

Dale and Patrick were smiling, too. "Nah," I said. "Let's try something different."

Dale took the lead and found a deer trail heading up. The sun was creeping above the eastern hills in front of us, its blossoming warmth simmering through us and adding a crispness to the rich mix of smells coming from all the life stirring and growing and decaying and dying around us: the little buds of wildflowers so fresh and new, the trees, the ancient masters, and a stew of every stage of life in between. I sucked it in, like a new, enhanced more powerful version of air.

We walked slowly and the climb seemed effortless. We didn't talk. I didn't even think about talking. There were no thoughts in me that wanted to get out. I was a mute sponge, my senses only working one way trying to absorb all that I saw and heard and smelled and touched and tasted.

I don't know how long we had been walking when we came to a small clearing, rimmed—it seemed almost intentionally— with fallen trees. Dale sat down on one and the rest of us did the same, almost equidistant from each other, forming something close to a square. I sat on the remains of an old cedar tree, its outer layer soft with rot, but it still exuded its sweet spicy perfume. I knew it was where I was supposed to sit. Was it my Don Juan spot? Right then and there it was, though the odds against me ever finding this spot again were close to infinite.

Dale spoke. His voice shattered the sensory bubble I had been enveloped in, like glass breaking in a silent night, sharp and piercing.

"You know what's going on here," he said, looking long at Stu and then me. No one answered. I had no idea what "here" he was talking about.

"It's the battle of good versus evil, light against dark, God and Satan. You can call it any damn name you want, but that's what's happening and, hate to crack your eggs brothers, but the good guys are losing."

Still, not entirely sure what he was talking about—this day, the ranch, the world—I looked to Stu, who looked back wide-eyed, seeming as unready for this conversation as I was. Patrick, just a couple of days at Ash Valley, was studying Dale intently.

"Don't you see it?" Dale challenged me. His bright blue eyes were pulsing with intense psychedelic clarity.

"Man, I'm not even sure what you're talking about. For one, I'm tripping my brains out and I can see you are, too. And … is this about Jack and Sydney?" Dale waved his hand at me, as if to dismiss that suggestion. "The trees? Doing dishes? The Revolution? Other stuff going on? Man, I just can't get where you're coming from."

"Yes," he fired back at me. "It's about it all. Jack is just a dumb okie, a pawn. Sydney tells me she really loves me but he is a better fuck. Love is losing here, man. Society told her she was a piece of candy. And she bought it. It's Hefner and 'everybody needs milk.' Sorry, brothers. We came here to drop out but we let the evil in and it's seeping into all of us." He glared at me.

"You once told me my life was my politics and I didn't really see it—but now I see it clear, clear as that creek water on my face. This life is our politics? I see an ugly voracious beast prowling around looking for its next victim to devour. Revolution? See the dark and seek the light, my brothers, that's the only politics that matters, the only revolution that can liberate us."

Dale took a long breath and leaned against a fir tree that rose above him. He stared into each of us. His intensity glared with an urgent magnetism. As much as I wanted to not listen, not see, not be swept up into his trip, I couldn't resist it. And I couldn't tell in that moment if he was batshit crazy or crazy wise, onto something deeper than I had ever gone.

"In what guise does this rough beast visit us?" Dale asked. "Forest Service green? We should have known. We should have known …when they told us they were going to massacre these trees that a trap had been laid for us. These trees that were babies when Shakespeare was writing and knew the Indians who played in these woods before White people even knew they existed, lived through the American Revolution, through Thoreau and Marx and Mark Twain and Nietzsche and Freud. We're going to get front row seats to their destruction?

"Shit, we have the prime suspects: Wayne with his sugary tales and fancy tools and long fingernail and good drugs—shit, brothers, we're high out of our minds on pills he laid on us. Or Phillips' folksy hippie family rap? Or Jon's money. Or Stephen's down-home country competence that somehow keeps wooing the ladies to his bed. But maybe they're *too* obvious. The sheep in wolves clothing to distract us from the real beast.

"Or …" he looked slowly to each of us. "One of us? Look at Sydney? No one would have imagined her going where she has gone in the last month. I don't hardly know who she is. Mike and his Mao? Ben and his mellow militancy? Walter and his Ching and 50 chews a bite? Stu and his monastic devotion to dirt and pulling stuff out of it? Me? Look at me—am I insane? Probably. But I see, too. I see …"

He stopped. Looked down toward the mix of fallen branches and ferns and the thick layer of decomposing life in the clearing between us. It was like he was a wind-up toy whose spring had played itself out. The sounds of the forest—breeze in the trees, the cracks of critters moving in the distances— creeped over us. And beyond that, from another world, we heard the rumble of the faraway and forgotten party, some bass notes and a buzz of humans. Dale finally looked up and smiled.

"I don't really know what's been going on here," Patrick said. "But it's a beautiful place and the people I know here are beautiful people. How can we not make it work?"

"I don't know," Dale said, quietly. "Welcome, man. I hope you're right. I hope I'm wrong. But it's great to have you here. It *is* a beautiful fucking place."

Stu walked across the clearing and gave Dale a hug. I did the same. Then Patrick. Was he insane? Were we all? Standing awkwardly in the clearing, we all knew it was time to head back downhill, to see what was going on in the beloved valley.

It was hot, well into the afternoon, the sun high in the electric blue sky, when we crossed the creek back into the valley. I forgot how scared I had been trying to get across it earlier and just jumped. It was easy. We could hear the music and the clatter coming from the Main House, see naked people wandering up and down the road and a bunch of people gathered near the Second House, which was almost directly across the valley. Off in the distance, looking south, toward the front of the ranch, we could see people on horseback, not-quite-galloping toward us. We were sort of mesmerized by the tableau all around us, our ranch, so open and wide and now singing with a panoply of human activity, so alive, a jubilee across our 135 acres. We watched the riders come closer. It could of have been the opening scene of *Bonanza*, so Western, complete with the cloud of dust and the carefree cattle and that smell of hot grass and dry air. It was as though they were riding toward us with purpose, perhaps a message of some importance. They drew closer and slowed, bringing their horses to a stop not far from us. Only in the last few seconds did I recognize that Sarah was one of them.

I had been sure they must have been strangers, come to visit us on horseback—which made perfect sense in my Western fantasy. Yes, it was Sarah, breathless and luminous on Mona's back, shimmering in her overalls—and just her overalls, her still very white skin leering out from under them—looking like she had been born to ride horses. She looked at me, puzzled. My shock at seeing her and in that way must have been all over my face. I tried to smile.

"Ben? You all right?" she asked.

"Yeah … yeah … Yeah," I said. "You just look so … Wow."

"Good acid, huh?" She laughed. Only then did I notice the other two riders, Stephen and a woman I had never seen before, an exotic, beautiful woman, with copper colored skin and long black hair, maybe Mexican, maybe Indian. I tried not to stare at her, though I could see both Stu and Patrick were transfixed.

Sarah laughed again. "You guys, this is Loretta, a friend of Wayne's. She just arrived in time for the party."

We all stammered our hellos and welcomes and Loretta smiled. The horses were getting antsy. "I was going to take them down and show Loretta our house. You guys look like you are going to be flying for a while yet. We'll see you a little later." They trotted off laughing.

Stu still looked bedazzled. "Somebody tell me that wasn't a hallucination," he said.

"Oh no, " Patrick said. "She was the real thing. I mean really the real thing."

"What was her name?" Stu asked.

I didn't remember. I was still thinking about Sarah.

"Loretta," Dale said, with a leery look toward Patrick and Stu. "You guys … The beast sometimes takes on the form of the things you desire most."

"Fuck you," Stu said. "That was no beast, I may be tripping but I could see that. Loretta, I gotta remember that. Tucker, help me remember that."

"Sure," I laughed. "No problem." We started ambling, almost without thinking, toward the Second House.

The Hammonds and all their kids, Wayne and Tammy, Jon, Sheila, and Annie were hanging outside by the road and their "driveway"—just a packed-dirt extension of the road—where a keg of beer was set up, which made me suddenly realize I was really thirsty. We were met with hearty greetings and laughter as we mixed in. Phillip, Wayne, and Jon were also tripping and we exchanged the knowing looks that people tripping give each other. Mostly, I just smiled and zeroed in on the beer.

Oh, man, that was good. So cold. The bitter flavor was just right to startle my taste buds and the alcohol a bit of a leveler to my soaring high. My cup was suddenly empty and I quickly returned to the keg to refill it. Perfect. I saw Mike and Jeffrey— also tripping—walking up the road laughing, and Stu and I walked over to greet them with grins and giggles.

"Hell of a party, eh, boys?" Mike said. "Man, there's a lotttttt of people here and everybody's pretty fucked up. You two look pretty fucked up."

"Nah, just another day on the ranch," Stu said. "Who are you anyway?"

Mike laughed but Jeffrey's expression took a quick shift from shiny smile to deep concern. I tried to follow his eyes but only saw the cluster of people centered around the keg.

"What's wrong, man?" I asked.

"Ummm," he slowly shifted his eyes back to the three of us. "Nothing, man, nothing," he said but his eyes and his forced grin said otherwise. "I think maybe I'll get a beer."

"Great idea," I said and noticed my cup was nearly empty again. "It tastes so good."

As I followed him back toward the keg, I saw the three people on horses trotting up the road and moved toward them. Just before they got to us they veered off the road around a pile of scrap wood. I was just on the other side of that pile when Loretta's horse suddenly reared up and threw her. From where I stood it looked like she hit the edge of the pile and I saw her head land on a board with a nail sticking out and I saw blood. I think I screamed before I felt this wobbly wave of dizziness surge up through me and I collapsed.

I don't think I was out very long but the next thing I remember is Sarah and Stephen and Stu hovering over me, sort of concerned but sort of laughing, too.

"Ben, Ben," I heard Sarah. "Are you alright?"

I couldn't respond, couldn't remember where I was, what happened, why I was laying on the ground on this hot day with all these people murmuring around me. I stared up at Sarah. Now she looked really concerned. Stu repressed a laugh that I could see in his eyes. Stephen studied me like I was another species.

"Ben, I think you fainted," Sarah said. "Are you OK now?"

"Yeah, yeah … I guess so. I think so." Then I remembered. "What about that woman …" I couldn't remember her name. "She fell off the horse … hit her head. Blood?"

"She's fine," Sarah said. "A snake in the wood pile spooked her horse, but she's fine. She's right over there." She pointed.

I saw Loretta standing a few feet away with a beer in her hand. She raised her cup and smiled at me. I didn't see any blood.

"Better than you," Stu, next to Loretta, said, and the laugh came pouring out. And it seemed like everybody there was laughing, like the whole valley was ringing with laughter.

I struggled to my feet, Sarah and Stephen helping me up, and looked around. Everyone was staring at me.

"Hey, man, why don't you come inside and rest for a bit." It was Phillip, his eyes flaming. Anything to change the scene sounded good. Sarah walked with me into the Second House. Stu brought me a beer. I sat in a faded plush arm chair up against the plank-paneled wall.

"I'm OK," I said, wanting to not be the focus anymore. "I just have to sit for a while. You can all go back to the party."

Sarah looked sweet and forgiving. "I'll ride Mona back and take care of her and then come back, OK?"

"Yeah, sure. Thanks." I smiled and she bent down and gave me a warming kiss. Stu followed her out the door. Only Phillip remained.

"Man, what a trip, eh?" he said. "This acid. Powerful stuff."

"Yeah, I swear I saw that woman fall off her horse and hit her head on a nail. Shit. Freaked me out."

"It's OK, man. I swear it's OK. Glad to get a few minutes with you. Man, I can see what a groovy dude you are, all the love you got. Sometimes we get lost in such petty shit around here and you and me end up on different sides. But, man, I know—I know!—we're on the same side. We gotta get loose of the hang-up of sides and look at the love and reach for the cosmos. This place, this place, man, you think it's an accident you and me are here? Nah, man, nah. Ain't no accident. There are no accidents." He took a breath. I had nothing to say but he had swept me up from the verge of bumming out and I felt strangely comfortable in the relative quiet of the Second House where I didn't hang out very often.

Phillip was glowing, a light emanating out from his eyes creating an almost halo-like aura.

"You see, man, if you and me can get past all this bullshit, get down to the love I know we share, man, that could be a powerful thing for this place, take us to another level, like a transcendental plane where we can ride the energy of this place, become brothers and sisters in a way we can't even imagine now when we argue about who's doing the dishes or all that political bullshit." He lit a joint and passed it to me.

"Man, this place, this place …" He spread his arms and swiveled in a half circle, as if to embrace everything around him. "I know you know, I can tell man, especially now when we're both so blessedly high—this place was meant for us to do something fucking incredible, it's a new world man, for real. But it's not just a playground—man, we gotta tap into the cosmic vibes that ripple all over this place. You can feel them, now, right? Man I can feel them to my bones."

I pulled hard on the joint. I might have already been holding it for awhile. I'd lost track. Loved the smoke going down and the airiness of the buzz floating above the acid. I was digging Phillip's rap, like a show, I guess. And I did feel real love coming from him.

"Sure, man, I'm feeling all kinds of vibes," I said. I felt a big smile on my face but I couldn't come up with any more words.

That seemed to satisfy him that we'd had some kind of breakthrough. I couldn't say whether we did or not, but I was glad to have had that time with him.

Other people wandered in and I retreated to quiet observation, trying to lurk behind a defensive grin. Finally Sarah came back and told us folks were starting to build a bonfire by the ponds near the Main House. She and I headed that way together.

The sun had sunk below the western hills and the day was cooling. It felt good to walk up the road with my arm around Sarah's shoulder and hers around my waist—so much contentment in that embrace. She'd had a fun day riding her horse and seeing new people and I loved listening to her tell me all about it. Sarah grounded me always but especially when I was tripping. I was beyond my peak—think that happened about the time Loretta was being thrown from her horse— easing down, with the pot and beer I'd had mellowing the descent, but still pretty high. Sarah was so firmly right there, the smooth softness of her warm bare shoulder beyond the straps of her overalls, the relaxed grip of her hand on my hips, riding the bounce of my stride, the naturally satisfying ways our bodies bumped as we propelled forward like two pieces of a strangely coordinated contraption. As she talked, warning me and filling me in on all the people who would likely be around the bonfire, I felt this deep and gushing sense of love and gratitude for her, that she was so right there for me, that she, above all others, always seemed to be. Why did we even have to go to the bonfire? I thought. But we were moving inexorably toward it, part of a loose and wobbly parade of people moving from the Second House in the same direction.

The bonfire was already blazing when we got there. And, despite Sarah's warning, I was blown away by all the people, more than had ever been on the ranch. Maybe 50? 60? More? Lots of vehicles, mostly pickups, were parked on both sides of the road from the Main House almost to the garden. People surrounded the bonfire in the middle of the field between the Main House and the ponds, many tossing in logs and branches and chunks of scrap wood from a pile we had created the day before. I hesitated at the edge of the field and took it all in. People trailing us from the Second House passed us, some almost running toward the fire. Phillip walked by and turned and smiled, waving his hands for us to join the crowd. After a while, Sarah sort of nudged me toward the fire.

It was fucking cool. I grabbed a big branch as I walked by the pile and threw it into the fire, which flared in absorbing it. The heat was intense and the circle of faces around it were red with reflection and the contagious intensity. Everybody from the ranch was there, even the kids, all our visitors, and, I think, every freak from Drew to Days Creek. I didn't recognize a few faces, but they were all part of our scene now. As the sky darkened, the flames brightened and grew higher and higher.

We'd been there a while when Jack came marching across the field with an American flag on a pole. Somebody had found it in the root cellar, left over from Willie's days, and this seemed like the perfect occasion for it. Jack squeezed himself through between Sarah and me and got real close to the fire and dipped the flag into it. As it caught, he raised it up, and a mighty cheer went up from the crowd. He waved it around for a minute and then passed it to me. I was into it now, waving it with all my might, as it was engulfed in flames, people spreading out away from me, and someone started chanting, "Fuck the Flag! Fuck the Flag!" Sarah had backed away so I passed it to Mike who was nearby and the chant shifted to "Power to the People! Power to the People!" The flame had started to burn the pole, so Mike lowered the whole fiery mess to the ground. Patrick moved close to it and started to piss on it and quickly most of the men joined him, laughing insanely and now chanting "Piss on the Flag, Piss on the Flag." It felt glorious and celebratory, our declaration of independence from our diseased country and its putrefied symbol. And suddenly we were dancing around the smoldering remains, everyone joining hands and skipping in circles, our anger transformed to a powerful joy. "Love! Love! Love!" we sang into the flames, now a brilliant beacon of ascending light reaching high into the almost perfect darkness that had engulfed the valley.

Some folks, finally exhausted, just fell to the ground and the circles of dancers almost elegantly collapsed on top of them and each other, and we were all swept up in breathless laughter. And we just lay there for a while, eventually silent, the crackle of the roaring fire the only sound for a couple of minutes. Gradually, people sat up or rose to their feet. This had been— though thoroughly spontaneous—the fitting and spectacular finale to our 4th of July—like the finales at Camp Nonquitt when I was a kid, a dramatic barrage of the best fireworks, illuminating the sky and Buzzards Bay beneath it. Man, I loved those 4th of Julys. I loved America. I loved the flag. Could I ever love America like that again? The truest loves betrayed are the most painful, the most unforgivable.

People started wandering to their rigs or back to their places on the ranch. Sarah and I just sat there for a while, joined by Patrick and Stephen and Loretta. We were all spent, sharing soft talk, satisfied with the party we had thrown, what we had shown of our place. Loretta was smitten and relaxed. She seemed like one of us already. That had been a theme that had come out of our discussions about who we should invite to move on the ranch, "when it's right, we'll know it." And she was the first single woman to come along. That wasn't the first thing I thought of, but I remembered the reactions of Stu and Patrick when we first saw her and realized that balancing those numbers could help morale and stability. And she was cool.

I saw Stu and Jeffrey engaged in what looked like a heavy rap off by themselves near the root cellar. I walked over and sat with them. Jeffrey looked up. His eyes still had a psychedelic blaze to them. We had dropped the acid about the same time and I was in the empty spaciness of the aftermath but he still looked in the thick of it. But there was also some terror in his eyes.

"You OK?" I asked. "You still tripping?"

He looked so forlorn. "Yeah, I am." He stared off into space for a while. "I went to get some pot from the ammo can in the woods to help me come down. There was some mescaline powder . . . it must have spilled . . . and I must have inhaled some of it. Fuck, man. I'm so high and I don't want to be. Fucking Annie." Stu shot me a look like we were heading into dangerous territory.

"Fucking Wayne." Jeffrey stopped and pounded his fist into the ground. "Where am I supposed to go? I'm fucking tripping my brains out."

I didn't know what to say, except, "It's OK, man. Really, it'll be OK."—Nothing but words and with the state Jeffrey was in, I knew they were almost worse than nothing. It clearly wasn't OK. Nothing was OK for him right now.

"You can come to my cabin," Stu said. "Hang out, ride this out by the creek. Sleep if you can. Everything is crazy now. We'll see what things look like in the morning."

Jeffrey exhaled. Looked back and forth between Stu and me. "Thanks," he said, quietly now, "Fuck."

They rose to leave and I headed back toward the small group I had been with. Quiet laughter came from them. It seemed like the circle had gotten smaller, Sarah had moved closer to Stephen and she was gazing at him in that way that scared me and he had that aw-shucks grin that struck me as seductive. She turned toward me as I approached and smiled in a practiced way. Not like she looked at him. Was I imagining all this? I couldn't tell. My brain was so sapped I couldn't resist whatever thoughts jumped into my head and I couldn't make sense of them, couldn't play with anger or hurt or trust or faith. I only knew that Sarah walked home with me, holding my hand, and at the end of that long strange day, that was all I needed to know.

SUMMER/8

Ash Valley woke up the day after the 4th of July immersed in an acid aftermath: emptiness, entropy, emotional vulnerability. I slept until the day was already hot. Sarah and Moonbeam were gone. I lay in bed for a long time, listening to the creek, flashes of memories from the day before flitting through my head, like a mixed-up movie reel at double speed. I couldn't grab onto any of them. I didn't want to. I didn't want to think.

I stumbled off the loft and got it together to start a fire in the stove to boil water for coffee then dragged myself out to the creek and dunked my head in it. The startling cold water felt good, pierced through my numbness, opened a path to some place of wakefulness. I sat there a while, dabbing my feet into the water, dazed by the rush of the creek and the lightness of the air and the gentle blanket of an easy warm breeze. The smell of boiling water brought me back and I pulled myself up to go make the coffee.

The coffee was good, with powdered milk and brown sugar. It was hot, so I took tiny sips as I rocked slowly, staring out at the meadow. Blank.

I was nearly done with my coffee, which had gotten cold, beginning to feel the caffeine rush stirring in my gut, when Sarah came sprightly across the meadow—smiling, in the way she did when she knew we were on different planes of consciousness.

She chuckled as she kissed me quickly and asked "And how are you this morning—or afternoon, I guess."

"Is it afternoon, really?" I asked. She smiled. "I'm not sure yet. This coffee is really good and the creek is really cold. Beyond that I don't know much of anything. How are you?"

"Fine. Not a lot going on at the Main House. Hardly anybody there and the few who are look like you." She smiled again, a little smug in her unique clear-headedness. "Dale left, this morning, I guess. Heading to the East Coast. Wouldn't say when he might come back. Liz is leaving. Patrick and Rodger are going to ask to stay. I'd rather Liz stay and Rodger leave, but I don't think she feels all that welcome. Loretta hopes to stay around. I like her."

She presented all this news matter-of-factly. Another day of comings and goings at Ash Valley. I felt no reaction. I was glad that she had come back, that I didn't have to go to the Main House, see anybody else or hear anything more about anything beyond our little meadow. To pick a side or have an opinion. Sarah would smile and humor me and give me space to jell out. Sometimes life was so simple and good at our little house by the creek. On that day, that was all I wanted.

A couple of days later, both my and Jane's probation officers came to see us. They came separately but they coordinated their visits so they could compare notes about the reality of a given day. I met my PO, Gary Jones, at the Tiller Store so I could show him the way. Folks on a town trip had dropped me off early and I waited for him (after scoring a red hot pickled sausage from the store) leaning against the side of the building near the phone booth.

Tall with wavy hair, he seemed more like a country social worker than a cop. Driving along the river road, we chatted about Tiller. He used to love to come down here to fish, he told me, but hadn't done that in a long time. He asked sort of

general questions about Sarah and me and how we ended up
in Oregon. It was like a pre-interrogation. As we got further
upriver, he went on and on about how beautiful it was and how
lucky we were to be here. I think he really meant it. We turned
up the Forest Service road toward the ranch and he slowed
way down, both because of the road conditions and because
he really wanted to take it all in. Coming around a big turn, he
slammed on the brakes as a line of quail marched across the
road in front of us.

"Open the glove compartment," he shouted excitedly. I
fumbled a bit with the latch but got it open pretty quickly.

Sitting on top of a blank envelope that must have held
documents for the car was a service revolver. I recoiled,
slammed up against the back of my seat, and froze. He reached
past me to grab the gun, but by the time he got it cocked and
ready, the quail had scurried into the brush on my side of the
road. He smiled at me as he replaced the gun and shut the
glove compartment.

What the fuck? I was on probation for felony convictions
of assaulting two police officers with deadly weapons. Was
he testing me? Was he trying to set me up? I couldn't think
fast enough to react to either potential scenario. I just knew
I wasn't touching that fucking gun. He drove on as though
nothing had happened.

The rest of his visit was comparatively uneventful. He
was suitably amazed by the beauty of Ash Valley as we drove
slowly through the property toward our house where Sarah
was waiting to play the role of the dutiful country wife.
We emphasized that we were a "community" rather than a
"commune," a collaborative working arrangement that made
it possible for a collection of relatively poor people to live in a

beautiful place and develop a working farm. We talked about our garden and the hay and our plans to raise pigs and goats, to be self-sufficient and bring in enough income to pay off the land and cover expenses. We talked about all the structures— like ours—we had built or fixed up. Look how much we'd done, we told him, and we'd only been on the land a little more than two months. We were convincing and he seemed genuinely impressed and maybe even a little envious of our situation. Shit, I was impressed with our story—and a lot of it was true.

He asked about the connections among the various family units on the ranch, gingerly probing specifically about the Hammonds. We said we were cooperative in terms of the operation of the ranch and sometimes shared meals and food but had distinct living situations and that was particularly true of the Hammonds because of their three kids and the fact they had had their very own house since the day they moved on the land. That was what he and Jane's PO had to determine: were we living together (against the rules) or just cooperative neighbors (not). Jones indicated he was not inclined to pursue the matter but noted that Jane had a trial coming up and, especially if she were convicted, her PO might force the issue. But, he told us, in a sort of friendly confidential way, that it was most likely that Jane would be the one who would be forced to leave.

I think he liked me, liked Sarah, liked the place, liked what we were trying to do. He didn't see me as a danger to society and would not be monitoring me all that closely. He had me sign a document called "Conditions of Supervision" with sixteen rules that I agreed to, of which I only actively violated four routinely:

• I shall not correspond nor associate with any ex-convict.

• I shall not indulge in the use of any intoxicating liquor or narcotic drugs.

• I shall make every effort to find and maintain gainful employment.

• I shall avoid evil associates and not frequent improper places of amusement. I shall respect and obey the law and at all times conduct myself as a good citizen.

Jones gave us permission to go to Philadelphia for Sarah's brother's bar mitzvah, but we could only be gone fourteen days and had to give him specific dates, which we hadn't really decided on yet. But we told him September 1–14, which seemed liked it would work.

After about an hour, he was ready to leave and asked me to ride with him to the gate. On our way out I showed him where we were planning to plant an orchard, the barn we were setting up for the pigs, and where the logging would be if we lost the lawsuit. He shook his head at the prospect of a skinned hillside where that raw and irreplaceable forest now looked down on us. It was almost like he was a friendly uncle paying a visit. When we got to the gate and I started to get out to open it, he held up his hand to stop me for a second.

He looked serious all of a sudden, "Can I give you one piece of advice?" he asked.

"Sure," I said and settled back into the passenger seat, expecting a longish conversation.

"Get a door," he said, not quite smiling. I was confused. Our house didn't even have walls, still in summer mode, with just a roof over our living area. We were a long way from a door.

"On the outhouse, on the hill across from the big house."

I couldn't help but laugh, though I tried to stifle it. "No, seriously," he said. "On our way in. I look up and see a pretty young woman just getting off the stool." He paused and looked pleadingly at me. "Seriously, that's not something people want to see, not something they should see. Not something I want to see."

"OK. Sure."

"A door. Before I come back. Really."

"OK."

He sort of motioned me out and I opened the gate for him and waved goodbye. From the pistol to the outhouse, not the sort of visit I was expecting.

The flow of visitors continued: Blivon and Falcon from Champaign-Urbana; Kenny from Boston who'd been with us at West Campus and then lived near Jeffrey on Dana Street; Timmy, my freshman year roommate, en route with three others in a van bound for South America, they said; my youngest sister Kim and her boyfriend and his little dog; a couple of Little Eddie's friends, who had played music with him in Miami or Boston or maybe in the fancy nut house before he escaped to Mountfort Street. People were on the road that summer and a destination in the mountains of Oregon was too good to pass up. They'd hang out for a couple of days or maybe a week. We'd smoke a lot of pot (if we had any), drink beer and alcohol if somebody showed up with some, swim in the ponds, and wax rhapsodic about how cool it all was. Then we'd take a picture and off they'd go to their next stop.

Matthew, a leader from BU, both in the student government and the Movement, showed up with his girlfriend Sylvia. They weren't really looking to stay but they did want to hang for a while as they figured out where they would go next. They didn't want to go back east. Matthew had always been solid and Sylvia was just as conscientious. They kept a low profile and made a point of helping out wherever they could.

One day two men and a woman from two communes near Grants Pass showed up, cool friendly people. I had written a letter to one of them a while back, from an address I got at the Renaissance Faire, and they had heard about our lawsuit to stop the logging and wanted to know more about it. Wayne and Jon told them where things stood with that. We also talked about how our respective communes tried to organize and get stuff done. Theirs had both been going longer than we had and had more cohesive group identities, hippie spiritual kind of stuff. It seemed to me like they had their shit more together than we did, but the stunning beauty of Ash Valley gave us kind of an unearned impressiveness and we had a ranch full of people—including me—with great bullshitting skills. They were clearly taken aback by how much pot we smoked. One afternoon, as yet another joint circulated among the people spread around the living room and kitchen of the Main House, and I went to pass it to one of the visiting communards, he looked at me almost desperately. "I've had enough," he said, "Don't I look like I've had enough?" That wasn't a concept that had much currency on the ranch.

SUMMER/9

Beneath all this hippie tourism and the story we could spin for outsiders, the ranch was flailing. Our ambitious work plan with crews and a schedule and clear tasks had evaporated in the acid and smoke of the 4th of July and the constant stream of visitors. We all kind of did our own thing and if our things overlapped that was cool, but that didn't happen much outside of supper, which Walter was still organizing and trying to maintain as a shared activity. Most of us showed up for that, except the Hammonds.

The cracks and divisions that had been developing just got deeper as collective activity waned. The Hammonds and Wayne and, now, Annie and Jon (and sometimes Sheila, depending on who she was sleeping with) had coalesced as a group—partly because they seemed less and less interested in the collective energy and vision the rest of us had, and we more and more didn't want to have anything to do with them.

Sydney and Jack were kind of their own faction, though they still connected more with the core Boston group. Walter tried to straddle the divide, partly because of his closeness to Jon. Jeffrey was in a similar position until Annie started hanging out with Wayne, which changed everything for him. Stephen tried to stay out of the ongoing drama but had contributed a lot to it by sleeping with Paulie and then Sheila, which had made a staunch enemy of Jon. Paulie and Mike, Stu, and Sarah and me were still pretty tight with each other and united in our resistance to the influence of Wayne and the Hammonds. Loretta, who had moved in with Stu, and Patrick and Rodger, who had moved into the cabin Dale had been staying in, were still trying to figure out just what the fuck was happening on this beautiful land but tended toward our side of things.

We couldn't entirely escape connections around the big common challenges we faced, mainly the lawsuit to save the trees and the need to raise the money for our balloon payment, the due date still nearly a year away but always on our mind. As things had developed, Wayne and Phillip had become our main representatives with the lawyers. Dale and Sydney had been part of that team, but he was lost and gone for now and she had been eased out of the conversations. Jon had also taken a keen interest since he had arrived. So, it was people who we didn't really trust who were taking the lead on that.

After the initial thrust around housing, when Wayne and Phillip were righteous contributors, they had less and less interest and involvement in common projects and seemed to gravitate toward things that took them off the land. We had to try to keep some lines of communication open around the lawsuit. Similarly with Wayne and his pot-selling scheme to raise the $20,000 we needed. We were happy to believe that could work and he was working with our money, but … He'd come back from his "business" trips with several ounces of great pot and a little spending money—which we were always happy to see—and that would mollify us for a while. But when the smoke cleared, his reports on his progress sounded increasingly like bullshit and our underlying mistrust just kept growing. We couldn't really afford to cut ties while he was still out there with our money.

One afternoon, a few of us were hanging around the Main House in the heat, reading and shooting the shit, and we saw little Greg come running up the road, looking like he was crying. He could barely catch his breath when he got to us, but we could tell from his tears and the frightened look on his face that something really bad had happened. "Billie … ," he finally blurted out. "My mom ran over Billie …On accident … He's dead, I think." Sarah hugged him tight.

Paulie and Walter just took off running up the road toward the Second House. The rest of us just looked around at each other in stunned silence. Billie was our little male goat, as cute as can be and sorta the foundation of the goat herd we had hoped to build. Our grown female goat Sheika had dried up and now Billie was gone. Our goat project just wasn't happening. Sarah and I put our arms around Greg between us and started slowly walking toward the Second House to try to see what we could do to help.

All this tension was further intensified by an outbreak of scabies—tiny bugs that get under your skin and itch like hell. Everybody got them, I think, except the Hammonds, which gave them even more reasons to avoid us. Scabies spread when people live close together and share bedding or towels or, mostly, by skin-to-skin contact. Not bathing regularly was another cause that applied to most of us. We'd swim a lot and splash Dr. Bonner's over us, but we rarely used hot water which had to be heated on a wood stove. People sleeping around a lot is the perfect way to pass around scabies. Not sure how Sarah and I got them since I wasn't sleeping around and I was pretty sure she wasn't or Little Eddie or Walter. But we were all—in other ways—on top of each other, especially in the early days. Scabies can take a month or more to develop.

At first, people thought it might be poison oak, but it didn't look like poison oak and, as it spread around, somebody looked it up and we decided it had to be scabies, something none of us had ever heard of before. The itching could drive you crazy and nothing seemed to help. I made a rare call (from the Tiller phone booth) home to wish my father a happy birthday and to beg him to send us something that might end our misery as well as any other medical supplies he could pull together. He told me about something called Kwell that was made specifically for scabies. I think he was pleased I had turned to him for help. Though I had regular correspondence with both him and my mother, I hadn't talked to them since my mother's birthday, right before we had moved on the land.

The scabies were eating away at Sarah and me as much as anybody. Even though we were firmly on the same side of the growing split on the ranch, I had a sense of a growing distance between us. Most days after we'd head up to the Main House in the morning, we'd go our separate ways. She'd go off to the horses with Loretta, Paulie, and Stephen or hang out around the Main House with Walter and Little Eddie.

I'd putter in the garden with Stu. We were between the busy seasons for the garden but there was always something to do. Or I'd try to help somebody fixing a vehicle—a constant activity. It seemed more and more, Sarah and I would go on different town trips with different people. In the evenings, we'd head home after supper with Moonbeam and have a quiet evening at our place, reading or sometimes playing a card game by the light of the kerosene lamp. We still made love with some regularity, but she never seemed as into it as I was and I could never really tell if I satisfied her. Sometimes it seemed like she was going through the motions out of a sense of obligation—

without the sort of passion we'd had before, when even if I was clumsy and fumbling, as I often was, I had no doubt that she was all there. She could be voracious in her sexual appetite once we got past the preliminaries. But we hadn't been there in a while.

We'd been on a long intense run since the trial. We'd immediately switched into preparations for the wedding and the trip to Oregon. And once we were in Tiller, the drive to find land and then to move to the ranch and then get the garden in and to make our house livable had propelled us with this potent sense of common purpose. Now, we were trying to figure out where we fit as individuals and as a couple into this anything-but-normal but still quotidian rhythm the ranch had fallen into. And with all the sexual escapades going on all around us, I couldn't help but wonder if Sarah might want to see what another man might do for her. Stephen?

I could see something in their exchanged looks that set off alarms. Or even Patrick, who she also seemed to take special notice of since he showed up. I had no real reason to suspect anything—except this pervasive feeling that I was somehow failing her.

SUMMER/10

I woke up early. Made a fire and coffee. It was another beautiful morning, blue, blue, blue as consistent as the gray of winter but so much more invigorating. I sat outside on our wood chopping stump, with Moonbeam loyally at my feet, and sipped the coffee, trying not to scratch the scabies patches that had been expanding across my chest. Stu and I were going to town later to see Earl about brake parts for the red truck. I was hoping the package from my father would be at the post office so we could begin to get some relief from these nasty little bugs.

Sarah was still sleeping soundly. I could hear her quiet, rumbling snores coming from the loft. She almost always slept later than me and I liked the peace of the morning time alone. Sometimes I wrote in my journal or tried to get caught up on letters. It was always easier to write in the daylight of the morning rather than by kerosene lamp at night. This morning I wrote a letter to my sister Carey, who was still living in Boston. Just as I was finishing, I heard Sarah stirring. I was kinda anxious to get going so we could do our town trip and get back with time to work on the brakes.

I went in and around to her side of the bed, stretching up to give her a kiss. "Good morning," I said with a smile.

She smiled back. "Good morning," she said. "You been up long? It looks like it."

"Yeah, hoping to get up to the Main House in not too long. Stu and I are going to see Earl. Want some coffee?"

"Mmm, not yet. In a bit."

I made myself busy. I filled up our water containers from the creek and split some wood to stack by the stove. I made Sarah a cup of coffee and set it on the ledge of the loft. She gave me a questioning look.

"It's getting cold," I said. "And I would like to get going soon."

"Fine," she said. "Just give me a little time to wake up."

I could have just gone myself. But we almost always walked up together unless one of us had a real early commitment which almost never happened. It wasn't like Stu and I were on any schedule. I was just ready to get going and it didn't seem like there was any reason why she couldn't go soon.

I walked past the ash trees back down to the creek. The day was warming but it was still chilly in the shade of the trees. The creek churned along, so fresh and clear. Trying to defuse my impatience, I watched it for a few minutes, picking up sticks from the bank and tossing them into the current, following them as they twisted and twirled downstream. I went back to the house, sure I'd given Sarah enough time for whatever she was doing, or at least enough to start to get it together.

She was still in the loft, sipping coffee. "Are you really going to be ready soon?" I asked through the opening where our front door would someday be.

"Yes, just relax." She was getting impatient with my impatience.

I poured myself a little more coffee and sat in the rocking chair, looking out toward the meadow. The sun had cleared the hills around us and gave a gloss to the grasses that were turning golden as the days since our last rain kept increasing. I picked up a *Harpers* magazine from the top of the dresser and started leafing through it. I could feel my foot tapping out an incessant rhythm that felt out of my control. I realized I had already read every article in that magazine. I tossed it back on the dresser and turned back toward Sarah. She was off the loft but was fiddling around with something in the storage area beneath it.

"Come on," I said, "Really, when are you going to be ready?"

She looked up at me, with an expression somewhere between disgust and pity and said, "Four minutes and thirty-seven seconds. Is that all right with you?"

I stared back at her. Then stood and grabbed the nearest thing, a small wooden dining room chair—something Sarah had bought at a secondhand store, one of only three places to sit in our house—raised it above my head and smashed it into the floor with all my might. The crash shook our tiny house as the chair splintered into a dozen pieces. Sarah, only four or five feet away, stared at me, still holding a last jagged piece of the chair in my hand, with a deep horror, like she had no idea who I was—and then left without a word. I, too, was stunned to silence and knew I shouldn't go after her.

After I watched Sarah disappear across the meadow and onto the road, I threw the last remaining shard of the chair in the opposite direction, beyond our toilet stool, toward the end of the meadow where we never went. Turned and stared at the shattered pieces scattered across the floor. Fell into the rocking chair, buried my head in my hands. I felt the same question that Sarah's look had shouted at me. "Who are you?"

I felt completely alone, like the ride in the paddy wagon after the cops had grabbed me at Northeastern. In an instant of violent rage, I had killed the world that existed up to that moment and couldn't imagine the world that would be there whenever I could face it again. At Northeastern, I was swept up in a violent scene and I could still find a way to see that act of violence as righteous. But this …? This was crazy and dangerous and scary—to me. What was Sarah thinking as she stormed away from me?

Where had that come from on a beautiful morning in our sweet little house by the singing creek?

Scared that I was losing Sarah, I gave her a reason to abandon me. Frustrated that I could not cut through the drama and the bullshit that was keeping Ash Valley from being what I wanted it to be, I became one of the crazies, creating drama in what had been—for all appearances—an island of stability.

Me? The mellow conciliator, the optimist, the let's-talk-this-through extremist with both Sarah and the group? What a fucking lie.

Was I going to fuck this up, too?—in our perfect little house, on our perfect piece of land, with the woman I loved and my best friends in the world. I'd learned to use tools and work hard with my body. We canned food, chopped wood, fixed wheel bearings, ate salads out of our garden and fresh eggs from our chickens. Why couldn't I be what I needed to be for Sarah to love me, to help make this place work.

How was I going to face Sarah? What would I say?

Later, I heard the rumble of a rig coming up the road. Man, I didn't want to see anybody. But it was the white truck with just Stu in it. Maybe I could handle that. He pulled over to the side of the road and climbed out. He was smiling a little grimly as he approached.

"Looks like I'm going to have to bail your ass out again," he said, "And don't ask me for a cigarette this time." Sarah and I had just quit smoking. It was Stu that had got me out of jail after my Boston arrest.

Fucking Stu, even in my deepest depths he could make me laugh. "I don't know, man," I said. "I think I might rather face the Boston courts than Sarah right now."

He raised his eyebrows and looked serious. "Yeah … what the fuck, man?"

"I don't know. I got crazy. A whole bunch of shit that has been fucking with my head all came pouring out at once … and I took it out on this poor chair." I looked back toward the house where the bits of chair were still spread out over the floor.

"Well, that's one way to make kindling," he said shaking his head. "Let's clean this up and then I'm under orders to take you to town to go see Earl. Sarah said that seemed to be real important to you."

I grimaced. "Shit. I sort of forgot about Earl and town." I shook my head. "Do you think she will ever forgive me?

"You're an even bigger idiot than I thought," he said really looking serious. "She's worried about you, but for some reason I don't really understand, I don't think she's quite ready to give up on you yet." That helped.

"But she's not quite ready to see you, so let's go see Dr. Earl. He can set you straight."

Earl was a great tonic. Of course, he had the brake shoes we needed. He rustled them out of one of his sheds. He found a bin with an assortment of blackened metal parts. He'd stare in there a bit and then reach in and pull one out and examine it, pulling it up close to his face. The first few he tossed back in. But then he found one that seemed right and ran his thick fingers along the edges.

"Yes, this one'll do the job," he said and handed it to Stu. He dug around some more and finally found a suitable mate.

"Yes, I think these will do the trick for you boys." He charged us $10 and then we sat in his living room for a while, drinking instant coffee and listening to stories about his son down in Tule Lake. He asked how things were going up on the ranch.

"That sure is one beautiful spread," he said. "You getting a good jump on firewood?" He asked. Earl had stacks of split and seasoned firewood covered with tin roofing all over his property. Stu and I looked at each other. It 'd been hot and dry for weeks.

"Well, we're getting a start on it," I lied. "I think we need to do some work on our chain saws."

"Now's the time," he said. "It could be a long winter up there."

We nodded and started wrapping up the visit. We could tell Earl was always glad when we came and he grounded us in real-life Oregon in ways we often lost track of at Ash Valley. I always left there feeling like I'd learned something I didn't know I didn't know, and his unconditional acceptance of us flailing kids left a deep warmth as we headed back upriver.

The package from my father was at the post office, almost grudgingly handed over by the postmaster, Mrs. Potter. She didn't like us and she made a point of letting us know that. The package had obviously been tampered with. I asked about why it seemed to have been opened.

"Nobody here opened it," she said, not looking at me. "Looks like it was pretty poorly packed to me."

It was no use arguing with her. She finally looked up to convey that she didn't give a shit that we knew that she opened our mail and I returned as hostile a look as I could muster. The important thing was, relief from the scabies was in hand.

We were greeted like heroes when I announced we had the Kwell, and everybody in the Main House crowded around as Little Eddie opened the first package and read the instructions—lots of warning about keeping it away from your mouth and eyes and using gloves when you apply it. This was heavy duty stuff. It got passed around the room like the best Colombian anybody'd ever seen. I stood away from the frenzy and sought Sarah's eyes. She looked back, switching from the amused observation of Kwell-mania to a sad and questioning look, not angry. I motioned with my head toward the door and she slightly nodded her understanding and we headed outside.

We walked to the ponds, exchanging awkward small talk about the package and Mrs. Potter and Earl. We sat on the bank and got silent for a while, both of us staring down. Finally, I looked up and took a deep breath,

"Sarah, I'm so sorry." She looked up, now full-on sad. "I don't know why I did that. I know I scared you. I scared me, too." It was really quiet, the gentle movement of water through the ponds and into the small creek along the edge of the meadow murmured louder than I ever remembered.

"I didn't know that I was that angry, that I had that kind of anger in me. It didn't have anything to do with when we were going to the Main House … obviously … Fuck."

She stared at me, deep questions and now some anger and tears mixing in her eyes. "I just feel out of control of everything … and maybe that was like the last thing I felt any control over at all … Fucking time … being on time when, shit, nobody even cares about time. Nobody here has a fucking watch. Why is that the thing that snapped me? Fucking time."

She just kept staring.

"But it can't really be that. Right? So … Been thinking all day about this, talked to Stu some. I'm scared … scared that I'm losing you, shit, that I may have already lost you." No reaction. "I feel this distance and with all this sexual triangle stuff." She looked pissed now. "I just feel like I don't know what's going on with us or how to make it better." Her expression didn't change. "And us going back to our house and feeling at least there everything wasn't constant chaos and drama. That no matter what, I had you to …"

"To what, Ben?" She was hurt and pissed and sad. And nothing I'd said had really helped.

"To keep each other sane, to talk through stuff … I don't know … to be together in this. I just haven't felt that for a while. And I know part of that is that I feel so helpless in trying to make this place work better. You and Stu and Stephen and Walter other people just have things that you're doing and can just kind of roll through all the drama. I feel useless and it freaks me out when I think I might lose you. Sometimes the way you look at Stephen scares me. Maybe I'm just being paranoid, probably, I hope …"

She shook her head, stared hard at me, now mostly angry, "Shit! Ben."

"I know, I know … It's not fair. I have no reason. I guess sometimes I think I wouldn't blame you … I'm sorry … carrying all this shit in my head and it just exploded today. I'm just so sorry. I love you so much."

It was quiet again. Her expression softened.

"Well, at least you said it out loud, maybe that will help you see how absurd it is. I'm not sleeping with anybody else," she said. "I'm not thinking of sleeping with anybody else. OK? It's ridiculous that I even have to say that to you. If I'm thinking about trying something different, you'll be the first to know. OK?" I didn't say anything but she wanted a response from me.

"OK?"

"OK. I'm sorry …" She cut me off.

"It's my turn, now … And I sense that same distance or whatever you want to call it. You get so intense, Ben, with me at least. Maybe this morning wasn't really about the time, but you get intense like that about so many things. Like sex, which is a major turnoff. It's like you're always trying to prove something—to me, to yourself, I don't know—and it's like you always want me to prove something to you. It's just too much. It wears me out. It makes it hard to be around you sometimes. Yes, it's insane here but when you get that intense, you're not helping anything. You make it worse … for me at least. I miss our quiet mellow together times in the evenings, too, but I think it's changed because you bring all the angst and intensity home with you instead of leaving it behind when we walk up the road."

She smiled, a kind and forgiving smile. "I love you. You know that. I want to be together with you on this, to get through the insanity and getting things going in a better direction. It will happen. This current situation with people so divided just can't go on much longer. You just have to relax, have faith in me—and Stu and Mike and Paulie and Jeffrey and Walter and Little Eddie and Stephen. Patrick and Loretta look like they will be good additions. Look around at this beautiful land and think of our cool little house. I know it will work out right but you've got to learn how to relax.

"You scared me this morning. I wasn't really afraid of you hurting me, but I saw all that intensity that I've seen building in you come out in a really scary way. And I won't put up with that. You've got to learn better ways to deal with that shit if you want to make things better between us."

I was staring at the ground, but when I sensed she was done, I raised my head slowly and looked into her eyes, now calm and open. "I know," I said. "I'll try."

She reached her hand out toward me and I took it in my mine.

SUMMER/11

The garden was thriving. We were eating early heads from the broccoli, getting the last of the radishes and the first planting of lettuce. Zucchini was coming on strong and tassels were forming on the corn. Even the tomatoes were starting to show hints of red. Willie Campbell got us a pregnant sow. He said she should have 10–15 piglets in about a month. Our plan was to raise those pigs, keep a sow and a boar for future breeding, slaughter one for its meat, and sell the rest to get a cash flow going. We had set up a stall in the goat barn with a fenced area on the lower level behind the barn for her and any other pigs to root around in. She was huge—something like 400 pounds, Willie told us—but kind of cute and she was definitely freaked when we dragged and pushed her from Willie's truck to her stall.

Paulie and Sarah hung around with her for a while, giving her treats and trying to help her get comfortable. We immediately named her Martha, after the wife of Attorney General John Mitchell, the chief pig in Nixon's world. I think it was Eddie's idea. After getting to know her a bit, though, I felt kind of bad for naming her for such an asshole.

Stu had to go to Portland to deal with the draft. Supposedly it was for induction. He'd passed his physical last winter, including the mental exam, despite taking LSD right before it. But after he'd received his "Greetings" notification to report for induction, he'd gotten that letter from the shrink in Eugene that Dougy had sent him to, saying he had that "group delinquent disorder," so we weren't that worried. We couldn't imagine him suddenly being put into a uniform and getting his hair buzzed and being shipped off to some training camp. We just knew one way or another, he just wouldn't fucking go.

We dropped him off at the freeway in Canyonville to hitch to Portland. Sarah, Paulie, Sydney, Jack, and I had gotten up at four in the morning to pick beans at a farm just outside of town. They charged just 8 cents a pound if we picked them ourselves. It was quite a scene, mostly little kids out there picking beans for the farmer—and our small band of freaks among them. One girl who was thirteen or fourteen told us she'd worked the day before from seven in the morning until two in the afternoon and made $3.15—less than 50 cents an hour. And it wasn't easy work. I'd made a dollar an hour detasseling corn in Illinois when I was fifteen, six years earlier, an equivalent kind of work.

It was close to seven by the time we started and we worked until noon when it started getting hot and we decided we had enough for the day. We had a good time and everybody worked hard. We couldn't screw around too much or smoke the joints Jack had brought, with the kids around us working so hard. Most of them went back to work after a quick lunch break, where they ate peanut butter and jelly or bologna sandwiches they'd brought in little brown paper bags. They weren't quite sure what to make of us but they were nice enough and even gave us a little advice on the best picking techniques. We ended up with 70 pounds, which somebody figured would make 30–40 canned quarts, a good start on a winter food stash.

We treated ourselves for our hard morning's work with an array of snacks from the Canyonville market: cheese, cookies, pickled sausages, Twinkies, chips, sodas, and a half-case of beer—which we started devouring, along with Jack's joints, as we headed upriver toward Tiller.

In the mail that we picked up at the Tiller Post Office was a letter from Luke. The letter was mostly about his upcoming visit, which he now planned for the middle of August, a couple of weeks away. He went into a lot of detail about the logistics of picking up his daughter Rita from her mother in the San Francisco Bay Area.

But mostly he was freaked out because I, somewhat offhandedly, mentioned in my last letter that there was no electricity at Ash Valley. He was planning on spending five hours a day writing a book and he had been using an electric typewriter for ten years. He said he would have been "so bummed out it would have been unbelievable" if he hadn't known about the lack of electricity before he came and had shown up with his typewriter ready to work. He was still freaking out about the challenges and was reaching for solutions—like somehow hooking his typewriter up to some kind of dry cell battery or hanging at some friend's house that had electricity.

We did have a generator, but we weren't going to run it five hours a day, so he could type. He did also mention the possibility of borrowing a manual typewriter, which seemed like the most sensible solution to me. It also occurred to him that no electricity meant limited lighting (kerosene lamps and candles) when it was dark outside—so he was concerned how his schedule could jibe with our work schedule. I had told him that we tried to do most of the heavy work, which he said he wanted to do, in the mornings, which would also be his optimum writing time. And an important part of his trip was to spend time with his daughter that would also impede on his ability to do what he might consider a fair share of the work.

I had to laugh. Stoned and tired while reading Luke's letter, I mused about what he thought about us and what we were doing. We were his fantasy of a commune in the country. His fantasy was based a lot on what he wanted it be, how he had imagined it in his last months in his prison cell. That was colored by what I wrote in my letters, in which I did want to impress him, to talk about the stuff I thought he cared about, and to sort of justify—for both him and me—Ash Valley in the context of the deeply political revolutionary reality he lived in. I don't think any of it was dishonest …just colored. If you took the letters Sarah wrote to her folks and compared them to what I wrote to Luke, you might have a hard time recognizing that they came from the same place. Or communications from anybody on the ranch to anybody outside.

We were all living in the Ash Valley of some odd combination of our individual dreams for it, our varied experiences of its day-to-day life, and our diverse expectations of where we were heading. And our friends and family outside the gate had never experienced anything like it—not the physical, natural setting, not the primitive living conditions, not the communal ethos—so their imaginations had to answer all the questions our communications raised for them.

How could Luke be so out of touch with our reality that he assumed we had electricity or that our work schedule was anything more than a rough framework of intention? He didn't really blame me for not telling him about the lack of power but he was clearly blown away that I had just casually mentioned it. It was going to be a trip for him to be on the ranch. I was a little leery and definitely feeling responsible for the intense sort of energy he was sure to bring, but mostly I was curious and kind of looking forward to seeing the effect he would have on us—and the effect we might have on him. For all his intensity—and undeniably strong ego—I did like and admire him.

Back at Ash Valley, we found out Stephen had left with Sundance in his black truck, with no indication of where he was going or when he might be back. In his usual taciturn way, he told Walter, who just happened to see him loading up his rig, he needed to get away and nothing more.

But two new people we had sort of been expecting had showed up: Brian and Sandra. It was particularly ironic to welcome Brian with Stephen leaving and Luke's letter still jostling around in my brain. Brian had buzzing East Coast energy and no manual skills and was at the opposite end of the countercultural spectrum from Luke.

We met Brian in our early days at Boston University and he ended up being a roommate with Mike and Stu and me at Mountfort Street for a while. He even had a date with Sarah before I'd met her. He was a year ahead of us but still lived in the dorms when we were freshmen and soon enough was part of our pot-smoking, LSD-taking, rock-and-roll loving tribe. He wasn't exactly apolitical. Like all of us, he was against the war and racism and capitalist greed and he'd been with us at Marsh Chapel in 1968 when we tried to create a sanctuary for a soldier who went AWOL in protest of the war. That was kind of a defining moment for that era at BU, though the soldier was dragged out of there one morning and taken off to some stockade and a dire future. The imagined power of the defiant community that formed and its actual powerlessness to protect that brave young man left deep impressions on a lot of us.

But Brian was more of a poet than an analytical or political thinker. And when politics got too personal—and specifically related to women's liberation—Brian recoiled. He thought of himself as a lady's man (in contrast to Stephen who didn't advertise it but seemed almost magnetically attractive to women). I'm glad somehow Sarah had slipped by Brian. When he lived at Mountfort Street, where our wall decor was mostly slogans and drawings our friends had scrawled on our white plaster walls, above the doorway to his bedroom he painted: "To ye virgins, make the most of time," a quote from some 17th century poem. Most women who visited our apartment laughed or raised their eyebrows when they saw that. But some seriously political women's liberationists got pissed and threatened to conduct a guerrilla raid to paint over our walls.

They never did that but Brian's defensiveness about that issue was a constant theme in our frequent political discussion—especially as women's liberation moved from the fringes of the Movement to become more and more a central part of it. And that drove him further and further from the political stuff that Mike and I, especially, were into.

Sarah and I had met Sandra when we were in Boston waiting for the trial. It was hard to get a sense of her because Brian had such a dominant personality. He tended to fill any vacant spaces in a conversation and she didn't seem the type to compete with him. I think she was a bit younger than us and had an open smile and curly brown hair that dangled around her shoulders. She was about the same height as Brian, who was shorter than all of us, except Walter. He had very long hair when we first met him but had cut it off during one of his many bad acid trips. Now it was long again and he wore it in a thin pony tail.

It surprised me that they had come with the intention to stay. I thought Brian was one of the many who would talk about joining us but never would. He was a real East Coast city guy from my perspective, grew up in New Jersey and never really seemed enthusiastic when Stu and I fantasized long ago about getting some land, moving to the country and getting our hands dirty. But here he was. I liked him despite all the ways he could annoy me. He told great stories. He was funny. He was, really, a fine poet. And I'll always be grateful to him for helping Stu get me out of jail and having a cigarette for me.

But what was he expecting from Ash Valley? Hard to imagine.

SUMMER/12

Stu returned, undrafted. Of course. He got a ride all the way from Days Creek with Russ, who had been our neighbor when we were in the Red House. They brought a couple of six-packs and it didn't take much to get everyone who was anywhere near the Main House to stop what they doing and join in a midday celebration. Stu was happy and surprised to see Brian and Sandra. Stu and Brian got along great when we were all roommates at Mountfort Street, often standing up together against Mike and me when we got too political for them.

When everyone had gathered, Stu told us what had happened at the induction center. "They put a bunch of us in this big blank room, fifty or sixty of us in a warehouse kind of place, and told everybody to take their clothes off. I looked around and everybody was doing it. Some looked a little freaked out, but they started doing it anyway. And I thought, 'what the fuck, I'm not doing it.' And I didn't. I just stood there. Some of the other guys were looking at me, like they were wondering why I didn't have to do it. The army guy up front just kept looking at me. I just stood there. Finally when everybody else was naked and I still had on all my clothes, he pointed at me and told me to report to this other room.

"When I got there, there's one guy sitting behind a desk and he told me to sit down. As I did, I handed him the letter I got from Dougy's shrink. While he was reading it, I decided I didn't want to sit, so I stood up and just started pacing, back and forth, back and forth, in this small office. When he finished reading the letter, he looked up at me and I was still pacing. He didn't say anything for a minute or two. Finally, he said, 'OK. I tell you what I am going to do, Mr. Martin, I'm going to classify you 1y, which means we are going to delay your induction for a year, with the hope, that something will change in your, ummm … ' He paused for a minute, like he couldn't quite think of the right word. I was still pacing, but watching him closely. ' … Your condition,' he said. He asked me if I understood, like my 'condition' made it hard for me to grasp what he was saying. I said. 'Yeah. Does that mean I can go now.' And he said I could.

"I couldn't fucking believe it. It was too easy. But man it felt so good walking out of that place totally free to the blue sky and sunshine. I felt bad for all the guys back in that room … but I couldn't do anything to help them. Now you assholes are stuck with me."

It was a drag that the army was still drafting kids for a war we all knew was both wrong and doomed to failure. But submitting to the draft, joining the army, being part of an immoral and pointless war (for Americans) didn't make any sense if you could avoid it. What about the kids who got sent in place of those of us who resisted or refused—one way or another? Man, we didn't want anybody to go. Us going too wouldn't help anybody.

From the time I had first gotten involved in the anti-war movement, fighting the draft, trying to stop the government from forcing kids into the army and the war, was a central part of it for me: doing draft counseling, helping kids understand their legal rights *and* illegal or creative ways to beat the draft. I understood why some chose not to fight the draft and go … whether it was out of fear of the consequences or a sense of duty. And it was absolutely wrong that it was easier for rich kids to get out, which it definitely was. But if you believed the war was fundamentally wrong and were willing to fight to stop it, it seemed to me, then not going, by any means necessary, was the right thing to do, even if fear was part of that decision.

I was safe from the draft now that I had two felony convictions, but I certainly hadn't planned that.

The egg production from our chickens had dropped off dramatically. Instead of close to two dozen every day, we were getting less than a dozen, which didn't go far among the more than twenty-four people who were on the land. We asked folks like Earl and Willie and others who raised chickens what the problem might be and got a few answers. The most common reason that chickens stop laying eggs is age. Their production dwindles as they get older and eventually stops. We didn't really know how old most of our chickens were. They'd come from a variety of sources. The initial batch came from Phillip and Jane. Some they had raised from chicks, so they'd still be reasonably young. But others had been given to them—and that's how we got the rest of our flock, too. There was a good chance that many of those were past their prime laying years. The other reason was stress caused by overcrowding. We just kept adding any chickens anybody would give us and now realized that the coop and its yard weren't big enough to handle them all. So, after some discussion, we decided to do a culling to get rid of the hens who weren't laying to make more room for the ones who were.

When we assigned duties, somehow I ended up being assigned to be the executioner, to wring the necks and chop off the heads. Stu and Paulie were charged with catching the chickens to take to Sarah and Mike, who were the judges. We'd found an article in *Mother Earth News* that had a list of ways to tell if a hen had stopped laying, things like whether the comb was rich or pale in color and whether the abdomen was soft and supple rather than tight and hard. We had blocked off part of the yard around the coop. Patrick's job was to put the exonerated chickens in that area and Jack would bring the condemned chickens to me and the chopping block. Walter, Sydney, and Loretta would dip the dead chickens in a pot of boiling water and pluck them. Eddie and Jeffrey had some pressing reason why they had to be in town that day. Brian and Sandra were a little too new to country living to get into the process but they hung around to offer moral support. Wayne, Annie, Jon, Sheila, and the Hammonds made it clear that they wanted nothing to do with it.

I'm not sure how I ended up with the worst job. People jumped in to volunteer for the other jobs. I really didn't want to be one of the judges—and Mike and Sarah were perfect for that: clear criteria, yes or no. And plucking seemed terribly tedious and foul in a drawn out way compared to what I imagined was the quick gruesomeness of the execution. And I guess I was still trying to prove—to myself? To others?—that I could handle the full gamut of this self-sufficient country life, despite, in this case, my lifelong aversion to blood, probably initially implanted by my father's sometimes graphic dinner-time stories of the surgeries he'd performed or the occasional slide from some bloody operation that would appear in the midst of the myriad sunset shots he took on trips to northern New England with my mother.

I'd killed things before, but just like bugs or fish. I might have killed a rabbit driving when I was a teenager. My girlfriend and I were driving next to a park when a rabbit ran in front of the car. I tried to swerve but we heard a thump underneath us. My girlfriend wanted me to stop—but what were we going to do? If that thump was the rabbit then it was pretty definitely dead. Did she want to try to save it … or bury it? I kept going. She was pissed at me for a while after that.

But this was hands-on mass killing. When Jack tried to hand me the first victim, she was squirming so much I couldn't hold her and she got loose and we, with help from Sydney and Loretta, had to chase her down again. This time, Jack steadied her while I squeezed her tight with my left arm and grabbed her by the throat with my right hand. He let go and I raised her in the air and whipped her around like a cowboy readying a lasso. I could feel her neck snap but I kept spinning, wanting to make sure she was dead. When I stopped, I lowered her and grabbed her feet in my left hand and kind of flipped her across the chopping block, a thick round of Douglas fir. But she was still squirming so I moved my left hand to the center of her back to hold her down.

Her body was startlingly warm. Her head was limp and her neck stretched out. I took the hatchet up and swung down hard. It landed and sliced the neck but didn't quite sever the head, so then I did it again—and then again to be sure. The head fell off the block and I let off the pressure on her body—and all that remained of her rolled off the block. Then … the fucking chicken with its head cut off was running maniacally around the front yard—just like in the cartoons— blood dripping from its neck. Jack was laughing at the antics of the dead chicken and at my clumsy attempt at slaughter.

Finally I caught her and hoisted her by the legs and passed her to Sydney who gave me a sympathetic smile and dipped her remains into the pot of boiling water.

Jack was still laughing when he went back to the chicken yard to get the next one. I was shaken and still actually shaking. It wasn't as straightforward as it sounded: wring the neck, chop it off. With my bare still-soft city hands, I was taking the life out of a being that was not really ready to die and it resisted with whatever means it could. Willie or Earl, real Oregonians, could do that like they were chopping wood or bucking hay. I felt a little kick in my gut and a sting in my soul with every one. But I was determined not to give in to that.

I killed twenty chickens that day. I got better at it, snapping the neck more efficiently, holding the feet while I swung the hatchet, to keep the headless chicken from gallivanting off, making sure my blow was hard and true. I never stopped being clumsy or queasy, but I saw the job through.

The worst part of this day that would come to be known as Bloody Tuesday was this: The reward we planned for all of us was to have a chicken barbecue feast. By the time we were done, it was hot in the afternoon and we built up the fire in the pit in front of the Main House where we'd been boiling water to get the dead chickens ready to pluck. Sarah butchered three of the chickens into pieces and we set them on the grate over the flames. Eddie and Jeffrey had brought back a case of beer, maybe to assuage their guilt for copping out on the chicken culling. We had worked ourselves into a festive mood, though I was still shell-shocked as we knocked down the beers and reveled in the smell of roasting flesh.

But the chicken was inedible, too tough to chew no matter how determined we were for it to be this longed-for taste treat. With Stephen gone and the Hammonds off in their own world, there was no one there to remind us that chickens too old to lay eggs were too old to barbecue. We took little solace when Walter and Sarah told us these old withered hens might work all right in a soup or stew.

The day after the chicken massacre the ranch was eerily quiet. I felt sort of hungover, not from the party—there wasn't enough beer to cause that—but from the blood on my hands. When I had tried to sleep, I kept seeing severed chicken heads flying off the chopping block or headless chickens eluding the outstretched arms of the front yard posse trying to capture them for the plucking pot. It was a troubled and fitful night.

Sarah and I lingered quietly around our house long into the morning, drinking coffee and reading. We eventually decided to try to do something productive and walked a little ways down the road to sort through the scrap pile across from the Second House to find boards to fill in the walls of our house. The open-air design—nothing between the eight upright poles that defined the shape of our house and the border between interior and exterior—was wonderful for the summer but we would need real walls as the days got colder. Our plan was to use 1-inch scrap wood—of which there was still a plentiful supply in piles all over the ranch—horizontally between the poles. We'd cover that with tar paper, and then use bark slabs— the outer layer sliced from logs to make them square in the milling process—running vertically as our siding. Bark slabs, essentially waste in the process of turning logs into lumber, could be had cheap from mills around Roseburg or Medford.

Cold weather was still off a ways, but getting our house closed in was one of the things on our list that we hadn't done much about, so this could be kind of a token start, and a good semi-mindless task for the day after a slaughter.

We dug through the scrap pile for maybe an hour, found about twenty decent boards out of the 140 or so we'd need. We stacked them off to the side to haul to our house in a truck sometime later. We agreed that was a sufficient accomplishment for this hot, sluggish day and that we deserved a swim.

We went straight to the ponds, not stopping at the Main House. From the road I could see the remains from the work for the day before: the bloodied chopping block, the charred grate above the firepit, vestiges of feathers scattered around the yard. Whether it was real or an imaginary memory, I swear I smelled the moist dank odor of boiled feathers and the thick sticky stench of drying blood. I didn't even want to walk by that scene.

Nobody was at the pond. We shed our clothes and I dove in. Sarah eased in from the bank. The summer had warmed the water, which had been startlingly cold for our first spring swims, but it still offered a deep refreshment. Sarah was more of a wader than a swimmer and avoided getting her hair wet, but I could tell it felt good for her, too, as she splashed the water up over her chest and gingerly dipped her face, holding her hair up out of the water. She looked good. Nakedness was so routine at Ash Valley that it had lost some of its erotic power, but just the two of us alone in the sultry afternoon air was different from the usual workaday nudity.

I swam across the pond, remembering most of the crawl stroke I had learned on the beaches of Buzzard's Bay. This was tamer water in a wilder place but I still felt the rush of gliding through wonderful wetness. From the far end of the pond, I waved to Sarah, who was just kind of lolling in the water not far from the bank. She smiled as she waved back. She looked really good. Just as I started my swim back to her, I saw her climb out of the water.

When I got out, she was lying on the water bed, still naked, beads of water sparkling all over her. I smiled big at her and she could tell what was on my mind. She smiled back in that way she had … acknowledging the obvious but not necessarily assenting to it.

Since the chair incident, we'd been getting along really well. In a shitty and inexcusable way, I had broken the dam that was backing up all the doubts and paranoid fantasies that were polluting my head. Her stern forgiveness had pushed me toward the absolute trust she deserved and a real effort to learn to be honest about my feelings, a deep challenge for me—and reminded me why I loved her so much. Her frankness, her uncalculated honesty, and her mind-blowing loyalty were, in some ways, frightening to me. I couldn't match her, and deep down, I still struggled to believe that she could love me—and when I started reveling in self-doubt, a part of me had to doubt her, too, as though the only way I could feel less unworthy was to imagine, to create a reality, where she was just as—or more—unworthy as I was. But when she forgave me at the same time she challenged me—because she did see something in me that was worthy of her love—it made me want to try harder to feel worthy, to become worthy.

I lay down next to her, as the water bed rippled under my weight. She was flat on her back. I was on my side not quite touching her. She was almost dry and I was still soaking wet. I reached my arm across her to embrace her opposite shoulder. She smiled, more open now, then turned her head toward the Main House, as if to gauge just how alone we were. There was no one in sight. It was almost absolutely quiet, the only sounds the faint trickle of the nearby creek and a whispering breeze through the trees surrounding us. Maybe a bunch of people had gone to town, or maybe everyone was just mellowing out like us. I didn't care. I was thrilled to have this time in this place with just Sarah.

She rolled to her side, now directly facing me, and we kissed, long, slow, extra wet. That first kiss, the opening kiss, the entry kiss into the otherworld of intimacy always sent pulses of jubilant charged energy through every channel of my body, making every nerve sing, ready to dance. We drew in tight to each other, my wet mingling with her dry, and eased into making love in the open-air sunshine on our little island of near privacy on this ranch full of people. The water bed rolled with us until our motion raced ahead of its rhythm and it became almost a counterpoint, slapping our joined body on the downbeat and leaving us without support as we rose. In the midst of the heights of our passion, we laughed and awkwardly tried to adjust. As we finished, our laughter and overpowering satisfaction combined as we held each other tight and kissed softly as the water bed slowly calmed.

"I love you," I said.

"I love you," she said.

We drifted off to something like a nap as the sun slinked down over the western hills behind us. We were startled to wakefulness by a commotion at the Main House. We heard the raised voices of Walter and Stu and agitated yelping from some dogs. As we rose and stared in that direction we saw Moonbeam trotting across the meadow toward us. When she got close, we saw some things sticking out of her face, which we quickly recognized as porcupine quills. She looked at us, pleadingly. We couldn't help but laugh at first, but realized it was not funny for Moonbeam, as she futilely threw her nose about and made motions toward rubbing it into the ground, but quickly realized that only made it worse. We pulled on our scant clothes and led her to the Main House, where we could join forces with the other dog owners and maybe find some pliers for the extrication process.

Stu's big white dog Winter had the most quills, thick across his face and extending down his neck to his upper chest. I couldn't imagine how he had gotten them there, but Winter, as lovable as he was, was kind of dumb. That was surprising because his sister Moonbeam was the smartest dog I ever knew. She was intense, the clear leader of the Ash Valley pack, and ferociously loyal. Stu had them both for a while but then gave Moonbeam to us as a wedding present even before we got to Oregon. It said something about him that he chose the big all-white lovable lug over his sleek and smarter German Shepherd-colored sister.

Abby, Walter's dog, who was also pretty smart, had about the same array as Moonbeam, a half dozen or so on her snout.

So our first focus was on Winter. Walter and I tried to hold him still while Stu gripped each quill with the pliers as close to the skin as possible and tried to yank it out quickly, causing as little pain as possible. Pain was inevitable because the quills were barbed so they ripped the skin on the way out. Sarah and

Paulie—Quinnman had not joined the others on their run into the woods—tried to cover Winter's eyes and talked softly to try to calm him down. He was strong and freaked out. Keeping him still was a challenge. As sweet as he was, he couldn't help but struggle against our restraint and snap at Stu as he yanked the quills out.

It was an arduous process to get all the quills out of those three dogs. When Walter pulled the last one out of Abby, who went last because she seemed to be the least freaked out, we all just kind of collapsed in the front yard, where no one had bothered cleaning up the vestiges of the chicken slaughter of the day before. Little Eddie brought out a joint. I inhaled desperately when it came around to me. Blood and death and love and pain, lazy carefree moments and unavoidable hard shit thrusting itself in our face. What a life this was.

SUMMER/13

The simmering insanity boiled over. And it didn't take much to raise the temperature those last few degrees. Most everybody was hanging at the Main House, drinking coffee and rustling up something for breakfast, when Mike came in and asked if anybody was heading into town or if there was a rig that he and Paulie could use.

I told him the red truck was running OK and they could use that, but, from across the room, Jon felt it necessary to say to Wayne, just loud enough for everyone to hear, "They sure as hell can't use my bus."

Mike had turned toward me to acknowledge my offer, but quickly shifted his look toward Jon. "Did I ask you anything, man? Fuck you and your stupid bus."

"At least my stupid bus runs reliably because I don't let people like you use it."

"People like me? People like me?" Mike scanned the room with a questioning look. "What the fuck does that mean?"

"People who don't take care of anything. People who don't respect other people and their things."

"Well, I sure as hell don't respect you and fuck your things, man. You're right, I don't respect your things. You show up with your moving van and your money and you think that makes you a brother." Mike pointed a finger at Jon and took a couple of steps toward him. "Well, you ain't my brother, man, and you never will be."

"I feel exactly the same about you," said Jon, sort of straightening himself up in the chair where he sat.

The whole room was tense. Wayne stood up, sort of easing himself in position to block the path between Mike and Jon. "C'mon you two," Wayne said. "Is this really about a trip to town?" Mike stopped and leaned back against the kitchen counter, shaking his head.

"It's bullshit, man," I said, turning to look at Jon from the bench by the table, "you're only partway in. You've always been only partway in. Sarah and I have put every cent we have into this place and so have Mike and Paulie and Stu, most everybody else, I think—some people didn't have much, but they put in what they could. We all know you've got a pretty healthy money stash that could help a lot, but …"

"My money is my money," Jon said, staring back at me. "I've put money in. I've given money to the lawyers for the tree suit, but I didn't come here to support people like Mike."

"Then you aren't really here, are you?" Paulie said. She was standing near the fireplace. "Either you are all in or you should just leave. We don't need that kind of energy."

Annie stood up from the floor next to Wayne and moved toward Paulie, with her arms outstretched, sort of like she was going to give her a hug. "Ah, you don't really mean …" she started to say when Paulie threw a mild punch into the side of her face, sort of a closed fist slap.

"Get the fuck away from me," Paulie said. Everybody gasped. Annie withdrew with a horrified look on her face.

"Hey, come on, what is this?" Phillip said. "You people are out of control, man. Lighten up."

"Us people?" Sarah said. "You mean the people who do most of the work, have put up most of the money, are trying to figure out ways to make this work together rather than doing our own thing and hoarding money and stuff?"

"I mean you people who are so fucking intense about almost everything," Phillip responded. "You're always up into everybody else's trip. She fucking just threw a punch, man. It's a fucking bummer, man."

Jane was smiling through all of this. "We just all need to mellow out a little bit," she said. "Take some breaths. We're all trying to live together in love and sometimes that gets a little hard. Relax. Smile. Love your neighbors." She beamed as she looked around the room. Sarah and I looked at each other, dumbfounded by Jane's willful blindness. But her rap was so out of kilter with what was really happening in that room that it shut down the exchange.

Phillip got up and left, with Jon, Sheila, Annie, and Jane, still smiling, not far behind. Wayne lingered a while and asked if anybody needed any help working on their houses. It'd been a long times since he'd done anything like that, made himself available for the common good—aside from whatever it was he was doing when he was out supposedly raising money for our balloon payment. His query was met with silence. Since his prolonged absences and the thing with him and Annie, none of us really trusted him anymore. And his clumsily transparent effort to weasel his way back into the good graces of those of us on the other side of the ever more obvious split wasn't going to help him.

"Cool," he said to the roomful of hostile faces, as he headed out the door. "Catch you later."

It was quiet for a minute after the door shut. Then Stu said, "Well, that went well." And the lingering tension was released by a round of laughter.

"Fuckin' Paulie," said Eddie, in amazement. "That was quite a punch. You've been hanging around Mike too much."

Paulie had a sheepish look as though she couldn't even quite believe what she had done. "I'm glad that happened," Mike said. "It was going to happen sometime. Might as well get it over with so the people who really want to be here can start getting it together without those assholes."

"Something got broken there," Walter said, with a touch of melancholy. "Breaking don't necessarily mean fixing." Walter still had some loyalties to Jon, but it was increasingly clear that Jon had picked the other side in this dispute, the side of the Californians who were latecomers to the dreams of the Boston core. Jeffrey was in much the same position, but was less sympathetic to Jon since he started cozying up to Wayne, who Jeffrey would never forgive for what happened with Annie.

"And Wayne's still got our money," Stu said. "How does this play out?"

"Do you think they might want to split the land up—them on part, us on part?" Jack asked. Sydney shook her head.

"That's not going to happen," Sarah said. "Look, there's a lot more of us than them. Can you imagine how terrible that would be?"

"But what if Wayne somehow comes up with money," Jack asked. "I mean, they could try to kick *us* off."

"Fuck that," Mike said. "He's not going to get the money. He's just fucking around out there. We've got to get our money back and kick him and all of them the fuck off."

"It's just that easy," Stu said, kind of laughing, kind of not. That's where things got left. Our newcomers Brian and Sandra and our visitors Matthew and Sylvia were blown away by the whole discussion, such ugly shit in such a beautiful place.

SUMMER/14

Sarah and I took the Karmann Ghia to Eugene for a major shopping trip to pick up Luke and his not-quite-five-year-old daughter Rita, who had flown up from the San Francisco Bay Area, where Rita lived with her mother. It was great to see Luke. He looked healthy and seemed relaxed.

We had a good time eating steaks and drinking wine with Dougy and Jill the night they arrived. Luke doted on Rita. He'd been away for two years, as she turned from a barely verbal toddler into an alert and engaging little girl. I'd never really spent personal time with Luke. It was always and only at political meetings and demonstrations, with him in a leading role. Our correspondence did slip into personal areas but it was more about our personal connections to bigger things like the Movement and the Revolution. It was cool to see him just reveling in his freedom and digging being a dad.

As we went through the gate onto the ranch the next morning, I looked toward Luke in the back seat. I saw the same amazed gaze that most newcomers showed when they first saw the sudden openness of the valley and the dense green steepness of the hills rising above it. I could only imagine how this vista compared to the images he had conjured in his prison cell. I envied him that rush of possibility, like the one I had known when I first saw the gray-green mysteriousness of this place four months earlier. I hadn't been off the land in a while, and now, coming back to it, I was struck by how brown and dusty the valley had become. The long string of dry hot days had transformed its hue and light and texture. It was still breathtaking and welcoming to me, but the stark clarity of the view from the entrance came as a shock.

Luke and Rita were greeted warmly when we got to the Main House. Some people had no idea he was a big-time revolutionary back in Boston. And those who did, who might have been intimidated by the thought of him coming to the ranch, seemed put at ease by how mellow he seemed and how focused he was on Rita. Eddie was gone, visiting his parents in Miami, so Luke and Rita took his room on the upper level of the tower annex.

They went to bed pretty early, and Sarah and I were filled in on what had happened since we left the morning after the big blowup. Nothing much had changed in the dynamics between the two sides of the split, Mike told us. But our side had resolved to push forward with the positive energy toward creating the ranch we envisioned through truly communal social and work structures and to let the negative people who refused to join that vision organically purge themselves. We'd stop trying to force them to be part of our trip but, for the time being, allow them to live among us. A sort of containment—less stress and more energy to focus on the garden, our houses, our collective education, getting ready for winter.

Luke had come with big plans for working on his book as well as getting to know Rita again and joining in on communal work. I don't know if he got much writing done (on his manual typewriter) that first morning, but the two of them showed up for breakfast kind of late. They had quickly bonded with Brian and Sandra, who lived in the lower level of the tower annex. Sandra had immediately connected with Rita but even Brian and Luke seemed to hit it off, an odd couple for sure. Both had lived in New Jersey at some point and found common ground talking about that. Luke seemed intent on being relaxed and getting to know people rather than pushing anything political. He and Rita came out to the garden for a while to help us turn over a couple of rows where our spring lettuce had bolted and we were going to plant some fall lettuce. Rita had fun alternating between running around and hanging with Luke as he earnestly wielded a shovel into the still moist and loose soil. The creek running down from the ponds had diminished significantly but maintained a sufficient flow to keep water on the garden. Rita played in the rows behind Luke, sifting through the just-turned soil with her little hands. She got excited when a big juicy worm squirmed out of the dirt. "Look Daddy," she shouted excitedly as she tried to pick it up.

"Oh, no, honey, don't." Luke freaked out a bit. He was a city guy through and through. The rest of us laughed. He looked up and around at us with a smile and then bent over toward Rita and helped her gather up the worm. She gingerly touched it and smiled at her dad.

"We love worms in the garden," Stu said toward Rita. "They help keep the dirt nice and loose so it's easy for the plants to grow." Luke dropped the worm back into the soil. Rita continued to watch it intently.

After lunch, Luke fulfilled one of his prison dreams, stretching out on a blanket and laying naked in the hot afternoon sun. He had taken a few hits off a joint. Like most visitors, he was amazed by the amount of pot we consumed and started declining hits the fourth or fifth time a joint came around. But he was good and stoned and he lay in the sun with a beatific smile on his face.

It was Sandra who noticed first that his skin that had been pale when we went out to the garden in the morning was turning red. She broke his trance and suggested he go inside.

He was sunburned all over and it didn't take long before the pain set in and became overwhelming. Somebody suggested a jump into the pond. The sun was still powerful and centered over the valley, so he covered up and with Rita, Sandra, Sarah, and me walking with him, made the short trek and dove in. He got some quick relief but the water wasn't very cold and the sun was inescapable. Back inside, a few of us squeezed the juice from the leaves of one of our aloe vera plants growing in pots on the porch and tried to spread it on his burns. But his body was big and the yield from the leaves was slight.

Luke's orientation to Ash Valley was further complicated by a bad case of the runs—from some bad water? Or the radical shift in diet?—which kept him close to the Main House and its outhouse. I don't imagine he got much writing done and he wasn't available for ranch work, though there wasn't a whole lot of that going on in the hottest days of the summer. Some of us were plugging away at getting our houses ready for fall and winter. Sarah and I were slowly creating walls by putting up the scrap boards between the exterior upright posts. We started on the backside facing the trees on the creek bank, leaving our view onto the meadow as open as possible as long as we could. Stu could always find things to do in the garden. Walter and Mike kept their focus on preparing meals and making bread, with help from others.

The Main House continued to be the central meeting place for all but the Hammonds, who more and more kept to themselves at the Second House. Wayne, Annie, Tammy, Jon, and Sheila lived in the Main House, so some interaction was inevitable. Walter and Brian and Sandra straddled the divide, maintaining an almost cordial relationship—and everybody went out of their way to be nice to Rita, and, to some extent, Luke, though I think Wayne and Jon were intimidated by both his physical stature and his reputation as an ex-con revolutionary. We all loved Tammy so we tried to avoid direct confrontations with Wayne when she was around. But the unnegotiated ad hoc truce was awkward, so the times when the opposing sides mixed was limited mostly to meal times and a few chance encounters during the day.

There was little opportunity for the full-on community discussion about the "Ranch and the Revolution" that I had anticipated, hoped for, during Luke's visit. One day, when Luke was beginning to feel better, most of our folks were gathered at the pond, Rita having fun splashing in the water with a few of the women. Mike, Matthew—who had known Luke in the Movement in Boston—Luke, Brian, and I, watching them from the bank, had a chance for a bit of a rap.

"So what do you think of our crazy hippie commune?" I asked Luke, a question I'd been wanting to ask for days.

"Oh, man," Luke answered with a gentle smile, "What a beautiful place. And I love you guys—and Sarah and Paulie and Sandra and Patrick and, of course, Stu. Stu is great. And Loretta. You know, the good guys." He looked around and took a deep breath. "You all have been so kind to Rita and me and that's really what I've realized is most important to me." His expression got serious. "But, man, the internal contradictions here are so intense. With Jon and Sheila and Wayne and Annie." He hadn't seen much of the Hammonds, but he knew they were on the other side. "Shit, man, this is, on a much smaller scale, of course, like SDS a couple of years ago.

There's no way for you to do any of the stuff you really want until you figure out how to deal with that, the enemy within."

"Right on, man," Mike said. "We've got to get rid of them." Everybody nodded. "Yeah, I know that's not going to be easy." Luke went on. "I gotta say, from prison, writing to Ben, I underestimated the challenges you all face. Shit, I underestimated the challenges we all face trying to build some kind of realistic revolutionary movement among White kids. Just getting our shit together, man."

Maybe for the first time ever, I saw an expression that showed more questions than answers on Luke's face.

He scanned our little group, the girls playing in the water, and leaned backed with his palms flat to the ground, looked up into the forest rising behind the ponds. "I don't know, man," he said bringing his gaze back to me. "This place could be an escape, a bunch of White freaks smoking dope and talking bullshit," he smiled as we all chuckled. "Or it could be some kind of revolutionary outpost, where we learn about living in noncapitalist, nonsexist, nonracist ways and provide critical support to the battle in the cities against the pigs. I don't know. I don't even know what's possible now. But I know right now, with my sunburn healing and the shits gone, I'm glad to be here with my daughter and you all. Maybe we'll figure out the rest somewhere down the road."

Luke relaxed as the days went on, sort of adapting to the flow of the ranch. He led a couple of yoga sessions in the front yard of the Main House, with Rita, Sandra, Paulie, Walter, me, and various others. Luke looked good up in front of us. His skin still had some of the scabs from his burn but the color had turned to a mellow bronze and he was lean and strong from his prison workout regimen. You could sense that Brian, who nervously sipped coffee as he watched us from the porch, was getting increasingly uncomfortable with a bond that seemed to be growing between Luke and Sandra, mostly around Sandra's instant affection toward Rita. Annie and Sheila sort of lingered as they passed on their way down to the Second House, which had become the headquarters of their faction, tempted to join in but knowing that would be seen as a betrayal of their menfolk. They had fallen in step with Jane's version of the good hippie wife, deferring to the strength and wisdom of their men.

Luke also taught Rita to shoot with our .22 rifle at a makeshift target range behind the Main House. We set up beer cans on a stump and a few of us joined in. Big Luke surrounded his little daughter from the back and curled his finger over hers on the trigger. After a couple of wild shots, they knocked the can off the stump and we all cheered. Luke looked proud. Rita looked around at all of us, smiling but a little dazed, too. This country life was full of surprises for a city kid. Some of us Ash Valley folk believed we all needed to learn how to shoot—for hunting, most immediately, but also in some vague future, maybe for self-defense and maybe even in our Revolution to come. Even Sarah got into the target practice, though for her it was more about the competitive challenge than any sort of training. We also had a 30.06 (which had killed the White House's TV) and Stephen's 12-gauge shotgun.

Luke, Mike, and I had a few chances to talk about the political situation in the outside world. Luke seemed to have cut off connections to what remained of the Weathermen, who were now mostly underground. His focus, he said, when he got back east would be on organizing prisoners, a natural enough next step for someone fresh out. Because of drug busts, political arrests, and the growing number of pissed off Vietnam vets who were ending up in prison, some small cracks were opening in the once impenetrable racist barrier between Black and White prisoners.

Revolutionary consciousness among Black prisoners was high, fueled by the stuff that had gone down at Soledad and San Quentin prisons in California first brought to light by George Jackson's truth-telling book, *Soledad Brother.* Black prison activists killed by guards, followed by guards dying, followed by sweeping charges against other Black prisoners. And then national headlines when George's younger brother, Jonathan, and two others charged into a courtroom to free three Black militants, on trial for assaulting a guard at San Quentin after another Black prisoner had been gassed and beaten to death in his cell. They also took the judge and four others hostage, hoping to exchange them for George and other prisoners. Jonathan Jackson, two other militants, and the judge were killed. The lone militant survivor of the raid and well-known activist Angela Davis, who wasn't directly involved but was linked to the gun Jackson used, were charged with murder. The Revolution was real among the Black vanguard. The three of us knew we had to connect to that somehow, but the distance between San Quentin and Ash Valley was so vast, none of us had a realistic notion of how to do that beyond trying to support Luke in his prison work. But even that was a theoretical project at this point.

In the doldrums of one hot afternoon, a commotion arose around Stu's cabin. Luke's screams rang across the valley. Rita had mistaken a jug of gasoline for water and poured some into a cup for a make-pretend tea party in the cabin while Luke was sprawled in the shade of a nearby tree. One sip and she started gagging. Luke darted into the house, smelled the gas on her breath, slung her over his shoulder, and ran toward the creek, screaming for help. Patrick was nearby and got to a deep pool in the creek about the same time as they did. Luke held Rita up, while Patrick poured water down her throat from a clean jug he kept refilling. A few of us who had been hanging around the Main House and the ponds had rushed to the scene and surrounded the three of them, in frightened silent support.

After a terrifying fifteen minutes, they stopped forcing the water and Rita's breath slowly came back to something like normal. She looked wrung out and dazed as she draped over Luke's shoulder. A tear dribbled down Luke's face as he noticed all of us around him for the first time. Nobody said anything as we started slowly shuffling toward the Main House.

For the last couple of days of their stay, Luke was almost wholly focused on Rita, with Sandra hovering close by, much to Brian's dismay. We got big hugs and smiles from both of them as they loaded into Matthew and Sylvia's VW bus for the trip to Eugene to catch the plane for the trip that would eventually take them to their respective homes on opposite coasts.

Luke got the sunshine and air he'd fantasized about in prison and the time with Rita, time that turned out more intense than he could have possibly imagined. Who knows what that meant down the road for them. I don't know if he got any writing done. Maybe he was humbled by it all and maybe that was what he needed most with all the grand plans and strategies he'd readied for his life after prison.

I was wrong in all my expectations for his visit. I thought maybe he could do what I couldn't do, fit Ash Valley into the bigger picture of the Revolution, show us, tell us, lead us. Show me who I needed to be, all that I thought I should be. But he couldn't be what I needed him to be any more than Ash Valley could be what he needed it to be. He got sunburn and diarrhea and faced a frightening medical emergency fifty miles from the nearest hospital. He made some new friends who didn't really care about his rhetorical skills or his political critique but connected with him and his daughter as interesting guests to our fledging community. I got to know that someone who intimidated me with his brilliance and commitment was flawed and confused and could be just kind of a cool guy to hang out with—and who couldn't save me from myself.

SUMMER/15

It was just like some fucking old Western movie—head 'em off at the pass. Except it was the gate at the ranch where the showdown went down. Walter had overheard Jon and Wayne talking about splitting and had sprinted—as best he could—to Stu's cabin to alert him and Loretta. Stu ran—he was a little faster than Walter—to the tractor, which was at the edge of the garden while Walter, like a latter-day Paul Revere, spread word to Mike and Paulie. Mike and Walter headed back toward the Main House while Paulie came to tell us.

Stu did head them off at the gate with the tractor blocking the road. Walter and Mike got there just after Jon's VW bus had been forced to a stop. There was a lot of yelling and threatening going on by the time Sarah, Paulie, and I pulled up behind the bus in the red truck.

"You can't stop us from leaving," Jon was yelling at Stu and Mike, not making eye contact with Walter, who had emphatically shown what side he was on and it wasn't Jon and Wayne's. "I'm just taking Wayne to Eugene to get a plane. What the fuck are you guys freaking out about?"

"You can leave," Mike said. "We'd love for you to leave, but you need to give us our money back before you do."

"I don't have it, man," Wayne said. "It's out there working for us. I just need a little more time."

"You've run out of time," Stu said. "We've stopped believing any of your bullshit. Give us our fucking money back and I'll be happy to never see your lying face again."

Wayne looked around at all of us: Stu and Mike up in his face. Walter right beside them, Paulie, Sarah and I filling out a half circle facing the bus, where Wayne was almost pinned against the passenger side door. Jeffrey, Patrick, Loretta, Sydney, and Jack had walked down the road and stood behind us. The will of the people was staring him in the face, pissed and determinedly united.

He smiled. He had us good for a while, but his con had been called and now he could only try to negotiate an exit. "Fine," he said, "but I don't have any money to give you. Give me a couple of weeks and I can probably get it."

"Fuck that," Mike said. "He's got money." He nodded toward Jon, who was watching nervously from the front of the bus.

"Oh yeah," Jon said. "I'm just supposed to give you some money." He tried to laugh but he was too tense to make it sound like anything beyond a distorted inhalation.

"Well, if you want to leave here with all the shit you brought—and we do want you to leave—and you want your buddy to leave with all his shit," Mike said, "Yeah, we do want you to give us some money. Our money."

"Hell, if you want to leave at all," Jack spoke up from the back row. "If you want your bus to ever move again," he laughed, "we need to see that money."

"If you trust Wayne so much," Sarah said looking back and forth between the two of them, "then you should trust he'll pay you back." An angry laughter riffled among us.

Wayne looked at Jon and eased his way to the front of the bus. The two of them walked out of hearing range of the rest of us and talked for a while.

Nobody in our group said anything, just exchanged determined looks. Walter's was kind of goofy. Confrontation was not his thing, but he was kind of our hero in this showdown and he wasn't quite sure how to act.

Wayne and Jon made their way back to the front of the bus. "How much money are you asking for?" Wayne said.

"Two thousand, five hundred dollars," Stu said. "That's what we gave you. That's not even getting interest or anything like that."

"Well, you sure smoked a lot of his pot," Jon said.

"OK, fine, we'll call that interest. Two thousand, five hundred is what we want." Jon and Wayne looked at each other,

"OK," Jon said, grim-faced. "Obviously I don't have that kind of money here. I have to go to the bank." For Jon, this had become a business transaction.

"Obviously," Stu responded with a smirky smile, "we don't trust you to go and come back with the money." He thought for a second. "How about if Mike and me ride with you to the bank." He looked over to me. "Tucker can follow us and bring us back here."

Jon hesitated. Wayne was still smiling, shining it all on. He had another sucker on the line. "OK," Jon finally said. "Man, I can't wait to get away from you fucking people."

I backed up the red truck. Jon backed up the bus and Stu and Mike climbed in. Jack moved the tractor off the road. Sarah opened the gate and waved like a beauty queen as I passed her, following the bus down the road. I bet Jon had his 8-track turned up loud.

SUMMER/16

They were gone: Wayne, Annie, Tammy, Jon, Sheila. With Eddie, Stephen, and Dale off the ranch, Jeffrey had settled in to his almost completed house up in the woods above the road, the Main House was not overcrowded for the first time since we moved on the land. Walter finally had his own bedroom upstairs and Brian and Sandra had the tower annex all to themselves.

Philip and Jane and their kids were still in the Second House, but it was like a separate property, isolated and mostly functioning independently from the rest of us. Open hostilities had ceased. We were cordial and occasionally had to coordinate around the lawsuit and other ranch business but any pretense of them being part of our commune was gone. We tolerated their presence—for now while Jane's legal stuff was hanging over her. They didn't hassle us.

The whole vibe had changed. We had space to live and space to create the sort of communal relations and structures we needed. Our enemies were gone, leaving the cohort of friends that had been the basis of this undertaking from the start. The Boston core had prevailed, shedding the Southern Californian pseudo hippies who had weaseled their way into our trip with good drugs and sweet-smelling bullshit—that includes Phillip and Jane, who were gone from any influence, and Jon, a peripheral (in my eyes) Boston kid who picked the wrong side. And we had seemingly absorbed Jack and Loretta who were Californians but had allied with us and seemed happy to follow our lead.

The absence of so much of the tension that had been building almost from the beginning was liberating and we could savor our presence in this amazing valley in all new ways.

The solid, deep-blue days of late August were crispy hot, and the hue in the valley had shifted completely to a brittle golden brown. The creeks were slowing and the ponds were stagnant and almost warm. We tried to do our work before the sun's blaze overwhelmed us: watering and harvesting the garden, finishing our houses, picking hundreds of pounds of tomatoes and potatoes and onions from farms in the valley north of Canyonville, and canning shelves full of whole tomatoes and sauce and, even, our very own ketchup—all prepped over a wood stove. Sometimes, unavoidably, the canning would run into the afternoons and Sarah and Sydney and Walter and those of the rest of us who occasionally pitched in would drip with sweat over what minimal clothes we happened to wear.

But most afternoons were unapologetically and necessarily languorous. We would still dive in the ponds for quick relief but they were thick with algae and almost bathwater warm and the afternoon sun was relentless over them. So the best relief was the shade of the front porch of the Main House or our individual houses. Our house was great with its open walls and double shade layer of our roof and the full-leafed ash trees above it.

If we were lucky a soft breeze would blow through. And we could even go dangle our feet or dunk our heads in the creek, which was about half its springtime flow but still invigoratingly cool. We'd spend afternoons reading or piddling around on low-energy house projects. Occasionally, if the breeze was right and it wasn't *too* hot, we might slip into some laid-back lovemaking and let the afternoon drift off in torpid napping. Summertime and the living did seem pretty damn easy.

Matthew and Sylvia, our friends from Boston, came back with the good news that they had found a place on the main stream of the Umpqua, west of Roseburg, where they could move into in mid-September—and the horrible news that George Jackson had been killed. Jackson—the Black revolutionary, author of *Soledad Brother,* accused along with seven other Black prisoners of the murder of a White guard at Soledad prison—was shot and killed at San Quentin prison. Three White guards and two White prisoners were also killed. Details were still sketchy but there was one unambiguous fact: George Jackson was dead.

Jackson had been in prison since 1960, when at age 18 he was sentenced to one year to life in prison for allegedly stealing $70 from a gas station. He had pled guilty on the advice of a White public defender though he claimed innocence. He had been promised a short county jail sentence. But he had served more than eleven years on that sentence when he was killed. He was less than a model prisoner early in his prison years. Then he began reading and studying history and revolutionary theory and trying to be the sort of inmate that a parole board might look favorably on, taking correspondence courses and lining up a job on the outside, a requirement for parole. *Soledad Brother* is a collection of his letters beginning in June 1964 and they reveal both his growing revolutionary consciousness and his frustrations year after year with the parole broad. He came to realize that his consciousness was much more dangerous to authorities than his petty crimes—and that they would never let him out of prison alive.

"We attempted to transform the [B]lack criminal mentality into a [B]lack revolutionary mentality," he wrote:

International capitalism cannot be destroyed without the extremes of struggle. The entire colonial world is watching the [B]lacks inside the U.S., wondering and waiting for us to come to our senses. Their problems and struggles with the Amerikan monster are much more difficult than they would be if we actively aided them. We are on the inside. We are the only ones (besides the very small [W]hite minority left) who can get at the monster's heart without subjecting the world to nuclear fire. We have a momentous historical role to act out if we will. The whole world for all time in the future will love us and remember us as the righteous people who made it possible for the world to live on. If we fail through fear and lack of aggressive imagination, then the slaves of the future will curse us, as we sometimes curse those of yesterday. I don't want to die and leave a few sad songs and a hump in the ground as my only monument. I want to leave a world that is liberated from trash, pollution, racism, nation-states, nation-state wars and armies, from pomp, bigotry, parochialism, a thousand different brands of untruth, and licentious usurious economics.

We were eager to know the details of what happened on August 21 at San Quentin. But we didn't need any more information to know why George Jackson was dead.

The sky was as blue as it could be and the valley sparkled in the sunshine, but a dark somberness hung over us as we sat in the shade of the porch at the Main House. What did we have to do with George Jackson? Did we even qualify to be a part of "the very small minority [W]hite left" that he saw as allies. We—or some of us, at least—talked about being that, aspired to being that, but what did these days of looking after ourselves in this fantasyland contribute to getting at the monster's heart to liberate the world from his right-on list of the evils perpetuated by the American Empire. He called on us to shed fear and foster "aggressive imagination." When would we be ready for that? Would we ever?

A life sentence … no a death sentence … for—allegedly—$70. I was convicted of two felony assaults of police offers with deadly weapons. I was guilty of one. And I walked out of that courtroom to marry my love, to go on smoking dope and partying my way clear across the country to land in one of the most beautiful places on Planet Earth. Privilege. White skin. How many George Jacksons were dead or getting their bodies and souls tortured in prisons or living in internal colonies, daily oppressed by an occupying army of pigs who had no restraints on the cruelty they could impose? How many Ben Tuckers, guilty and free, smoked dope and rapped righteously about revolution, knowing they could turn on the privilege any time things got tough?

We decided to dedicate our garden to the memory of George Jackson—so far a bunch of city kids working to turn a patch of pasture into a food-producing garden was our most revolutionary act. Jack took the wooden "National Forest Service" sign we had hung somewhat mockingly (we had liberated it from the road) on the garden gate and carved "George Jackson Memorial Garden" on the back side. We all gathered by the gate and ceremoniously hung it up. But, shit man, we had to do more. I hope everyone understood that we had to do a lot more than that.

SUMMER/17

Stu and Patrick dropped us off at the Medford Airport. They were picking up chicken feed and doing other errands before heading back to the ranch. Sarah and I were going to Philadelphia for her younger brother David's bar mitzvah, our first venture out of Oregon since we had arrived in March. What a trip! Even just hanging out at the airport was a goof. We had sort of forgotten how far our standards of hygiene and appearance had deviated from those of straight America.

We really hadn't been immersed among straight people since we had been on the ranch. At the airport, we were surrounded. Our hair had gotten much longer and wilder. I had stopped shaving, so a wispy Ho Chi Minh–like growth was hanging from my chin. We only took showers when we visited friends in Eugene. At Ash Valley we jumped in the ponds or heated water from the creek to wash with Dr. Bronner's Peppermint Soap, which also served as our shampoo. Our cloths were worn and faded from being—very occasionally— beaten clean with creek water and hung to dry in the blistering sun.

We had the last flight of the day out of Medford, going to San Francisco where we'd get an overnight flight to Philly. We had a long wait and there wasn't a hell of a lot to do at the Medford Airport. We only had a few dollars of spending money anyway. Sarah's folks had paid for our tickets and we wouldn't have to pay for anything once we were back there. But just watching people slowly fill the waiting area and, especially, watching them check us out was fine entertainment for a while.

But then, there was a buzz of activity around the gate where the airline people had started checking people in. Sarah went up to see what was going on. She hovered on the edge of the crowd and then looked back at me, question and concern showing on her face. I could see her talking to some of the other people around her and trying to get up to the desk. Finally, she came back, pissed and teary.

"They cancelled the flight," she said. "Our plane couldn't get out of San Francisco. Fog or something."

"Shit," I said. "Will they get us on another flight."

"Tomorrow," she said, her anger the one thing holding back her tears. "There are no more flights tonight."

"Shit," I said, "so we have to spend the night in the airport?"

"We can't," she said. "They close the airport." The tears were coming now, as the airport started slowly emptying of the other people who were supposed to go on our plane. "Ben what are we going to do? We have no way to go anywhere. We don't have nearly enough money to stay in a motel."

"They won't pay for us to stay someplace? That's bullshit."

"No," she was really sobbing now. "Because it's weather or something. I don't know. You go talk to them."

I went up to the desk and no, they were very sorry but they couldn't pay for us to stay somewhere and we couldn't stay in the airport. Wasn't there somebody we could call?

No. I walked back to Sarah, her face red with tears, distorted and forlorn. The airport was almost empty. What *were* we going to do. The airport was in the middle of nowhere, surrounded by farms and fields, no good place even for us to crash with our bags.

Just as I got back, a very straight looking woman approached Sarah, with a man close behind. "Are you alright, dear?" she asked Sarah.

Sarah gushed out our story. Stranded. No money. No car. Nowhere to go. "Oh, it's OK, honey," the woman, who was maybe in her mid-thirties and had neatly trimmed blond hair that hung to the middle of her neck, patted Sarah on the back. "We have a tent that you could set up in our backyard for the night. We don't live far from here."

Sarah looked at her in amazement, cried harder for a few seconds, then reached to hug her. "Oh, thank you, thank you!"

The woman accepted Sarah's hug a little hesitantly and pulled back. "We have to bring my mom back for the flight in the morning anyway, so it would be no bother for us to bring you, too." She looked at me for the first time and nodded with a tolerant smile. The airport was starting to shut down, with loud clanking echoing around as the roll-up metal baggage doors were being closed.

"Wow," I said as I reached out to shake her hand in the midst of the racket. "I'm Ben and I'm awed. Your kindness is amazing."

Her look back seemed to contain a question. She limply shook my hand. "I'm Louise and this is my husband Herbert." He reached his hand, also seeming a bit leery, toward me.

It was suddenly dead quiet. "And I'm Sarah." She was smiling and wiping her tears away. "You don't know how much this means to us. Thank you. Thank you. Thank you."

The lights were going out and Herbert reached to pick up Sarah's suitcase as I grabbed mine and we headed toward the exit. Louise's mother was waiting by the door, regarding us with skeptical curiosity as we said hello. She smiled, concerned, toward Sarah.

They offered us Oreos when we got back to their place and Herbert and I set up the tent while Sarah and Louise chatted.

As we nestled into the sleeping bags they had provided, Sarah and I talked about how lucky we were that these people took us in even though it was apparent that they were more than a little freaked out. We'd probably be huddled outside somewhere around the airport building if not for them.

Herbert tapped gently and firmly on the tent in the morning, to let us know that it was time to get up for breakfast before heading back to the airport.

The breakfast was outstanding, stacks of pancakes with butter and syrup and more bacon than we could all eat, and good percolated coffee with real cream and sugar. The conversation was stilted and slow. What were safe topics between us? Sarah answered their questions about our trip, that we would spend time in Philadelphia with her family and then a few days in Illinois with mine. When she mentioned my family, Louise and Herbert looked at each other, confused.

"What did you call him?" Louise asked.

Now Sarah was confused. "What do you mean?"

"What did you say his name was?" Louise asked, pointing at me.

"Ben," Sarah said, surprised at the intensity of the questions. "His name is Ben."

Herbert and Louise looked at each other and looked back at us with a relieved laughter

"Oh, thank goodness," Louise said, "We thought he introduced himself as God last night at the airport." It was kind of chaotic when we made our introductions. I couldn't remember exactly what I had said, but they obviously had misheard something.

Sarah and I looked at each other, shocked and then laughing. "And you still brought us into your home?" I said. "Wow."

"Well," Herbert said, with a shy smile, the warmest he had been since we met, "it was kinda too late to back out at that point, and, well, what would it say about us if we left God and his wife stranded." He chuckled. "It sure made for an interesting conversation between us after you all went to bed."

"But we're glad to know that you are Ben," Louise smiled at me.

Holy shit—truly holy. What was that conversation like? How did they sleep? A long-haired slack-bearded near-penniless man in shabby clothes claiming to be God was in their backyard, steps from their kids and her mother. What love moved Louise to comfort the tearful young woman, to persuade the shy and protective Herbert to take her and this strange man into their home, their life—even after they thought he thought of himself as God? They could have—I'm sure they thought as they lay in bed with us right outside their window that they should have—run from us when they had the chance. But they gave us Oreos and made us breakfast and found in their hearts the love to be kind to truly strange strangers. Kindness with no reward, only risk. I suspect they were religious people and their religion taught them to be kind. But this was not an act of doctrine but of the heart. The holiest of loves, it seems, come to us unexpectedly in the strangest times and places.

That bizarre night in Medford was perhaps the perfect preparation for our ten-day whirlwind tour of the Old Country, a week in Philadelphia, three days in Illinois.

Philadelphia was a rush of family and parties and putting on costumes to try to cover just how country we had become in the wilds of Oregon. It was centered around celebrating the passage to manhood of Sarah's younger brother, David, but was shadowed by a gathering darkness of illness that seemed to be overtaking Sarah's older brother, Harry, who was struggling to get through medical school—some rare neuromuscular disease that caused a distortion in his neck that tilted his head to one side.

But they were all so thrilled to have Sarah there to celebrate, to comfort, to be a glue among them all. They were even gracious when Sarah excitedly pulled from her suitcase a bunch of beets we had brought from our garden, a few little dots of Ash Valley soil still clinging to them. They did love her so.

Maybe for the first time I could appreciate the connections and complexities of Sarah's family and the love that permeated it all—and how Sarah was instrumental to all that. I even began to feel a part of it, no longer needing to compete for her love. With the mind-blowing kindness of Louise and Herbert still reverberating in my head, their lesson in meeting a situation that could have been utterly uncomfortable with acceptance and grace, I could see that Sarah's family had made the similarly loving effort to accept me. All I had to do was to accept them back. Not really difficult, it turned out. So when her dad took me shopping for clothes for the bar mitzvah and other social events—bright colors and stripes, flared pants, wide-collared shirts—I went along and relaxed into small talk about baseball and family and some of our successes on the ranch.

Illinois was a different scene entirely. Quiet at home with my parents and my youngest sister Kim. Easy and plentiful drinking and getting high with my friends at night after my parents faded. My mother and father seemed to be in a perpetual state of exhaustion. My dad worked at an emergency room in Kankakee, 100 miles north. He stayed up there and worked long shifts four days a week and had long weekends at home. My mother worked full time at a mental health rehabilitation facility in Decatur, a little less than an hour west, commuting every day with a carpool. They were happy to see us and my mother, especially, perked up when old friends dropped by. But there wasn't the sort or exuberant intensity that seemed almost constant in Philadelphia. We had serious and quiet discussions about the ranch and politics and what was going on with my other sisters.

Kim, who had graduated from high school the previous spring, helped out my parents with cooking and cleaning and had a part-time job at a department store at a nearby mall. She had come out to Oregon, to Ash Valley, with her boyfriend early in the summer, the only member of my family to visit us. So she knew better than anybody the radical cultural shift we were navigating. She was glad to have some of her generation's energy in the house and went out with us a couple of nights. It was great to see all my friends. A few of them had come to see us in Oregon, too, and most of the rest promised to come soon. Not much serious talk happened then, but it was a good time—and the only times I felt completely relaxed on the whole trip.

While we were traveling from Philadelphia to Illinois, a rebellion broke out at maximum-security Attica prison in New York. In the aftermath of an altercation between inmates and guards—triggered by the guards mistaking horseplay for a serious fight in the prison yard—prisoners seized control of significant parts of the prison and took about forty hostages. The rebels quickly organized themselves and presented the authorities with a list of twenty-seven demands for such basic human rights as access to legal representation at parole hearings, an end to racial and political persecution, a stop to physical brutality against them, more humane treatment like decent medical care, an end to unsanitary conditions, and access to decent food and water in adequate amounts. They were demanding to be treated like human beings. We watched the first reports on CBS News in my parents' living room—television, such a strange presence after we had killed ours in the early Tiller days, making it all immediate, exciting, and frightening. It was just two weeks since George Jackson had been killed.

During our long flight from Chicago to San Francisco, I was swept into a torrent of thoughts about our time in the East and what waited for us back home in the West. We had told the tale we told outsiders about the ranch. Oregon was great. Our land was great. Our house was great. The garden was great. We had stockpiled an amazing amount of food for the coming winter. We had a few people who didn't work out, but they were gone now and we could focus on working together toward our common goals: self-sufficiency, community education, changing the world. It was a good story and enough of it was true that we could tell it with conviction. But when we had left the ranch, the reality was the euphoric buzz that we all felt after getting rid of the opportunists had dissipated. Significant differences among those who remained about work ethic, communal commitment, visions for the future were suddenly glaringly apparent now that our common foes were gone. We had no real plan for raising our balloon payment and no source of ongoing income. We needed government handouts in the form of food commodities (canned meat and vegetables, dried eggs and milk, blocks of cheese) to fill out our food supplies. Our animals—goats and chickens and pigs and horses—were stagnating at best, costing us more than we got from them. Our vehicles were as unreliable as ever. Most of our shelters were functional and not far from being ready for winter and we'd done well putting up tomato sauce (and ketchup!) and canned beans and sacks of onions and potatoes. We hadn't made much progress with our firewood stash, which seemed like a ludicrous thing to be gathering when it was so hot, day after day. But we had now slipped into September and the rain and the cold could not be far away.

But for all that sometimes-hard-to-face reality that our distant perspective had made clearer somehow, the reality of the Old Country was scarier. We couldn't come back. We couldn't live the lives of the people we loved in Philadelphia or Urbana. All that comfort and convenience and cleanliness came at such a high price.

Sarah's family sort of put on a show for us and made us characters in it, not a phony sort of show, but a brave face kind of show. David, who didn't seem all that religious to me, played his role at the center of things—not because of any sort of ego trip but because it brought his beloved big sister home and gave the family a joyous focus that diverted their minds from the deep but mostly unexpressed concern about Harry's illness and increasing difficulties for his father's clothing manufacturing business, facing withering competition from international manufacturers. Her father shared my parents' perpetual exhaustion, which showed through when he took off his wanting-to-smile face and drifted off to sleep on the family-room sofa. And there was a desperation in the unwavering ebullience of her mother, pushing the role too far. But even in the ready smile and the unflappable optimism, it peeked out: a desperation borne of the certain knowledge that Sarah would leave and the looming trials would be evermore present. "Maybe," she would softly say to Sarah about our life in Oregon when she broke role just a bit, "it won't be forever."

My parents didn't even pretend that their lives were a model for us or that Urbana might be a good place for us to live. But they were also not convinced that what we were doing in Oregon made any sense. They saw it as an interesting experiment and, I guess, hoped it would keep me out of trouble and that we wouldn't get hurt. My friends mostly thought it was cool and a little bit crazy. None of them seemed particularly interested in joining us.

Past the love and the friendships, all I could see back east were old stories and old patterns. People wearing themselves out "making a living"—what a crazy fucking term—professional jobs or get-by kind of jobs, even selling dope or playing music, maybe going to school or scheming the government somehow or other. And spending the rest of their time recovering or escaping from whatever it was they did. Dope, alcohol, TV.

I wouldn't trade places with any of them. I knew we had serious struggles ahead at Ash Valley. But I still believed as deep as I could get that all that we dreamed of was still possible. In that place, that beautiful open valley, protected by miles of mountains, watched over by the ancient forests, nourished and cleansed by the singing creek, sheltered by the pristine blue or impenetrably gray above us, dazzled by the sun and the moon and the stars or the absolute pure darkness that cast their spells upon us. With those people, the *us* that we were becoming, that we would become if we could finally figure out how, the *us* that was worthy of that valley. We didn't have to play by the rules of the Old Country. How could *we* fail?

On our way home, we spent a night in San Francisco with Shelley's friend Sally and went out to eat at an outrageously good restaurant in Chinatown. There were some good things in the city, I guess.

In a newspaper we picked up at the airport the next day, the news was all about the full-on attack by New York State troopers to end the rebellion at Attica. Authorities were still pretending to negotiate with the prisoners when the pigs dropped tear gas into the prison yard and opened fire with a variety of weapons, including shotguns. When the smoke cleared, twenty-nine rebels and nine hostages were dead and many others injured. Motherfuckers.

Just by chance, we ran into Patrick, who'd been visiting his family in Vermont, at the San Francisco airport. He got on the same flight to Medford as we did. We were almost home.

SUMMER/18

It started really feeling like home when we turned north on the Tiller-Trail Highway. Scattered funky houses and ramshackle trailer parks slowly gave way to the dense fir forest as we climbed toward the summit. This was such an exotic foreign land when we first arrived last spring, and now I could feel the tension that had built up in my body as we traveled in the East ease as my senses were awakened by the crisp green smells and the brilliant late-summer light filtered through the towering canopy. Ash Valley was just a few ridges to the northeast as a crow might fly. I could almost taste it.

After we crossed the South Umpqua in Tiller and headed up the road along the river, still singing with its diminished September flow, the now familiar houses sped by and finally yielded to nothing but the river and the trees. That other world was behind us. By the time we reached the Forest Service road that led to the ranch, I sucked deep the distinctive sweetness of the air that was our breath, that enveloped and gave life to us and *our* place. Home had never meant so much to me before.

And it was a true homecoming. In addition to Patrick, Sarah, and me, our wandering brothers—Eddie, Dale, and Stephen—had all returned. We were whole again. No trace left of Wayne and Jon and Sheila It was sad to also lose the adorable innocence of Wayne's daughter Tammy but it was the price of having him gone. The Hammonds were isolated, neutralized. Sarah and I were refreshed and renewed. Having seen the Old World, with knowledge of all the possibilities of the new one locked into our bones, we were more committed than ever to make it work. It felt like a new start.

Patrick had gathered up a few things from home, now committed to Ash Valley for the long haul. Eddie had brought back some great Colombian and we spent that first night partying and telling the tales of our travels. Stephen as usual didn't say much but whatever he had seen out there made him want to come back to be a part of us. Dale, who had spent some time in his old home town of Richmond, Virginia, was changed: somber but seemingly shed of the bitterness, determined to find a place for himself, without Sydney by his side, on this land. He, too, had seen the desperation, the emptiness, the fervid pointless enterprise out there.

We all brought back echoes of the news from Attica and other evidence of the deterioration of the American Empire. The last place he stayed, Dale had heard John Lennon's brand-new album and had stayed up all night learning the chords and the lyrics to two of the songs, which he played for us. We all joined in as he played them over and over—as we demanded—and we picked up on the words.

"Gimme Some Truth."

"Imagine."

The next morning—after a wonderful night back in the sweet loft of our partially enclosed little house—Sarah and I ambled down to the Main House to see if there was anything to eat. Almost everyone was there, there was some pancake batter left, and the stove was still hot.

We shot the shit for a while about the previous night's party and our travels and then Eddie suddenly got serious and focused on Sarah and me.

"So when I got back and you guys were gone, it just felt like everybody here was feeling pretty down. Getting rid of Wayne was cool, but that didn't really solve all of our problems. Like how the hell are we going to get the money to pay for this place, to pay for lawyers to stop them from cutting the fucking trees? Jon had the money to help but he turned out to be an asshole, too. So that left us with people we mostly liked"— he shot a quick look at Mike with a questioning look. Mike grimaced back at him. Eddie laughed: "Just kidding man." Mike gave him the finger but with a big shit-eating grin.

"No, seriously, it just seemed like everybody was in kind of a daze. So one day Stu and I took a walk down the road and found this cool little cave on a hill near the front of the property."

"We just knew we had to do something to change the vibe here," Stu said. "It just wasn't feeling good."

"Yeah," Eddie said. "So we smoked a joint in this cool little cave."

"Of course," Stu said.

"And I told him about my neighbor in Florida where I got this Colombian from."

"Good dope, man," Walter said with a smile. We all agreed.

"And he kinda let me know," Eddie went on, "that there was a lot more where this came from."

"Far out," I said.

"So Stu and I thought, maybe that was the solution to our money problem." It was quiet for a second.

"So I guess you're talking about dealing it," Sarah said. "Do you want to do that?"

Eddie smiled innocently at Sarah. "I think I can do it. We need to find a partner who can help us with money. We can't spend all that money we got back from Wayne. It's going to take us a while. I have the connection for the pot, and I know some people who would love to be part of this deal … so …

you know … for the people," he smiled again at Mike, "I'm willing to do it."

"I sorta remember a cocaine deal from our Boston days," Sarah said, smiling knowingly at Eddie and then me. "That didn't go so well. You and Ben did most of the snorting and there wasn't a lot of selling going on."

Everybody laughed. Patrick had walked in, picking up on the conversation. "Sorry I missed that," he said.

"Yeah," Eddie chuckled and then looked seriously at Sarah. "I think I've learned some stuff since then and besides Jeffrey says he'll help me. We can keep each other focused on the business stuff."

"Do you want to do this?" Sarah asked Jeffrey.

"Well," Jeffrey said with a sort of reluctant grin. "Some yes. Some no. How else are we going to raise that kind of money? $20,000 is a lot of money." He grinned. "But it is kind of a thrilling business. It will take a while and it'll mean spending a lot of time off the land, in Florida, which is not my favorite place to hang out."

"You guys will be taking a big risk," Walter said.

"I know," Eddie said. "But this all did kind of fall in my lap. It's seems kinda cosmic really. We need the money, right? It's the same kind of thing that Wayne was supposedly doing, but you know you can trust Jeffrey and me. Right?"

"No question about that," I said.

"Look," Stu said. "This just kind of came along right when we need it. Eddie and Jeffrey are into trying to make it happen. Let's let them give it a shot—if it seems too risky or if they decide, for any reason, that they're not into it, they can stop. When did we let silly things like laws and risks get in the way of what we want to do. If nothing else, it'll probably mean we'll have a steady stash of good dope."

"There is that," Mike said, smiling as Eddie lit a joint.

"Like Mr. Natural says," Walter chimed in. "'Dope will get you through times of no money better than money will get you through times of no dope.'"

"And maybe we'll end up with both," Patrick said, taking the joint from Eddie.

Some kind of consensus was signaled as the joint moved slowly around the room.

Money for hope.

Fall

FALL/1

Fall crept in. The nights had gotten cold. An early frost killed much of what was left in the garden. We had hoped for another month before the first killing frost. A few sunny days had allowed Sarah and me to finish the first layer of our siding boards on our walls. We were ready to cover that with tar paper but we were stalled by four straight days of cold rain. All the windows were in but we still didn't have a door. I hoped that this was just a taste and warning of the rainy season to come and not the thing itself. All of us still needed some spells of dry weather to get our houses completely closed in and to accumulate the firewood we would need to heat and cook throughout the winter—which people who seemed to know expected to be colder and wetter than usual. But we didn't have any real idea of what a usual winter at Ash Valley might be like.

The total officially living on the ranch was now twenty-two, counting the five Hammonds. But Jane had to turn herself in to the county jail for sixty days for the welfare fraud rap, and the kids were going to stay with some of their friends in town, so Phillip would be the only one living on the land for a while. Brian and Sandra had announced they would be leaving soon, going back to Boston. That wasn't a surprise. They never seemed entirely at home, and, as the weather began to turn and the prospect of a winter with wood heat and no running water loomed in front of them, they decided to pack it in. We'd miss Brian's wit and Sandra's innocent sweetness, but they had always seemed more like long-term visitors than committed commune members. No hard feelings, no deep sense of loss at their departure.

As we were sitting out the rain one morning at the Main House, folks who had left on a town trip about an hour earlier returned suddenly and rushed into the house. Jack blurted out that an urgent message had come to the Tiller Store for Sarah. Her father was in the hospital. She should call home as soon as possible. Sarah freaked, of course, and she and I jumped in the back of the white truck to head back to Tiller, where the nearest phone booth was. I held her hand tight as we bounced around while Stu navigated the river road as fast as he could.

We got dropped off by the gas station near the phone booth, and the other folks headed to Canyonville. Sarah was frantic and crying and increasingly frustrated and angry as she ran into repeated dead ends on the other end of the line.

Calling from a phone booth was a pain in the ass anytime but much worse when you felt desperate and were trying to track someone down through a bureaucratic maze. Nobody was home at the Stein's house and once she found out from an aunt what hospital her father was in, it took her a while to locate her mother, who was in the visitor area of the intensive care unit. Her father had had a heart attack the night before, at which point he was put in the hospital—and then had another earlier that day. He was not doing well. Sarah's mother and her older brother were camped out by the ICU, with no idea what they were waiting for, but with some sense that it could be the unthinkable, though that was never said out loud. He was just barely in his fifties.

"I have to be there," she said as she hung up the phone. She was crying uncontrollably but had this fierce sense of focus behind the tears. "Oh, Ben, I have to get there now. It's my father. It's bad. He's in critical condition. I can't believe it." I pulled her in as tight as I could but she wasn't looking for comfort, she needed action. She pulled away. "Oh, when will they be back? I don't want to wait for them."

We had to get back to the ranch for her to pull together a few things for the trip and then to Medford, the closest airport. We hoped for someone else to come by who could give us a ride but no one turned up. Sarah paced and cried and occasionally blurted snippets of her conversation with her mother, "She sounded scared. She never sounds scared. She tried not to but I could hear the fear in her voice … She only gets to see him for five minutes every hour and she says he's got tubes coming out all over and he's barely conscious … She tried to say everything was going to be all right but I could tell she had her doubts."

We got to Medford late that afternoon and got her a standby ticket for the late plane to San Francisco and then the overnight flight to Philly. We didn't say much as we picked at food at a nearby burger joint. I said I'd call her the next day and come if she thought I should. We talked about stuff I could do while she was gone. There was not much we could say about her father. We both knew that he might die, but she couldn't face that and I didn't know how to talk about it or even if we should—like it might be some kind of jinx. So we told each other how much we loved one another, held hands and squeezed, shared occasional deep glances into each other's eyes but I had no words that could make anything better.

It was a long quiet ride back to the ranch. For the first time, I slept up in our loft alone. Moonbeam and our kitties Mocha and Kachina were warm company but the absence of Sarah made for a cold night.

I couldn't call her the next day because there were no running vehicles on the land. The white truck had died just inside the gate to the ranch after I got back from Medford. Patrick and I spent most of the day trying to get it going with no luck. By the time we gave up, it was too late to start hitchhiking to Tiller. I was freaking out thinking about Sarah and her dad. I knew she was expecting my call.

In the daylight that was left, Patrick helped me get a start on putting tar paper on our house. We still didn't have a door and holes in the walls still needed patching but I made a fire in our cookstove and felt pretty toasty when I sat next to it to write Sarah a letter, even though I would talk to her before I could even mail it. I just needed to tell her how much I missed her and was thinking about her. We had written lots of letters to each other when she was in Philadelphia and I was in Boston or Illinois, but it had been so long since we'd been apart, it felt strange.

Frost still coated the ferns but it was a crystal blue morning when I walked the steep downslope that "our'" road became after it left our property on its way toward the river road. I danced and shook to stay warm as I had to wait about forty-five minutes before I saw any rig besides a log truck. But fortunately that battered old pickup stopped and picked me up. A gruff guy with a stiff beard, maybe in his forties, sort of grunted and nodded as I climbed aboard and he told me he was going into Tiller. Perfect, I told him, that's just as far as I needed to go. He lit up a camel straight and offered me one—which I happily took even though I had theoretically quit smoking, along with Sarah, a couple of months before. He was camping up by the South Umpqua Falls and needed some ice and other supplies. He never asked about me or what the hell I was doing hitchhiking in the middle of next-to-nowhere. Fine by me.

Sarah was relieved to hear my voice. She said she had written me a letter, too, just because she needed to. And then the full story came out in a rush. Her brother Harry had met her at the airport when she had arrived about 10:00 in the morning and took her immediately to the hospital. She got to the ICU right at 11:00. The five-minute visits happened every hour on the hour, so she went right in.

"He really looked bad, real drawn out and pale," she said, her emotions making her voice start to quiver. "He looked real glad to see me and he started crying." She paused. "He asked me to wipe his eyes for him." I could tell she was crying now, but she went on. "I was really upset but I tried to stay cheerful because I didn't want to upset him."

"Oh, Sarah," I said. It was silent for a few beats.

"He didn't know I was coming. My mother didn't tell him that they had called me, afraid that would make him think he must be really sick. She told him I had called to say some packages he had sent had arrived and when they told me he was in the hospital, I just had to come to see for myself that he was all right. But then he kept asking her if anything in the packages [which we hadn't really gotten yet] was broken."

She took a breath and filled me in on what had happened before she got there. Her dad had chest pains during a scout meeting—he was an advisor to David's Boy Scout troop— which apparently was the first heart attack. After getting a ride home, he went to a doctor, who took him to the hospital. He was admitted and the next morning, while lying in his room, his heart stopped beating—heart attack number two. An intern just happened to come into the room just then and pounded on his chest and his heart started up again—and he was sent to intensive care.

"So, it was—and still is—really serious," she said. "What if that intern hadn't walked in his room at that very moment?"

Another long pause. "He's getting better now, but it really freaked him out, not so much that he might die but that my mother couldn't handle it or that he'd be an invalid or a burden, which he couldn't handle."

He seemed better with each subsequent visit, she said, and later that day he was taken off the critical list, which meant they could visit him longer and he would soon be moved out of intensive care.

We talked every few days while she was there, but we kept writing each other increasingly long, intense letters. Somehow the combination of the gravity of Sarah staring at the possibility of her father's death and the sudden distance between us broke through the routinized soft uncertainty that had lingered over our relationship since I had smashed that chair in stupid anger at her. And there was so much more space in writing for me, especially, to explore and complete thoughts. When our relationship had faltered, when I failed her by abandoning Woodstock and she failed me by not standing up against her parents and coming back to Boston for our sophomore year, it was letters that lifted us again—pen-to-paper explorations and rambling explications of what this thing was that kept pulling us back to each other—with more depth and staying power than our also frequent, but ephemeral, phone booth-to-phone booth calls.

Her letters focused, of course, on the ongoing drama around her father, its effect on her mother, and the grim reality of mortality.

In Oregon, it was hard to believe it could really be bad, that it could really happen to him. But it did. Ben, I really love him. We've had lots of disagreements in the past, but he's really such a good person. One thing more he said—'I'm not ready to die yet. I've got too much love in me.' Tonight at 7, just my mother went in and he was real upset and said he was afraid of being buried and said that maybe she wouldn't believe it but he talked to his dead mother all last night. He was upset that they would have to change their whole life style. She kept saying she didn't care—she just wanted to be with him. He was crying saying they couldn't even sleep together for a month—that's how long he'll be in the hospital. It's so sad— he's really scared and my mother is trying so hard to be strong but it's real hard on her. She hasn't slept for three days.

But she also addressed me with a passion I had not felt for a long time.

"I miss you so much & love you so much. I love you more today than I've ever loved you before, but not, I'm sure, as much I will love you tomorrow."

My letters were as supportive as I could be of her and her father and her family. I filled her in on the happenings at the ranch. But the quiet nights alone in our house gave me lots of time to think about her and how things had gotten twisted between us.

"First—I love you very much. I felt lost in my head a lot this summer. I know that was hard on you. I got caught up in this crazy contradiction of thinking analytically that monogamy was a source of pain and evil but being desperately scared of losing you. The day you almost left taught me a

lot—I see that day as a turning point in a lotta ways. I could never deny how much I love you and how much I enjoy living with you. Somehow— for my own sake—I need to reconcile my intellectual reasoning with my gut feelings. I think maybe I am beginning to come to terms with reality again. I miss you so much. I can't wait to see you."

Meanwhile, spots in the valley and the lower-elevation rim surrounding it were brightening with yellows and reds deepening on the oaks and ashes. The increasingly cold nights left a dense morning fog that slowly yielded to the rising sun and rich blueness overhead and delightful warm days.

Life and drama continued at the ranch. The vehicle situation added a layer of tension; it was harder to escape. We had one reliable vehicle, Stephen's truck, available to us. Roger had stayed in Eugene. Stu and Loretta had hitchhiked home when he decided to stay longer than they wanted to. The Karmann Ghia was parked in Medford while Eddie was doing his thing in Florida. The red and white trucks worked sporadically, and Phillip's Willys was off-limits to us because, with Jane in jail, the kids were mostly staying in town and we accepted that he needed to reserve his rig to be able to get back and forth, as well as visit Jane in Roseburg. That meant I usually had to hitchhike to Tiller to call Sarah, which made it close to a full-day activity.

And Phillip continued to spread his bad energy all over the ranch. We all were sympathetic to Jane's situation and the challenges with the kids but he used that cynically to his advantage. He never offered to let us go along on his town trips, never even told us when he was going. He helped himself to our supplies and tools and meals and dope without giving anything back or helping in any way.

He had, with our unspoken approval, removed himself from any attempt to build communications or develop collaborative plans, convinced he could hold his privileged space in the Second House but isolate himself from everything else happening on the ranch. Word even got around that he was planning to ask us to allow some friends—Jerry and Susan—to move up into the house that Little Eddie was vacating to move back into the Main House, since he was going to be traveling so much. Jerry and Susan were renting in Tiller and that's where the Hammond's kids were staying. But no way we were going to let them move on. When the kids came to visit one day, Greg told me what an asshole Jerry was. That was good enough for me. And we had no intention of giving Phillip any new allies. Besides we had already decided that Patrick and Roger would move into that house.

Other things contributed to an overall "lack of spirt"—the words Stephen used when he came to hang out with me one day, after bringing us a bunch of logs to cut into firewood that he hauled behind the tractor. Brian and Sandra had pretty much checked out. Walter seemed grumpier and grumpier by the day, still cooking and offering up the occasional sharp one-liners but less and less enthusiastic about the big picture of what we were trying to do. Jack and Sydney did their own thing, sometimes in synch with the rest of us, sometimes not, and they didn't seem to give a shit when they were called on it.

Come to think of it, they were mostly united with us when we came together against people like Wayne and Phillip, but not so much about our long-term projects and visions. Dale went about with a quiet intensity, a strangely muted version of his former self. He did more than his share with communal projects and worked hard on his house in the woods above the Second House, convinced, he shared with his closest friends who helped him when he needed it, that Sydney would come back to him when he had a house for her. We didn't argue or try to convince him that he should let that go. We knew he was past listening to that and the subdued Dale was easier to handle than the maniacally jealous one. But we missed the Dale who had been such a hearty friend and helped lead us to Oregon.

And even Moonbeam was acting strange, didn't even want to go home with me from the Main House one night. After Eddie returned from his fundraising exploits, Moonbeam nearly killed his dog, Micro, a tiny miniature Dachshund. Three of us had to pull Moonbeam off his throat or she would have killed him. That upset Eddie a lot—and me, too. Maybe Moonbeam missed Sarah, too. We all did.

But Eddie had brought back some fine Colombian, the first sample of the product he would be selling for our balloon payment. A bunch of us (eight!) worked together to prepare and plant hairy vetch seeds in the garden, a cover crop to prepare the soil for an even better garden—next year! Mike, Stu, Dale, and I worked together to put up the bark siding on Mike and Paulie's cabin and then ours. Most of our houses were done. I finally hung the door to our house and filled most of the remaining gaps in the walls. Thanks to Stephen, we had a decent stash of firewood, which I cut to stove-size lengths, split, and stacked against the back wall of the house. I loved doing that work. I was determined that Sarah would come back to a virtually complete house, warm and cozy, a loving shelter from the cold and rain. And, with lot of help, it was ready.

And so it went. Death and distance. Joy and production. Disharmony and distrust. Preparation and forward-thinking. Dead vehicles and dead-ends. Love trying to find its way like our little creek moving around ever-changing obstacles, fighting toward the promise of the river.

And the valley took little notice, its wide-openness unaltered by we specks who dallied within it. Its flowing grasses shifted hues as they did long before us, its days and nights slowly giving and taking from each other as they always had. The valley's seasons took no account of us and never would.

FALL/2

It was almost like the honeymoon we never had after Sarah came back from Philly. We hadn't been apart since before our wedding. And she came back to *our* house, sealed and completed on the outside, the fulfillment of the vision we'd had when we first imagined our meadow as our spot four months earlier. I didn't exactly carry her across the threshold but the moment of release from the intensity of her time with her ailing father and her desperately loving family and my time shifting between the ongoing communal circus down the road and the strange solitude at this far end of the valley had swept us inside as if entering a new world.

I quickly made a fire to chase out the chill while Sarah took in the total interiorness that now defined our space. The fire crackling to life as I shoved the biggest pieces of wood I could into the small cookstove fire box, I turned and saw her leaning again the center pole, watching me and smiling . . . with relief and gratitude and fulsome love. We kissed and kissed and, almost without separating, she led me up the ladder to the loft, where the heat was already taking over.

In the days that followed, we worked together to finish a few more interior touches: a cold box, which was a 2×2 wooden food storage space that extended out of the exterior wall with a door on the inside made of 1-by planks to block off heat; a 6-foot long waist-high cabinet along one wall for dishes, nonperishable food, and other kitchen supplies; and a 4-foot table that could be folded down flat against the wall to save space. The table sat in front of the window looking west out into the meadow and the hill beyond, a splendid panorama for morning coffee, evening meals, letter writing. Sarah and I delighted in working on these finishing-touch projects together. She had also brought some things back from Philadelphia, a spice rack that we hung next to the stove and a marionette that we first hung on the wall (but had to move to a less accessible spot because it was at just the right height for the kittens to attack), and some smaller knickknacks—a covered dish that would make a great stash holder, a small tarnished metal tea pot, a single pewter candlestick, an antique scale. She placed all of them with great care in little nooks and crannies.

I loved watching Sarah add her domestic touches to the house. Sarah had worked hard through all the stages of building our house, but the digging and sawing and hammering and scurrying around on the roof with boards and tar paper and shingles was, in a lot of ways, more my thing. But making the space within the structure harmonize and resonate as ours, really ours, was all Sarah—fulfilling the crazy dream she'd had ambling though Allston New Year's Eve 1969. She'd spent twenty months refining that vision of gracing our home, if ever we found it, with just the right things. Though sometimes she could drive me a little crazy, lingering long in some funky shop, looking for that just right thing, it made me crazy happy to watch her make this collection of fir poles and salvaged wood into our undeniable home sweet home.

After I had mentioned to my mother in a letter that I hoped to spend the winter reading and writing, she offered to buy me books to support that effort. Somewhere along the way, I had picked up a catalog from a San Francisco-based distributor of New Left and revolutionary books. I made a list for her:

Vietnam Will Win by Wilfred Burchett

Away wirth All Pests: An English Surgeon in People's China, 1954–1959 by Joshua S. Horn

Soviet Marxism: A Critical Analysis by Herbert Marcuse

The Dialectic of Sex: The Case for Feminist Revolution by Shulamith Firestone

The State and Revolution by Vladimir Lenin

Trial by Tom Hayden

White Man, Listen! by Richard Wright

Our Revolution by Leon Trotsky

Bolshevism (The Practice and Theory of) by Bertrand Russell

Living My Life by Emma Goldman

Value, Price, and Profit by Karl Marx

The Communist Manifesto, by Marx and Friedrich Engels

Monopoly Capital by Paul Baran and Paul Sweezy

Weatherman by Harold Jacobs

Strategy for Labor: A Radical Proposal by Andre Gorz

Ten Days that Shook the World by John Reed

Total Loss Farm: A Year in the Life by Raymond Mungo

The Rebel by Albert Camus

Seize the Time by Bobby Seale

The Anatomy of Revolution by Crane Brinton

The Second Sex by Simone de Beauvoir

Jail Notes by Timothy Leary

We Are Everywhere by Jerry Rubin

Steal This Book by Abbie Hoffman

War and Peace in the Global Village by Marshall McLuhan

People's War, People's Army by Võ Nguyên Giáp

A Dying Colonialism by Frantz Fanon

The Price of My Soul by Bernadette Devlin

Malcom X Speaks

An Essay on Liberation by Herbert Marcuse

Revolution in the Revolution? by Régis Debray

Castro's Cuba, Cuba's Fidel by Lee Lockwood

Patterns of Anarchy, edited by Leonard I. Krimerman and Lewis Perry

The Red Sun Lights the Way Forward for Tachai, China Publications Center

I never thought she would send them all.

FALL/3

Walter was the next to leave. His usually ebullient spirt had been sagging for a while. He was essentially living alone in the Main House since Brian and Sandra had left. Eddie had moved back in but he was gone more than half the time. Visitors would hang out there but there were fewer and fewer of them as the responsibilities and chill of fall had overtaken the seemingly unending party of summer. It fell to him—even when Eddie was there—to keep the house together, still do a lot of the cooking, and, despite his frequent reminders and our repeated oaths to do better, clean up after us. So often, nights at the Main House ended in all of us staggering out as stoned as could be. Nobody, not even Walter, felt like cleaning up then.

And Walter was lonely amidst our crowd. For all the sexual intrigue and changing partners of our first five months, Walter never did find even a short-term mate. About half of the remaining people were coupled, snuggling up in our freshly winterized houses. Of the single men, Dale, Jeffrey, and Stephen had all been on one side or the other of the sexual dramas and were, it seemed, resigned to being single, at least for the moment. Who knows what Eddie was up to all the times he was gone. And Roger ?... I still didn't quite get why Roger had been allowed to stay. Liz, who seemed more naturally compatible with the ranch, had left long before. Roger was there ... but he never seemed really to be there.

It all weighed Walter down, and I guess he didn't see much hope of things getting better as the weather turned cold and dark and our population dwindled. He'd been right at the core of it all going back to the early Boston days and the first days at the White House in Tiller. He was especially tight with Dale and Sydney, Jeffrey and Mike (for all their differences). They had all lived, at different times, at 1387 Commonwealth, one of our main hubs in Boston. He shared our love for all the live music we had seen and he and Stu could talk for hours about which of those early Allman Brothers concerts was the best. He and Sarah had developed a special bond—two headstrong Scorpios—during the time on the ranch and often stood together in group discussions advocating responsibility around food and the kitchen and that our Revolution shouldn't even contemplate violence. He and I loved to spar intellectually.

He opened my eyes to notions of spirituality—the I Ching, astrology—that I hadn't thought about before. He told me that one of the things I said that made some sense to him was one of my favorite cliches "your life is your politics." He always made me laugh. We'd miss him.

He was the first of our core to give up on the ranch. Somehow, we failed to make him feel a part of what we could still become. Maybe that was because we had still not articulated what that was clearly enough. Or maybe he saw too clearly that he didn't want to be a part of what was growing organically among us. Or, maybe in the end, he was just too horny to face the prospect of a winter without a woman, eighteen miles from the nearest speck of civilization.

Whatever the reason for his leaving, it did jolt us into a new round of stock-taking. Maybe losing Walter, along with Brian and Sandra, and eliminating the Hammonds from any influence in the group, narrowed the spectrum of ideas and visions about what we were, so we might be able to focus better on what we wanted to become. Maybe he had to go not just for his own sanity but so the Ash Valley commune could become something more than a bunch of people living on beautiful land, getting high.

We were now at fourteen people—not counting the occupant of the Second House, who would be gone soon. It felt like all those who remained were committed to living out the winter. We all had made ourselves decent places to live. We had stockpiled food. We had a reasonable start on the firewood we would need. I wrote to my parents:

We are trying to grow and regroup from our experiences from the past summer. It was a difficult summer in many ways. We made many mistakes. People that we trusted took advantage of us. We saw many shocking aspects of ourselves. We didn't have any agreements, no rules, let it flow—and sometimes it got very scary where it flowed to. It's all new— or it seems that way to us. We don't believe in the rules of this society any more. No way. We're playing to not get caught. We're outside the law. But it's not good or very satisfying to build a life of only opposition. Even if one understands entirely the evils of Amerika, that leaves one dependent on the evil for his purpose, like the people who are horrified that the Vietnam War might end and that we'd have no good issues to protest. We have to build—are building—something new. But at first, it was like walking in the dark and just bumping into one thing after another until you really start to doubt the existence of light. Sometimes it is easiest to conclude that life is purely haphazard and nothing matters, including us, so we might as well just party ourselves along and watch Amerika die from a distance. But we can't do that because of our sense of internationalism and our great desire to make the world a loving, trusting, productive family. And our outrage.

They murdered George Jackson, you know, and 43 at Attica. Now I hear they have shot H. Rap Brown and that the people of Pittsburgh are smashing windows and fighting cops to celebrate their World Series victory.

Things are moving. 1972 looms as a heavy year. We must begin again, this time a little more aware of things, to build a tribal feeling to develop a workable group arrangement. This is to be done in conjunction with freaks on similar trips across Amerika and our brothers and sisters everywhere struggling to overcome human misery and exploitation.

We're closer now that our numbers have dwindled, that we made it through such insane times together, that we have not lost that great spirit that has got us through so many things and that once again—finally again—we're beginning to push each other, to learn from each other, to truly share with each other. I feel better and closer to understanding many things than I have in a few months.

Love,

Ben

FALL/4

A string of mostly dry, cool days continued for a couple of weeks into October. They were a gift. We could see snow on the tops of mountains not far from us and we knew rain was coming any day. But we were given the time we needed for more preparation, including most of us joining in to plant hairy vetch on two more fields: one for a herb garden down by the reservoir and one for an orchard planned for an area between the goat barn and the creek. With living spaces more settled and comfortable than they had ever been, we had found some kind of rhythm of work and play and a balance between communal engagement and space for individuals or couples to do their own thing.

When Eddie and his Karmann Ghia were on the land, we could take slow rides from one end of the property to the other, back and forth, cranking out tunes with its cassette player, windows open to spread the music throughout the valley. *Low Spark of High Heeled Boys*, *Who's Next*, and *Aqualung* were the only tapes we had but we could—and did—listen to all of them over and over again. We didn't do it often, but it was easier than trying to use the generator and it was a great rush when we did it.

The lawsuit to stop the logging was stalled in the creaky machinations of the court system. It could be months before any final decision was made. But that also kept the Forest Service from proceeding with the sale and the chain saws and trucks off the mountain.

Little Eddie's venture was going well. We had a healthy stash of the products he would be peddling—several different types of Columbian pot—and our expert collective opinion was that it was righteous stuff. Now that he'd made the initial connections and the momentum was building toward the deals that would start bringing in real money, Jeffrey became his partner. Eddie had the connections and was really smart in assessing situations and planning strategy but could also be impulsive and occasionally delusional. Jeffrey had more experience in the business and a calm level-headedness that could temper Eddie's weaknesses. And they had a special connection.

They really knew how to talk to each other. A couple of Eddie's girlfriends ended up being Jeffrey's girlfriends and that didn't even seem to put a dent in their friendship. Jeffrey had been reluctant to participate in the dealing to raise money for the ranch when Wayne was supposedly doing it, but I guess it was different for him with Eddie. This would mean both of them would be gone, off the land, for long stretches. But the general unspoken sense among the rest of us was that was not necessarily a negative for them, especially Eddie, who was always eager for town trips, especially when there might be a cheeseburger (something we never had at the ranch) somewhere along the way.

FALL/5

Sarah and I made a major town trip, all the way to Eugene, to shop at Waremart, a big, cheap store where we could buy things in bulk. It was always a celebratory time when a town trip returned loaded with fresh supplies. Mostly we brought back staples like wheat (to grind for flour) and rice and coffee and cooking oil, but we'd usually get something extra like beer or wine or cheese (a highly valued taste treat at Ash Valley). Whoever was anywhere near the Main House would help unload whatever rig had managed to make the trip to be in position to get first crack at any special thing that showed up. So on this particular day, most of whoever was on the ranch at the time was in the living room of the Main House, drinking beer, eating cheese and crackers, feeling good, shooting the shit.

Mike came in and surveyed the scene and saw a 10-pound bag of sugar on the kitchen counter. "What the fuck is this?" he asked. "I thought we weren't buying sugar." Sugar, white sugar in particular, was frowned upon on the ranch, like white flour, an overly processed food without a lot of nutrition, an addictive substance in the products and kitchens of America. We normally didn't buy it, but we were in the thick of canning season and canning things like jam went a lot smoother with sugar than with any alternative.

"We bought it just for canning, Mike," Sarah said. "We won't use it for anything else, just canning."

"If it's poison, it's poison, man. Am I right?"

"It's not poison, Mike. If we're going to try to can all this jam and stuff, we need to use sugar, and we'll be fine. And that's it—we'll just keep it for canning."

"Fuck that, man. If it's here, I'm going to eat it for whatever I want, whenever I want."

Stu jumped in, "Hey, Mike, that doesn't make any sense. You say it's poison and then that you'll eat it whenever you want. They bought it for canning, let's just leave it for canning."

"That's exactly it," Mike said, as though his argument was just common sense. "They shouldn't have bought it, but since they did, I'm going to eat it and nobody can tell me that I can't."

"Mike!" Sarah was red with exasperation. "What the fuck?"

"In fact, I'm going to have some right now." He walked to the other side of the kitchen counter, opened a fresh-from-Eugene bag of tortillas and pulled one out. "I'm going to have me a sugar burrito." He opened the bag of sugar, stuck his meaty hand in and pulled out a fistful and then sprinkled it over the open tortilla, rolled it up, and took a bite. "Yum, yum," he said with a big smile and a six-year-old's glare toward Sarah.

FALL/6

Late one afternoon as I was splitting wood outside our house, Stephen's black truck pulled up along the road. He got out looking kind of beat but smiling.

"I got a deer," he shouted across the meadow.

"A deer?" I yelled back. "Far FUCKING out!!" I ran across the meadow to check it out. Moonbeam eagerly ran ahead of me. Sarah, who'd been inside, was right behind us.

I gave Stephen a slap on the back as he led me toward the rear of the truck where the young buck lay, blood stained around his upper chest and his eyes dead open. Moonbeam and Stephen's dog Sundance had their front paws up on the truck bed, panting heavily.

Sarah, joining us, winced at her first glance, and uttered an involuntary "Oooh" before registering what this dead once-cute deer would mean for us. "Cool," she said, just a little bit reluctantly.

Stephen beamed with pride. More than ever, living in his lean-to in the woods, he kept to himself. He'd show up for meals or to smoke some dope and he always pitched in when he saw we needed help. He'd wander down to our house now and then, usually bringing something like firewood or some beer if he'd been in town, to shoot the shit for a while. But he seemed happiest when he could be alone and pursue his own things. He found ways to both be a part of our communal trip and to spend enough time apart to maintain a reasonable level of sanity. And in the relative calm that had settled over the valley, everyone seemed to be cool with that. He gave enough to the communal whole that he earned his solitude. But, as we admired his kill, his face showed how good he felt when following his own path also served the collective good. He knew how excited everyone would be about the deer.

"Where did you get him?" I asked.

"About ten miles up the road, and a little ways up into the woods," he said, adrenaline still animating his usually soft-spoken voice.

I'd gone out with him a couple of times and we saw some traces of deer, but never got close enough to shoot one. We didn't talk much but enjoyed each other's company, though I could sort of sense that I was more of a hindrance than a help with the objective of actually killing a deer. He'd shot a few ducks who came to our valley as a rest stop on their way south and some quail who would pop up in the woods by the road. I couldn't seem to kill anything. Sarah and I had a .22 rifle we kept at the house. It was not nearly powerful enough to kill the deer that occasionally wandered into our meadow, usually in the early mornings. And, besides, we liked that they felt comfortable hanging out near our house. It would hardly be neighborly to try to shoot them there. But even when I tried to kill something I failed.

One day, walking down the road with the gun, I saw a full covey of quail, marching one by one about 18 inches apart across an opening in the foliage on the uphill side about six feet in front of me. It was like a shooting gallery. I got off four or five shots but didn't hit a damn thing. Another time, walking the creek with Stu, we saw three decent-sized trout in a pool about three feet deep and four feet across. How could I miss them? Shooting fish in a barrel. I made three shots and perturbed them a bit but didn't even clip one. Stu was laughing so hard that I almost just threw the rifle at them. Probably would have had a better chance of doing damage.

But Stephen was a real hunter. After a couple of minutes of us all admiring the dead animal, Stephen said, "Well, I better get this thing gutted. Wanna come help?"

"Sure," we said together and climbed up and sat on the back edge of truck bed with legs hanging over, the deer between us. The dogs followed eagerly, with great hopes, as Stephen eased down the road.

Word spread quickly that Stephen had killed a deer and soon everyone was gathered at the Main House. Stephen, Sarah, and Jack did most of the gutting and butchering work but everyone hovered around trying to help get rid of the waste and keep things clean. The dogs were going crazy. It was a real celebratory happening: fresh meat.

We decided to cook three steaks that night. The rest was wrapped up in paper to take the next day to our recently rented freezer locker in Days Creek. The temperatures were cold enough that it would keep overnight in the root cellar. We also decided we would pull out a roast from the locker for Sarah's birthday, which was just a few days away. Too bad, we didn't have a place to keep it until then but we just couldn't count on the temperatures being that cold during the days. And it was a good excuse for another town trip.

The steaks were great, three steaks shared among us along with fried potatoes and onions and a sprout salad. We hardly ever had meat. Never bought it. We got boiled canned chicken in our government commodities handouts, but you'd have to disguise that in lots of rice and soy sauce. But even that stuff went fast. Our diet generally was vegetarian but not by a moral or dietary choice. We didn't have any committed vegetarians left among us. The chickens were still producing eggs, though that seemed to be diminishing again for reasons we still hadn't figured out. We relied heavily on dried beans (especially lentils) and rice, as well as the commodities foods which featured cheese, powdered milk and eggs, cooking oil, corn syrup, the canned chicken, and an unidentifiable meat product that was so disgusting we fed it to the dogs—and all the stuff we had gathered and canned (green beans, tomatoes in various forms, pickles) or stored (primarily potatoes and onions). So the venison steaks were a treat, indeed.

We had just sort of flowed into a somewhat loose but workable organization of roles that we had failed to achieve through so many group meetings in the past. We rotated cooking duties, two people each night responsible for the evening meal, which we agreed would be a common meal, but we also agreed it was OK for folks to occasionally eat at their own house. We even (sort of) welcomed Phillip (and his kids when they were on the land) to eat with us without expecting him to contribute, though he would sometimes show up with some bread or fruit.

Mike was the primary baker. Stu was (always!) the prime mover and planner for the garden. Paulie, with help from Sarah and Loretta, looked after the non-pet animals (horses, goats, chickens, pigs). Sarah also kept track of our money. Dale had taken over interaction with our lawyers about the lawsuit. Patrick and Stephen took the lead on locating firewood and organizing work parties to gather it. Eddie and Jeffrey were doing their thing off the land. I was charged with correspondence with other communes and activists and setting up historical and political education sessions. Sydney and Jack … well their roles did not seem quite as clearly defined but they mostly did their share with the meal preparation and communal work session. Roger was kind of the same, but less so. But, for a time, we functioned relatively smoothly as a group.

FALL/7

Mike made a honey cake for Sarah's birthday and we were
able to put together a mishmash of candles for her to
blow out. We didn't do much in the way of presents. I wrote
her a poem:

> blue sky clear sunshine
>
> plays against the soft brightness
>
> of Fall's fine colors
>
> it's your birthday again, my love,
>
> and this time we celebrate
>
> surrounded by oregon's incredible green
>
> in a land of our own,
>
> in love and growing—

Other folks made cards for her. Her parents had sent a
nice sweater and a whole package of goodies like Tastykakes, a
Philadelphia sweet treat, and almond candies. My parents sent
a check, which we planned to use to buy some new goats, and
all my sisters sent cards. Katherine sent her a Yahtzee game,
which was cool, another activity for the nights that were getting
noticeably longer every day. This was Sarah's 21st birthday.

As she closed her eyes to compose her wishes—she
always gave her wishes a lot of thought—I couldn't help but
think of where we had been on her birthday the year before
and what she might have wished for then. We were living
in an apartment in Brookline, sort of add-on roommates to
our friend Leslie (who had been Sarah's good friend in high
school before they both came to BU) and her sister Janice

and another woman named Anita. We slept in a roll-out sofa bed in the living room of the three-bedroom apartment with one bathroom. Anita hated us. We could never be really alone or ever feel comfortable in any way. That was during one of those periods when my trial was supposed to be imminent so everything was super-temporary but then the trial got postponed once again and we were stuck. We were close to broke. Sarah was working at Angel Memorial Hospital and I had just started working at Boston Children's Hospital. But I couldn't stand the thought of spending Sarah's birthday night in that fucking claustrophobic cold living room. So I booked us a room at a cheap motel nearby, a wild extravagance for us.

After work, we took the subway over to Harvard Square for an early dinner at Mr. Bartley's Burger Cottage. After delicious burgers (grilled mushrooms and onions on hers; cheese and peppers on mine) and their best-in-the-world onion rings, they brought Sarah a brownie with a candle in it and I quietly sang "Happy Birthday" and she closed her eyes to make her wishes, so many possibilities then: a new place, the trial over and all that behind us, some clarity about our fate, and what else? What about the parts of her that didn't revolve around me, a smart, beautiful twenty-year old woman forced to face so much, so young. Had I left any room for her to wish anything for herself? She opened her eyes and smiled and blew out the candle.

We took the subway back to Coolidge Corner, and we were both nervous as we checked into the motel. Sarah pretended to look at brochures in a corner of the lobby. It was the first time we'd done anything like that, sort of pretended to be a married couple. But the desk clerk didn't seem to care. He took my money and handed me a key to our room. I felt like I'd gotten away with something serious, like I just talked my way out of jail or something like that.

And what a wonderful night it was, alone together in a tired and tight little room overlooking Beacon Street. The double bed and privacy were all we needed to make it feel like a honeymoon suite. It was hard going back to the rollaway.

Now, so many of the things we had wished for a year earlier having come true, it was harder to know what she might be wishing for beyond the obvious number one of her father and brother's health. About her role on the ranch? About us? About getting through the winter? Everything seemed so immediate and so changeable here. There was something complicated about living in the midst of a wish granted but tarnished by the intermittent tedium of reality. Could we take the freedom and escape and committed togetherness and found paradise of the past year to another level—or were we just trying desperately to hold on.

For all her natural, blurting honesty, Sarah held some things tight and deep, maybe so deep and tight that they were outside of her consciousness until, unless … I'm not even sure what it takes … the broken chair maybe. … her father's illness … the prospect of me going to prison … but all those things were still about others. Maybe in those quiet seconds with her eyes shut and the candles burning, she dug into that deep well and wished for something for herself and herself alone.

FALL/8

The rains came, steady and cold. A couple of mornings we even woke up to a beautiful white blanket of snow all over the valley. Looking out on our meadow with all its greens and browns and yellows and reds gone, hidden by a pure and uniform white, I felt like a kid waking up to the prospect of a day free from school, unexpected possibilities as far as I could see. But in those early November days, the rains took over by midday and washed the white away.

I got knocked down by a nasty cold for almost a week, spending my time keeping our woodstove stoked and curling up in the loft with a book while Sarah went off and did her thing with the animals and hanging out at the Main House. As miserable as I felt, there was a lot of comfort in the warmth of our little house and the relative mellowness of the communal scene that allowed me the space to take the time I needed to get better. By the time I felt well enough to get back to work—gathering firewood, trying to keep vehicles running, and so on—and back into the communal flow, I realized that I hadn't left the land for three weeks, a personal record, I think. I dug that and had no desire to break that streak anytime soon.

Jane got out of jail and her probation officer told her she had to be off the land within a week. It was the end of months of awkwardness, after all "their" people left and Jane went to jail and Phillip maintained his claim to the Second House and a stake in the land, though they never put any money toward the land payments or our communal funds. We loved the kids, and Greg, especially, was always happy to see us though those opportunities became fewer and fewer during the final weeks.

Kathy, on the cusp of being a teenager, was more distant. She had lots to be pissed off about—her mother in jail, her father more then willing to pawn her off to the folks in town. Maybe she even felt betrayed by all of us, the chaos of her life a result of the failure of adults to get along.

We were all happy to see Jane free. Seeing the cops come on *our* land and take her away and then watch the legal system lock her up and separate her from her kids was a gut punch to all of us and our illusion that our little valley in the mountains ten miles from the nearest neighbor was some kind of liberated zone. Even in that last week, Jane had a sweetness that made it hard not to like her. Sort of like the kids, she was caught between Phillip's opportunism and hippie-flavored chauvinism and the still-not-clearly-enough-defined goal the rest of us seemed to share of developing truly communal relations and rooting out the sexism we all had been indoctrinated in so effectively. But Jane with her stoned-out Christianity and her "shine it on" approach to any conflict played the role of the good submissive hippie wife perfectly. She validated all Phillip's worst traits, so, law or no law, she needed to go, too.

That last week, we were friendly in a "nice knowing you; glad to see you go" kind of way. After Stephen and Jack, they were the first "outsiders" to join the Ash Valley project and they had been important contributors in the early days. But as we watched them leave, finally fully exhaling with relief, it was clear their most important contribution was showing us a way not to go.

FALL/9

Little Eddie's parents showed up on a cold and drizzly night. Eddie had gone to Medford to meet them and the three of them pulled up in a rental car loaded with groceries—$180 worth, Eddie told us, including about $80 in steaks. I'm sure Eddie made sure they knew that if they wanted to eat anything besides lentils and fried potatoes they had to bring enough of the kind of food they wanted to eat for all of us. After we all had eagerly helped unload the many bags from the car, Eddie's mother dug into her deep-pocketed purse and pulled out a whole bunch of those little bottles of liquor they give you on airplanes: bourbon, scotch, vodka. Those proved to be great icebreakers as people hustled around the kitchen cooking steaks and potatoes and putting together a huge salad.

Eddie's folks were rich. I never understood exactly what Eddie's father did but I think it had something to do with real estate speculation and development in Florida, which, I guess, was booming. We had been introduced to Eddie as a rich kid who escaped from McLean, the mental hospital outside of Boston, where people like James Taylor and Sylvia Plath and Robert Lowell had been patients—a nuthouse for rich people and celebrities. When he escaped during a field trip to Harvard Square, he found a friend of his from summer camp who was in Boston and a friend of ours. That friend was afraid Eddie's parent would know to look for Eddie at his apartment so he sent him to the place he was sure would take him in: Mountfort Street, #9, with its sign on the door that said "Welcome All!" Stu, Mike, Brian and I did welcome him, of course, and from then on he would forever be known as Little Eddie. He was fifteen. And he *was* crazy in ways different from the rest of us—but also different from what they tried to fix at McLean—and dangerously smart.

Eddie was the oldest of four siblings and his parents seemed young compared to mine and most of my friends. Maybe it was just that sort of youthful mirage that money sometimes creates. But they were good sports, jumping right into the party, stationed in the middle of the central table, asking all about us and what we were doing. As I joyfully gulped down the shot bottles as fast as I could, I tried to imagine what they thought of this place that Eddie was part of now. Was this the place for the kid who was so out of control a couple of years ago that they committed him to a mental institution? Maybe they just saw that Eddie felt a part of something outside of himself for the first time, surrounded by people who loved him and whom he loved. Yeah, it was downright primitive and we did a lot of drugs, but maybe they saw that he had a sense of purpose he hadn't shown before, though I can't imagine they knew the specifics of how he was trying to serve the people. And maybe his father, who Eddie sometimes hinted was cavorting on the edges of legality in his business dealings, would have been proud of his son for his strategic and enterprising wheeling and dealing.

After the cocktails and the lavish feast, which we devoured with a rapidity that clearly shocked his mother, Eddie asked his folks if they wanted to smoke some pot. His mother graciously declined, but his father, with the same kind of "what the fuck" look on his face as Eddie showed when we just didn't stop consuming whatever drugs were in front of us until they were gone or we passed out, shrugged his shoulders and said, "Sure." He was engaging and smart and funny—like Eddie—

and got silly with the rest of us as the joints went 'round the table. Eddie's mother looked on, amused and weary from a long day of traveling and the intensity of the evening.

It was a trip how people slipped into our reality once they came through our gates, if they didn't make a quick getaway after an initial glimpse like Sarah's aunt. Eddie's parents just rolled with our outrageousness, fed it, even, with their booze and steaks. An evening with their son and his friends, and everything was cool. I couldn't imagine my parents or Sarah's adapting so quickly or willingly.

So it was kind of ironic that the next day's mail brought a letter from Luke, the first since he had been on the ranch in August. He said he was surprised and a little disappointed that his time on the ranch was mostly about him learning from us: "I learned a lot there, in fact, some of the little resentment I had was that I feel I was a little more open to people teaching me what they know, which was a lot, than they were really receptive to hearing what I know or at least wanted to teach … At the time, the contradictions around Jon and Sheila, Phillip and Jane, etc, were heavier for you than the contradictions around the pig." Some famous person once said, "All politics is local." It turns out that even applies to the chaos of the counterculture in 1971.

In some ways, Luke was as out-of-place at Ash Valley as Eddie's parents. The rich folks and the revolutionary. Though it seemed like we were much closer to Luke culturally and politically, we met Eddie's parents, on that particular night at least, on the common ground of hedonism. And that was a much more accessible realm than our political consciousness that Luke had hoped to penetrate and maybe even transform in some way. Even with the main sources of our interpersonal contradictions that Luke had witnessed gone, we still would have a hard time defining what our collective consciousness was. Most of us would even have a hard time defining our individual consciousness the way Luke thought about it. Luke tried hard to roll with us. Partly, I think, because he really needed an emotional and psychic break after prison, and the laid-back vibe of the ranch gave him space. But partly, also, because he thought it was what he should do as a revolutionary. So there was always an awkwardness to it. "Trying too hard," as Sarah would say. And we never really gave him space to lay his revolutionary vision on us.

Hedonism had always been at the heart of what we as a tribe had in common. Drugs, sex, and rock and roll. And the relative deprivation that we seemingly had volunteered for at Ash Valley had added "normal" food to that list. Show up with a carload of store-bought groceries and a shitload of hard booze, and we were instant comrades. Wayne had won us with his PCP-laced pot and it took us months to see through his smoke-and-mirrors bullshit. Eddie's folks only wanted to be part of their son's world for a short spell. And they succeeded magnificently.

Luke's letter went on to say that he was questioning a lot of his assumptions about the Revolution. It's not going to happen as quickly as he hoped, like in the next five years, but, he wrote, "People who want a revolution in 5 years will be able to make one in 20 or 30. But people who say they think it will take 30 usually don't want one and just use '30 'as a numerical representation for 'who gives a shit.' That's what scares me about thinking in longer terms, it risks being fed into the strong revisionist, sell-out tendencies among [W]hites who translate that as meaning, 'Oh, wow, great, that gives me 29 years to fuck around.'"

He said he was planning to come west to the Bay Area to see Rita and wanted Mike and me to drive down to see him. He said he also wanted to see Sarah and Paulie, too, at some point, but that he knew they wouldn't be excited about meeting up with him for "heavy discussions."

"Part of the problem is that the verbal level that we—you, Mike, me—— discuss 'politics' on is still wrong, still bullshit, not revolutionary. For certain, there is a thing called the revolution, which will be partially determined by our reality, that is [W]hite male revolutionaries, and when we get together despite a lot of problems, we are often able to connect. But often with women, and specifically with Sarah, for example, these 'conversations' are not seen or felt as revolutionary but rather, the many contradictions still in us affect her more negatively than the kernel of true humanity hidden in the bullshit. So it's not exactly a question of different strokes for different folks as much as different people will discover in different ways the key to why they want to collectively destroy the system and perhaps die in the effort to build something better, and probably, for Sarah, that way is not gonna be with discussions with Luke Vaughn for a while."

It made sense, I guess. And I would like to have that kind of conversation with Luke and Mike. But the challenge for us "White male revolutionaries" at Ash Valley was that we had to get beyond what was comfortable for us to discuss among ourselves and what women like Sarah—or even nonpolitical radical men like Stu—detect as bullshit if we wanted to get to any kind of consensus. What is this revolution and what is our part in it? On those 135 acres and among the fourteen of us, we didn't have the luxury of excluding the people who asked the hardest questions.

There was no way for Mike and me to get to the Bay Area in later November to see Luke, even if we wanted to. But all the same, I was thrilled for Luke to consider me this close a comrade that he wanted to include me in this discussion to figure out just what was to be done to make our Revolution, and I was eager to continue the dialog through correspondence.

FALL/10

Rain, rain, rain. It beat on the shakes of our roof like down-pouring waves of the ocean or the whooshing rush of river rapids, the power of water in motion interrupted, engulfing me, isolating me from everything but the dry cozy island of our little house. In my island I found a freedom I had never known. The freedom to spend day after day reading and thinking. Now it had been a month since I'd left the land.

Sarah and I would check in at the Main House in the morning, but there just wasn't a lot of work going on. Sometimes we'd both go back to our house, sometimes Sarah would hang out, dealing with food preparation or tending to the animals. Sometimes she'd go along on town trips to help with shopping and other errands and to make a call to her folks. Her dad was doing much better but she still wanted to keep in regular touch. Most days, I was more than happy to stay on the ranch and feed the woodstove at our place and work my way through magazines and the pile of books my mother had sent me. She had sent almost everything I requested. She didn't seem that concerned about us living primitively or controversially, but she did worry about me letting my mind atrophy because of drug use or mental laziness. She couldn't do anything about my drug use, except occasionally lecture me about what my father's alcoholism had cost our family, but my list had given her an opportunity to try to stimulate my mind. So what if most of the books were radical or even communist, at least I would be working the bloody muscles of my mind, as she might say.

It worked, I guess. I read and took notes and pondered. The rain, the creek, the winds that occasionally swept our meadow were the perfect background for thinking deep and hard. Some choice quotes from the books she had sent me:

"There are no limits to the power of people. In a specific situation it may remain latent and quiescent but when events require it, this power can become violent, as tempestuous as the tide at its fullest, something no enemy can restrain. ... the moment of revolt is an unforgettable day in the life of the oppressed."

—Bo Nguyễn Giáp, in *Vietnam Will Win* by Wilfred Burchett

" ... a revolutionary in every bedroom cannot fail to shake up the status quo. And if it's your wife who is revolting, you can't just split to the suburbs. Feminism, when it achieves its goals will crack though the most basic structures of our society."

—Shulamith Firestone, *The Dialectic of Sex*

" ... history has not yet found any other way of securing progress than that of pitting the revolutionary violence of the progressive class against the conservative violence of the reactionary class."

—Leon Trotsky, *The Proletariat and the Revolution*

" ... and socialism, in turn, defines a new human existence. Its content and values are to be determined by free time rather than labor time, that is to say, man comes into his own only outside and beyond the entire realm of material production for the mere necessities of life. Socialization of production is meant to reduce the time and energy spent in this realm to a mini-

mum, and to maximize time and energy for the development
and satisfaction of individual needs in the realm of freedom."

—Herbert Marcuse, *Soviet Marxism*

" ... no revolution can be truly and permanently successful
unless it puts its emphatic veto upon all tyranny and centraliza-
tion, and determinedly strives to make the revolution a real
revaluation of all economic, social, and cultural values. Not mere
substitution of one political party for another in control of the
Government, not the masking of autocracy by proletarian slogans,
not the dictatorship of a new class over an old one, not political scene shifting of any kind, but the complete reversal of all
these authoritarian principles will alone serve the revolution.

—Emma Goldman, *The Revolution Betrayed*

"I maintain that the ultimate effect of white Europe over
Asia and Africa was to cast millions into a spiritual void; I
maintain that it suffused their lives with a sense of mean-
inglessness. I argue that it was not merely physical suffering or economic deprivation that has set over a billion
and a half colored people in violent political motion."

—Richard Wright, *White Man, Listen!*

"The first duty of a revolutionary is to get away with it."

"Smoking dope and hanging up Che's picture is no more a
commitment than drinking milk and collecting postage stamps."

—Abbie Hoffman, *Steal This Book*

"Within two years of Liberation, Chinese volunteers were helping the Koreans to repel US aggression and it became necessary to mobilize the people to protect their health from the dangers arising from the use of germ warfare in Korea. A patriotic health campaign was promoted in response to this need. Tens of millions of people of all ages, guided by sanitary workers who supplied the know-how and the necessary materials, waged a war of extermination against the "four-pests"—flies, rats, bedbugs and mosquitos.

"The unprecedented success of this campaign has been acknowledged by many western observers. In many parts of the country, flies were virtually eliminated; an astounding feat in the fly-ridden Orient and one that could only be accomplished by an unusually united and responsive population."

—Joshua S. Horn, MD, *Away with all Pests*

From my little spot on the west slope of the Cascade Mountains in southwestern Oregon, I reached across space and time to get into the heads of my predecessors and contemporaries who had the audacity to believe that they could reimagine, recreate, remake, revolutionize the very fundamental arrangements of how human beings lived together, who risked being thought ridiculous—and much worse—to plot out a world where war and racism and mindless consumption and devastation of our planet were not "normal," not "just the way things are," not the "inevitable result of human nature." Where "peace" and "love" were not trippy hippie platitudes but the core lived values of the human community.

And we were part of it. Right? We had to be part of it. Why else would we be here?

We took a photo of Mao from one of the books my mother had sent to me—a Chinese propaganda book called *The Red Sun Lights the Way Forward for Tachai*—and hung it in the Main House. On it, somebody (it looked suspiciously like Stu's handwriting) had altered his name to Chairman Mao Tse-naise and added a quote from Mr. Natural: "Oh, yeah, he's our man!" OK, yeah, humor, satire, irreverence were part of our "revaluation" of ALL authoritarian principles. But we also needed somehow to seriously figure out how we fit, how we could be part of the enormous power of the people which—if the people can eliminate all the flies in China—was the only power capable of smashing the authoritarian, oppressive, straight-ass rulers of the world.

We had to be part of the people reclaiming the world or we were just drinking milk and collecting stamps—smoking dope and feeding the fire. And in these books I thought I could find some help in convincing my brothers and sisters of that.

FALL/11

Activity around the Main House picked up as we prepared for Thanksgiving. We were ready for a big party. We'd survived seven months. We had purged the primary sources of our dysfunction. We were at a comfortable number of people on the land. We all had decent places to sleep. Our garden had been productive despite its late start, and we had gathered and preserved or stored pounds and pounds of food from nearby farms. Our chickens still laid eggs. We had pigs fattening up. We had put up a reasonable amount of firewood. Our appeal on the logging was still stuck in the clogged machinery of the court system, which meant not a tree had been touched, no roads had been built. The virginity of the forest was intact.

Two years before, the Mountfort Street boys—Mike, Stu, Brian, and me—had thrown the Beggars Banquet Thanksgiving bash with people overflowing the apartment's four rooms. We had a turkey and lots of other food and alcohol and endless joints—and some fine LSD. Sarah wasn't there. She was still living in Philadelphia. Tripping my brains out, I desperately tried to talk to her on the phone but I could barely get thoughts from my brain to my mouth. We still didn't know what we were and I wanted more than anything for her to tell me that we were really a couple in love and committed, but all I could do was make her laugh at my feeble attempts to form sentences. Last year we had been in Philadelphia, a fine and warm family gathering, a respite from the bleak interminable waiting in Boston. But Sarah's parents had suddenly taken me, alone, for a drive and a challenging conversation about our plans. What if: jail? Not jail? Marriage?

Not marriage? Oregon? What would we do in Oregon? I had stumbled through all my attempts at answering those questions, leaving them as freaked out as ever about what kind of life their daughter could have with me.

Now, we had answered all those questions. We had so much to be thankful for.

We made a list of all the people to invite, other freaks living in the Tiller Valley and our friends in Eugene—almost twenty people altogether—and let them know that anyone else was welcome. We made an elaborate menu, all of us taking responsibility for at least one thing. We had a huge shopping list and Sarah, Mike, and Sydney went to Roseburg to buy supplies, including several bottles of hard liquor, bourbon, vodka, tequila—a rarity at Ash Valley (the little bottles that Eddie's mother had brought had whet our appetites). Stu and Patrick had tinkered with the generator to get it running and we made sure we had plenty of gas so we could play music. We had stacked up extra firewood for the stove and the fireplace at the Main House. A lot of the food was also prepared in stoves at our individual houses.

We started making breads and such a couple days before and got the turkeys in the ovens (nobody had ever cooked a turkey in a woodstove before) early Thanksgiving Day itself. The feast we offered included three turkeys, mashed potatoes (my thing), stuffing, real butter (a special treat), gravy, various kinds of squash, corn, green salad, banana nut bread, fruit bread (Sarah's), a real chocolate cake (not carob!), and a couple of pies (apple and blackberry). We still had a plentiful stash of Colombian pot and all that booze.

It had been stormy rainy all day, hard rain and stiff winds. The ground and even the road was starting to get soggy.

Richard, an environmentalist friend from Eugene we'd met through our lawsuit, and a woman friend named Wendy had shown up around noon and said the river road was getting a little hairy with thick rain and tree branches and debris swirling around. They helped us with the final preparations as well as some pre-feast toking. We had told folks to show up anytime and we'd figure to eat mid-to-late afternoon. As what little light the hidden sun had provided began to disappear over the western peaks, we were ready. We fired up the generator and put the Dead on the turntable. We even opened the first bottle of bourbon and sipped on it a little nervously as we waited for more people to show up.

They never did.

Finally, Mike said, "Fuck it, I ain't waiting no more," and, with a stoned grin that swept around the room, started piling food on his plate, and the rest of us followed, attacking the spread, fourteen of us determined to devour as much as we could of this bounty that easily would have fed thirty or forty.

We ate and we ate, like we hadn't eaten for months, like it was our moral obligation to consume and enjoy this food at a higher level than we had ever eaten food before. When we could eat no more of the turkey and stuffing and potatoes and squashes and salad, we manically cleared them away, piled the dirty dishes wherever we could, passed joints as fast as we could roll and light them, and then dug into the cakes and pies, forgetting plates, diving directly in with forks and spoons until they almost instantly vanished.

Joints kept coming and now the liquor bottles were passed, swigs replacing the tentative earlier sipping. Even Sarah, who rarely drank anything alcoholic, took her swigs and fought the involuntary grimaces that contorted her face. But then she smiled and drank more. We turned the stereo up: *Concert for Bangladesh, New Riders of the Purple Sage,* more Dead. We were all dancing and laughing and clapping, stuffed and stoned and drunk and jubilant. Sarah, especially, was illuminated, moving with rhythmic wildness, reaching out to me to pull me into that frenzied, passionate motion. I wanted to be there with her and let myself go and felt the urgency of her touch, of her closeness, of every part of her gyrating, flowing, beautiful body. But in that moment, I was not enough for her. Somehow we came against the bench next to the dining room table, and then, suddenly somehow, she was on the table, never slowing down, never breaking her rhythm. And we all were mesmerized by her—by her luminous beauty set free by her raw and dazzling dance. We all loved her letting loose up above us like that, for all of us—and we clapped along, loud and joyous. And she danced until the track went silent and the needle crackled at the end of the side. She looked down at me, breathless and satiated, and I helped her off the table. Everyone seemed to take a deep breath before someone put another record on, a little softer, a little mellower.

I'd never seen Sarah so drunk, never really even seen her drunk at all, but it was a lot more than that. I'd never seen her show so openly to others that free, passionate wildness that came alive in the best times of our lovemaking. It could be so powerful that sometimes she scared me. Could I ever really satisfy that part of her? And I knew that that passion was not just a sexual, physical thing. It was intrinsic to so much that was fundamental about her. Her fierce loyalty. Her quick judgments of situations and others, good and bad. Her unflinching and sometimes harsh honesty. The intensity of her love—in every sense of that word. She'd been through a hell of a year of joy and pain and struggle and, often, putting all her intensity into supporting others—me, mostly, but her parents, too, and the family that we were trying to create at Ash Valley. She deserved to be on the table in the center of us, the star of our Thanksgiving, the physical expression of what it had meant to come this far.

I hugged her tight. She was sweaty and supple and breathed heavy and warmly into my ear.

"Let's go home," I said. I knew in a way that I hadn't fully appreciated lately how lucky I was that she loved me. I was glad to share her intensity with everyone for a while, but now I was mad with the desire to have her to myself.

"Yeah," she said, with a soft smile. We rustled up Moonbeam and covered up to make our way out into the rainy night.

FALL/12

Sarah and I staggered through the rain to the Main House sometime midmorning the next day. Mike, Paulie, Stu, Loretta, and Patrick, and Dale were drinking coffee, picking at leftovers, and beginning to try to clean up from the chaos we'd left. Stu stoked a good blaze in the fireplace. Everyone was bleary-eyed and dragging and greeted us with slow-nodding half-grins.

"Looks like you guys made it to the suburbs and back," Stu said.

"I don't remember exactly how we made it home last night," I said, "but we did wake up in our bed this morning, so …"

"Bet Sarah just could've danced all the way up there," Paulie said.

Everyone mustered a subdued laugh.

"I don't know what you're talking about," Sarah said, trying to look innocent through bleary eyes.

Richard and Wendy from Eugene peeked their heads out from the bottom of the stairs. They had slept in our old room upstairs.

"This party just keeps on rolling, eh?" Richard said as they headed toward the leftovers. He and Wendy looked as hungover as the rest of us.

"Never stops," Mike said with raspy mock enthusiasm. "NEVER stops."

We all nibbled on the remains of the turkey and hunks of bread. We had water heating on the stove for the piles of dirty dishes and pots and pans that covered every horizontal surface. Somebody lit a joint.

"Hey," Patrick said toward Richard and Wendy, "I heard you talking about some airplane hijacking. What was that all about?"

"Yeah, they were talking all about it on the radio on the way down yesterday," Richard said. "Some guy hijacked a plane out of Portland heading to Seattle, said he had a bomb. In Seattle, he let all the passengers off in exchange for parachutes and 200 grand."

Everyone kind of stopped what they were doing. "Holy shit!" Dale said. "Then what happened?"

"The plane took off again. Headed to Mexico with just the crew and the hijacker but he jumped out somewhere early in the flight."

"With the money?"

"Yeah, of course, with the money."

"Who was this guy? What was his trip?"

"They don't know much about him. White guy, forties. No note. No kind of political statement. They called him …" Richard scrunched his forehead.

"D.B. Cooper," Wendy filled in. "And they hadn't found any trace of him, last thing we heard yesterday."

"Do they know where he jumped?

"Not exactly," she said. "The plane was heading to Reno for a fuel stop. They think somewhere in Southern Washington or maybe Oregon, but they don't really know."

"Cool," said Paulie.

"Seattle to Reno?" Dale said. "Shit that would go right over us—be a perfect fucking place to jump, just beyond the most populated areas not quite into any real wilderness." His eyes got big. "Hell, yes. D.B. fucking Cooper."

"Cool," said Paulie, "We'd be the perfect place for him to come. He could hide out. We'd take care of him."

"We could split the money—we could pay off the land—and he'd still have 100 grand for himself." Dale took a big toke and let it out with a wild smile. "D.B. Cooper, man."

"I think they were thinking he's somewhere farther north," Wendy said, "if he even survived the jump." She was trying to keep the conversation based in some of the known reality of the situation. What fun was that?

"But they don't know, right?" Paulie said. "And even if he did jump somewhere away from here, who's to say, he wouldn't find his way here somehow?"

"It's a long shot at best," Patrick said, somewhat seriously, "But we'd certainly welcome him. Who knows?"

"Sure," I said, "There's a lot of space in these mountains, but we are pretty far from any neighbors … I know, I know it's fucking crazy, but crazy shit has happened in this last year—I mean how did we end up here?"

Sarah shot me a scoffing look.

"You fucking guys," Mike said. "He ain't coming here. He ain't bringing us his money. And he ain't going to clean up this fucking mess."

"Besides," Stu said. "Where would he sleep? We just got everybody straightened out and he shows up and we've got to figure it all out again. And, maybe he's a fucking asshole—200 grand or no … will he do his own dishes?"

Even Dale and Paulie laughed, if a little reluctantly, at Stu's assessment and slowly we began scraping and washing dishes.

Of course, Mike and Sarah and Stu were right. The odds of D.B. Cooper showing up and saving us were at least as steep as the mountains between his possible landing points and our valley. But we all did think it was cool that this guy pulled off such an audacious act and seems to have gotten away it, and nobody got hurt—except maybe him—in the process. It was a perfect fairy tale that somehow he would stumble upon Ash Valley and embrace us—and we, him. And as the rain dragged on, with the snow line creeping farther and farther down the hills toward us, I'd be lying if I said that D.B. Cooper, as long as they didn't catch him or find him dead, didn't maintain a steady presence in my head as a lurking answer to many of our questions.

FALL/13

Dale and Roger grabbed a ride with Richard and Wendy up to Eugene. Neither gave any indication of when they might be coming back. With the rain and the cold now settled in, we spent most of our time inside and the sense of the space we lived in shrunk significantly, which seemed to increase the restlessness of those two. It was hard for Dale to have Jack and Sydney in his face all the time. Roger had no real connection to anyone, and the awkwardness of his presence felt heavier and heavier for most of us—and for him, too, I expect.

Loretta went to Miami to help Eddie and Jeffrey in their endeavors to raise money. She flew out of Medford, also with no idea of when she'd be back, which was also true of the two men. Eddie and Jeffrey were no doubt serving the common good at the opposite end of the country and had our full support, but we also couldn't help but think that the sunshine and warmth (and ready cheeseburgers) of Florida made their duty a little less onerous.

All that left us with nine people on the ranch, the lowest our number had ever been.

Stu and I decided to walk the property to check out the water level of the creeks at various spots. The rain, with occasional flurries of snow, had been hard and steady for days and our little Ash Creek had swollen over it banks and cruised toward the river with a new sense of urgency. We sort of got trapped by a newly created creek running about fifty feet across the valley floor from a low spot in the dirt mound around the reservoir to Ash Creek. We were coming at it from our house, so to avoid it entirely we would have had to go all the way back around the reservoir. I saw a spot close to the reservoir where the stream narrowed some, so I decided to take a run at it and try to jump over it. My lead foot barely reached the opposite bank but it was so soft and muddy that I slipped back into the flowing water and was shocked to find it coming up to my chest. It was fucking cold. I scrambled to the bank and had to slither my way up, with no firm ground to grab onto. I struggled in mucky mud to get to my feet. I was soaked and muddy almost to my neck, but I could hear Stu's wild laughter over the rushing water and pelting rain. "Yeah, you fucking try it," I yelled across to him. He was looking for a narrower and shallower crossing point. A little ways farther toward Ash Creek, he found a spot where the flow seemed a little more spread out, but he didn't make it all the way across either. He ended up in water up to his waist, but he was able to walk his way out without getting quite as immersed as I had been. We'd seen enough to report back to the Main House, where we headed as directly as we could now, that the water all over the ranch was fucking high and getting higher. We were thankful that Stephen had the fire roaring as we shed all our wet and muddy clothes, to the amused delight of all who were gathered there.

Mike and Paulie moved into the Second House, with most of us helping, lugging boxes of books and kitchen supplies and their few pieces of furniture across the soggy valley floor to the road where we stacked them into the back of Stephen's truck for the short trip. It was a celebratory undertaking, reclaiming liberated territory. Sarah and I had to walk by there at least twice a day and in the last few weeks while Phillip held out, vibes were so bad that we tucked our heads down and hustled past. Now, it was a warm and welcome part of our ranch again. Mike had more space in the kitchen area for baking than he had in their cabin. Paulie was closer to all the animals. It provided an alternative space to the Main House with a decent-sized central area where a bunch of us could hang out.

One night, as though someone flipped a switch, the rain turned to steady snow. The incessant patter on our roof quieted to a slow thrumming and then to an enveloping silence. When we woke, the marshy brown surface of our meadow was coated with a pure white icing. White surrounded us, the road a flat white shelf, the hills white-highlighted trees soaring out of thick white blankets, our uncovered outhouse, twenty feet from our front door, an entirely white box.

Sarah and I tried to outlast each other, hoping the other would be the one to clear the snow from the toilet seat and experience the unavoidable chill on our bare ass. Sarah almost always held out longer than me.

This new setting was stark and wonderful and embracing and constant—big chunks of snow, falling steadily, so thick, like petals from a flower, so quiet but so substantial, they turned the very air into a plush curtain of white. The green and brown and gray of our fall world was gone and we lived in a white, white, white world—winter a few weeks shy of the solstice.

FALL/14

For one of my cooking nights, Mike taught me how to make yeast bread. I always loved when somebody— mainly Mike—made bread, but it seemed like a special skill, almost magical, turning flour and water and yeast into that wonderful stuff that sometimes I'd dig my hands into when it was still warm and it would thrill me all the way down to my tummy. Now, Mike was going to reveal the magic to me.

We started in the early afternoon, with good fires going in the fireplace and the cook stove. We basically followed the recipe in the *Tassajara Bread Book,* but Mike had developed his own style and techniques in the years he spent working in his father's bakery and since we'd been on the ranch, working with more basic tools and ingredients. I ground the whole wheat into flour with our hand-crank grinder, sixteen cups worth for the four loaves we were planning to make. I worked up a good sweat and stripped off my top layers down to my long underwear. Mike had exacting standards about how fine the flour should be. When I finished a grind, he'd grab a handful and run it through his fingers, shaking his head in disapproval until—after running it through three times, adjusting the grinder to be finer and finer—I finally got the approving smile and nod. We had heated some water on the stove and mixed that with cold water until Mike's finger thermometer determined we had the right lukewarm temperature to mix it with the yeast. We added honey to spur the growth of the yeast and some dry milk to make the bread a little smoother in both texture and taste, according to Mike. I mixed all that up—with Mike admonishing me to keep the strokes smooth and gentle:

"You ain't whipping it," he said. "You just want to blend it all, make sure all the solid shit dissolves."

Then I added about half the flour, a cup at a time, stirring briskly. As the mixture got thicker, Mike took the spoon and showed me how to beat it, going up and down in short strokes and making small circles at the top. He handed me back the spoon and watched me closely: "Up and down," he said. "Now you gotta beat the shit out of it and scrape all that stuff that sticks to the sides back to the middle." He watched me for a while. "Yeah, OK that's pretty good. Now keep going until it's all really smooth." My right arm started getting sore. I'd never appreciated how physical making bread was.

We covered the bowl with a towel and set it close to the stove to rise. Mike took a book and sat in the far corner of the living room. I sat by the kitchen table, staring at the bowl. Every once in a while I'd get up and lift the towel to check on the growth of the dough. "Quit fucking doing that," Mike shouted across the room, "It'll just make it take longer."

Finally, he said it was ready for the rest of the ingredients. Everything now would be "folded" in, using a spoon around the edge of the dough and flipping it toward the center. No more stirring. That would fuck up the strength of the dough, he said. We poured in some oil and sprinkled on some salt and Mike showed me how to fold, turning the bowl slowly with his left hand as he folded with the spoon in his right. He handed me the spoon. It was an awkward motion. "Don't fucking stir it, man," he said. Gradually as my motion got smoother, his scowl gave way to an accepting grin. As I added more flour, the dough got really thick.

"Don't worry, man," Mike said. "Keep going. You'll know when it's ready." Soon after, the dough came away from the sides and bottom of the bowl and formed kind of a cohesive lump, standing on its own.

We dumped the lump onto a floured board and Mike showed me how to knead the dough, folding it in half and pressing down with his finger and the tips of his palms to push the top half into the bottom half, rocking his whole body into the thrust of his hands into the dough, then turning it a bit and repeating that process. He nodded to me to take over. It felt good, deeply sensual, immersing my hands in the dough and driving them into it with all my strength, feeling the dough stiffen and stretch. Mike tossed fistfuls of flour on the top of the dough when it got sticky. Eventually, it turned shiny and smooth. We put it back into the bowl, brushed some oil on the top, covered it with a damp towel, and let it rise for another hour. Mike returned to his corner and his book. I took a walk outside.

It was almost dark when I got back. The dough had nearly doubled when we took the towel off. Mike said, "This is the fun part," and punched his right fist into the dough as deep as he could get it. He did that about five times and turned it over to me, saying to do another twenty-five or thirty punches. Man, me and this dough were connecting in all kinds of ways. It *was* the fun part. We covered it up again and left it for about forty-five minutes. After that, I dumped the dough back onto the board and, following Mike's instructions, formed it into a circle by folding it from the outside into the center and pushing down on it. We put the smooth side up, cut the dough circle into four roughly equal pieces and let them sit for a bit. Mike took one of the sections and shaped it into a loaf: kneading it to make it more compact, rolling it into a log shape, flattening the top, and squaring off the ends, flipping it over and pinching the seams all the way along the bottom. He put some oil in a bread pan and then the dough, seam side up and then flipped it so the now-oiled smooth side was up. He worked around the dough with his finger tips to make if fit more uniformly in the pan. It was all fluid motion for him, like his hands were a finely tuned bread-shaping tool. He looked at me matter-of-factly and said, "See?"

He talked me through the process with the other three sections, but I was clumsy and forgot some of finer points along the way. But I did get them all more-or-less into the right shape and they all fit snugly into the bread pans. We gave them about fifteen more minutes to rise in the pans, then I cut some slits across the tops, and brushed them with a mix of egg and water. Then put them in the oven. We didn't have any accurate way of knowing the temperature of the oven, but Mike had a pretty good intuitive sense of how hot it was and played with the dampers to get it to what seemed right to him.

The smell, man. The smell of baking bread is one of the greater sensual joys humans can experience. But this … this was my fucking bread, man. Mike had lit up a joint and Sarah and Stu and Patrick were hanging out and laughing about something. I hadn't really even been aware of when they came in or of their presence while we were in the thick of the bread making. I took a hit on the joint and sat as close as I could to the oven, breathing as deep as I could, digging the deepening, ripening smells coming at me. Mike said we needed to keep a close eye, but warned me about checking too often. He said it would probably take about an hour.

Finally … finally, he pronounced them done and let me pull them out of the oven. He tapped them with his fingers and they made this full hollow thud that confirmed they were ready.

They were so fucking beautiful … all four—an almost-glowing shiny golden brown, uniform across the tops. Mike said to get them out of the pans right away, so I worked a butter knife around the edges and knocked around the outside of the pan to loosen them and then, ever so gently, flipped them out and, with my bare hands, put them on at the cooling racks. I loved the feel of their almost-burning heat on my hands.

I lined them up nicely on the cooling racks to let them sit for a while. I felt this incredible sense of accomplishment and pride and looked at him with a big smile. Mike, now pretty stoned, looked back at me, also smiling, "Hey dude, you did it," he said.

"Yeah," I said, feeling kind of sentimental and dreamy and fucking proud, looking around the room at the rest of the people smiling back at me.

"But it is just fucking bread, right?" Mike said arching his eyes.

"Yeah, I guess," I said but feeling no slight. "It is just fucking bread."

It didn't take long before the munchies overtook our patience of letting the bread cool. The five of us devoured the first loaf before anybody else even showed up for dinner. `

FALL/15

One gloomy afternoon, Stephen shot a porcupine. He came tromping into the Main House, carrying it carefully by its feet, and he smiled, kind of mockingly. "Look what I got," he said, not quite sure if he should be proud or not.

"What the fuck?" said Sydney. "What are you going to do with that?"

"Hell if I know," Stephen said. "Eat it? Seems like you should be able to eat it. The son-of-a-bitch was just kind of waddling down the road and I thought of all the goddamn quills we've pulled out of our dogs and I hadn't seen anything else to hunt, so I shot it. It was pretty fucking easy. I figured we could do something with it."

"Sure," said Jack. "I bet we could eat that sucker. Skin it. Get rid of all the fucking quills. Gut it and then just boil the shit out of it. Make a stew."

Sydney made a face.

"Sure you do all that and then let me know what you think," Stu said. I was skeptical, too. You never hear about anybody eating porcupine.

"People eat porcupines," Patrick said. "Not anybody I know, but I think in some places—like Africa—it's a regular thing."

Sarah and Paulie seemed curious about it. "Worth a try, I guess," Paulie said. "There's enough of them around here— could be a whole new thing for us."

Mike kept his face in his book. He didn't seem to want to have anything to do with it.

"Don't matter to me," Stephen said.

"Shit, I'll skin it and gut it," said Jack. "I'm sure I can figure out something to do with the quills and the skin."

"I'll try to cook it," Paulie said. Sarah offered to help.

"I don't want that thing anywhere near my house," Mike said.

"Relax," Paulie said, "We'll do it here."

Jack took the dead porcupine outside. He pulled the picnic table under the porch roof to get out of the slushy snowy drizzle and laid out a bunch of newspapers and started working on it. Patrick was out there, too, offering advice and lending a hand when he could. All the dogs hovered close by. They all had tried to get at a porcupine. Porcupines don't run or hide. They just dared you to try to find a way around their quills. Our smarter dogs eventually learned to avoid them; a couple never did. But all of them were keenly interested in this dead thing lying on the table.

Paulie and Sarah got a big pot of water heating on the stove and sliced up some potatoes and onions. Stu and I brought in wood to keep the fires going. The water got close to boiling just about the time Jack finished up with the skinning and the gutting. He had a big smirking smile when he brought in a bloody disgusting looking blob of meat and dumped it in the pot, to which the veggies were already added.

Nobody had any idea how long to cook it, but the consensus seemed to be that it should be at least a couple hours. As the water came back to a boil, a nasty dank and sour smell filled the house. Sydney and Mike were driven out first and went to their respective houses. Stu, Patrick, and I decided it was a good time to go out and work on getting one of our chain saws running; we still needed a lot more firewood. Sarah remembered some organizing she wanted to do up at our house. Jack and Paulie and Stephen hung in there, though eventually they opened the outside door for some ventilation despite how cold it was outside. They all hung close to the fireplace and kept the fire going strong both for the heat and the smell of the wood smoke to counteract the odor coming out of the pot.

We all kind of wandered back into the Main House just as it was starting to get dark. The room was really hot for seven or eight feet from the stove and the fireplace and chilly everywhere else, so we shut the door. The smell had somewhat dissipated but still was oppressive. The "stew" in the pot had a slimy topping of grease that reflected the light of a kerosene lamp on a shelf above the stove. We all filed by, checking it out and turning away with various expressions of disgust.

Jack finally spoke. "Well, are we going to eat this fucking thing or what?"

No one responded except by moving farther away from the pot and shaking our heads.

"Go for it," Patrick said, laughing.

"Fuck it," said Jack, and he grabbed a fork and pulled a chunk of meat from the pot and put it in his mouth

His eyes widened as he turned toward the door and got outside as fast as he could to spit it all out.

"Fuck!" he said. "That's fucking awful."

The house almost shook with our outburst of laughter. Jack came back in, pained and laughing, too. "Get that fucking thing out of here," And the laughter went up another level. We couldn't stop. Patrick helped Jack dump some of the hot water out of the pot into the sink and then carry it outside and toss the whole thing out fifteen or twenty feet away from the house. The slop melted the thin layer of mushy snow on the ground forming a disgusting little puddle. The dogs were ecstatic. We were all ecstatically relieved that we didn't have to eat that thing. Everyone quickly volunteered to help put together a meal of fried potatoes and onions with a few eggs mixed in. That staple of our diet never tasted so good.

But it took a few days until the house was completely rid of that smell.

FALL/16

Ileft the land for the first time in more than seven weeks. Earl, our friend in Days Creek, had gotten himself an oil stove so he was giving away a bunch of firewood. He had several cords of wood stashed around his property, and he was giving us first crack at it. We took a couple of trucks down to load up. Two of our three chain saws weren't working well, so we also needed to take them into Canyonville to get them fixed. With snow settled into the valley and more coming every day, we were realizing we didn't have nearly enough wood to get us through the winter. We were heating seven houses and cooking with wood. We were burning through it like crazy.

I felt a little sad to leave the ranch. I was proud of my long run and had developed a comfortable rhythm of time at our house of reading and writing and hanging out and cuddling close with Sarah, time at the Main House hanging in the mornings and most dinners, and doing chores and spending time with everyone else on the land. We had almost no visitors and relative calm among us to match the hush of the snow that had become the defining characteristic of the valley. I felt a real sense of personal peace and purpose and freedom and a deeper than ever connection to the land. I was a little afraid that driving out that front gate would make all that vanish.

But it was always great to see Earl. He directed and chatted while four of us made quick work of filling up the two trucks with a mix of madrone and fir, well-seasoned and bone dry as it had been stored in a few of the many structures that dotted Earl's property. A drippy rain was falling in Days Creek. The snow had switched to rain with the drop in elevation about half way between the ranch and Tiller. Earl loaned us a couple of tarps to drape over the stacked piles in the truck beds. After we secured them, pulling them taut and tying them down to Earl's satisfaction, he invited us to "set" for a while in his small house.

Earl was proud of his new stove and had it cranked way up. Already warmed up from loading all that wood and our multiple layers of long underwear, shirts, and jackets that had become standard for us moving around in the deep chill of the ranch, we were all kind of knocked back by the wave of heat that greeted us as we filed into his living room and tried to squeeze into the small space. Earl took his spot in the rocker close to the stove, with his old dog Queenie curled next to him. He had a big smile as we all started shedding and undoing zippers and buttons on our outer layers.

"She sure does put out the heat, don't she?" Earl asked, scanning the room. "I bet you boys would like some coffee." He didn't wait for an answer. He went into the small kitchen right off the living room and turned on the burner under the tea kettle. Five minutes later he came out with hard plastic cups, two at a time, in which his Nescafe instant coffee crystals were dissolving into the hot water. When we all had our cups, he passed around a sugar bowl and a spoon.

"How are things going up on your ranch?" He asked. "Lots of snow?"

"Yup," Stu answered. "Lots of snow, close to a foot already. Is there usually this much snow up there this time of year? I don't remember hardly any snow in Tiller last winter."

"Well, you are up quite a bit higher than Tiller. But I do believe it's a little early for you to be having that much snow."

"We're doing OK," I said. "But all this snow so early makes us realize how much firewood we're going to need and the snow makes it harder to get at it now. We really appreciate you helping us out with all this wood."

"Well, it's my pleasure. I've got no use for it anymore. I've got to tell you boys that folks down here are saying you all are leaving, can't handle the snow and the cold. They don't see you so much anymore?"

We all laughed.

"We ain't leaving," Mike said, "Don't you worry about that. We're doing better than ever because some people did leave, some people that were kind of working against us. Now we've got a good group of people working together."

"It's little harder for us to get out with the snow," said Stephen, "and it's pretty good just hanging out up there. The snow is real beautiful. I guess people don't want to leave as much."

"Well, I sure am happy to hear that. I know you fellas here have been at it from the start. You did have a lot of people up there last summer. It's probably good to get it down to the ones that really want to do the work and get along. You just let me know if there is any way I can help. I've probably got another load or two of wood out here and you're welcome to it." He smiled and reached down to pet Queenie.

Fucking Earl. What a guy!

FALL/17

Willie told us it was time to kill John Mitchell—the pig, our male animal pig, not the attorney general. Martha (named, of course, for John's wife), our sow, was pregnant and due soon. With winter coming, feed costs would go up and we were unlikely to get him any fatter. Willie guessed he was about 250 pounds, a little below what he should be but not bad for our first attempt at raising pigs and still good for lots of meat, which we all were looking forward to. The weather was right: cold! So we'd have time to get him butchered up and then get the meat down to our freezer locker in Days Creek.

Willie said he would help us and told us to be ready first thing in the morning. So a bunch of us gathered at the Main House just after dawn. Based on his instructions, Stu and Jack built a big fire in the pit in the front yard. We put a 50-gallon drum of water on there to heat up so we could scald the dead pig to make it easier to remove hair from the skin. Stephen loaded up our 30.06 and, over a joint with our coffee, we decided Mike would be the executioner. He talked the toughest and I'd killed all those chickens, so I was glad to have somebody else with blood on their hands.

Willie showed up just about the time we finished the joint. I'm pretty sure he could tell we were stoned by the grin he greeted us with. We invited him in for some coffee and he ran down the process to us. We'd been over it a couple of days before, so it was just kind of a refresher.

"OK, we should get on 'er," Willie said. He looked around the room with the same grin we'd seen earlier. "You boys ready for this? It goes fast."

We all assured him we were. Most of us jumped into the back of his pickup for the short ride to the goat barn, but Sydney and Jack stayed behind at the Main House keeping the pit fire stoked to heat the water.

Willie backed his truck up to the short deck leading into the goat barn. Patrick and I volunteered to lure John, the pig, out of the barn. Inside, we opened the door to his stall and started scattering a path of some grain-based hog food to the barn door. We hadn't fed him for a day or so, so he was eagerly scarfing it up. We continued the path out the door, on to the deck. Mike stood with the rifle where the deck met the road, Willie behind him, Stephen with the sticking knife, just to his side. Paulie, Stu, and Sarah were on opposite sides of the deck between those guys and the barn. After we spread out the last of the grain, Patrick and I went next to Stephen, essentially forming a chute to steer John to his death. The pig ate his way out of the barn, delightedly gobbling up his grain treat. Just before stepping off the outer threshold, he seemed to suddenly realize he was surrounded and raised his head to look around.

"Now!" Willie shouted. Mike pulled the trigger, scoring a square hit in the center of the pig's forehead. John dropped to his side, motionless for a beat, and then his legs started kicking spasmodically into the air.

It was dead silent. Everybody but Willie was stunned, immobile, staring at this hulk of an animal, suddenly surely dead but still moving with a forceful energy.

"Stick him!" Willie shouted. "Stick him!" He looked at Stephen, who held the specially sharpened knife but seemed to have no idea what to do with it, transfixed, like the rest of us, on John's dramatic death scene. None of us moved.

Willie grabbed the knife from Stephen and rushed to the dead pig, rolled him on his back, felt for the right spot where the torso moved into the neck, and jabbed the knife into it, twisting it back and forth. When he pulled it out, blood flowed quickly around the throat, onto the deck, spilling over to the ground, staining the snow bright red.

Willie wiped his brow, stood up and looked around with something between amusement and disgust. The spell seemingly broken, we shuffled in our places and averted our eyes. "I told you it goes fast," he chuckled. "Now let's get this pig hung. I don't think I can do that by myself."

Now we all eagerly rushed to help, hoping to make up for our dereliction. It was hard for us all to grab a hold on the dying pig, but we did manage to drag him close to the rear end of Willie's truck where he had a hoist. We awkwardly lifted up his butt end so Willie could attach the ends of a chain from the hoist around his rear legs and then stood almost like spotters as Willie worked the hoist to lift the entire carcass in the air. Blood flowed out the hole in his neck. We all looked around at each other, still mostly stunned, but somebody laughed—it must have been Paulie who started, but soon it was all of us, even Willie.

Mike, still holding the gun, jumped in the cab with Willie and the rest of us followed behind as the truck eased its way down the road to the Main House. The blood dripping from John Mitchell's throat laid out a slowly diminishing red line in front of us in the snow centered between the tire ruts our vehicles had worn in the road. We felt somewhat triumphant, but also, once again, humbled by how inept we were at so much of the nitty-gritty of ranch life. Beneath the bravado earned from participating in a gruesome kill, was the certainty that it would have been a bloody fiasco if not for Willie—sorta like barbecued old chicken or porcupine stew.

Sydney and Jack greeted us as Willie maneuvered the truck to back down the front yard of the Main House toward the fire pit and the steaming water. We all gathered round the hanging pig, still swinging from the bumpy jerky last 20 feet of the ride. It felt almost ritualistic. Nobody said anything, but the exchanged looks, reluctantly grim smiles, low awkward laughter felt like we were engaged in a ceremony without knowing any suitable liturgy. We'd taken a life and it felt more sacrificial than the deer or the mass of chickens. This pig—this bloodied corpse—had had a name and now the sight and smell and weight of its death hung between us.

Willie couldn't take that for long. He cleared his throat and as we all looked at him, he said, "Hey, we still got a lot of work to do."

Using the hoist, we dipped the hanging carcass in the hot water, then raised it out to scrape off the hair and dirt from the skin. Then Willie moved his truck so the corpse was away from the scalding barrel and hanging over a tarp to catch all the funky shit falling off the pig. And Sarah, studying instructions from a recent issue of *Mother Earth News*, took our sharpest knife and went to work on removing the head.

Sarah was hard focused. She plunged the knife down to the bone in the back of the neck just below the ears and then sliced an incision all the way around the neck. I could hardly watch. She gritted her teeth as she severed the windpipe and the gizzard. Patrick grabbed the head as it started to fall and twisted and pulled until it came off in his hands. In an almost involuntary act of triumph, he held it up high—like something out of the *Lord of the Flies*. But for the rest of us, that gesture brought only mild laughter, no frenzy. John Mitchell in his death had ceased to be a symbol or any kind of metaphor. He was becoming meat.

Sarah smiled a little grimly as Patrick lowered the head to a table and started to clean and trim it. Sarah set to work on the rest of the carcass: splitting the breast bone, opening the belly, removing the entrails, heart, and lungs, splitting the backbone and then the entire carcass with a saw. She was resolute, unfazed by all the blood and slimy innards, calm, and most definitely in charge. Most of the rest of us just loitered around her, helping as we could, disposing of waste parts, helping position the carcass for her best access, encouraging her.

With the carcass split, a couple of us could now handle carrying a half. We removed the two halves from the hoist and carried them up to the root cellar for a 24-hour chilling. Sarah was exhausted but glowing with a sense of satisfaction for getting through some hard-ass disgusting work. The next day she was at it again doing the cleaner and more directly fulfilling work of turning the carcasses into cuts of meat: hams, bacon, picnic shoulder, Boston (!) butt, loin, spare ribs, neck bone, head and jowls, feet, and various type of trimmings for sausage. We wrapped most of it up in paper to take to the freezer locker, but we kept a loin roast and some of the belly meat (uncured bacon) to eat right away. Man, that meat was delicious!

Sarah was a star with that pig. The Jewish girl from suburban Philly wielding a butcher knife like some grizzled guy from South Philly's Italian market. I don't know why I was still amazed at the breadth of her abilities and willingness to take on tough stuff. She was great with numbers, at making our little cabin feel like a cozy home. She was fiercely honest and frighteningly loyal and capable of such powerful, embracing love that I often struggled to feel worthy of it. But then … butchering a fresh dead pig? Taking it on and getting it done. Wow.

I suppose the ranch brought some of that out of most of us. City-kid Stu becoming a top rate gardener. Shy Paulie finding a voice to help guide us through the bullshit that bogged us down. Mike mastering wood-stove baking and occasionally even showing his delight in sharing his creations with all of us. Stephen, for all his steadfast individualism, trying to find ways to be part of our often amorphous community. Eddie spending any time at all in our wilderness home. Jeffrey embracing the peace and solitude of his cabin on the hill. And the two of them serving the people in a critical and dangerous way, trying to secure this place for us all. Loretta, the newest of us, had joined in their effort in maybe the most dangerous way of all. Sydney and Jack still stalwart as residents of Ash Valley despite their apathetic resistance to creating a truly conscious and functional community. And even me, learning to build and fix things with my hands, overcoming my natural klutziness that had led my father to mockingly call me his "mechanical genius." The ranch allowed us *and* forced us to alter who we had been.

But Sarah. Wow. After all that we had been through together over the past two-and-half years, how could she still stun me with these new revelations of all that she was and could be. It was thrilling and frightening to me. But I was so proud of her—and she was obviously but modestly proud of herself—as we devoured delicious pig meat over the next few weeks.

FALL/18

The snow kept drifting down, frozen drizzle, accumulating a foot and half in the deeper spots now. The valley was quiet except when somebody got ambitious and got the chain saws going to cut some firewood, the roar ringing from one end of the ranch to the other—maybe stirring some of us to pull ourselves away from whatever fire we were next to go help out and maybe score a little wood for ourselves. We were all barely staying ahead of what we were burning and we hadn't even officially entered winter.

There wasn't a lot else we could do beyond trying to keep vehicles running, the road clear enough to get out, cooking, reading, indoor crafts, planning for next year's garden (Stu with some consultation with whoever was nearby as he pored through the seed catalogs he'd accumulated and Rodale's *Organic Farming* book), or trying to figure out how to make our community work better AND be part of the coming Revolution (me with my books and notebooks at the table next to our woodstove).

Here's one analysis I came up with:

We are here because:

a) we are a group of friends which has grown over the years and has had a long-standing, often vague, goal of living together.

b) due to certain common perceptions of death culture & common liberating experiences we felt the need to leave our home towns, drop out of school, quit our jobs, leave the city, and live on the land with a group of people who we felt close to.

Some of these perceptions are:

1) death culture sucks (self-explanatory)

2) we sensed a need to break away from the incredible
dependence on technology and learn basic rules of survival

3) we have to be as independent of death culture as possible—therefore we must grow our own food, raise our own
animals, make our own bullets, make our own books

4) we are better able to cope with things
in the country than in the city

5) we are better able to cope with things
with a group of people than alone

6) we are better able to cope with things in Ash Valley with this group of people (this is a ? I'm sure)

**Some perceptions that I think are held by most of us
but not all of us are:**

1) that we are a developing revolutionary element in a pre-
revolutionary period in our society. The groundwork is being laid

2) that the revolution is necessary for the positive future development of the human race

Some perceptions held by some of us but not all of us:

1) that if we get our shit together to live produc-
tively on this land and get high spiritually and learn
to love that we will be able to overcome death culture without a violent, authoritarian revolution

2) that preoccupation with and preparation for
a violent revolution leads to an abundance of nega-
tivity and an authoritarian nightmare

Going forward

c) we all want to express our creativity, to
do what we can ...

d) we all want to learn about the earth

e) we all want to find a good way to live

f) we all want to take advantage of the potential of this land for supplying people with very cheap
or free organic grains and vegetables and fruit.

No answers, for sure. I was just trying to corral the questions.

In the same notebook, Sarah had made her Christmas list.
She was working on a watercolor poster kind of thing for Mike
and Paulie with a sunrise and a quote from Chairman Mao:
"Never before have the masses of the people been so inspired,
so militant, and so daring as at present." And a similar thing
for Patrick with a rainbow background and the beginning of
a Wordsworth poem: "My heart leaps up when I behold/ A
rainbow in the sky:/ So was it when my life began;/ So is it
now I'm a man;/ So be it when I shall grow old,/ Or let me
die." She was crocheting a blanket for Stephen, doing macrame
hangings for Jeffrey and Sydney and Jack, crocheting hats for
Stu, Loretta, and Eddie. She hadn't come up with an idea for
Roger but we hadn't seen him for a while.

I didn't have a Christmas list, wasn't really planning to do
anything. Don't think many people were. But Sarah was into it,
so that was cool. We were already in the midst of Hanukkah
and Mike had used that as an excuse to make some challahs,
which were fabulous. Nobody had a menorah and we did not
do any of the rituals (four Jews were left among us: Sarah,
Mike, Paulie, and Stu).

All this seasonal stuff was really about the Winter Solstice. The days were really getting short. We got less than eight hours of daylight and with the usual lead gray sky, it felt like less. Mornings were slow for Sarah and me. It was hard to get out of bed and get the fire going in the cold and the dark—and to be the first to hit our open-air shitter, to scrape the snow and ice before experiencing the rude shock of bare ass to chilled seat. We'd make our hobo coffee and linger. Listen to the surging creek. Bring enough firewood in for the rest of the morning and the coming night. Putter about until we could find the motivation to bundle up for the mile-long walk to the Main House, following our freshly frosted ruts in the snow, a different undertaking from when the road was dry and bare. Some days, just a few—if we had enough food to get us through—we talked ourselves into not going and just hung out at our place with Moonbeam and our cats.

But most days, we did make it to the Main House, as did most everybody else. We kept it warm in there. And it was mellow. People reading, cooking, shooting the shit, making plans for the next town trip. We were doing a lot fewer of those because of the constantly tenuous condition of our vehicles and because road conditions were rougher especially on the two-mile slope from the river road to the ranch. They kept the river road clear most of the time—to keep the log trucks going—but we never really knew until we ventured out. That also had reduced the flow of visitors to almost zero.

Usually, at some point in the day, some people would get it together to go out and do something—firewood, animals, vehicles—for a couple of hours then return red-faced and chilled and huddle close to the fire and relate whatever successes or failures they'd had or talk about next steps or get someone else involved in what they were trying to do. For the most part, there was an absence of the bullshit, quibbling, and keeping score that had so often come between us.

We were almost out of dope, so we tried to stretch it out, keeping the dwindling stash at the Main House and only breaking it out when we had something approaching a quorum (though there was no formal understanding about that) usually after dinner. Eddie, Jeffrey, and Loretta were off doing the dealing thing and there was some sense that they should be back soon to replenish the stash. But we never knew for sure when they might show up. We saved the last for a solstice celebration.

We had three joints left to share among the nine of us on the longest night of the year. We had a subdued party. No alcohol. We just savored the last of our stash and shared quiet reflections and some easy laughs about all the crazy shit that had gone down. Another season of challenges and growth. We were still here and things were good. The full of winter still loomed ahead, but we seemed ready and we knew now that the light was coming back.

As the days had shortened, the walk back to our house at night always seemed longer. It was another level of dark when the clouds closed in the sky. We were glad to have Moonbeam and her keen senses walking beside us. But on the night of the solstice, no clouds blocked the dramatic light a quarter moon cast over the snowscape of the valley, a warm white light, an angelic light, like a halo over all the land, over all of us. Sarah and I held hands and were humbled and silent as we moved through it, guided and protected by its divine luminosity.

GUY MAYNARD

Winter

WINTER/1

Christmas was all blue and white. The snow had tapered off over the past few days and the gray dome that so often hovered over us had opened to a deep rich chilled blue. The sun emerged midmorning and made the icy snow spread over the valley sparkle. It was fucking cold but the brightness of the day still cheered us. A few of us took advantage of the dry day to cut down a couple of decent-sized fir snags not far up the hill across from the Main House and drag down six-foot pieces to the front yard and cut them into firewood-sized rounds. We got a roaring blaze going in the fireplace and Jack made a big batch of fried potatoes.

It was a low-key day. No carols. No Santa. No Jesus. But Sarah handed out her gifts, which everybody seemed pleased with. And Paulie had made some blue and green striped candles, one for each house. And Sydney had done little paintings on some cedar planks that Jack had sanded down and adorned with some carved curly-q details on the corners. Good gentle vibes all around.

A kind of holiday, I guess, though not all that distinguishable from the rest of our winter days, which focused on keeping warm and eating.

The dry clear days held through New Year's and the transition to 1972 came and went quietly. No booze. No dope. Sarah and I were early to bed to snuggle under our covers and celebrate the second anniversary of our first lovemaking on the mattress on the floor in faraway Mountfort Street. In the tender aftermath, to the sounds of our woodstove crackling and the creek rumbling through the tranquil, frozen night, we reflected on the year we had just lived through: trial, marriage, cross-country road trip, Tiller, the ranch, the chaos, the purge, Sarah's dad, the sun, the rain, the snow, the incredible peace and love that at that very moment filled our funky cabin to a point of bursting. It was too much, impossible, but we had lived it, every bit of it. What wonders might now lay ahead of us?

WINTER/2

In the next day's mail, I got a letter from my probation officer, saying that as of the first of the year, because of a change in territory assignments, my case would be transferred to his partner, William V. Hamm. Seriously. Maybe our next pig should be named Bill.

Around the same time, Patrick was up in the woods behind his place scouting for firewood when two bedraggled hound dogs wandered into his path. They had tags identifying them as belonging to a man from Canyonville. They eagerly followed Patrick back to the valley where they scarfed up a couple bowls of dry dog food under the suspicious watch of the rest of our dog pack. The next trip to town, Patrick called the number, and the man who answered told him he'd been hunting for bear up in those woods (bear!). He was greatly relieved to hear that his hounds had been found alive and said he'd get up to the ranch as soon as he could to pick them up.

Well, he did and he was so grateful that he brought a couple of hound puppies to give to Patrick: a Black and Tan and a Walker Coonhound. Patrick welcomed them. They were full of life and insanely cute. He immediately named them Maggie and Molly. When Sarah first saw them at the Main House, she instantly fell in love with the Walker hound, Molly. She was particularly adorable: big, floppy ears, hanging well below her prominent jutting nose; droopy eyes framed in black, their deep brown pupils somehow vacant and piercing at the same time; a smooth coat blending deep black and honey brown with accents of pure white. Right away, Sarah started begging Patrick to give her Molly. I thought she was kidding—at first.

Patrick, who had already developed an attachment to both hounds, thought so, too. He'd earned them fair and square, after all. But Sarah was persistent, using whatever argument she could muster: all the work that raising two puppies at the same time would be; Patrick's cabinmate Roger already had a crazy dog, Bro; the brother and sister (both Scorpios no less) communal sharing thing; that she and Molly had formed a love-at-first sight connection. Patrick tried to resist. I tried to talk her out of it. One dog, especially a dog of Moonbeam's eminence and intensity, was plenty for me, and how would Moonbeam put up with this little runt of a puppy? But our arguments were useless. Sarah was determined and unlike the monkey she tried to talk me into during our transient winter in Boston, adding Molly to our family was not completely crazy. When we left the Main House that night the little coonhound meandered along beside us.

It was an especially long walk home that night. We had to coax Molly forward on her little legs as she stopped to smell whatever presented itself to her always active nose. Moonbeam was especially impatient, clearly wondering what this little beast was doing tagging along with us. Finally, at about the goat barn with all its glorious pig shit for Molly to revel in, I picked her up to carry her the rest of the way. She did not object. After we finally got home, Sarah was triumphant and delighted to curl up with our newest family member in the warmth of our loft.

WINTER/3

Steady snow returned, giving us more than two feet on the valley floor. We could see the patterns of our lives in the paths we had created as the snow deepened. We made two parallel ruts in the road when we had running vehicles, mostly with Stephen's one-ton, the best in the snow. But even that usually reliable rig was down now. Sarah and I followed one of those ruts between our house and the Main House, keeping it tamped down. It widened out past the Second House, Mike and Paulie's steps added to ours—and even more from the goat barn from all the foot traffic to attend to the horses and take care of Martha and her eight darling piglets. With no vehicles moving, lately the ruts were getting filled in beyond Shantytown, to the front gate and down the access road. But there were well-defined paths across the valley, from the three houses along the creek.

The tractor was down, too. That meant gathering firewood involved carrying all the gear—chain saws, oil, gas, axes—off the paths through the ever-deepening snow farther into the woods in search of standing snags, and then hauling what we cut back to the Main House or disbursing it to individual houses. It made hard work harder. We were now getting two or three day's worth at a time. Next year ... next year would be different. We had some small snags in the ash and oak woods around the reservoir, not far from our house. One morning I woke up and we didn't have enough wood to build a big enough fire just to make coffee. We didn't have a chain saw or even a bow saw at our place, so I took our axe and chopped down a little dead oak about fifty feet away and then chopped it into stove-sized pieces. We burned all of that in about forty-five minutes. We spent most of the rest of the day hauling a chain saw and accessories down to our house, cutting up some more of the little oaks and ashes and one pretty substantial fir from the woods above the road—about a hundred yards away—and dragging them through the snow. That maybe gave us a week's worth.

We all spent more time at the Main House, which was where we gathered most of the firewood. Some nights we didn't even start a fire at our house. The walk from the Main House heated us up and, as soon as we got to our house, we'd just jump under the covers on our bed with Moonbeam and Molly and our cats, Kachina and Mocha, bundling around us.

Stu and Stephen hitched into town one day to check out a 1955 Chevy station wagon that we'd heard about through Earl. They ended up buying it for $100. We hoped to use that for town trips, to try to reduce the demands on our pickups, so we'd have them available for more work-related stuff. But the SW—as it was to be called—broke down ten miles away on its first trip to the ranch. Stu said it was something pretty simple with the fuel line. He and Jack hoofed and hitchhiked to fix it the next day and had it parked in front of the Main House by nightfall. Stu swore it would be a good and reliable car.

Patrick, Paulie, and I got to try it out the next day with a trip to Canyonville to do some collective laundry which had been building up for a while (and to grab a burger at the Airport Cafe). We also stopped in to see Earl, who had just had a short stay in the hospital. He was feeling better and his spirits seemed good. He was really happy to see us. He sung the praises of the SW. It ran just fine for us that day .

Around the same time, Stephen hitchhiked off the ranch to take one of his periodic breaks, leaving us with eight. He was never gone very long on his mysterious forays. Maybe he had a warm honey someplace. In Stu's most recent check-in call with the folks in Florida, Eddie hinted that they would be heading home soon. We also kind of expected Dale to come back any day, though with him we also knew we might never see him again.

For all the hassles with the vehicles and firewood, I had no desire to be anywhere other than Ash Valley with those seven? Eight? Twelve people? Reading, eating, gathering firewood, feeling so warm beneath the covers in our loft surrounded by deep chill. The all-encompassing presence of the snow blanketing everything, confining our movements, lighting the grayest of days, brought with it a kind of liberating grace. This couldn't last. The roads would clear, people escaping the cities would come and see us. All kinds of work would be possible and necessary. Something would happen with our court case. The world would come back into our valley and we would have to go out into it more. So, for now, I was more than content to relish this simplicity and the stillness that winter had given to me.

WINTER/4

One morning savoring some coffee as we watched the snow glide down to lay a fresh topping on our meadow, our house warmed by a quick hot fire from small oak logs from a nearby snag, we heard a busy scratching sound from under our floor. Sarah and I looked up curiously at each other. The dogs and cats were laying on the floor between us and the stove, so it wasn't them. Moonbeam and Mocha perked up quizzically toward the sound. Molly, content and warm, couldn't be bothered. I stomped on the floor near where the sound was coming from, near the center pole, and it stopped. But in less than a minute it started up again.

I slipped on my boots and grabbed a jacket and went outside, followed by Moonbeam and Kachina. Molly didn't budge. The pie-shaped spaces between the floor-supporting joist (resting on pier blocks) under the house were still mostly visible but it was hard to get a very good look in there because of the snow, which was close to three feet deep just beyond what the roof overhang kept clear, about 18 inches from the exterior wall. But I could see signs of some disturbance—small footprints melded together?—in the snow near one piece of the pie, while all around it the snow was pristine, untouched. Moonbeam got almost frantic, shoving her nose in the opening as far as she could. She was convinced something was under there. I grabbed a shovel and flashlight from the house and cleared the snow away near that section and lay on my belly to peer in as best I could. "Holy shit," I yelled loud enough for Sarah to hear and come out. The narrow end of the pie slice, next to the center pole, was crammed with a wild array of stuff from our house: pens, nut shells, pieces of dog food, shredded paper, and most amazing of all, the little stash dish Sarah had brought back from Philadelphia, which had gone missing a week or so ago. We had figured that one of us had just put it someplace strange (each of us blaming the other). But, no. We had, it seemed, a formidably skilled pack rat.

I couldn't see it in there. All our commotion must have sent it skittering away. We left the rat's loot where it was and returned to the warmth of the house, sort of laughing about this resourceful rodent that had taken up residence under our house and sort of freaked out that it had such apparently easy and total access to the insides. Mocha was obviously no use in deterring it.

I decided the best idea was to shoot it with our .22 rifle. I cleared the snow more thoroughly from the area around the opening to the "crawl" space under that piece of the pie. I made a firm and clear path from our front door to that spot. If—the next time we heard it rustling around down there—I could sneak up to that spot without spooking it, I could just shove the barrel of the gun into the opening and fire. There was some clearance under the joist but not much. The rat would have no place to go from the tip of the pie slice except toward me and the bullet heading toward him. I brought the rifle home from the Main House (where I kept it in case I got a surprise visit from my probation officer) that night, loaded it with five bullets, and left it right by the door so I'd be ready.

Sure enough, soon after we woke up the next morning, we heard the noises from under the floor. Sarah was still under the covers in the loft, so I motioned to her to stay there and keep all the animals up there and be as quiet as possible. I slipped on my boots, grabbed the rifle, and eased out the door. I could still hear the rat fussing with his stuff as I went out. I hustled to my prepared spot, stuck the rifle in and aimed straight down the middle of the pie slice and fired five shots as fast as I could.

Sarah came rushing out. Moonbeam ran ahead of her and Kachina and, even, Molly behind her. All noise from the rat's lair had ceased. I shone the flashlight in and saw no sign of the rat, dead or alive. His accumulated booty was more scattered than it had been. I figured I either wounded him and he was able to slip away somehow, to, hopefully, die somewhere else (a rotting dead rat under the house would have maybe been worse than a living thieving one). But there was no sign of blood that I could see. Or maybe I just scared him enough to drive him away for good. Either way, it felt like some kind of victory.

Sarah brought out our broom and stretched out with the handle to reach into the under-house space and painstakingly recover our stuff. It's amazing what that little fucker had taken. The stash box was still in one piece. Some of our best pens were there and—in ripped, now mostly illegible pieces—some of my brilliant notes. We never did hear from him again.

A couple of days after that, when we wandered up the Main House midmorning, we were surprised to see Roger casually drinking coffee, as if he never left. He nodded a greeting with a slight smile. He'd been hanging out in Eugene, crashing with Richard or Dougy and Jill. He didn't say much about anything he'd done, just that he'd hung out with some cool people but the city finally got to him, so he and Bro had hitchhiked back, arriving last night after Sarah and I had left to go to our house.

WINTER/5

Dale was the next of our absent comrades to return. He seemed mellowed out, refreshed, showing some of the solidity that had made him a stalwart friend and one of our leaders in earlier days—before Sydney shook up everything for him. He'd been staying in Eugene, mostly at Richard's house. He and Roger had run into each other a few times up there but didn't spend much time together. Like Roger, he got a yearning to be back on the land, I guess, and he felt ready. He'd gotten a ride to Canyonville with one of Richard's roommates who was heading to California. And then hitchhiked to Tiller, where, by pure chance, he connected with Stu and Mike, returning from a town trip in the SW.

He had brought a few joints, gifts from Richard, one of which the three of them smoked on the way up the river road, so they were all laughing and smiling when they pulled up to the Main House. Dale looked good, and, after the hugs and greetings as he climbed out of the car, he got serious, took a deep breath and did a slow 360 of the snow-covered valley. "Man, I just forget how fucking beautiful this place is when I've been away too long. It's just too much to hold onto when you're not surrounded by it. Unreal, man, fucking unreal."

He lit up a joint as soon as he settled into a spot at the kitchen table. We'd been dry for a while so we all gathered in a tight circle around him. That first deep pull felt good. Good stuff. He lit another as Mike carefully fingered the tiny roach to get the last bit out of the first one.

We all got nicely stoned and gradually spread out around the room to the various sitting spots and Stu tossed a couple of fir rounds on the fire. "So, how the hell you been?" Sydney asked.

Dale smiled at her. "Good," he said, with almost a smile. "I've been good. Richard's is a cool place to stay. Good people. And I got to hang some with Dougy and Jill. I heard some music, played some music. Eugene is all right. But it is a city." The room greeted that comment with a hum of collective approval.

"I met with the lawyers a couple of days ago," he said. The mood shifted and everyone stiffened. "The judge has scheduled a hearing for March on our appeal of his ruling that we can't even sue the fucking Forest Service because we are just landowners." He paused and looked around the room.

"So … what do they think our chances are?" Sarah asked.

"Not good," Dale said, scanning the room, almost laughing, "I mean, shit, we've known that all along, right? A bunch of hippies suing the fucking government?"

"I thought they were going to do research," I said, "find some precedents."

"Yeah, they did. They found some stuff, where people sued about roads and dams and shit like that, but the damages were real specific and they didn't *stop* anything, they just got some compensation. The lawyers said we'd have a hard time translating our damages into money—and even if we could, they'd still cut the fucking trees." He smiled. "Sorry."

"Fuck that," said Mike. "I ain't going to sit here and watch them cut those trees down."

"What are you going to do, Mike?" Sydney asked. "Shoot 'em? Blow 'em up?"

"I don't know, man, we've got to do something, right? Motherfuckers!"

"It's not over yet, right?" Paulie said. "Who knows maybe something good will happen?"

"And even if we lose in court, there's other ways besides guns and bombs to stop them," Patrick said.

"Yeah," said Jack. "Maybe we dose their water jugs … Maybe we have a big party and invite people to set up camps all over the hillside—and stay."

It got quiet for a bit.

"Fuck 'em all," Stu said.

"We've got some time to think about it, right?" Sarah said.

"Yeah," Dale said. "We do have some time, a couple of months to the hearing, and the lawyers have not given up. There's more appeals we could do. And, man, shit's happening out there. It's 19 fucking 72. Nixon's running again. Some group called Movement in Amerika planted bombs in safe deposit boxes in nine banks in big cities last summer with some kind of delayed fuse and they just sent a letter to newspapers saying where they were before they were set off and that this was a warning of what could be done down the road if they keep fucking with the people. Shit, just the other day in Louisiana a couple of cops and a couple of Blacks got killed and a whole bunch of cops and people got hurt in a shootout. Shit's happening. Maybe not the Revolution—it ain't exactly clear, but shit *is* happening. Where do we fit in all that? Where do our trees fit in all that? Do we? Do they? What do *we* do if the Man comes crashing into our piece of paradise?"

What could all those books I was reading tell me about how to deal with this? Not an abstraction. Not something theoretical. Not Cuba, not China, not San Quentin. Our very own living breathing contradiction. The Man and his machines versus us and our dreams. Cutting those trees right in our face would be a triumph for everything we hated: capitalism raping nature for the joyless, wham-bam orgasm of material gain, the poisonous tentacles of death culture squeezing the spirit out of this valley. But we weren't armed except for a couple of old rifles or trained in any kind of resistance, violent or not. We weren't even united on what sort of resistance we'd be willing to do.

"Yeah," I said. "Like Dale said, we've got to decide how we're going to connect with the revolutionary stuff that is going on. If the fucking lawyers can't save our trees, then we've got to find ways to work with people who can. Right?"

"Sure, Tucker, sure," Stu said. "You and Mike get that all figured out and let us know how to do that. For right now, what about we kill that last joint and welcome Dale home."

Mike kind of snorted but everybody else laughed in agreement. Dale nodded to me as he fired up the last joint. I didn't have a plan. I couldn't even translate the Revolution that I could sometimes see so clearly sitting by my woodstove in my snow-covered cabin to anything most of my brothers and sisters could relate to. Mike and I could riff on political strategies. Dale could bring his cosmic darkness-and-light vision to the discussion in a way that acknowledged the class and race and economic struggles in the real world. Patrick was always game for deep and probing discussions of how we change the world. Sarah, Stu, and Walter (while he was here) advocated for us to become the peaceful, mellow example of the possibility of the power of collaborative living and organic farming as an alternative to the straight world. How could we do that with fucking bulldozers ripping roads through the virgin forest and screaming chain saws wiping out the trees,

Faced with an imminent threat and a perfect opportunity to demonstrate the power of the people to stand up against destruction, greed, and evil disdain for the precious 1,000 year-old treasures that had been such gracious hosts to us, we could do no better than beg to a court system we knew to be corrupt to its core.

And I had nothing better. The joint came around and I took a long deep toke and felt another surge of that wonderful fuzzy consciousness and laughed with everybody else as Dale told a story about Dougy and Jill pulling together a great steak and prawns meal with shit Dougy and him shoplifted from Safeway.

WINTER/6

We got a package of medical supplies from my father: antibiotics, cough syrup, cold medicine, salves and lotions for burns or cuts or other skin irritations (including more scabies-killing Kwell), vitamins, non-narcotic pain pills, medicine for vomiting and diarrhea, and a whole bunch of other stuff. He had been promising me this comprehensive medical package for a while and he really came through. The package had clearly been opened.

The woman who ran the Tiller Post Office still hated us, had from the first time Dale or Sydney walked in. She would love to find something incriminating in one of our packages, something to help her run us out of the valley. She had done a lot of petty things to annoy us besides routinely opening our mail, which was so common people had started writing notes to her with their letters or packages. "Hello Mrs. Potter. Hope your day is going well." Both incoming and outgoing mail was often delayed or lost. She was rude and dismissive of us, sometimes ignoring us at the post office window while she sat nearby drinking coffee. We couldn't really do anything about it. She had the only game in town. But at one point when she pissed Walter off, he had cast a spell on her to fall into the pit at the dump, where we had deposited our TV in our early days in Tiller. I didn't doubt Walter's powers in such matters but we hadn't yet seen or heard about any fulfillment of that curse.

A box full of medicine was too tempting a target for her. But my father, well aware of Mrs. Potter's hostile nosiness, had anticipated her probing and inserted a letter on his University of Illinois Health Service stationery. It was very official-looking and professional-sounding. He described the contents of the package and our situation living far from any physician. "I feel these medications are essential to their well-being and good health."

His letter concluded: "By law, you are entitled to open this package and inspect its contents. I can, however, as a physician, assure you that this package contains no narcotic habit-forming drugs, no stimulants, amphetamines, or other drugs banned by the FDA. I have taken great care in packing this package and hope that by writing this letter truthfully to you as to its contents, inspection will be unnecessary." Right on, Dad. Mrs. Potter was particularly grumpy when she begrudgingly handed over that package.

A few days after that package, we got another dose of good medicine. Liz, Roger's former (?) girlfriend, and Pauline and Mike's friend from Amherst, arrived unexpectedly. Maybe Roger knew, but I'd never heard she was coming back, until one day Roger returned from a town trip to Canyonville with her. After she left without Roger last summer, she spent some time around Amherst and then with her family in Florida before the call of Oregon or Roger drew her back. It was hard to tell what their relationship was. Patrick had offered to move into the Main House so she could move into the cabin he shared with Roger. But Liz said no, she was fine sleeping in the Main House—without Roger.

When she had been here before—at the height of our summer craziness—she was almost too linked to Roger and it became apparent that he cared more about securing his own spot on the ranch than the two of them staying together. So she was sort of abandoned by him and not able to establish an identity of her own in the raging interpersonal chaos going on among the rest of us just then. So she split.

It was smart of her to stay separate from Roger, though there still seemed to be some kind of awkward connection between them. She jumped right in to ranch activities, helping Paulie and Sarah with the animals, pitching in trying to keep the Main House together, and helping with meal prep. She even got out there with the usually all male crews cutting and toting firewood. She was obviously glad to be back on the ranch and to be welcomed this time—and we were happy to have someone so willing to work and who brought such fresh positive energy. I didn't really know her before but quickly grew to like her and accept her as a solid sister.

WINTER/7

We had a bad outbreak of distemper among our cats. In the first wave, five of our thirteen cats died. Sarah and my cats were doing OK, maybe because our house was so separated from all the other houses. But then Kachina started throwing up and not eating, we got a bunch of serum from the vet, but that only helped cats who weren't sick already. We gave Mocha one of those shots and gave Kachina some pills to treat the active disease. Sydney's cat had recovered after showing distemper symptoms and then taking the pills. But they didn't work for Kachina and we had to watch her slowly die an agonizing death. Kachina was a fluffy soft gray and a sweetheart, good buddy to Moonbeam and had welcomed Mocha and, more recently, Molly. Almost everybody who had cats—except Sydney—lost at least one. It cast a depressing pall over the whole ranch, as we dug into the frozen ground to bury them all. Fortunately, Mocha survived and her ever-entertaining kittyness help lighten things up and fill the empty spot left by Kachina.

A succession of rainy days started to wash away the snow to reveal patches of slowly thawing mud, especially in the ruts on the road where Sarah and I walked every day, the mud becoming more of a challenge than our snow paths had been.

But all of our moods were lifted when, finally, we got word that Eddie, Jeffrey, and Loretta were coming back, flying into Eugene. Eddie had given Stu the traveling details and an only slightly cryptic message: "A small package of value will be coming to you shortly." We all knew what that meant. Our drought would soon be over.

Stu and Jack were dispatched in the SW to pick them up. (After winter had set in, Eddie left the Karmann Ghia with a friend in San Francisco. Bye-bye tunes.) The rest of us tried to spiffy up the Main House and gathered extra firewood. We had pulled from our freezer locker the last of the pork roasts from John Mitchell. We wanted to welcome them home and ease their transition back to winter ranch living after spending more than a month in the land of ready cheeseburgers and abundant sunshine.

The flurry of activity helped keep our wild anticipation at bay, until darkness started settling over us and we all were gathered in the Main House, our ears arched toward the road, awaiting the sound of a car echoing across the valley.

When we finally heard the first faint rumbling of that sound, we all came alert and, trying to be as restrained as we could, eased our way out the door and into the yard to follow the lights that slowly grew brighter and closer. But we soon realized that the vehicle was not the SW but some little white sports car. Confusion mixed with our excitement as we looked around at each other, with questions none of us could answer. When the car pulled to a stop in front of us, Jeffrey stepped out of the front seat, with his loaded smile. Eddie scrambled out of the tight back seat right behind him, shaking his head and slowly loosening up to a raucous laugh. Richard, our Eugene environmentalist friend, came around the front of the car, with a wide-eyed grin. And Jack came around the back, stretching himself out and smirking. No Stu. No Loretta. No SW.

It was a big hugging mob for a few minutes. The steady rain did not deter us. We couldn't even really formulate questions at first. It was good to see them all. And it must have felt like some kind of monumental relief and release for Eddie and Jeffrey to be at the end of their long trip, safe in the peace and quiet of the ranch. As the mob separated I saw Jeffrey nod toward Richard, who moved around to the trunk of the car and opened it. Eddie and Jeffrey moved quickly and pulled out two suitcases with huge smiles now. "Anybody want to get high?" Jeffrey said matter-of-factly.

We reconvened inside. Eddie pulled a tightly wrapped block out of one of the suitcases and carefully unfolded the wrapping to reveal a brick of beautiful Colombian buds. He grabbed a chunk, loosened it over the paper, and started rolling joints. Jeffrey joined him.

We were all in awe but still didn't know what happened to the SW and its crew. Sarah finally asked.

Richard spoke as Eddie lit the first joint. "I got a call from Jack," he said. "He and Stu had broken down just outside Eugene and they needed to pick people up at the airport and get them back to the farm. Could I help? I said 'Sure, but I only have room for four, especially if they have luggage.' And, he said 'oh, yeah, they have luggage' and laughed, which gave me a hint as to just what that luggage might be." We all laughed. Jack told him that Stu was going to stick around to try to get the SW fixed, so room for four was perfect. After Richard picked Jack up, he made it clear exactly what the luggage was, and Richard was still willing to make the drive.

The joints started coming fast and the dope was very good so the buzz came on quickly. "And that's just the beginning of Richard's heroics," Jack said.

Richard smiled. He was getting as high as the rest of us. "Yeah, we took back roads out of Eugene because of the nature of our cargo." He paused to take another hit, then continued the story as he exhaled. "Not far out of Eugene, we picked up a county sheriff who hung on our tail for a while. I was getting the feeling that he was about to light us up, so I swerved onto a small country road and took off. That little Fiat isn't all that fast but it's mighty nimble, and I know how to drive it pretty well. I lost him on those curly curvy roads. We weren't far out of Eugene, so we spent the rest of the trip on real small roads, looking over our shoulders the whole way."

"Man, you should've fucking seen him," Eddie said. "Like a fucking race car driver. I'm glad I was in the back seat. I was just hanging on, trying not to look."

"I do race it some," Richard said with a big grin. "Me and that car are tight."

"We're so lucky you showed up." Jeffrey said. "Out of the all the intense, complicated shit we had to deal with in Florida that was the scariest time of all. Some Podunk sheriff in Oregon on our tail."

We all joined in praising and thanking Richard.

"And there's more," Jeffrey added, "Loretta is flying into Medford tomorrow, and Richard said he'd pick her up. We gotta do something about the vehicle situation. I don't even want to think about what it would have been like if Eddie and me were stranded at the Eugene airport with our two suitcases."

We all agreed, but our focus was on the joints still going around and the report on how the business in Florida was going. They had brought us three pounds of different strains of Colombian pot, samples of the product they were selling.

Jeffrey explained the differences: one brought sort of a mellow slow high, the second produced a wave of energy before a sharp crash, the third just knocked you on your ass from the start. Eddie had pulled out the last of those and it was living up to its description. Things were going well with the sales, too, Jeffrey told us. They had connected with their old Boston dealing buddy Charles Vernon to get cash to invest. The supply was as stable as you could hope for, but timing and coordination were continually challenging. They had a couple of buyers who had prospects of moving serious quantity, but had started with relatively small orders, 10 or 20 pounds with the hope that would lead to much bigger sales. The three of them needed to go back in a few weeks to follow-up, building up to selling in hundred-pound lots. It would take a while, they told us, but they felt pretty good about having the $20,000 we needed for our balloon payment by June, when it was due.

The joints had slowed. We were all so high and the news was so good, it felt almost like a rebirth of the crazy, magical optimism we had felt when we first found Ash Valley. It was meant for us to be on this land. It was inevitable and things would happen to make it so, no matter how far-fetched they might seem. And especially for it to be this "us" that had remained or returned, the core of those of us who had dreamed of a country home in the West back in Boston, plus a few who had earned their spot by living through all the ups and downs that had brought us to this point.

Jeffrey and Eddie, man, servants of the people. Without them, we had no hope to make our payment and stay on the land. It was so great to have them back, laughing among us.

Richard and Patrick picked up Loretta at the airport the next day. She flew separately from Eddie and Jeffrey because they didn't all want to be on the same flight and it was kind of a dry run for Loretta, who would be playing a bigger role in transporting product in the future. Loretta and Richard must have hit it off on the trip back to the ranch because they ended up in the same bed that night. When he left for Eugene the following day, he had a big bag of pot and a big smile on his face. I think he felt his heroism had been well rewarded.

Having Loretta back, Stu's return with the running-for-now SW, and Stephen reappearing as nonchalantly as he had left a week or so earlier, meant, for the first time in a long time, everybody who was part of the ranch was on the land: Dale, Eddie, Jeffrey, Loretta, Stephen, Patrick, Roger, Liz, Sydney, Jack, Mike, Paulie, Sarah, and me. Fourteen of us.

WINTER/8

The rain tapered off and we were treated to some sweet, clear, surprisingly warm days. Having everybody home, a good stash, and a break from the cold dreary wet days lifted everybody's spirits. The pressure to constantly replenish our firewood stash eased a bit. Thanks to Eddie and Jeffrey, we had a little bit of extra money to buy food to break us out of the routine of fried potatoes or lentils in various forms that had defined our diet for a while—and surprisingly our chickens had dramatically increased their egg production, giving us about twenty a day. Even though we were just barely into February, it felt like spring—"when the world is mud-luscious"—we all seemed to glow with the crisp vitality of renewed hope.

Sarah's friend Sally finally made it. She'd been saying she was coming since we first moved on the land. But she got sidetracked in San Francisco along the way—not an unusual thing to happen—and ended up hanging out with a guy named Stick who she'd known from Ohio, both of them part of the ongoing mass migration of young folks from the Midwest to the West Coast. Stick was cool, nicknamed for skinniness, very mellow and, like Sally, a Pisces.

Sally and Sarah had been tight going back to their elementary school days in suburban Philly. They were like sisters. About the same height as Sarah, Sally had blondish hair that sort of flipped at her shoulders and a natural easy smile. The two of them could fill many dialog balloons at a rapid pace. Since Sarah and I started hanging out, our encounters with Sally were sporadic but always, it seemed, at significant times. The two of them were together at Woodstock, when

I (with Stu) left in the early chaos of that event before Sarah and Sally got there, delayed by the intense traffic. They never saw any music either. Then, Sarah and I ran into her, by pure coincidence, among the half million people at the November 1969 Moratorium Against the War march in Washington. On our first trip west, Sarah, Mike and I had stopped to visit at her Ohio college a couple of days after the Kent State killings. Mike got arrested wandering around the nearby Miami University campus jacked on speed, the night a building was bombed. He really didn't have anything to do with it and we somehow got him out of jail the next morning.

Maybe her presence at Ash Valley was some kind an affirmation that, having survived the worst of winter, we were here to stay.

They had come at a perfect time, spirits up, weather beautiful, decent food. They took long walks in the valley and up into the still snow-covered hills. Sarah and Sally rode Mona and Morning Star, though Sarah had to take it easy with Mona, who was due to drop her foal any day. They beamed with the delight of two giddy young girls as they trotted across the valley in the low winter sun.

Sally and Stick helped with all our chores whenever they could. Stick quickly volunteered his van to do an emergency run to Canyonville after Loretta got thrown off Morning Star (again) and landed hard on her wrist, which turned out just to be a bad sprain.

One night early in their stay, they enthusiastically jumped up to do the dinner dishes, and Patrick immediately invited them to stay on permanently, an invitation quickly backed up by everybody else as the post-dinner joints began circulating around the room. They laughed and Sally said, "Watch out. You might never get rid of us."

It was a boost for all of us to again see new folks come to the ranch and fall in love with it, reminding us how special it was, how lucky we were. Not quite ready for the communal commitment, Sally and Stick talked instead about trying to find a nearby place, a cabin on a small piece of land. They would be great neighbors. I know that would make Sarah very happy.

Little Eddie's birthday came. He was turning 18. Unbelievable, man. He was a kid, but he was in the thick of this thing and we'd put a lot of faith in him—and pressure, too—with the future of the ranch hinging on this dope deal. Jeffrey was the perfect counterbalance to him—at the ripe old age of almost 22—mellow, cautious, organized. Eddie was intense, impulsive, too smart for his own good, and wickedly funny. Sarah and I had bonded with him in our winter of waiting in that drafty apartment in Cambridge just a little more than a year ago. He, with help from Jeffrey who lived not far away, kept me stoned in all kinds of ways, and we talked deep and meaningful bullshit long into the nights: books, politics, that far away place called Oregon which our friends were beckoning us to. Sarah, three and a half years older than him, became his surrogate mom, making sure he ate and slept and did his laundry and was his source for practical advice, which was an ongoing need. And he sorta tried to listen. It was only fitting that Sarah made a huge batch of lasagna—his request—for his birthday. That night was topped off by a smoke-out, where joints just kept coming and coming to determine who would be the last person conscious. Sarah and I and Sally and Stick were early losers, stumbling to our respective sleeping spots while the contest was still going strong. It came down to Stu and Eddie, long after the rest of us were asleep, with the two of them finally agreeing to a draw, both acknowledging that the other would never quit.

Sarah, Sally, Paulie, and Sydney went to Medford to a giant flea market. They bought a bunch of canning jars, and Sarah bought an old needlepoint piece in a classic frame with the words, "Hope Springs Eternal."

Willie arranged to sell Martha's piglets for $25 a piece, giving us $200 total, some nice spending money but hardly the sort of cash flow that we needed. He also made arrangement to get her bred again.

All our seeds were ordered. Stu had planned out the garden thoroughly. As we watched the snow slowly recede from the valley floor, we grew more and more anxious for more warm and dry days, so we could go to work and get our hands back into the ground.

Something close to a normal rhythm of life had settled in the valley. It was a good time.

WINTER/9

Somebody picked up an *Oregonian* newspaper in town, which had news of an intense round of bombing strikes against North Vietnam, shitting all over the supposed peace talks in Paris. The North Vietnamese delegation walked out. But Nixon was going to China, the first president to go there since it had become Red China. Hard to tell what that fucker was up to. A friend from Tiller who came up to sample our new stash—the news of which spread quickly among the small freak community—told us that a *New York Times* article reported about some massive computer study that said society faced a total collapse within 100 years unless there was quick action toward halting population growth and industrial pollution.

Heavy shit happening in the outside world. There was also good news that was heavy in its own way: Angela Davis was released on bail from prison after sixteen months. Apparently some White farmer put up most of the bail, which was over $100,000. Cool.

The mellow vibes at the ranch were disrupted when Jeffrey returned, after a trip to Eugene with Eddie and Jack, with a big old white Buick sedan followed by the other two in the SW.

Jeffrey climbed out of the car, smiling. Eddie and Jack followed, also smiling. Dope had been smoked. "What the fuck is this?" Mike asked.

"It's our new Eugene-express car," Jeffrey said, laughing. "Ain't she pretty."

"I didn't hear nothing about us buying a new car," Mike said.

"Don't worry, Mike," Eddie said, with a little sneer. "We bought it to serve the people."

"Did anybody else hear about this?" Mike asked.

Nobody said anything. Jeffrey looked around. Not smiling anymore. "What the fuck, man? We're moving lots of pounds of pot for this place. We can't be fucking around with cars that are likely to break down at any minute."

"So it's just for you guys?" Dale asked.

"Yeah," Jeffrey said. "We'll use it to drive to Eugene and leave it at Richard's, so we'll be sure to have a running car when we come back."

"I get that," Sarah said, smiling "But still it would have been good for you to tell us or ask before you did it. That's how we're trying to do money things, just to keep things smooth."

"It cost 150 bucks, man, and we're out there raising thousands of dollars for you."

"For us," I said.

"Yeah, yeah, for us," Jeffrey said, "but nobody else is out there risking their asses like we are. And if *we* could keep our fucking vehicles running it wouldn't be a problem."

"It's cool," Stu said. "You did it. It's done. Looks like the perfect straight car. Maybe next time just talk it over before you do something like that."

"Sure thing," Jeffrey said, still kind of pissed, looking over at Eddie, who raised his eyebrows in shared disapproval.

Sarah went over and gave Jeffrey a big hug and then Eddie. Most of us followed—not Mike and Paulie—and awkwardly tried to shift the conversation to something else—how the rest of their trip went, what'd been going on at the ranch—but it wasn't until we went inside and fired up a couple of joints that people really started smiling again.

We couldn't quite pull off my request for my 22nd birthday dinner—roast duck. Lots of ducks passed over and through Ash Valley, sometimes even hanging out in marshy low spots. Stephen had shot a few in the fall, but none lately. Sarah with Sally's help spearheaded the effort to make a fine meal of spaghetti, with real meat sauce, a cabbage salad, and some of Mike's fine bread. They even made a cake that resembled a Boston cream pie with yellow cake and real chocolate frosting and whipped cream between layers. It was all such a treat and I felt loved and appreciated, and content ... that was probably the most unusual sensation, just fucking content to be exactly where I was, doing exactly what I was doing. The best wish I could come up as I blew the mixed assortment of candles on the cake was for that to continue.

WINTER/10

A few days later, Jeffrey, Eddie, and Loretta took the big white Buick back to Eugene to fly to Florida. Stu had been planning to go to San Francisco to meet up with his mother and stepfather, who were visiting the city from their home in Massachusetts. Stu was going to hitchhike, but Sally and Stick decided it was time to head home, so he could catch a ride with them. On a sudden whim, Sarah and I decided to go along. It was the perfect time to leave. The weather had broken so roads were clear, but it was still too early, too wet to start working on the garden. And it would be cool to hang out in the big city, get a sense of what was happening before we all became totally immersed in our spring work. We didn't really know how we would get back but we were sure we could persuade somebody to give us a ride for the chance to experience our Oregon paradise.

That would leave only eight on the land, and both Stephen and Roger were talking about taking off sometime soon, which would leave a record low of six.

The trip down was a blast. It was the first time Sarah and I had made the trip from Oregon to SF. In our summer explorations in California a year and a half before when we had made it almost to the Oregon border, we had stuck strictly to the coast roads, almost no time on I-5, the central artery from Seattle to San Diego. On this trip, we hooked up with the interstate in Medford and, at Ashland, started climbing toward the Siskiyou Summit over steep curling roads with beautiful vistas. The Siskiyou Mountains form a natural dividing line between Oregon and California, though the official border is four miles south of the summit, followed soon by a California Agriculture Inspection station, one of the many which greet you as you enter the state on almost any significant road.

We had brought a good stash of the Colombian pot and had smoked a couple of joints before we hit the summit. The inspection stations were looking for agricultural products that might somehow contaminate California's vital produce crops. I had experienced it once before on our first trip from Boston to California, totally unexpectedly after driving (without a driver's license) all night through the Arizona desert. It freaked me out—suddenly all these bright lights and uniformed inspectors with no way around them. But it was mellow. The inspector asked me if we had any produce and I said, "No," and he waved us through. But that experience didn't stop me from getting freaked out again as we pulled into this inspection station, though we had opened all the windows to get the smell of pot out of the car, and Stick was very cool in responding to that one question. I pretended to sleep in the back, and just like that we were rolling down the mountain again.

My first view of Mt. Shasta had come just after the summit—and then you can see it for miles and miles, becoming more defined, more intense. As it got closer, Sarah, Stu, and I were on our knees right behind the front seats, trying to look around them to get a full view through the front window. Even the first peeks were awe-inspiring. We could see a perfect conical white peak rising way above everything around it. Immediately, you understand why people going way back saw Mt. Shasta as a source of spiritual power—man, it just exuded 14,000 feet of mesmerizing mystical energy. We got quiet in the van as we got our fullest view of it, just past the town of Weed. Wow!

We wound and climbed through beautiful dry forests leading to Shasta Lake. The farther we drove into California, the more the dominant hue shifted from Oregon's lush green to a crisp brown. Past the lake, we went down into the Sacramento Valley and it got flat and hot and kind of boring. Stu lit a joint and that helped pass the time until we stopped in Corning for munchies and gas. Corning—the "Olive Capital" of the world. A store/cafe had every kind of olive you could imagine. Olives stuffed with almonds, anchovies, artichokes, bacon-cheddar, blue cheese–jalapeños——just the offerings from the beginning of the alphabet—as well as a full menu of fast-food breakfast and lunch options complemented with olives in a variety of forms. We kind of made a scene, goofing on all the olive options, and finally ordered burgers and shakes (no olives in my shake), which were pretty tasty … And Sarah insisted on getting some cream cheese stuffed olives … just because.

San Francisco was cool. Sally and Stick lived in a funky first-floor apartment on Cole Street in the block just off Haight Street, with a couple of friends from Ohio. Stick's brother Hank and his buddy Artie, recent dropouts from Purdue University, had showed up just a couple days before, so with us added in, the place had a people-sleeping-everywhere, Mountfort Street kind of vibe—though a little more together and definitely cleaner than our old apartment. Like Mountfort Street, a steady stream of people flowed in and out, smoked a little dope, and shot the shit. Cool people. Everybody eagerly quizzed us about Oregon and our land. We loved talking about it, encouraging them to come hang out, telling them that one of our reasons for trying to build a self-sufficient commune was to serve as a retreat and revitalizing experience for city folks—and we hoped those kind of connections would give us places in the cities where we could go to keep us in touch with what was happening there. Sally and Stick joined in our enthusiastic, romantic tales of Ash Valley.

Haight-Ashbury was five years past the Summer of Love and seemed to be at least starting to recover from the crime- and hard-drug–ridden scene that had followed in the wake of the wilting of the innocence and idealism of the brief reign of flower power. There were still lots of funky buildings and plenty of people who looked down-and-out on Haight, but things seem to have lightened up since we had checked it out briefly during our stay in the city in the summer of 1970: fresh paint, fewer bars on the windows and boarded up shops. Less of a sense of the menacing paranoia that had made our earlier visit a short one.

Cruising around one day, Stu, Sarah, and I came across a "free store" and recycling center on Cole Street just on the other side of Haight from Stick and Sally's place. The free store offered mostly used clothes but also some pieces of furniture, kitchen stuff, books, and a bunch of miscellaneous other things. It was cool. People donated stuff and people could take whatever they wanted. Total honor system.

We got to talking with the guy sorta running the place. With long crunchy blond hair and an untended mustache/ beard combination, he introduced himself as Aries Rick. He and the store were part of the Free Earth commune. They were doing all kinds of far-out things besides this place. They had been an important part of the recent turnaround in the neighborhood. They cruised the streets to discourage and run out heroin pushers and petty thieves. They didn't really want cops patrolling their neighborhood and the cops were happy with anything that lessened the amount of crimes they had to deal with. Free Earth helped with the reconstruction of the neighborhood's distressed Victorian buildings with apartments and ground-floor businesses and shops. They offered repair, painting, and electrical services at reasonable prices or through barter. Their recycling efforts had led them to start a trucking company. They hauled furniture and equipment for businesses in exchange for goods and services. They organized against outside speculators who tried to take advantage of property values that had plunged during the darkest days of the Haight. They worked in collaboration with business owners and the neighborhood association to make zoning less restrictive so it was easier to rebuild and keep rents affordable. They had close to 300 people living in a string of houses on Cole and around the corner on Oak.

Rick's rap was well-rehearsed. Heartfelt to be sure. He knew his stuff and *believed.* Once he got rolling, we couldn't do much more than nod our heads and interject the occasional "cool" or "far-out." But then he paused and asked, "So where are you folks from? What's your trip?"

"Oregon" got an approving smile. But when I said the words *commune, 135 acres, in the mountains,* his eyes widened and focused in on me, then slowly scanned Sarah and Stu. "No shit, man?" he said, looking back and forth across the three of us. "Cool," he said. "I need to hear more about this." He looked around the place for a spot where we could all sit. We had just been standing a little ways inside the front door, sorta clogging the flow of people coming in and out. He pointed to a corner in the back next to a bunch of recycling bins, where we pulled up wooden crates to sit on in a rough circle.

Sarah, Stu, and I took turns telling him the history of our time at Ash Valley and our plans for more gardens, and orchards, and animals. More ways to raise the money to sustain ourselves. More outreach and connection to other communes. Developing ways to welcome city folks and other visitors without disrupting the flow of the ranch.

A couple of other Free Earth folks who'd been hanging around the store wandered over and stood behind us, intently listening.

Rick asked us a bunch of questions. About drugs. He nodded approval when we said we smoked a lot of pot, but didn't do hard drugs. He asked about where we were all coming from, our pasts and our paths to Ash Valley. About the locals and how we got along. At some point, a joint started going around and the conversation got looser. After an hour or so, we hit a lull and we were all just smiling a little awkwardly at each other—strangers breaking through to a point where we sensed something much bigger happening here but still unsure just how real that feeling might be when we took it back to our respective homes.

"Well shit, man," Rick broke the quiet and looked to his fellow commune members. "Seems like there's some synchronicity happening here that's worth pursuing. Maybe a few of us should take a road trip to Oregon to check out your scene. And anyone from your valley is certainly welcome to come by and hang out with us."

"Cool," said Stu, "Come up in about a month and you can help us plant the garden—the more the merrier."

Everyone laughed. "That sounds great," Rick said. "We'll see."

We gave them our postal address and rough directions to the land. We got phone numbers from them. We all hugged each other in parting.

Sarah, Stu, and I were quiet as we eased back the short distance to Sally and Stick's.

"The guy's got a good rap," I said as we stopped outside their building. "They're doing good stuff."

Stu and Sarah sorta nodded.

"A little intense," Sarah said after a bit. We were still pretty buzzed.

"Yeah," said Stu. "What did he say—300 of them?"

"Yeah, I think so." I said. "That's a lot. But it can't hurt to get to know them more, right?"

Sarah looked a little concerned. "I don't know. I mean it could. I think we should have learned our lesson about adding people in too quickly."

Just then Sally and Stick came bounding down the street. "Everything all right?" Sally asked. "You guys look a little dazed."

"We just had a long talk with a guy from a commune around here. They've got a free store just down the street. Free Earth, I think, right?" I looked at Sarah, who nodded. "Seems like they'd like to connect with us somehow. Do you know them?"

"I don't know anything about them." Sally said. "Are you guys into it?"

"Maybe," I said. Sarah and Stu shrugged

Sally smiled and said, "You guys look pretty stoned." She looked down at the bag Stick was carrying. "Want some ice cream?"

That shifted the mood. We all went inside and, with help from a couple of other people, demolished quarts of Mocha Chip and Peach Supreme.

I was more excited about the conversation with Aries Rick than Sarah or Stu seemed to be. In some ways, it could be just the kind of connection I imagined as I mapped out my vision for Ash Valley and our place in the Revolution: city folks, organizing, building community, creating enterprises that we could link to for mutual political, economic, and social benefits. They were more developed, more mature, much bigger than we were but maybe the connection could be a spur for us; their energy, shit just the people power they could bring, might be just what we needed to make Ash Valley the working sustainable farm and education center that we—or at least I— fantasized about.

I understood Stu and Sarah's hesitancy. We couldn't hold it together with twenty-five people when we tried to stretch beyond the core group with roots in the Boston scene. Things began getting better when we got smaller and more careful about who we invited to live with us. The prospect of being some kind of small adjunct to a big enterprise like Free Earth was scary on a personal level even if it fit into my theoretical scheme. Maybe they wouldn't be a good fit. But just the conversation—the excitement we triggered in Aries Rick's eyes—reinforced the notion I had about the larger role our ranch could play beyond our gate. It just added to the hope I had started feeling over the last couple of weeks at Ash Valley.

Like sending off our seed order to Burpees, the necessary first step to planting the seeds for our next stage of growth.

We never did get back in touch with Free Earth on that trip. We mostly played. A day walking around Golden Gate, stumbling across good music, sharing joints and laughs with strangers, admiring the phantom-like eucalyptus trees, grooving among the gardens where amazing arrays of flowers were just perking up and peeking out, napping in the sprawling meadows. One day a van load of us went across the Golden Gate Bridge to Stinson Beach, where we ran and danced to the roar of the surf to try to stay warm against the chilly wind, all of us pink-cheeked and exhilarated. Coffee and books in Berkeley. Brunch and cruising funky shops in Sausalito. Everywhere we saw people that somebody knew or met people who knew somebody we knew or thought we did or could have—immersed again in this great transient interconnected transcontinental migration that had eventually led us to our valley home. We shared our tales and heard of other's quests for their own versions of our Oregon.

Stu had been going back and forth between hanging out with us and with his mother Mary and stepfather Sam. On our last night, Sarah and I joined the three of them for dinner in a great Chinatown restaurant. We had fun with them. We drank wine and shared lots of laughter, trying to translate our Oregon experience to terms they could understand, but they still mostly didn't. But we laughed and laughed. The bond between Stu and Mary was obvious. She was as quick-witted and funny as Stu but as old-school as they come, which made her even funnier. And Sam, who understood us even less was a good sport. As we walked them to their Union Square hotel after dinner, we became part of the flow of tourists, mesmerized by the delights of old San Francisco. Sam was so moved by it all, he broke into merry song: *"Oh, how we danced on the night we were wed/We vowed our true love though a word wasn't said/The world was in bloom. There were stars in the skies/Except for the two that were there in your eyes."*

We all laughed and hummed along with him, especially when he switched up the lyrics of the second line to—"I needed a wife like a hole in the head." He smiled at Mary with a twinkle in his eye and she couldn't help but laugh and smile back. It was a great night, a perfect ending to our "vacation."

WINTER/11

We couldn't make it to our gate. Stick's brother Hank and his buddy Artie had offered us a ride home from San Francisco after hearing all the wonderful stories about Oregon and our place—and we were excited to show off the ranch to them. But we hit heavy blowing snow going over the Siskiyou Summit and Hank had been squeezing the steering wheel of his '63 Mercury sedan ever since.

The snow turned to howling rain when we got off the mountain, actually intensifying this nasty late winter storm that followed us all the way up I-5. When we finally made it to the South Umpqua Road, we slowed to a creep through a tunnel of flying branches and debris, littered with downed limbs and a couple of hefty trees that earlier travelers had chain-sawed passages through. Our crawl up the access road to Ash Valley was abruptly halted by a downed fir snag that completely blocked the road about 35 feet short of the gate. We were lucky to make it that far.

It was deep dark and still driving rain made fierce by gusting winds as we all buttoned or zipped up as tight as we could, covered up with hoods or hats, and steeled ourselves for the mile-long walk to the Main House.

We were all soaked and bone-chilled as we neared the house. We passed a darkened, quiet Shantytown, and could only see a feeble glow through the front window of the Main House. The desperate sense of relief of finally getting there was quickly transformed to stark alarm as we entered and, by the desolate light of a flickering kerosene lamp, saw Liz curled up in a blanket, surrounded by a few dogs, as close as she could get to the fireplace, where weak flames smoldered over damp wood, struggling to put out any heat at all.

The dogs jumped up to greet us. Molly and Moonbeam were excited to see Sarah and me. Winter rushed to Stu. Liz looked up with a half-smile. "Welcome back," she said. "Things got a little rough while you were gone."

Stu, Sarah, and I were speechless, trying to absorb the cold bleakness of that room and the dire specter of Liz's prostrate position, almost in the fireplace. Hank and Artie were silent, too, looking around, stunned. We were all wet and fucking freezing.

"Are you OK?" Sarah spoke first. "What happened?"

"I'm OK," Liz said. "Just fucking cold." … She paused and looked around at us. "You guys left. Stephen and Roger left. We had no running vehicles. The rains started and we hadn't been getting firewood because the weather had been so nice. Our chain saws were fucked up. We ran out of dry wood pretty fast. We had to ration what we had to cook food and have at least some heat here. We broke up a couple chairs we didn't think we needed and that small table that was in the loft, just to have something dry to try to start the fires. We managed to cook a pot of rice and lentils yesterday and have been rationing that with some sprouts. The dogs, too. We ran out of dog food. They've been eating sprouts and lentils. It's been fucking miserable the last few days." She stopped, pulled her blankets tighter around her, as she half sat up.

"Sprouts?" Sarah said and crouched to hug Moonbeam and then Molly. She looked up at me, pained.

Liz, now sitting all the way up, took a long look at us and realized we were all shivering. "You guys look really cold. Let me grab some blankets. Get out of those wet clothes."

"Oh, yeah, this is Hank and Artie," I stammered. "Hank is Stick's brother. Artie is his buddy. They gave us a ride back from SF—until we ran into a downed tree a little before the gate."

"Cool," Liz said with a grim smile as she pulled herself out of her covers and scampered up the stairs in search of something warm.

Sarah and I quickly decided to walk the extra mile to our house so we could get dry clothes and huddle under our own blankets. Stu also decided to get to his house, which was closer than ours.

When Liz returned with an armload of blankets, Hank and Artie took off their wettest outer layers and bundled up. We told her we were heading to our houses and we'd talk more in the morning.

"Yeah, that's what everybody else is doing—hanging out here most of the day and then huddling under their blankets at night." She looked so worn out and forlorn. "Sorry you guys came back to this shit."

We hugged her quickly and traded our soaked coats for some almost-dry ones hanging on pegs by the front door and said a hurried good night.

"Holy fucking shit," I said to Stu and Sarah after we got out the door, ready to push on into the still ravaging storm.

"Yeah," said Stu.

"I can't believe it," Sarah said. "What happened?"

"We'll figure that out in the morning. I'm too fucking cold to think now," Stu said, as he headed across the valley to his house with Winter following, while Sarah and I walked up the muddy road toward ours, Molly and Moonbeam right behind us. We walked as fast as we could and didn't talk.

Mocha screamed at us as we approached our house. She must have been hanging out underneath it. Who knows the last time she had eaten? The animals rushed to follow us through the door as we went in and found a bit of dry food to split between them.

I did feel real relief being in our house, which was freezing cold but dry. There were even a few sticks of dry firewood by the stove, maybe enough to make coffee in the morning.

We just threw off our wet clothes, dried ourselves as best we could, put on long underwear and sweaters, and climbed under the three layers of blankets on our bed. Moonbeam and Molly and Mocha cuddled close as Sarah and I held each other as tight as we could until the chill finally left our bodies. Sarah drifted off to sleep quickly but I couldn't get the scene at the Main House out of my head.

The winter we had been fearing had hit when we least expected it.

We'd only been gone ten days and everything had changed. Firewood was virtually gone. Breaking up furniture? Rationing rice and lentils. We were down to the last dregs of kerosene. It looked like, backed up against a wall of weather, everybody had just given up. It was as though, while we were gone some brazen spirit rustler had snuck onto the ranch and ridden off with whatever collective strength and resilience we thought we had. It was gone … suddenly and stunningly gone.

As the rain and wind pummeled the roof above me, for the first time since we first saw this valley, I couldn't quiet the unthinkable question: Did we really have a future on this land?

WINTER/12

We woke to the roar of the creek, streaming over its banks and rushing with great purpose. Otherwise, it was calm. No wind. Just a quiet drizzly rain, falling from a soft gray sky.

It was still cold, but we did have just enough dry firewood to make coffee and take the chill out of our house, too. We were too far from other houses for anybody to come and take our meager wood stash. We lingered. We knew it would be intense when we went to the Main House—firewood? Food? How had things slipped so far in the ten days we had been gone? We needed to clear the road—without a chain saw, it seemed. Once we did that, we'd have a least one running vehicle with Hank's Mercury. But the overwhelming thought in our minds was still, "What the fuck?"

Sometime midmorning with the fire dying in our stove, we bundled up and headed down. There was no sign of Mike and Paulie at the Second House. We were hoping to get some time with just them to get their perspective before encountering everybody at the Main House. But their house was cold with nobody there.

There was activity outside the Main House. Patrick had dragged a couple of small fir snags to the front yard and he and Jack were cutting them into stove lengths with a bow saw. Hank and Artie were splitting them and Liz and Paulie were taking them straight into the house to feed the stove and the fireplace. Everyone greeted us warmly. Hugs and smiles.

Inside, Mike was making pancakes, while Stu messed with the fire, trying to get more flames and heat out of the not altogether dry wood. It was a lot warmer than it had been last night. Mike greeted us with raised eyebrows and a grunt.

I was surprised at the relative normality of this scene, but there was a subdued vibe, the calm after a storm, I guess. There was just enough coffee left for Sarah and me to have half a cup each. It was gritty with the grounds that had settled to the bottom of the pot.

"What's happening?" I finally asked.

Mike looked at me with contemptuous disbelief. "Everything's fucking peachy keen, man. Just fucking peachy." He held the look, boring in on me. "We got the shit kicked out of us for four, five days, while you fuckers are gallivanting around San Francisco. What the fuck do you think is happening?"

He looked away. I stepped back. Sarah shot me a distressed look. Stu had stopped fiddling with the fire. Liz entered with an armload of firewood, and looked around at all of us frozen in a nervous silence and gently piled the wood next to the fireplace, like she didn't want to disrupt whatever was going on.

"Hey, man, I'm sorry. I can see that shit got rough," I said. "Sorry."

Mike had refocused on his pancakes, shoveling some onto a plate and handing it to Sarah, not looking at her.

"Thanks, Mike." Sarah said. "Sorry we weren't here to help, but everything seemed fine when we left."

"Well, things got not fine." Mike said. "And they ain't fine yet. You want pancakes?" He looked at me with a snarl.

"Sure, thanks," I said as he poured batter on the stove.

Sydney came in, also carrying some wood. "Welcome back," she said to Sarah, Stu, and me. "You guys missed all the fun. What's wrong with him?" She nodded toward Mike.

"He's pissed because we planned our trip to San Francisco just right." Stu said, "and had the nerve to have a good time."

"Fuck you, Stu," Mike said, but his anger had dissipated a little. Stu, and Sydney, too, had a way that I didn't, to temper Mike's outbursts. I guess he needed to tell us that he was pissed that we were gone for one of the most difficult times at the ranch and I, with my empty, clichéd greeting, had given him the perfect opportunity to pounce. But, it seemed, he'd got it out and moved on, though he would hang on to his scowl for a while. And his pancakes were great.

We got too focused on dealing with the aftermath of the storm to have any kind of deep discussion about what had happened in our absence. First thing we needed to do was to get Hank's car moving. After that, people could go to town, get our chain saws in to be fixed, and buy food for both humans and dogs.

Five of us walked the road to where the car was blocked. None of us, especially Hank, was into backing down the almost two-mile curvy, steep, slippery road. We needed to clear the road, so he could go forward into the ranch and turn around. We took turns using our not-especially-sharp bow saw to cut the snag, which was about 15 inches in diameter at the thicker end. That warmed us all up. After we made cuts where the tree sat on the opposite shoulders of the road, we were left with about a 10-foot log that we pivoted and rolled to the lower side. Hank drove through the open spot to the Main House where they loaded our two broken chain saws and Sarah and Sydney joined him for the town trip. After the car passed those of us still hanging out where we'd cut the snag on the way to town, we started cutting the log into rounds for firewood. The wood was fairly dry on the inside. After we finished that section, we worked on the upper part of the snag, maybe another 25 feet, with the thickness steadily diminishing toward the tip. We hoped to have working chain saws before tackling the lower section where it got to almost 20 inches in diameter.

We trudged back to the Main House, soggy and tired, but the fire was still going and we could relax with some sense of satisfaction that our recovery had begun.

Near dark, the Mercury pulled up and we all joined in unloading the groceries and then devouring some crackers and cheese the shoppers had bought. The chain saws wouldn't be ready for a couple of days. Once the car was empty, a crew of us loaded in to go back and collect the firewood we had cut earlier. It took three trips, some loading at one end, others unloading at the other end. Everybody helped. Don't think Hank was expecting his ten-year old sedan to become an all-purpose ranch vehicle, but it had saved our ass. Over the course of the day, we managed to get enough reasonably dry firewood to keep the Main House fire going for a while and to distribute some to each of our houses, enough to take the chill off at night and first thing in the morning.

By the time Sarah and I went home that night—after a good meal of spaghetti with meat sauce, bread, and salad—the rain had stopped completely and the temperature had risen a few degrees, so it was a pleasant walk, even in the mud. We were tired. We'd all worked hard, had a good meal, and smoked a few joints. The vibes were mellow, but a little short of celebratory.

I was still shaken by the state of the ranch we came home to. After all the talk in San Francisco ... the ranch I told people about was still a fantasy: people working together, working the land, becoming Oregonians, building models for how to live outside the system, models for our future, some sort of force in some sort of revolution. I talked so much and so enthusiastically that I bought into my own bullshit. And, it turns out, we were one bad storm and a few people gone from the precipice of collapse. Today was a little encouraging. We bounced back. But I couldn't shut down the thought that had kept me awake the night before. Could we ever be what I, what we, had imagined, what I had told all those people we already were?

WINTER/13

Stu, with some spurious assistance from Jack and me, had managed to get the white truck running. He, Jack, and Sydney headed into town, followed by Hank and Artie in the Mercury, just to be safe. They were going to have Earl check out the white truck and pick up the chain saws in Canyonville—and no doubt grab a burger at the Airport Cafe. If all went well, Hank and Artie would continue on to San Francisco, with promises of coming back sometime in the spring.

The rest of us spent most of the morning in a drizzly cold rain spread out around the valley gathering what firewood we could and distributing some of that to the individual houses. Then we lingered at the Main House after lunch, quietly reading or chatting and keeping the fire going.

Suddenly, unexpectedly, Dale burst through the front door. He had an almost manic look in his eyes as he looked around the room to assess who was there, no doubt noting that both Sydney and Jack were not. He smiled. "Hey folks," he said. "Y'all look pretty mellow. Pretty mean storm we had, eh?" He scanned the room again, with a look that seemed to have a lot of questions in it.

A muted chorus of greetings with nodding went back at him, as he pulled off his soaked coat and squeezed into a spot at the table.

"I saw Matthew and Sylvia right before I left Eugene. Their place on the Umpqua got flooded out. They were pretty freaked out."

"What a bummer," said Patrick with the rest of us echoing that sentiment. Their place was a sweet little cabin right on the bank of the main branch of the Umpqua River, 15 or 20 feet from the water in normal times. That *was* a kick-ass storm. "We had it pretty rough here, too—but, I guess not that bad."

"Well, you all seem alive, at least. The roads are clear. Where's everybody else?"

"Stu, Sydney, and Jack went into town," Sarah said. "Eddie, Jeffrey, and Loretta are still in Florida. Have no idea where Stephen is."

"Or Roger," Patrick chimed in.

"I ran into Roger a few times in Eugene," Dale said. "I thought maybe he had already come back and told you—that was why you all seem so bummed out."

"Told us what?" Paulie asked.

Dale looked around again, and took a long deep breath. "Well, I was planning to ease into this, but what the fuck … The lawsuit is dead."

A cold shudder went around the room. I think we all sorta knew this was coming but didn't think it would be this soon or so definite.

"Fuck," said Patrick, speaking for all of us. Otherwise it was quiet.

Dale was surprised. "Are we ready to arm up for the Revolution, Mike?" he asked.

Mike grunted. "That's shitty news," he said. "Guess we gotta figure out what we have to do next."

Dale smiled, a big exaggerated smile, and stared at Mike, "Are you all right?"

"Shit's been kinda heavy here, man," Mike said. "This is just another fucking thing we gotta deal with."

Dale scanned the room. "Wow. What's going on?"

"The storm was bad," Patrick said, after nobody else responded right away. "Not as bad as it was for Matthew and Sylvia. But a lot of people were gone. None of our vehicles or chain saws worked. We got real low on firewood and food and it felt kind of desperate here for awhile. We're still trying to recover from that. Right?" he said looking around for confirmation.

"That's about it," said Paulie. "It sucked and some of you weren't here to help when we really needed it."

Dale took that to mean him, though I think it was mainly aimed at Sarah, Stu, and me.

"Whoa, man," Dale said. "I didn't know what was going on here. You all should know by now that I'm a part-timer, can only take so much of this communal love. Don't count on me." He chuckled. But nobody else laughed.

"What happened in court?" I asked.

Dale explained. The judge had ruled that although we had a theoretical right to sue (a victory of sorts), the potential damages of the clear-cutting—harming water quality, creating hillside erosion, affecting our quality of life—were all speculative or unsubstantial. The Forest Service had convinced him that their practices would prevent the physical harms and that "quality of life" was subjective and irrelevant to these proceedings. Congress had given the Interior Department broad discretion to manage National Forests and the courts could not intervene, the judge said. So, he concluded, our case did not have sufficient merit to move forward. The lawyers said we could appeal but our chances of winning were almost zero. They would need more money because—this was Dale's evaluation—the chances of them winning some history-making decision were too low for them to work for free.

Somebody rolled a joint from our dwindling stash. Our mood lightened and we heard more from Dale about his time in Eugene, hanging out mostly with Doug and Jill and some fellow guitar players he'd met at a party. He played us a song off the new Allman Brothers album, which none of the rest of us had heard yet. The song was about "not wasting time no more." It was a good song and he played it well, sang it with heart. I didn't catch all the lyrics but I got enough to know that, for Dale, it was about getting over Sydney and figuring out a way to get on with his life. And the snatches of phrases I picked up—things about "precious days," and "pouring rain," and "just getting high," and trying again and again—and the urgency with which he sang the repeated theme made it feel loaded with immediate and resonant meaning for me and all of us at Ash Valley.

Wasting time?

The court news just piled on all the debris left by the storm. We had mostly cleaned up the physical effects of the storm but hadn't figured out a way to begin to deal with the psychic damage to whatever collective sense of purpose we had, that deep belief that we, those of us who made it this far, were meant to be on this land, together.

Was it just me?

We got high when we could. We had food to eat, always at least something. We, some of us, worked well together in spurts. Some of us had to leave regularly to be able to stay here for any time at all. Some of us just shined on any sense of broader purpose, did what they felt like, and dug living in such a beautiful place with no real responsibilities at all. Maybe all of us had all those parts of us to different degrees at different times.

What the fuck were "we"?

We had a lot to talk about. Since our return from San Francisco, there just hadn't been the energy or the inclination to get deep into what had happened. But now with the court case lost, Dale back, and an almost constant tension riffling just below the surface, it didn't seem like we could put it off much longer.

WINTER/14

Most of us were gathered at the Main House, bemoaning the fact that we were almost out of dope—again— and speculating about when we might see more. We heard the rare sound of a vehicle coming up our road. We looked questioningly at each other. All our rigs were here. It could be Willie but why would he would be coming?

A beaten-up, high-riding old pickup pulled up and a couple of strangers got out. Stu and I were first out the door to greet them but everyone was pulling on their shoes and jackets to follow us.

Stu offered a friendly greeting. The taller of the two strangers nodded and said, "Do you folks know a man named Roger? He claims to live up here."

"Yeah," I said, "We have someone named Roger who stays up here. Why? What's going on?" Everyone from the house was now there with us, with Liz nudging her way to the front. The tall stranger scanned the crowd, not sure what to make of us, but he zeroed in on Liz.

"Well, … we pulled him out of a sports car that had landed in a ditch along the river road." Liz gasped the loudest but all of us drew in a hard breath. "He missed a turn and ran into a tree. Him and the car were tore up pretty bad." Patrick put an arm around Liz and held her tight as she visibly flinched. A chorus of concern rose up. "We got him back to Tiller and got an ambulance for him. Pretty sure they took him to the hospital in Canyonville." Liz was shaking her head and tears started to come as others drew in to comfort her.

"Not sure what all was wrong with him. In some ways he's lucky that tree got in his way or he most likely would have ended up in the river." He was matter of fact. His buddy was looking everywhere to avoid looking directly at us, maybe not comfortable with our emotional reaction. The tall one went on, "Pretty sure he's going to make it. He couldn't talk much and what he did say didn't make much sense. But he said something about Ash Valley, so we thought we should let you know."

After a prolonged silence, Patrick spoke for us. "Hey, thank you guys for stopping for him—you made the right choice to get him to a hospital and thanks for coming up here to let us know."

"Sure thing," the other guy said. "Who knows how long he would've been out there if we hadn't come along."

They still weren't quite sure what to make of us but in this moment it didn't matter. They did the right thing for another human being and whatever bullshit might have put us on opposite sides of something or other in a different time or place was totally irrelevant. Led by Patrick, the men all shook their hands and the women gave them hugs, and they couldn't quite conceal their smiles as they climbed back into their truck. They knew they'd done a good thing.

We filed slowly back into the house, as conversations of shock and concern overlapped each other. It was quickly decided that Patrick and Liz would take the white truck into town to try to find Roger and to bring him back if he was healthy enough.

While Patrick and Liz scurried to get their shit together, Mike asked, "Where do you think he got a sports car?"

"I'm thinking it had to be Richard's," Dale said. "Where else would he get a sports car?"

"Do you think Richard would have let him take it?" Sarah asked.

"I don't know about that," I said. "He loved that little Fiat."

So making that tough phone call to Richard was added to Patrick and Liz's tasks for the trip.

It was late and dark before Liz and Patrick made it back—without Roger—so we were all pretty anxious, but nobody had left the Main House. It took them a while to find him. He was unconscious when he got to the hospital and basically incoherent when he first came to. They only had his first name, so he spent the first few hours as a John Doe in the emergency room. Then there was confusion about when he was admitted and where they put him. It wasn't like it was a gigantic hospital, but he got lost in some combination of his spaciness and the hospital not knowing how to deal with him.

He'd been hurt pretty badly, broken wrist and several broken ribs, as well as a few serious cuts. He would have to be in the hospital for maybe as long as a week. Liz and Patrick said he was conscious and pretty mellow by the time they saw him because he was heavily sedated—but still talking crazy. Roger told them he knew something terrible was happening at the ranch and he had to get there as soon as possible to save us. Richard had gone away for the weekend but he'd left his car. He was sure that Richard would completely understand why he had to leave so suddenly and why he had to take his car. He didn't remember anything about the accident or crawling out of the car. The only thing he remembered about the guys who picked him up on the river road was that they wouldn't take him to Ash Valley. He was, Liz said, really surprised when she and Patrick assured him that nothing really terrible had happened at the ranch. They knew that he didn't need to hear about any of the shit that had happened. Maybe somewhere in his crazed brain he knew something more than the rest of us. Patrick said he kept saying, "Are you sure?" And he told them that they should get back as soon as they could because he was sure that something horrible was going to happen.

This was all really hard for Liz. She had been trying to distance herself from Roger, but they'd been together for a long time and, obviously, she still cared about him and felt some responsibility to him and for him.

When Patrick called Richard, he'd already heard from the Douglas County Sheriff that his car had been involved in an accident and was totaled. Richard knew it had to be Roger. His roommates told him that Roger had heard that we'd lost the lawsuit for good and that put him in a frenzy and, before they could stop him, he found Richard's keys in his bedroom and drove off. Richard was pissed for sure, Patrick told us, but also concerned about Roger. He'd been aware that Roger was acting stranger and stranger his last days in Eugene. We'd all seen friends going through periods of getting strange, but they got past it, so Richard was hoping maybe it would pass for Roger, too. But now, we all knew, that it had just gotten worse.

Richard showed up at the ranch the next day. He'd stopped by the sheriff's office in Roseburg, where they gave him a shard of a magnesium wheel, a tangible memento of his car and a testament to just how wrecked it was. He had no interest in seeing the whole corpse. He also visited Roger in the hospital. Richard only had liability insurance, so it wouldn't cover anything for this accident. Roger swore he would pay him back for the car. But Richard told us he wasn't expecting anything to come of that. Neither he nor the sheriff were interested in pursuing any criminal charges. Richard knew that wouldn't bring his car back, only fuck up Roger's life more. And the cops, I guess, just didn't want to deal with it if they didn't have to. Another break for Roger—and us too. Richard had stopped at the site of the accident on his way up the river road and, seeing the damage to the tree and the imprint the car had left in the river bank brush, agreed with the guys who had found Roger that it could have been a lot worse.

Richard was subdued and teary talking about it. He loved that car, he told us. He'd dreamed about a car like that since before he started to drive. He'd saved for years to get it and only had it six months before Roger wrecked it. "Fuck," he said, "it's like losing a friend, not really replaceable." He was drinking a Coca Cola he'd brought with him, sitting at our kitchen table.

We tried to apologize, but none of it could really touch what he was feeling. Were we really responsible for connecting Roger to him? Were we responsible for Roger? He was part of us, but … not close enough for any of us to know how troubled he was, or what we might have done to help him. Who among us did we know that well? Did our connection or responsibility stop at the front gate? It was apparent that Richard didn't blame us for this singular act, but it couldn't help but change what he thought about this idyllic community we were trying to build. How did it change what we thought about that? We needed to be more careful about who we allowed to be one of us. Was that it?

We were lucky that Richard didn't want to pursue any legal or financial revenge. Cops poking around could have jeopardized our whole trip. Trying to compensate him would have eaten into whatever money we had raised for the land payment. Roger was lucky not to be dead. And we were all left with yet another reason to ask what the fuck we were trying to do.

WINTER/15

Sarah and I awoke to a drizzle tapping on our roof, the skies the bold gray of the flowing dress Sarah had worn at our wedding, exactly one year before. Our first anniversary. We chuckled as we lay in the loft, cuddling under our stack of blankets, delaying as long as we could facing the cold and the morning ritual of starting a fire, making the coffee, and doing our thing on the wet, chilled outhouse seat—me first, one of my most selfless husbandly acts. We'd chuckled through our wedding and the anticipation of the Oregon that lay ahead of us. It was only fitting to chuckle now—a year of marriage and Oregon behind us. And, suddenly it seemed, as much uncertainty as ever in front of us.

It had been a triumphant year in so many ways for the two of us. Getting here. Moving on this land. Building our house. Finding ways to be useful and productive in this community, facing challenges we never imagined with skills we'd never had. Overcoming our own problems, the problems many newly married couples might face and problems unique to trying to live as a committed monogamous couple in a communal situation where norms about sexual and other relationships were fluid—in a place close to the middle of nowhere.

And together we took pride in being at the heart of it all, central players in this undertaking at Ash Valley Ranch: all the houses, the garden, all the food we had grown and gathered and preserved, the hay and the animals, welcoming people, running other people off, the countless meetings trying to figure out among whoever was there at the time how to live and work together, the quiet triumph of making it almost all the way through the winter. We'd worked as hard as anybody to try to make it succeed.

Things on the ranch were shaky now, Roger's accident just the latest blow to any notion we had about the mythic magic of this place: that we were meant to be here, that we would become what we needed to be to earn our place on this land. Just by being here?

But alone in our bed, under our many layers of covers in our hushed and intimate celebration of our anniversary, we chuckled because we again, still, didn't know what the fuck was going to happen next, but like in the Philadelphia Holiday Inn a year before, we could celebrate our deep certainty that we would go through it together.

We had received acknowledgments from the outside world of the occasion. Sweet cards and letters from both our families. Two of my sisters and their male companions and an aunt and uncle had sent an amazing array of cheeses and crackers from a place called the Cheese Wheel. That package arrived the day before. We opened it at the Main House and it had been devoured in minutes by the six people who happened to be there at the time.

We were in good spirits when we finally made it down to the Main House on the morning of our anniversary and saw Stephen sipping coffee at the table. He grinned as we walked in. It was good to see him. So, everybody but the Florida people—Eddie, Jeffrey, and Loretta—and Roger were back on the land and all of us were in the Main House.

Stephen had been hanging out with a woman friend who had a place near Azalea, south of Canyonville. She'd been hit hard by the storm, too, and Stephen had been helping her clean up, get her road cleared, and fix some fences that held in her horses and her dairy cow. He looked relaxed and refreshed.

"That sounds pretty sweet," Jack said to Stephen, grinning. "So why'd you come back here?"

Stephen chuckled with his reticent grin. "Oh, I don't know," he said. "Maybe we needed a break from each other," he said. "She's used to living alone. And we were pretty much right on top of each other for a while."

"Well we all knew that," Stu said. "What was the problem?" Everyone laughed. It took Stephen a second but then he laughed, too, sheepishly.

"And I wanted to see how things were going here. I kinda missed you," Stephen said, looking with a mocking sweetness toward Stu.

"We coulda used you here a week ago," Paulie said, with an edge.

Stephen was a little startled by her tone. "I don't know that I could've got out of there a week ago," he said. It got quiet.

Something had shifted. Stephen looked around the room. Looked directly at me, questions in his eyes. I looked back, shrugging, no answers. "Something happening here you want to tell me about?" Stephen asked.

Dale spoke. "I just got back here a couple of days ago, but it seems they had a rough go of it here during the storm. Stu and Tucker and Sarah were gone to SF and you and me were gone. The roads were fucked. They didn't have any running vehicles or chain saws and almost ran out of food, did run out of dog food and decent firewood. Then, just as folks were cleaning up after the storm, I showed up with the news that we have lost the lawsuit about the trees. We're out of dope. Fucking Roger damn near killed himself, wrecking Richard-from-Eugene's sports car. So … people are bummed. Looks like some folks are looking for other folks to blame. And you walked into breakfast. Welcome home, man." He punctuated his summary with an exaggerated smile as he looked around the room.

"That's bullshit." Mike said, glaring at Dale. "Six of us got left here with no way to get off the land and the rest of you were off fucking around when the shit got really tough. People just come and go as they please and fuck the rest of us. What do you expect from us?"

"That's not fair, Mike," I said. "We all thought the worst of winter was over. It seemed like a good time to go before all the garden work. Nobody was expecting a storm like that. Shit, I didn't leave the land for two months through most of the winter. But you all just fell apart while we were gone. Breaking up furniture for firewood? What the fuck happened here?"

The cloud of tension that had been hovering over us let loose a downpour. "That is real bullshit," Sydney said, glaring at me. "We did the best we could but the weather was so shitty, we couldn't really do much of anything, so we hung out in our houses and just tried to stay warm. You would have done the same thing."

"You couldn't have worked together to get some firewood or for somebody to get to town for some food …" Sarah asked, "at least for the dogs? You had lentils and canned stuff you could work with, but the dogs? Sprouts?"

"We didn't have enough firewood to really cook anything," Patrick said, trying to be calm. "And we had no idea the storm would last as long as it did—or that you would be gone as long as you were. We kept thinking it'd be better the next day or something good would happen, somebody would show up, but it just got worse and worse … and no sign of any of you to help."

"Sounds like you all got helpless all of sudden," Stu said. "I guess that wouldn't be so bad if you weren't trying to blame us—who weren't even here—for your helplessness. Truth is I don't think that much about people who aren't on the land. Fuck 'em. I just do what I need to do here."

"I don't blame you guys," Liz said. "And not everybody here was so helpless, some people came here before anyone else was up and helped themselves to the eggs the chickens are still laying and grabbed some of the firewood we were saving for the Main House fireplace."

"Fuck," Patrick said. He wasn't calm anymore. "I thought it was strange that the chickens stopped laying right when we needed it most. Who was it?" But we all knew it wasn't Patrick or Liz or Mike or Paulie. All eyes turned toward Jack and Sydney.

"What the fuck," Paulie said, looking back and forth between Sydney and Jack. "You really did that? When you knew what was going on for the rest of us? Fucking assholes."

Jack and Sydney looked at each other, like they were debating whether to try to deny it. And they didn't: "Fuck you guys," Jack said. "We had to look out for ourselves. You coulda got up early and got 'em if you wanted them."

Dale almost seemed to relish this revelation: "I didn't think that's the way things worked around here."

But Sydney wasn't backing down. "I guess you haven't been around here enough to know how things work. Some of you just assume you deserve the privileges you get. Why do Ben and Sarah have their own cute little cabin off by themselves? Who knows what they've got stashed there? Why do Mike and Paulie have the whole big Second House? Why can't we ever use Stephen's truck? How can you come and go as you please and still act like you're part of this? I'm sick of all the hypocritical 'what's mine is yours' bullshit. I love my eggs in the morning." She sneered at Liz: "Fucking snitch."

There was a stunned silence for a second as Sydney's defiant stare moved around the room to put an exclamation point on her statement.

"There's nothing good about this place anymore," Sarah said, tears seeping out of her eyes.

Then almost everybody started talking at once. I didn't have anything to say to that. I could see Stephen pull himself back, wondering why the fuck, indeed, he'd come back to this place.

Finally, Stu stood up and shouted loud enough to be heard above the din. "Would you all just shut the fuck up?"

We seldom heard Stu get that loud. Jack and Sydney bolted out the front door. Quiet again.

Those of who remained sat in that quiet for a while, staring anyplace we could find except at anybody else. I finally caught Sarah's eye and she nodded and we both got up and headed for the door without saying anything. I shut the door behind us quietly, like we were leaving a room where a group had just watched a beloved friend die.

The drizzle had let up but the deep gray clouds hung low over us; We didn't say anything until we were almost to the goat barn.

"That was horrible," Sarah said, looking straight ahead. "But not really surprising, I guess."

"Yeah," I said. "Horrible, really horrible." We took a few more quiet steps. I took a long breath and stopped. "I think maybe it's about time we start thinking about leaving this place," I said softly.

Sarah stopped, too, and turned to look directly in my eyes, sad, but kind of smiling, too. "Yeah, me, too."

I put my arm around her shoulder and squeezed her close to me. "I can't fucking believe it," I said, more shocked than angry.

"Me, neither," she said, and put her arm around my waist. "Where will we go? What will we do?"

We started walking again, slowly. "I have no idea …" I said. "I didn't think …"

Sarah suddenly pulled herself away from me and said, loud and urgent, "Look," pointing toward the field below the goat barn, "Mona!" she said.

Her horse Mona was lying in the field, with, we came to realize as we focused in, a new foal by her side. We moved quickly down the short slope to where she—they—lay. Mona looked at us, relieved? Happy? Tired? then back down at her beautiful foal, a silky tan with white stockings on two legs, wet with birth and the enveloping moisture of the field. Sarah gingerly approached Mona, while I tried to keep Moonbeam and Molly away. Sarah softly stroked Mona's forehead and gently scratched around her ears. The horse moved her head into Sarah's easy touch. Pleased. Sarah looked up at me with a content and proud smile. A fine anniversary present.

WINTER/16

We eventually left Mona and her foal. Sarah was going to town with Liz and Paulie a little later and we wanted to have some time together at our house before she took off. Walking past the Second House and the reservoir, Sarah was still smiling about Mona.

"There's still a lot of good things about this place," she said.

"Sure are," I said. "Could you leave Mona?"

She didn't answer right away. "That's when it gets hard. Mona. *Some* of the people … No, *most* of the people. Really. Our house … "

We were quiet for a while until we came to the meadow with our house greeting us from the other side, always a jolt of joy.

"Yeah … our house … and *most* of the people for sure," I said. "And the garden we're about to plant. I know it's going to be great."

We both stopped before we went in the door and looked all around. "And just this beautiful fucking land …"

We hugged once we got inside. And sat facing each other.

"Things are just not right now," Sarah said.

"Yeah. I know."

Long quiet, the creek singing loud to us. "… and the creek." I said, "Man, I'd miss that constant soundtrack of this place."

"Not the shitter," Sarah said. "I wouldn't miss the open-air shitter." We laughed. Another long pause.

"Maybe we need to leave to figure out what we would need to come back." Sarah looked confused.

"If Eddie and Jeffrey come through and we make that payment, we'd still have the land to come back to. It doesn't have to be forever. Maybe we just hit the road. Get some new perspectives. I don't know. It's not like we have to get out of here right away. We're not desperate. Right? We could stick around to help plant the garden. Make sure we have a decent vehicle. If those guys don't come through, we won't be here anyway."

"Whoa. Sounds like you've been thinking about this."

"Well, yeah, I guess. Since the night we got back—and nothing that's happened since has stopped me thinking about it. I've been hoping something would, but I guess it's easier for me to think about if I think there's a chance we could come back. That it would be more of a break than, you know … leaving."

"Yeah, I don't know. I like the idea of taking our time. This is happening pretty fast."

"Yeah."

We just sat there for a while. Sarah petted Moonbeam, and Mocha climbed up on my lap, starting to purr as I stroked her. Molly stretched out on the floor, close to the stove, maybe just wishing there was a fire going. Happy little family in our cozy little house. I looked around, and I couldn't keep my brain from imagining what it would feel like if? when? someday, maybe soon, this wouldn't be our house anymore. I didn't like it.

Walking back toward the Main House, we saw smoke coming out of the chimney of the Second House, so we stopped in. Mike, Stu, and Patrick were there, huddling round the woodstove.

"Hey, did you see that Mona had her foal," Patrick asked, excited.

"Yeah, so cool!" Sarah said. "We hung out with her for a while on our way up here. So cool!"

"Yeah, that's where Paulie is," Mike said. "Couldn't get her away from there."

"I'm heading that way now. We're supposed to go to town to do shopping …"

"Is gas for the tractor on your list?" Stu asked. "We just need a few dry days to get a start in on the garden."

"If it wasn't, it is now," Sarah said. She was lingering by the door, ready to leave. "I bet you boys might find something to talk about. I know Paulie, Liz, and I will."

We all laughed. Sarah left and I sat down to fill in the circle around the woodstove. The four of us. Friends, brothers, since West Campus at BU three-and-a-half years ago. Then Mountfort Street, where this very foursome had spent so many hours in variations of this circle getting high and talking deep about everything from rock and roll (a lot of rock and roll!) to revolution to the twist and turns of the tribe that was forming among us and our friends to the silliest shit you can imagine four boys storming into their twenties talking about. There had been lots of comings and goings over the time we had known each other, sometimes we weren't sure if and when we might see each other again. But here we were in a funky old ranch house in the middle of a mountain valley in Oregon's Cascades, closing in, it seemed, on another crossroad.

"Well, what do you think she could possible mean?" Stu said. "What in the world do you think we need to talk about."

Patrick and I laughed. Mike kinda grunted and rolled his eyes: "So much bullshit."

"Endless supply," Patrick said. "Too bad we can't put it on the garden."

I laughed again, but nervously. I had to get it out. Everything I said would have been bullshit if I didn't. "Yeah, Sarah and I are thinking about leaving. At least for a while."

"What?" said Patrick.

"Seriously?" Mike asked.

"Well, that's not what I was expecting," Stu said. "Assholes." But after a beat or two he smiled.

"I know, I know. Never thought it would be us. But, man, ever since we got back from San Francisco … You should have heard me down there. Right, Stu? Man, I was so high on this place … Maybe that's it … Got so far out there on my own bullshit … the realities that smacked us in the face when we came back were just too fucking cold. I really thought we were close … but man …"

"Close to what?" Mike asked.

"I don't know. Close to having our shit together … to having some kind of common understanding of how we could live together … some common fucking purpose. I don't feel that, man."

"Some of us do." Patrick said.

"Yeah for sure … or for sure some of us to some extent. The four of us, Sarah, Paulie … But then … Liz seems right on but she hasn't been here that long. I love Stephen, but you know he's going to do his own thing, sometimes that works for us; sometimes, not. Dale? Dale was as close to a leader as we ever had in the early days, but now we never really know what Dale we're going to get … and he could be gone in a flash, Sydney and Jack? … well, Sydney is our sister to the core, but they've shown us their response when shit gets rough. Lying and cheating is part of their scam. Eddie and Jeffrey?—solid brothers, doing the dirty work for us. They seem to like being part of our commune most when they're off the land and away from us. Loretta, like Liz, a new and righteous sister, but …

"We've done better when we get rid of people … sources of conflict, but then new conflicts come up with whoever is left.

"I read my books and write grand plans sitting in my house, how we can work better together, how we tie into political shit going on outside of here, but when I walk down the road and hang out at the Main House, try to translate some of that … I can't make it fit this place, these people. My crazy ass vision of a true collective, working together, learning together, being part of a revolution just seems like a stupid fantasy now."

"You're right," Mike said with a thoughtful smile. "That is a crazy ass fantasy. What's amazing is how much of that crazy ass fantasy we had sitting getting stoned at Mountfort Street has come true. We got this land, man. But, we all brought our own fantasy here. I agree with a lot of what you say, what you want, but I don't have as much trust or faith in other people as you do. The core of us was a bunch of friends who liked to get high and listen to music in Boston, who decided to get the fuck out of the city and that was cool—but we were never like comrades in the revolution. Look at fucking Walter or Brian. Brothers for sure but not revolutionaries. We were friends and that was cool—but then we started letting other people in— and most of them turned out to be assholes—Wayne, Phillip,

Stephen—who I know you guys like but he was a disruptive asshole to me—Fucking Jack, always a conniving asshole who saw a good scam and has been riding it for a long time. Jon? …" He rolled his eyes. "Fucking Roger … just crazy. Eddie, I love him but he ain't cut out for this life. Jeffrey, same shit …

"Man, I might be right behind you. I ain't going to sit here and watch them cut those trees. And I don't see this group getting its shit together to put up any kind of real fight."

He stood up to toss another stick of wood into the stove, with an expression that seemed to be both a period and a question mark.

"Fuck it," Stu said. "I don't need this to be anything more than it is. I've got my seeds. Give me some gas for the tractor and a string of dry days and I'm living out my fantasy. Some dope would be nice, too. I mean, for some reason, I like hanging out with you fuckers. Tucker laughs at my jokes when he's trying to be useful in the garden. Mike makes good bread and, uh …" He looked like he was at a loss for words. "I used to like it when he pissed off people like Wayne and Jon, but they're gone now. But his bread is good. Sarah keeps Tucker from floating off into the clouds and the only one here we can trust to keep track of money. Paulie is just a world unto herself and sometimes I like that world better than the other options. If you guys leave you would fuck up the ratio of somewhat sane—and I use that word as loosely as possible—people to nutjobs and assholes. Patrick and me and … ?"

"I'm not going anywhere," Patrick said. "I'm into making the garden incredible and planting an orchard and tightening up all the houses. Liz and Loretta are pretty sane. Stephen is all right with me, a good worker and a good guy when he's not screwing around—literally," he laughed. "There's so much promise in this place and once we make the balloon payment and figure out how to get some flow going, I think things will settle down. I think Hank or Artie or both of them may be coming back and they seem like solid dudes. I have hope. I agree with you, Ben, about the political stuff, but I think concentrating on making this a working ranch is the most revolutionary thing we could be doing now. Maybe, I hope, you and Sarah will get into some stuff, learn some stuff, make connections and come back to a much more together place that does fit into the whole revolutionary scenario."

"Man, that would be the ideal," I said. "I'm glad you and Stu are committed to staying and making thing work better as a farm, as a ranch—with Loretta and Liz and Stephen, even if he comes and goes, can contribute a lot. And those guys from SF do seem solid. I don't know … it sounds so good the way you talk about it. Sarah and I still need to talk. We haven't really made a final decision, but I just want you guys to know what we're thinking."

"Thanks," Patrick said. "But I have one question … If you do leave, can I have your house?" He laughed. We all laughed. But I didn't answer his question.

WINTER/17

Sarah and I walked up by the ponds to talk after she, Paulie, and Liz got back from the town trip. We talked a little about a phone call she made to both of our parents from the Tiller phone booth, thanking them for our anniversary presents and just catching up on news from them. She didn't get into the upheavals at the ranch, she said. All that was still too raw to try to explain.

She'd had a similar conversation with Paulie and Liz as I had with the guys at the Second House, though it seems that Liz and Paulie were more freaked out about the prospect of our leaving. Paulie was even kind of pissed, Sarah told me, but Liz just seemed shocked. Neither of them were happy with how things had been going but leaving had not come up as an option for them.

Sarah and I agreed that it was good that we had talked about it out loud to others. It seemed the best thing to do was to tell the rest of the people. Maybe, it could help us get past the bickering that had led the morning meeting to disintegrate, and we could seriously talk about ways for all of us to move forward in the coming weeks and months.

And it did, when we all ended up in the Main House late in the afternoon. It quickly became obvious that everybody was ready to try to pick up where the earlier meeting had faltered. Sarah set the tone by saying that she and I were thinking about leaving.

Even if there were resentments about the distance and comfort of our house and the relative stability of our relationship—important and somewhat rare psychic supports in that valley—I think everybody acknowledged that we had been sincere and solid in our efforts to make Ash Valley work.

"Not you guys," said Stephen, usually the last to participate in any group meeting, before she could say any more. He looked genuinely stunned. He was one of only four people who had not already been clued in on this. The other three—Sydney, Jack, and Dale—had similar reactions.

It was up to Stu to lighten the mood. "Hey, don't blow it you guys, our one-year plan to get rid of these two is finally working."

"We're pretty dense," Sarah laughed, "But we finally get it." She took a breath and said, "This is really hard. We love this place and all of you," she started to get teary as she looked around the room—then with a sad laugh, added "most of the time." A few people responded with nervous, hesitant laughter. She talked about a lot of the good things that she—and we—had experienced. "But nothing has felt the same since we got back from San Francisco. We never even imagined leaving before then and, now, it just seems like the right thing to do. This morning just brought a lot of the problems out into the open and moved us more in that direction. We haven't given up on the ranch but maybe we need a break, to get away for a while. Maybe gain some new perspective. We hope Eddie and Jeffrey come back with enough to make our payment, and some of this other stuff gets worked out."

"Well, you two leaving ain't going to make that any easier," Dale said.

"We won't leave right away. We're not in a big hurry." I said. "We'll stick around to help with the garden and other spring stuff, a month or two. You're not getting rid of us that easy. One thing I want to add to what Sarah said is that being in

San Francisco also stirred in me the need to get back in touch with what's going on politically out in the world. I haven't been real successful in tying what's going on here to those kind of things, so I'm hoping to make some of those connections."

"Anybody else thinking about leaving?" Paulie asked. "This is kind of a kick in the ass."

"Not me," Stu said. "I got nowhere else."

"Me, too," Liz said. "I'll be here as long as I can be."

"That goes for me, too," Stephen said.

"You know me," Dale said. "I'm the wind, never sure which way I'm going to blow. But I'll ride this current for a while."

Paulie was adamant about staying. Mike agreed but with an escape clause related to what was going to happen to the trees and what we were going to do about it.

"I'm sticking around," Dale said, "But we've still got serious things to work out." He wasn't subtle about looking to Jack and Sydney.

"We're staying," Sydney said, with Jack nodding assent, "but we won't be the scapegoats for the hypocrisy around here. Sorry about the fucking eggs, but we've put our share of work into this place and we're sick of being the outcasts in Shantytown, so we need to get real about what's going on here."

And we were off deep into a lot of the same old shit. But there was a different vibe to it. An undeniable transition was upon us that went beyond the change in the weather. The logging, the deadline for our balloon payment, the leavings. Everybody but Sarah and me and maybe Dale planned to stay for the foreseeable future or at least they weren't planning to leave. So the quotidian quibbles and quarrels had to be considered in the light of the very survival of this community on this land with these eleven or twelve people (plus or minus Dale and including the absent Eddie, Jeffrey, and Loretta).

Sarah and I sort of became spectators or commentators to this process. Sydney and Jack and Stephen and Liz became more earnestly engaged than they had been in these kinds of discussions. It was as though the subtraction of Sarah and me gave space to others, made it almost necessary for them to fill it.

We talked for a long time. It was one of the best and most honest sessions we'd ever had. Not enough to change the direction that Sarah and I had chosen, but enough to give us more hope that there might be an Ash Valley Ranch for us to come back to.

WINTER/18

March 14, 1972

Dear Folks,

Some pretty heavy things have come down in the last few days. Things have gotten pretty intense here since we returned from San Francisco. A long story but mostly it led us to start thinking about leaving Ash Valley. Yesterday was a marathon encounter session—Sarah talked to you in the break (thanks from me too for the check). I'm feeling a lot clearer about my own feelings and how most other people here feel. I have a real good feeling for what we have done here—we've developed a real closeness that transcends this ranch and this set of circumstances. It has become increasingly clear to me at this time given my abilities and my understandings and the state of the world that I can't settle down here. I believe we are at a point—that is, all of us—that is, history—that if the masses aren't moved to the left there will be an incredible onslaught from the right—the gov't is getting away with murder now and if things don't go right My Lai will happen in Watts, Oakland, South Side of Chicago, etc. Anyway, I feel it is real important now for people who have a consciousness about where history and this society are at to be turning people on to it as conditions—social, economic, etc—worsen in America or the upheaval that <u>is</u> coming will be a bloody mess and not a revolution.

At the same time, I feel a real stake in trying to keep this thing going—and an intrinsic attachment that transcends my physical presence. Our struggles center on working out relationships and working the land at the same time. It is my hope that we can develop an ongoing energy flow that will keep this place going. At the same time I feel that right now there are other places I should be. When I say right now, I mean in the foreseeable future. It's possible that won't happen—that this ranch will no longer be the scene of our activities at all. Some people are away gathering the rest of the down payment money and, when they return, money in hand we have many decisions to make as a group.

As for Sarah and my plans, it seems as though we will attempt to become mobile in, say,—and this is off the top of my head—6–8 weeks and to begin a trek to the south and then east—slowly—stopping places, getting into things—checking out what's going on—making bread to keep going—with an idea of getting a clearer sense of what's going on in this country and helping to spread and share some of the things we have learned and have come to understand. It is possible that other people may accompany us—there are any number of variations that could happen but that is what is in our heads now.

Weird things have happened here—many have been mind-blowing—but it's been, it is—also—so good on so many levels. We've avoided, for the most part, bitterness, spite, defeatism, or other such things that go along so often with human confrontation and tension. This valley has been filled with incredible confusion, misunderstandings, but it is also filled—and has filled us—with an incredible love.

I know the world beyond this valley is mixed up, filled with evil, and a thousand million different traps to fall into, but there are things that have to be done beyond this valley before I can settle back and let the creek lull me to dreamy peace. I feel good that I understand that—that I can act on it—I am always and forever looking toward to it all.

Take care. Power to the people!

Love,

Ben.

Spring II

SPRING II/1

The weather broke and the light stretched longer every day. When the sun eased through the clouds, the valley glistened with the fresh green of the pasture grasses and dots of wildflower color sprinkled the hillsides. Despite everything, Oregon spring was still a harbinger of hope and renewal. It had been spring when we first arrived and our hopes were fantastical and insane. Many of those hopes came true, but many had crashed hard into reality. Now as we shed the long underwear and top layers of blankets, a new hope was budding all around us. It couldn't be helped. Like the best of Oregonians, hope was stubborn, somehow coming back to start again with whatever resolve the winter had left us.

The tractor and all our rigs were running fine, the result of a focused effort in the last few weeks of waiting for things to start drying out, with many trips to Earl's for parts or advice or, sometimes, just the laying on of his magical hands. Once Stu made the call that it was time, we hauled load after load of a finely aged mix of barn straw and shit (chicken and cow and, even, some pig) onto the just barely not too wet soil of the George Jackson Memorial Garden. Stu was on his throne, behind the wheel of the tractor, directing us where to dump our wheelbarrow loads before he eased his tines into the dirt to make a glorious habitat for the seeds that he'd been gathering all winter. In the first, driest spots, we planted radishes and lettuces and our growing season had begun.

Most everybody helped some and the spirit was good. Meals got made. Clean up just seemed to happen. We even revved up our freshly tuned and sharpened chain saws and started building a wood supply like we should have had for the winter just passed. It wasn't like we had worked out all our problems. But the blowup following the storm had exploded the illusion that we were going to solve those problems any time soon. Maybe we had come back to the hippie ethic of "Do Your Own Thing"—a clichéd mantra that I, for one, had fought against since we first imagined a collection of people trying to build some kind of commune at Ash Valley Ranch. Some of us had envisioned a community of consciously shared values and responsibilities. Doing your own thing doesn't get you to that. Way back in the beginning, we pretty much drove Tim off the land because he was determined to do his own thing. He saw Ash Valley as a shared piece of land where he could pitch his tent and maybe someday build a house but he didn't have to help plant the goddamn garden if he'd rather work on a table for his own place. And we just kept shedding people whose thing did not intersect sufficiently with "our" thing of the moment, a never quite fully defined consensus of our values and responsibilities.

Now, we were all pretty much doing our own thing. It was cool that enough people wanted to work in the garden that we made great progress—or to cook or clean or cut wood. But our expectations of each other had diminished—at least mine had—and that led to a kind of peace among us and within me. But I couldn't shake an underlying regret that it took giving up to get there.

I loved working in the garden. The camaraderie was genuine and deep. Stu kept us working and laughing. By being part of the transformation from the rough clumped dirt to almost straight furrowed rows ready for the succession of seeds as the season progressed, I felt a link to the future of

Ash Valley even though I wouldn't be around for the harvest of most of it. Sarah spent some time in the garden but she also spent lots of time with Mona and her foal, like the garden, a developing love that she would leave behind. Moonbeam also gave a litter of four puppies that Sarah enjoyed and cared for. We both continued to try to pitch in where we could to the general good of whatever (commune? cooperative?) Ash Valley had become.

Maybe what Ash Valley was or could be would get a lot clearer when Eddie, Jeffrey, and Loretta returned, which could be any day. We had received indications that things had gone well, but no details about what that meant.

And Sarah and I had started doing our own thing in forming our plans and beginning our preparation for our departure. We'd head first to San Francisco, spend some time with Sally and Stick and try to reconnect with the Free Earth folks we'd met earlier. Then, we'd meander east aiming toward Champaign-Urbana, Illinois, where I had lived during my high school years and where my parents and two of my sisters still lived. A lot of my friends were still around, so it could be a good base from which to figure out our next moves. We would also be much closer to Sarah's family in Philly, which was important to her.

And C-U also fit perfectly into my vision of how the Revolution would develop, based on all my readings and note-taking through the long quiet winter and continuing correspondence with Luke Vaughn and ongoing discussions with Mike and Patrick and others.

The concept—not original to me—was that the Revolution would be built from communities that broke free from America, built their own organizational infrastructures and institutions—participatory democracy, free schools, organic food production and distribution, free medical clinics, worker-run industries—and developed a culture liberated from corporate control and commercial considerations. Black communities like Oakland were already moving in that direction and places like Berkeley and Santa Barbara and Ann Arbor and Madison, and even C-U, had vibrant youth communities with fledgling counterculture scenes that could grow into liberated zones. These free communities would shine in their humanity and livability and joy and fun, attracting more people and expanding their institutions. Our revolutionary war would not be one of terrorism and battles, but of building sane and humane institutions and defending them long enough for the decaying structures of the old order to shrivel and die from their own decrepitude. A renewed Ash Valley and other places like it could serve as models and retreats and as training grounds and educational centers for the builders of these new communities.

C-U had all the elements necessary to build that sort of liberated space—lots of students and young people, a youth culture based around a thriving music scene, a core of experienced activists, and a somewhat tolerant liberal community that could provide material and political support. I had been part of the music scene and involved in the civil rights and anti-war movements. I'd been president of my high school class as a sophomore and nearly again as a senior when I ran a serious campaign addressing racism and other intolerances. I saw myself bridging the youth culture and the political movements to help build on existing counterculture institutions like food and record-store cooperatives and helping to create new ones.

Sarah was not as focused on the political stuff as I was and not entirely convinced that Urbana was an ideal destination for us, but she couldn't come up with a better alternative, so she accepted it as a next step where we would be closer to East Coast friends and family and could decompress from Ash Valley. And then … who knew?

SPRING II/2

The anticipation of the return of the Florida folks had been building for weeks. The June 5 deadline for writing Willie Campbell a $20,000 check was creeping closer and closer, and finally, through our haphazard lines of communication, we knew they were on their way.

It was an unusually warm day for early April. Most of us were in the garden planting broccoli and cabbage when we first heard and then saw the Buick sedan cruising up the road. As they neared us, they slowed to a crawl and Little Eddie rolled down his window. "Glad to see a little fucking work getting done around here," he shouted as Jeffrey kept the car rolling until they pulled up in front of the Main House.

We all dropped what we were doing and moved quickly out the gate toward the car. Eddie and Jeffrey climbed out and stretched, smiling and big-eyed high. Sarah, who'd been working closest to the garden gate was first to reach them and gave them both big hugs, as the rest of us arrived to surround them. Mike, who'd been working in the kitchen, ambled up from the Main House. We were a giddy mob. Jeffrey finally held up his hands to calm things, and said, "Hey, we got great stuff for you. Give us a little room and we can do some show-and-tell." We backed off while the two of them went to the trunk to pull out a couple of suitcases. Stu and Patrick pulled the picnic table out from under the front porch overhang and moved it toward the middle of the front yard in the sunshine while others pulled up some chairs to sit on or found places to stand. We left one side of the picnic table open for Jeffrey and Eddie to plop down their suitcases and sit down.

I leaned on a hoe I'd been using in the garden, Stu and Mike standing beside me. Sarah sat in front of me, on the bench of the picnic table, opposite the boys dramatically opening their suitcases. Underneath a layer of clothes, which they tossed to the side, were several tightly wrapped bricks of, we all assumed, sweet strong marijuana. Eddie and Jeffrey had proud-parent (really hip parents!) smiles as they watched us behold their offerings. We'd been out of pot for a while, though the generosity of neighbors and visitors kept us from going too long without getting high.

"Looks like a lot of pot," Stu said. "But is it any good?"

"Oh, it's fucking good, man," Jeffrey said, his eyes twinkling as Eddie ripped opened one of the packages.

"It's so fucking good, Stu," Eddie said. "I guarantee it's going to put you on your ass." He quickly rolled a joint, lit it, passed it across the table to Sarah and started rolling another one.

As Sarah exhaled with a little cough and passed the joint to me, she asked, "Where's Loretta?"

"On a bus," Jeffrey said, "with the rest of it. This," he pointed to the pile of five bricks they'd pulled out of their suitcases, "is just a taste to get us by until she gets here."

"Fuck," Patrick said, laughing like most of us, and then taking a hit on the first joint.

Sarah was concerned about Loretta. "That's a long way for her to come by herself," she said. "And dangerous."

"She'll be fine," Jeffrey said. "She was ready for it. You wouldn't believe how straight she looked."

"Still …" Sarah said.

"Yeah, she's a true sister," Eddie said. "But don't worry, Sarah, really. She's going to be all right. Really. She'll be here day after tomorrow."

By this time, the joints were so plentiful that almost everybody had one in their hand and it was hard to find anyone to pass to. That stuff was fucking good.

"You guys did good," Paulie said, giggling. "What about the money?"

It went quiet. We were all already pretty stoned. It was the most beautiful day of the spring so far. So blue, so sunny, so stunningly warm. All of us—all of us—outside in the center of it, the deep green valley stretching out as far as we could see north and south, the still virgin peaks east and west embracing us, the earth drying under us, the garden, the houses, the smell of bread, our long absent brothers returning with tangible fruits of their herculean endeavors, the joy we'd known in the best of days sparking among us around that old picnic table.

Jeffrey drew a deep breath. "Yeah, we need to talk to you about the money." His unease was palpable and spread quickly, "I guess we may as well do it now." He looked to Eddie.

"Yeah," Eddie said, looking around, with a consoling sort of smile. "The good news is that we were able to raise a lot of money, enough money for the balloon payment—and bring you back a lot of pot." He was matter-of-fact, not celebratory. The rest of us shared looks of confusion. "But," he said, with a practiced forcefulness, "Jeffrey and I don't want to live here anymore, so we aren't going to give it all to you." He looked to Jeffrey and then, sort of defiantly, toward the rest of us.

"What the fuck?" Paulie said. Mike matched Eddie's defiant look. Stu recoiled. Dale shook his head and looked away. Sarah turned toward me as stunned as I was.

"What the hell are you going to do with it?" Sydney asked.

"Wait a sec," Jeffrey said. "There's more." Everybody focused back on him. The joint passing had stopped. "You might like this part better. For all of you who have been here most of the time …" He looked around. "Sorry, not you Liz. … For everybody else, though, we're going to give you each a pound of pot and a thousand dollars. You can do whatever you want with it."

It was quiet again. Jeffrey smiled and took a toke. "So," Eddie said, earnestly, "if enough of you want to pool that money, maybe sell some of the pot and put it toward the land, that's up to you." He passed a joint to Sarah who passed it, without taking a toke, to me. I took a long, deep pull.

Another pause as, I think, most of us tried to do math in our, by now, really stoned heads.

"But that won't be enough," Patrick said.

"Well, that'll be your choice, " Jeffrey said, "Maybe you can renegotiate something with Willie … Eddie and I have thought about this a lot, talked about it a lot. We worked really fucking hard to raise this money …"

I was more than confused—deeply befuddled. First, I was fucked up, higher than I'd been in weeks. Had been ecstatic when it seemed like it all worked: good dope, enough money (I had assumed), the land secured, another magical breakthrough in the saga of Ash Valley. Then I was pissed. They went out there for us, while we kept things going—with challenges for sure—for all of us, and they earned enough money for us, including them, to hold on to this land—and then they decided to keep a lot of it (we didn't even really know how much money they had made in total) for themselves, seemingly dooming any future in this valley. Then … their offer of a pound of pot and a thousand dollars—double for me and Sarah as a couple—was almost perfect for the two of us. A stake and a healthy stash for us to leave with (Jeffrey and Eddie didn't even know yet that we were leaving). Except there would be no Ash Valley Ranch for us to come back to. This rapid-fire range of reactions ricocheted around my altered consciousness. I didn't know what the fuck to think. Were Eddie and Jeffrey assholes or heroes?

"So, who would put their money back toward the land?" Patrick asked.

Sarah answered: "Well," she looked to Jeffrey and Eddie, "Ben and I are planning to leave …"

"What?!" Jeffrey and Eddie said simultaneously.

"You guys?" Eddie said, looking at us with shock and some concern.

"Yeah, in a month or so. That's a long story. But I think everybody understands," she said looking around. "This deal is sorta ideal for us." She looked back at me. " … Though I'm sorry for the folks who want to stay."

"And …" I managed to pull an almost coherent thought out of my head "… we'd hoped to have Ash Valley to come back to …"

"Well, you could still put your shares in," Paulie said. Sarah and I looked at each other but didn't respond. I think we both knew that didn't make sense for us.

"So …" Sydney said, moving on, "with Ben and Sarah out of it, I count eight of us. Eight grand isn't 20 grand—isn't even close, really."

"There's Loretta, too, right?" Patrick asked.

"Yeah, she's definitely earned her share," Jeffrey said. "And I think she'd like to stay."

"OK," Sydney said. "Maybe nine grand."

"We could sell the pot," Paulie said, "How much could we get for it?"

"$350 a pound," Eddie said. "Maybe a little more out here."

"So maybe another three grand," Sydney said. "If we all sell all the pot. Which we all know ain't gonna happen. And all of us put in all our money. We'd be left with no money and no pot. And still short. How does that sound?"

You could almost hear the calculations going on in everybody's head. There were no other sounds but a distant rustling in the trees in the hills above the ponds across from us.

Stu broke the strained silence. "I can't make that add up to anything that makes sense," Stu said. Sad, but seemingly resigned. "We'd have to hope Willie would cut us some slack."

"And then what?" Mike said. "This was our shot right here. Fuck!"

"Sorry guys," Eddie said. "I know this wasn't what you were expecting, but we're trying to be fair. And … maybe … with what seems to be going on here, maybe it's best for all of us."

"You did your thing, and did it well, but you lost the spirit of the land somewhere along the way. Maybe we've all lost the spirit of the land. Maybe we never really had it," Dale said. "Money's really got nothing to do with that. Too much darkness here. The land doesn't give a shit who stays or goes but it has to drive out the darkness. Looks to me like that's what's happening here."

It got quiet again. Fucking Dale. Sometimes his raps got close to being deep and wise, sometimes they struck as just stoned bullshit. Sometimes, like now, it was hard to tell the difference. A warm moist breeze drifted across the yard as people stretched and stirred. Eddie lit another joint, as if getting just a little bit higher would push us past this conundrum of ambivalence, a long-awaited resolution that wasn't fully satisfying to anyone, except maybe Eddie and Jeffrey. But even they were not getting all they might have wanted out of this. They were doling out close to $15,000 in cash and dope that they (with only Loretta playing a supporting role) had worked hard and risked big to earn. That could have helped them a lot in whatever they were going to do next. And there wasn't a whole lot of gratitude coming back at them. The best the rest of us could do at that moment was to not be pissed at them. Some people could not get that far.

What right did I have to be pissed? Despite the new onslaught of joints that I was fully partaking of, I could do the basic math that told me that even if Sarah and I had thrown in all our shares of pot and money, we still would have been more than $5,000 short. But that didn't really make me feel any better. I couldn't shake the realization that had come to me as I grokked the reality that Ash Valley Ranch as we dreamed it and known it was really dying—and that Sarah and I had delivered the first of what would be the final blows to kill it.

SPRING II/3

Loretta arrived on schedule with two suitcases full of bricks of the fine Colombian. She'd had a smooth trip. She did look amazingly straight. Her smooth black hair newly and neatly cut so it hung just over her shoulders, a light blue shirtdress that hung just above her knees over dark tights, and some shiny black low-heeled pumps with a strap and buckle across the front. While the rest of us ogled the bricks of pot, she grabbed some of her real clothes from the pile that had been tossed from one of her suitcases and changed into some homey jeans and her favorite peasant blouse and worn boots. "I'll never wear those fucking clothes again," she said when she came back to the homecoming party in the Main House, where Eddie and Jeffrey, with scales and baggies, were ceremoniously distributing the pot out to each of us. We all cheered when Loretta returned. She was a true hero.

We tried to put off as long as possible telling Willie that we weren't going to make the balloon payment on time. But he knew something was going on when Sarah and I told him we were leaving. The nine people intent on staying (Stu, Paulie, Mike, Patrick, Loretta, Sydney, Jack, Dale, and Liz) finally told him and he said he was open to working something out, but he would need some good faith cash soon and the assurance of a steady flow of money after that. Stephen was still around, too, but remaining shy of a commitment beyond the next day. Artie (from SF, buddy of Stick's brother who had been with us the fateful day we returned from our trip to the Bay Area) had come back and jumped right into the thick of things and seemed like a new strong contributor. Aries Rick, from the

Free Earth commune, who we had hung out with on that SF trip, visited with a couple other commune members. They liked what they saw and were especially intrigued by the transition that was happening right in front of them. Maybe they could play a role in filling the looming needs of money and new energy and people.

The weather had all the usual promises and disappointments of spring. Strings of warm, dry days followed by sometimes long stretches of gloomy gray, wet, muddy days, reminders of the soggy Ash Valley we had found and fallen in love with a year before. As Sarah and I began our rough countdown of the time we had left, I cherished those days as much as any. After all that valley had given me, I would celebrate each remaining day just as it was. And when the sun did break through and the blue, blue, blue sky stretched over the surrounding peaks, I breathed the warming air deep, deep into me, hoping somehow I could carry it with me wherever we were going.

We had dope and money, like we'd never really had. And nobody was really pushing community norms on anybody else. Life on the ranch felt more relaxed than ever, for us at least. Resignation, acceptance, quitting—all apt descriptions of our new relationship to the land and its people—made things easier.

Work continued through it all. The garden when we could. Vehicles always. Firewood. Shoring and finishing up houses. Patrick was funny when he came to visit us in our house. He'd always come often to shoot the shit, smoke a joint, but now we could see in his eyes that he was already beginning the process of moving in, imagining how he would fill this small eight-walled space with his life when it was his, which it would be soon.

For Sarah and me, there was also the work of getting ready to leave. Everybody agreed that we could sell the red truck, which had been ours before we moved on the land, with the money going toward a new vehicle, something more reliable and bigger. We, especially Sarah, was determined to take as much of our house with us as we could, including our big and heavy cast iron wood cookstove and the rocking chair she had picked up at a Medford flea market. Earl helped sell the red truck for $150—just $50 less than we paid for it, and soon after we saw an ad in the Roseburg newspaper for a 1948 Ford bread truck for $500. We fell in love at first sight. It was plenty big enough and oh, so classy. Like something out of our childhood. At first glance, it resembled a giant loaf of bread. It was a big rounded box, with a snubbed nose and a classic grill that almost looked like a smile. A soft yellowish green. Low to the ground with dual tires in the rear and a simple, six-cylinder three-speed engine. Folding door on the driver's side and a sliding door for the passenger. When I sat in the driver's seat, I felt like I should be leading a parade. Sarah and I were too instantly smitten to do much negotiating on the price, but $500 was about what we were expecting to pay, so we felt good about it, especially when it got a nod of approval from Earl, who after all had been a graduate of the first class of the Ford Motor Company's mechanics school.

Earl said he was sorry to see us go, but that he understood why we'd want to go to Illinois, which he'd heard had some of the best soil in the world and he was sure we could make a go of it if we got into farming.

Because the bread truck rode so low, I had to take it real slow up the road to the ranch, but everyone was impressed when we pulled up to the Main House to show it off.

We parked along the road across from our house, where it sat for a couple of weeks while we organized and packed our stuff. We didn't dare drive it across the meadow. The ground was still soft from the spring rains and we were afraid it might not be able to get down and then back up the small slope from the road. So everything had to be carried the 30 or 40 feet across the meadow.

Our wood stove had to be the first thing loaded. It was so big everything else had to be fit around it. When we asked for help one morning at breakfast, everybody volunteered to come up to join in. We didn't need that many people but everyone wanted to be part of it, offering support and advice and lending a hand as they could. We had other stuff to load once the stove was in, lots of books, kitchen stuff, treasures Sarah had accumulated. And as one person after another said they would come help it became a happening, an odd sort of party that nobody wanted to miss. A going-away party. A last hurrah. An ending. A beginning.

Eddie and Jeffrey brought joints and Eddie immediately lit one up as we all gathered in front of our house. It was a soft gray morning but not raining and warm enough that nobody was wearing more than a sweater. We had to take the front door off to make the opening wide enough to get the stove out. We didn't even have walls when we had brought it in, just the upright pole framing. Patrick carefully supervised the removal of the door, making sure no damage was done. Then a couple of us went to either end of the stove with a couple in front to try to get it far enough away from the wall so we could get behind it to detach the top piece, which rose about three feet above the surface of the stove and had a couple of shelves for stuff like matches and lid lifters—where Sarah had carefully arranged knickknacks that were now safely packed away. We passed the top piece over the stove body to the two in front who passed it to two others who were by the door opening who passed it to two more waiting at the door. Our cabin suddenly seemed so small as six of us, really too many, tried to surround and get a grip on that stove and maneuver it toward the door. But we just kind of pushed and pulled and wrestled it side to side until we got it lined up with the door. Two people slipped out and, then, the other four of us pushed and wiggled it to the edge of the floor. It was heavy in an awkward way, bottom-loaded and low to the ground so it was hard to get under it. We lifted it just enough to get it off the floor and pushed. And gradually we felt the weight shift from us to those outside. And then all the weight was gone. It was out the door and moving slowly but steadily across the meadow, two people on each side and one behind. A little giddy with the seemingly sudden lightening of our burden, those of us who had been inside took a breath and then ran to catch up as everyone was surrounding the stove, now being lifted up the slope to the road, everyone on the downhill side pushing and those on the uphill side guiding and trying to pull. We ran around that cluster of effort to jump in the back of the bread truck, and the uphill crew carried it toward us, and then, with the downhill crew behind them almost lifting them up with the stove, pushing and passing it to us. And we yanked it to rest in the back of the truck. And stepped away. A hearty cheer went up and everyone kind of hugged the people around them as convulsions of laughter broke out among us. From inside the truck, I caught Sarah's eye—she was in the midst of people pushed up against the back of the truck—and she was beaming.

"You better fucking put that to good use," Stu said.

"Fucking A!" Mike said, trying to smirk but he couldn't hide his laughter.

Eddie lit another joint.

We did eventually load the rest of our stuff from the house. We had put our dope stash in mason jars, which we placed in empty three-pound coffee cans, into which we poured wax and then stuck a wick into that. Candles. Six of them. Very innocent. Hippies make candles, right? We made room for our three dogs—we were taking one of Moonbeam's puppies who we had named Layla back to Illinois to give to my good buddy Scottie, trying to copy how Stu had given us Moonbeam. We also had two cats, Mocha and a relatively new cat we had named Quasar, traveling with us. We put the rocking chair right behind the engine compartment, a third passenger seat.

We spent one last bittersweet night in the loft of our empty house. We made love one last time to the song of the creek, strong in the voice of spring rains and snowmelt and smooth with purpose and certain destiny. Love, love, love. Our love was certain, but our purpose and destiny were as speculative as trying to guess Oregon's spring weather

The next morning, we loaded the dogs and cats into the bread truck, and fired it up. We stopped by the Main House for coffee and some biscuits left over from last night's dinner. One last round of hugs and goodbyes. Some tears, so much love.

And we left.

Aftermath

June 1972–September 1973

Things did not go well. We went from the ranch to Eugene to say goodbye to Dougy and Jill and to stock up on supplies for the trip. As we were leaving Eugene, going up a big hill that led to the interstate, the bread truck's engine began to cough and sputter. We managed to get back down the hill to a supermarket parking lot. Dougy connected us with a mechanic friend who told us we had blown the head gasket, which meant taking the engine apart and then rebuilding it. We had to get the truck towed to the mechanic's place, where he, with some small help from me, made the repairs over about a week. We paid for the parts, gave him some pot, and promised to give him more money when we could.

The truck rode fine to San Francisco, the first stop on our grand adventure. But I struggled with the three-speed's clutch on those steep hills, and parking our big rig was near impossible. And we did have three dogs and two cats, so we were not unobtrusive houseguests. We didn't stay long and made the decision that given our load and some fresh doubts about our rig, we best forego our plan to check out some of the youth communities along the way—like Boulder, Colorado, or Lincoln, Nebraska—and head straight to Urbana, to establish a base for further explorations.

But … after a day-and-a-half of relatively smooth sailing, we had a flat tire about fifty miles east of Salt Lake City. We had dual tires in the rear, and the flat was on the outside one on the driver's side. We didn't have a spare. After much debate and discussion, we decided that Sarah should hitchhike (with the wheel and tire!) back to Salt Lake. The tires were an unusual size and no place closer was likely to have one. We didn't want to both go and leave the truck, the animals, and all our things (including our pot-stuffed candles) sitting by the side of the road unattended. Sarah would have an easier time hitchhiking—a woman clearly in distress with a big old wheel by her side—and it was probably better for me—the man—to stay. I was freaking out as I waited, sitting in the truck, cars whizzing by, trying to imagine what Sarah was going through. A state cop did stop to check things out and eyed me suspiciously and judgmentally when I told him I'd allowed/ sent my wife to hitchhike alone back to Salt Lake. But he left without seriously hassling me. It seemed like forever, with dusk settling in, before Sarah returned, smiling, with a repaired tire and two helpful guys. We got back on the road, but the trip now had a threatening cloud over it—and we had a long way to go.

We had two more flat tires. But the tire folks in Salt Lake had told Sarah it was OK for us to ride on three tires in the rear—or even two (placed on the outside), which is what we were down to for the last wobbly hundred miles. So we hobbled into Urbana ... and things did not get better.

We stayed with my parents initially. They were going through tough times: my father trying to stay sober; my mother dealing with that and a stressful new job. And us with our menagerie and my revolutionary plans only complicated their lives more. Early on, I did go to a big meeting at the University of Illinois where the agenda was exactly what I had been dreaming of in my house by the creek—how to bring various factions of the Movement together to deal with the ongoing attacks on black militants, the US still deep into Vietnam with its bombs and mines and "advisors," and the anti-war Senator George McGovern the likely nominee of the Democratic

Party to oppose Nixon for the presidency. But I didn't know anybody there, had no standing, and the discussion quickly devolved into unproductive bickering between factions, mostly about whether to focus on the election or militant action. I sat in the back, didn't say anything, and left without making any connections. I never did. Over time, I did consolidate all the notes and incomplete essays from my winter days reading and writing by the creek into a twenty-five page manifesto. I sent it to Luke, who in an almost gentle way told me how fucking naive it all was. In Champaign-Urbana, it turned out, the people I wanted to hang out with, like most people on the ranch, had no interest in hearing that stuff from me, and I had no interest in hanging out with the people who might.

It took Sarah and me about a month to realize that we had made a huge mistake, not about leaving the ranch but about leaving Oregon. We never used the woodstove. After a crazy trip to New York for a friend's wedding in the bread truck, we parked it at the farmhouse we lived in, and it only moved when we moved to another farmhouse and parked it there. We bought a 1963 Chevy Bel Air station wagon after we sold 20 pounds of awful marijuana that was growing wild in a field behind one of those houses for $200 to a dealer friend who cut it with some decent pot. We got jobs, both of us eventually with the University of Illinois civil service—Sarah running a Xerox machine in the civil engineering department and me running an Addressograph machine in the School of Agriculture. I made some address plates for Stu, so he would get every publication the school put out. He never thanked me. We survived the almost mandatory boredom of those jobs by listening to the Watergate hearings—hearing Nixon get slowly skewered day by day was the highlight of our year.

Scottie refused our offer of Moonbeam's pup Layla, who managed to take some bird shot to one of her eyes when she was running with Moonbeam and Molly in the fields around one of our farmhouses and also lost the use of her legs when she was grazed by a car. One-eyed and three-legged. We were happy to still have her in our family.

Once we were out of my parents' house, we had some good times with them and my sisters who were in town. We did have a lot fun with our friends … really, my friends. Sarah never did get comfortable with her primary identity being the wife of Ben Tucker, who in the fading past had been a minor somebody in that town.

It took us a year to raise enough money to head back to Oregon in the Bel Air station wagon with a U-Haul trailer and a special portable cat box to accommodate Mocha's litter of kitties, our pet numbers increased from our eastward trip. We got somebody to haul away the bread truck without charging us, and we took the woodstove to an auction. Sometime later, we got a check for $15.

Blowing a wheel bearing going over a pass heading into Yellowstone made our return trip as stressful as the trip east.

Meanwhile, back at the ranch, those who remained gave Willie Campbell $5,000 without getting a new contract or a commitment for just how long that would allow them to stay. Discussions about raising more money to keep Willie happy seemed to focus on cattle, and Willie even suggested setting up a paid camping area for tourists. That was not well received by our friends, Paulie wrote to us.

The garden thrived with bountiful crops of peas and corn and melons and "a ton" of tomatoes, according to Stu, and folks did get a good jump on firewood. Patrick wrote that he, Stu, and Willie dammed the creek behind our house to create a new creek running in front of the house to feed two new ponds in the "park" between our meadow and the reservoir. It was hard for us to visualize that.

"Everybody" went to a free concert at the Renaissance Faire site outside of Eugene featuring the Grateful Dead and the New Riders of the Purple Sage, a fine time by all accounts.

And the population of Ash Valley continued to fluctuate and dwindle. Jeffrey and Eddie moved to a place in Wolf Creek, about twenty-five miles south of Canyonville. Four Free Earth folks moved up and started filling some of the vacated spaces. Mike headed to San Francisco to hang out with the Free Earth people there. Stu reported that news to us like a baseball story, a trade of Mike for the four Free Earthers. He said it was still to be decided who got the best of the deal. Stephen drifted off.

Sydney went to San Francisco. Jack did not go with her right away but eventually followed. Paulie, too, went to San Francisco to reconnect with Mike. Liz went back east. Dale headed to L.A, with plans to go to Richmond, Virginia, his hometown, and then on to England. By the time the garden was playing itself out and the rains started coming back, Patrick and Stu were gone, too, leaving only Loretta and Artie from our days—none of the original Boston tribe. Not long into the fall, word got back to us that a couple of the newer folks, in preparation for a big, planned heist of a San Francisco stereo store to finally raise a full payment for Ash Valley, got busted trying to rob a gas station in Oakland.

When Sarah and I came back to Oregon in summer of 1973, we went to Tiller, where Stu, Patrick, Liz (with JT, a long-time friend, who should have been at Ash Valley but never made it) were still living along the South Umpqua, closer to town. More folks from Free Earth came and eventually took over the ranch. It seemed like a whole new community of freaks had sprung up around the river. Our Ash Valley time had earned us some credibility and we were welcomed into that community. But Sarah and I were looking to live in a bigger town, with more possibilities for jobs or school and I, despite all my failures, was still determined to connect with some kind of political movement.

We tried Ashland, but housing was scarce and expensive, so we set our sights on Eugene, where we had friends to stay with while we searched. And when we had finally settled, we made trips to Tiller often and we became a Eugene base for all of our friends from the South Umpqua.

2024

Sarah and I recently celebrated our 53rd wedding anniversary and soon after, the 53rd anniversary of our arrival in Tiller. We have a forty-eight-year-old son, who is a good man with a wonderful wife and a five-year old daughter who brings effervescent joy to our life. I have been clean and sober for forty years. We have lived in Eugene ever since we returned from Illinois. We expect Stu and Patrick and three generations of their families to join us and three generations of our family for Thanksgiving as they do most years. Patrick and Stu never left the South Umpqua Valley.

We also remain in active, if sometimes infrequent, contact, with Liz (and JT), Mike, Eddie, Jeffrey, and Walter, as well as some of the Free Earth people who followed us at Ash Valley. Stephen, Jack, Sydney, and Brian have died. Most of us who are alive are retired now, having lived long and winding lives as an antiques dealer, magazine editor, grower and seller of plants, a bank technology vice president—who somehow managed to never surrender his freakdom and who morphed into a hipster DJ—volunteer fire chief, a music industry executive, a Colombia-educated lawyer, caterers, a novel author. That's only the bare surface of our lives. Each one of the others could write their own book and I would look forward to reading them all.

I wouldn't trade that year in Ash Valley for anything. We made or cemented lifelong friendships. We learned that we were capable of doing hard manual, mechanical labor. We learned

we could live without running water or electricity or phones
in what Walter would later describe as "squalid" conditions.
I had more time for peace and reflection than any other time
in my life, a wonderful way to recover from the struggles and
challenges of our year waiting for the trial. It was a hell of a
place for a honeymoon. I learned a lot in my readings. We all
learned a lot living every day. Sarah and I grew as individuals
and as a couple. And somehow we left with no hard feelings,
but rather with great feelings of love for almost all of the
people who spent most of the year with us. Ash Valley was a
perfectly disinterested host—and I will be forever grateful for
the chance to grow into that land.

But we did fail. We did make mistakes.

We were "young and stupid," Stu says now. Jeffrey is
gentler, calling us "naive." We were not careful enough about
who we allowed to join us. We had unrealistic expectations of
ourselves and each other. We each held on so tightly to things
most important to us as individuals (for me, the relationship
with Sarah) that we never achieved a true communal ethic.

Maybe it was stupid to even believe such a thing was
possible. Our celebratory drug use was often out of control
and contributed to distorted thinking and stupid decisions.
Our scheme to raise the money for the balloon payment
actually worked; it was our failure to work together to make
ourselves—individually and collectively—worthy of that land
that kept it from ever being truly ours.

But we were young and stupid enough to try, to risk being
ridiculous—sometimes, often, truly being ridiculous. We, like
many others of our age at that time, really believed that we
could, that we had to, profoundly change the possibilities
for our lives and for the world. Similar efforts—some far

more successful than Ash Valley—were taking place across the country and around the world. A Great Flood–worthy confluence of events (the war, Black rebellion, rock and roll, widespread joyous drug use, the pill, women's liberation, visible environmental degradation, gay rights, and so much more) exposed the rotten core of the culture and society we were supposed to grow into.

We were right in that assessment. We were right to try to fight that "reality." We were right to explore alternatives.

But, though many things have changed for the better since then, too much has not and too many things have gotten worse. The current MAGA movement is based on denying the truths exposed by the upheavals of the sixties and seventies and undoing what progress has been made in fighting the three fundamental evils of American society as defined by Martin Luther King, Jr., in 1967: Racism, Militarism, and Materialism.

The Revolution we hoped to ignite never happened. But as we went our separate ways from the ranch, most of us tried somehow to keep the spark alive: writing, organizing, growing pot, making music, building collectives and worker-owned cooperatives, marching against whatever new war or oppressive policy came along, contributing to our communities, trying, at least, to live lives true to the best of the values we cultivated in those time. Almost nobody among our brothers and sisters from that time sold out those core principles—compassion, cooperation, shared responsibility for each other, respect for all people and the natural world—for material "success." But we got older, had kids, needed incomes, got isolated from our tribes. Some of us were pulled down by drugs or alcohol. The fire of our Revolution slowly faded to the dying embers of another time.

I wish I, and we, had done more. Though grateful and fortunate for the life I have lived, I wish I and we could have sustained the intensity of our rebellion and been more effective. If young people today are angry at us for our failings to do more, I don't blame them. I hope they can do better. I hope I can keep finding ways to help. As the epigraph to *The Risk of Being Ridiculous* says, "May the passion, the experience, and even the faults of my fighting generation have some small power to illuminate the way forward." (From *Memoir of a Revolutionary,* by Victor Serge).

I find comfort and—still—inspiration in a common paraphrase of the teachings of the Jewish prophet Micah in the ancient *Talmud*:

> **Do not be daunted**
> **by the enormity of the world's grief.**
> **Do justly now.**
> **Love mercy now.**
> **Walk humbly now.**
> **You are not obligated to**
> **complete the work,**
> **but neither are you free**
> **to abandon it**

The land? The land abides. The land didn't promise us anything, "neither joy, nor love, nor light, nor certitude, nor peace, nor help for pain."

Ash Valley was an extraordinary living landscape of dirt and water, grasses and trees, valley and mountains, structures and pathways.

Some of us convinced ourselves that we were meant to be on that land, that it would teach or heal us, fill our deepest needs or set us free. But as Jefferson Airplane had told us, all of our dreams and all of our schemes didn't mean shit to any of it, even those trees we had tried to save—and were cut not long after we left. A worker-owned tree-planting cooperative whose members included Stu, Dale, Patrick, Liz, JT, and several Free Earthers replanted the east slopes over Ash Valley and did a good job. Trees have come back, but the irreplaceable wonder of the virgin forest is gone forever.

The Free Earthers as a commune were on that land for a couple of years. As most of them drifted off, much the same as we had, Willie started selling off chunks to individuals, including the Second House to a Free Earth couple we had become good friends with. A man who had been Little Eddie's neighbor in Miami and a key part of the Florida money-raising project, bought the meadow where our house was. He built a bigger and better house northwest of ours and our house became a storage shed until rot set in and it was torn down.

Eventually, Willie officially divided the place into five parcels. He kept the biggest parcel—closest to the front gate— for himself. He built a big, modern house in a nook just west of the road, just below the cave where Stu and Eddie had hatched the dope-dealing plan to make our balloon payment. Willie died in 2001, and his son lives there now.

Sarah, Stu and his wife Hazel, and I did a drive-through of Ash Valley a couple of years ago, on a pleasantly cool and brightly cloudy spring day. The first view, looking across the first opening of the valley to the reforested east slopes was … jarring. The shape was right; the openness to the sky was right; the crisp, moist freshness of the air was right; the green of the trees rising from the valley was right; even the hay barn still stood where the road bent toward the rest of the ranch. But … Willie's house was right there in our face; a pond was in the middle of what had been an open, flowing hay field; the hills were lines of uniform trees, like rows of broccoli or pole beans in a carefully planned garden. I tried to squint my eyes to distort my vision enough to see through the present back to my first view of the valley on that soggy rainy day in 1971—the wildness, the ruggedness, the immensity of possibility. I couldn't do it. "What came is gone forever, every time," Alan Ginsburg wrote in *Kaddish*.

As we slowly drove the mile and a half up the road, that sense of what was gone, what had changed, clung to Sarah and me. We saw no people. An essentially new house where the Main House had been. Small household gardens. The goat barn remodeled into a residence. The Second House refurbished. The reservoir and the "park" around it reconfigured in ways that made it unrecognizable. Small trees on the east edge of the road blocked the view into the valley, a view Sarah and I had experienced morning and night for most of a year. "Our" meadow had a new house with a driveway and a satellite dish. It was all so foreign feeling to us that we had to reassure ourselves that yes, indeed, we had lived there with all of our hearts, once upon a time.

I was glad we didn't see any people with a need to chat with them. "Yeah, we lived here, once, long ago." And they might be interested or they might not be. I'm sure they loved the land like we had, maybe more since they were there now and we weren't. Our story is a tiny blip in the story of that land, but that land will always loom large in the story of our lives.

Sources and References

Away with all Pests: An English Surgeon in People's China 1994–1969, Joshua S. Horn, M.D., Monthly Review Press, 1971.

Fruit of the Sixties: The Founding of the Oregon Country Fair, Suzi Prozanski, Coincidental Communications LLC, 2009.

I Ching, edited by Raymond van Over, based on the translation by James Legge, The New American Library, 1971.

"Dover Beach," Matthew Arnold, in *The Pocket Book of Modern Verse,* edited by Oscar Williams, Washington Square Press, 1972.

"In Just-," E.E. Cummings, *Collected Poems,* Harcourt, Brace & World, Inc., 1963.

"Kaddish," *Kaddish and Other Poems 1958–1960,* Allen Ginsberg, City Lights Books, 1961.

Soviet Marxism, Herbert Marcuse, Vintage Books, 1961.

Soledad Brother: The Prison Letters of George Jackson, George Jackson, Bantam, 1970.

Split, Lisa Michaels, Houghton Mifflin Company, 1998.

Steal this Book, Abbie Hoffman, Grove Press, 1971.

The Dialectic of Sex: The Case for a Feminist Revolution, Shulamith Firestone, Farrar, Straus and Giroux, 1970.

"The Proletariat and the Revolution," Leon Trotsky, originally published in *Our Revolution: Essays on Working-Class and International Revolution, 1904-1917,* translated by Moissaye J. Olgin, Henry Holt and Company, 1918.

"The Revolution Betrayed," Emma Goldman, in *Patterns of Anarchy,* edited by Leonard I. Krimerman and Lewis Perry, Anchor Books, 1966.

Vietnam Will Win, Wilfred Burchett, A *Guardian* book distributed by Monthly Review Press, 1968.

White Man Listen, Richard Wright, Anchor Books, 1964.

Acknowledgments

To Raymond Spore and Louis Rogers, teachers of Oregon.

To Brothers and Sisters: Keith Alexander, Wendy Belyea, Bruce Gordon, Larry Weissman, Seymour Joseph, Charlene Sawl, Cathy San Filippo, Ed Dake, Harry Steinman, Kenny Klein, Jimmy Phelan, David Nash, Jim O'Sullivan, Punky Fisher, Jane VanKuren, Kevin Kehoe, Marylou Stevens, Betsy Tarr, Richard (Momo) Anderson, Donna, Ricky Leibowitz, Alan Seltzer, Maxyne Strunin, David Graybeal, Patty Corwin, Blade Corwin, Erik Mann, Tan Dan Gregg, Libra Nancy, Risa Devore, Dan (Spud) Moore, Bob (Mouseman) McCarthy, and Jimmy Tarr.

To early readers: Shelley Maynard, Ross West, Betsy Tarr, Bruce Gordon, Kevin Kehoe, Don Marsh, Harry Steinman.

To Jeff Bolkan and Sharleen Nelson, who saw a trilogy.

To Judy, Albert, Jerry, and Steve Schwartz, who welcomed a mixed-up but headstrong young man into their family.

To my sisters, Trish Martin, Gale Maynard, Phyllis Maynard, and Valerie Maynard, who helped me to find the profound love that lived beneath the often-chaotic surface of our family.

To my mother, Peggie Maynard, who taught me to love reading, and my father, Guy Maynard, who always took me seriously, often when I didn't deserve it. To both of them for their love and years of intense correspondence and for saving all my letters, as I saved theirs.

To Corey, for the joy and challenges and love you have brought to my life. Being his father is the best thing I have done. And our joy is multiplied many times by Jordan and Jude.

To Shelley, for everything. It's impossible, our story. But I tried to tell it anyway. Love always.

About the Author

 Guy Maynard lived in New Bedford, Massachusetts, for his first thirteen years. He spent his high school years in Urbana, Illinois, and went to two years of college in Boston. He was lead singer in a teen rock and roll band, was active in the civil rights and anti–Vietnam War movements, worked as a carpenter, and was a member of a worker-owned construction company.

After receiving his degree in journalism from the University of Oregon in 1984, he was editor of a small community newspaper and then worked on a number of trade magazines in fields such as liquid and gas chromatography and geographic information systems. He was editor of *Oregon Quarterly*, the University of Oregon magazine, for seventeen years. He was editor of *The Elements of Building* (by Mark Q. Kerson) and *How to Build a Conestoga Hut* (by Erik de Buhr) and was co-editor of the 2003 collection, *Best Essays NW*. His essays and articles have appeared in numerous newspapers, magazines, and books. He lives with his wife Shelley in a 1930s-vintage house in the middle of Eugene, Oregon. Their son, Corey, lives in Austin, Texas, with his wife Jordan and daughter Jude.

Ash Valley is his third novel.

https://www.facebook.com/theRiskofBeingRidiculous

All GladEye titles are available for purchase at www.gladeyepress.com and your local bookstore.

Federation of the Dragon
Footman of the Ether
Jason A. Kilgore
Enter the ancient world of Irikara for high-stakes epic fantasy adventure in a mythical land filled with dragons and demons, dwarves and elves, magic and mages and gods.

Quilts of a Feather
Arlene Sachitano
An innocent birdwatching festival hosted by the parks and recreation goes terribly sideways when one of the event volunteers is found dead from a fentanyl overdose on the hiking trail. It's up to amateur sleuth Harriet Truman and her quilt group, the Loose Threads, to solve the mystery?

Coastal Coffee Club Mysteries
Patricia Brown

Five cozy mysteries follow retired poet Eleanor Penrose and her band of quirky friends as they solve mysteries along the Oregon coast.

Dying for Recipies
Patricia Brown
Follow the clues while enjoying twenty-two of Eleanor's scrumptious, mouth-watering recipes drawn from the pages of Patricia Brown's charming Coastal Coffee Club Mysteries series.

COMING in 2025 *from*

Far Side of Revenge
Anne Dean
A fictionalized account of the life of Brian Boroimhe and his rise to King of Ireland.

Black and Tan Fantasy
Randall Luce
In the turbulent and often violent nascent civil rights movement of the Mississippi delta, racial identities, culture, and attitudes collide and shift in this taut drama.

The Extraordinary Voyage of a Tall Ship in a Tiny Pool Far from the Sea
Donovan M. Reves
With gentle absurdity and copious humor, Donovan Reves weaves an exciting adventure yarn with a tender love story all set in a ridiculous landlocked tallship built in a tiny pond. As hard to describe as it is to put down, this tender fable evokes the magic of *The Princess Bride*.

RERELEASES FROM JASON A. KILGORE

The First Nova I See Tonight
Star pirates, alien lovers, tentacled mafiosos, this space opera offers a return to the beloved "zap gun" stories of the past!

Around the Corner from Sanity: Tales of the Paranormal
Fourteen short stories of spine-tingling horror will scare you AND tickle your funny bone!

Guide Me, O River and other poems